KING OF SWORDS

CHRISTINE CAZALY

Contents

PROLOGUE

The mines of Traitor's Reach lay silent in the aftermath of battle. Yet memory lingered, an echo of fading screams, the rise and fall of a silvered blade flickering eternally in the minds of ghosts. Together, they wailed. A long dirge of lament and horror.

But only one woman remained to hear them. She crouched, head cocked on one side like a carrion bird, poised over the fallen body of one old man. He lay on his back, his dead eyes fixed on the beyond.

Her long hair, dark as the blackness of the caves, brushed his rigid cheeks, and the woman tightened her hold on his crabbed, ancient fingers.

Hot tears seeped past her lashes to splash his frozen features. Face clenched in a mask of anger, she clasped her free hand around the hilt of Aequitas, her enchanted dagger, still buried in his heart.

"So easy to fool," she said, working it free. "They didn't even see it, did they? Always, they see only what they expect to see."

The old man's body, already stiffening, rocked in response as she pulled harder to remove it. It was as if he wanted to hold the blade. Keep it from her. "And you. You betrayed me to those who would see me fail." She set her jaw. Braced one hand on his bony chest. "I am not sorry. You shouldn't have helped them. I warned you."

His body released the blade all at once, and she tipped back on her heels, steadying herself on the stony ground that was soaked in his blood. She felt it sticky as poisoned honey against her fingers.

Grimacing, she scrubbed her hand against her gown. Stumbled to her feet. Somewhere behind her, another fallen body lay. Oswin of Hartwood. Plump as a yuletide goose. Equally lifeless. Equally useless now that his purpose was served. Beyond him, the ever-present darkness. And Cerys. Alone.

Teeth bared in a rictus grin, she swiped her face dry. Pressed the icy flat of the blade to her forehead and her own heart.

"A sacrifice to the Shadow Mage."

It was a murmur, no more. Her voice emerged cracked and harsh as the jagged rock walls. Somewhere in the blackness, a restless presence, the dark mind of an even darker god, shifted and settled. Satisfied.

Bowing her head, Cerys drifted into its dark embrace, her thoughts reaching, stretching like racing shadows before a storm. South. To her forces, where they lingered, waiting for her command.

Grim with intent, Cerys' mind touched the telepaths in every group. She could feel their anticipation, although they knew better than to answer her. Her command reached them. Cold as steel. Sharp as claws.

"I have the blade. The time of awakening is upon us. Rise and take what is ours. Find the book."

Chapter 1

Joran

Castle of Air October 1609

Way down in southern Epera, night had fallen early. A bank of lowering grey clouds smudged the late afternoon sunlight. Buttressed behind the thick stone walls of the Castle of Air, Fortuna de Winter's brocade sleeves rustled as she spread her arms to the heavy curtains of Petronella's bedchamber and drew them closed. The sumptuous blue velvet shut out the oncoming darkness and blotted the wind that howled around the castle battlements.

Joran watched his wife's nurse from his upholstered chair before the hearth, a hearty draft of Argentian red held loose in his grasp. He noted the graceful curve of Fortuna's body as she turned. Idly. In passing. As one might admire the masterly strokes of a talented artist, or a vista framed in flowers. Pleasing to the eye. Fortuna stopped by Petronella's highly decorated bedstead and placed the back of her brown hand on Petronella's pale, clammy forehead. The Grayling, tethered lightly to his perch at Petronella's bedside, turned his elegant head at her approach. Watchful.

"No fever this eve, Gods be thanked," Fortuna said. "The leg is healing at last. You'll soon be on your feet again." Her face wore a perplexed frown as she noted her patient's pallor. Her drawn features.

"I would wish you were not so tired," she murmured. "Perhaps 'tis the babe, draining your strength this time."

"Nay, I am well, Fortuna. I'll be up shortly." Petronella smiled up at her friend from her lace-trimmed pillows, "I have been abed much too long." Joran hid his trepidation for her health behind a toast as he raised his glass in her direction. Ever slender, Petronella's high cheekbones framed gaunt cheeks and hollowed eyes. Her face no longer bore the bruises caused by her recent riding accident, but a thin, triangular scar marked her broad forehead. A heavy splint still made a log of her left leg under the woollen blankets.

Fortuna busied herself preparing a nighttime draft for her mistress, and Petronella shifted uncomfortably. A frown dragged at her features as she put her hand low on her belly, where the hint of her third pregnancy marred the perfect symmetry of the bedclothes. Joran's gaze sharpened. "What is it? Is it the babe?" he asked.

"Nay, just a gripe," Petronella said. "I felt him move this morn."

"He quickened? You did not say." Petronella half shrugged. "I wasn't sure, but yes." She didn't quite catch his eye. Joran didn't need Farsight to understand why. Overrun with responsibilities, this was the first hour he had spent in her presence since rising at dawn. Placing his glass aside, he crossed the room in two long strides and knelt at her bedside. He caught her hand in his. Her heavy ring twisted under his fingers. Too big for her these days, but still impossible to remove. The crystal faces of its diamond shone dully, catching the warm red blaze of the fire, the yellow candlelight. Petronella wore its twin, the Ring of Justice, on a fine silver chain around her neck. It tumbled free of her nightgown as she shifted her weight. His mouth dried as he stared at it. Like Petronella's ring, the jewel glowed in the soft light of the chamber. He could feel its pull against his heart. It drew his gaze. A constant reminder of the mantle of power that was his birthright.

He remembered well its fragile weight in his palm. That brief contact six years ago, when Petronella defeated the Shadow Mage and regained her throne. Catching the jewel as she dropped it to him had awakened Epera's Mage light in his soul. His palms now bore the sigils of his dual heritage. From his gentle, doomed mother, Queen Gwyneth, he inherited the mysterious wisdom of the High Priestess, Goddess of Oceanis. From his despised father, King Francis, came the brilliant, crystal-clear light of justice and the unyielding willpower enshrined in the god of Epera, the Mage. Petronella had offered him a choice amid her battle. Wear the ring, join her, and rule the kingdom as the Mage decreed. Together, they would be bolstered by the power of the twin Rings—the Ring of Justice for him, and the Ring of Mercy for her. A perfect balance. He had witnessed the ring's immense power that day, along with its relentless demand to bind himself, body and soul, to Epera.

Touching a gentle finger to the fragile chain Petronella wore, his troubled gaze lingered on her satin skin. She said nothing, but he noted the slight hitch in her breath at the touch of his fingers. He snatched them away and bowed his head. He had also felt the weight of his father's legacy that night. The bitter knowledge that King Francis had abused that same power. Manipulated by Darius of Falconridge, Francis had used it to destroy Joran's gentle mother, Queen Gwyneth, as she lay recovering from his birth. In his grief and shame, Francis entrusted his newborn son to the orphanage in Blade, far from Darius's reach. It was the only good thing the broken king had ever done for him. But Joran had grown up wild and angry, abandoned and nearly driven mad by his untrained Blessed gifts. Volatile and reckless, he'd spent his early years on the streets, his forbidden magic simmering dangerously under the surface. It wasn't until Theda Eglion intervened and his uncle, King Merlon of Oceanis, took him in that Joran found direction. Even then, the scars of his abandonment and the chaos of his childhood lingered.

Meanwhile, Darius seized control. Ruthless and cunning, he wielded the Shadow Mage's manipulative power to turn Epera's Citizens against the Blessed. With Francis a shadow of his former self, Darius's influence only grew. He married his youngest daughter, Petronella, to Joran's half-brother, Arion—a child of Francis's second, Citizen wife, Ariana of Wessendean. But the union remained childless, and the kingdom spiraled further into despair, drained of both magic and hope. Then Petronella had risen to confront her father. A Blessed and powerful queen, she had wrested control from his clutches and earned the right to wield the Ring of Mercy. Joran had watched her fight, admired her strength. And yet, even now, he could not bring himself to take up the Ring of Justice. The memory of that day lingered—its power, its promise, and its warning. Joran's own history was a tangled web of violence, rage, and fear. He knew his strengths: telepathy, a sharp mind, and a siren's charm inherited from his Oceanian mother. But he also knew his weaknesses. He could not risk letting the ring's immense power amplify his flaws. Now, as he knelt at Petronella's bedside, the light of the ring flickered in the fire's glow. Its pull was undeniable, yet he resisted. It waited for him still, but he wasn't ready. Might never be. He shook his head. He knew his own nature. The risk was too great. For Petronella, their family – and for the kingdom.

He blinked, lifting his gaze to Petronella, who was staring at him with a complex expression of understanding and impatience. "It waits for you," she breathed, so softly he could be forgiven if he chose not to hear her. Hating himself, he sat back a little on his heels and dragged his attention from the symbol of Blessed power and the twisting weight of doubt and commitment it represented. Lowered his eyes so he did not see the disappointment in his wife's. Her hand tightened in his. She squeezed his fingers in quiet acknowledgement. Her own ring flashed white light as she connected briefly with its gentle wisdom. She didn't need to say anything else. She never did. "I am sorry, sweetling," he murmured, grazing the back of her hand with his lips. "I do not mean to neglect you." "Oh, Joran, I know," she replied. "I wish my leg would hurry its healing. I need to be on my feet. Not just lying here acting like a glorified scribe." She traced the growing stubble on his cheeks with a gentle finger, and he rose on his knees to drop a kiss on her soft mouth. "You will recover soon," he reassured. "Try not to worry." "I can't help but worry. Is there no news from Falconridge? None of Dupliss?" Petronella asked. Joran's eyes flickered closed, and he replaced his wife's hand gently onto her belly, conscious of the familiar prick of ire gnawing his innards like a wolf, muzzle deep in blood. "Contacting Falconridge is on my list of grim tasks this evening," he said. "But I fear any news will not be good. As to Dupliss..." He rose to pace the room, grinding one fist into the other. "The man is as elusive as the wind, still. Sir Dunforde guards Falconridge well. But just this afternoon, I received word of an uprising near Goldfern. Another at Temple Bridge. Our forces are scattered more thinly than I would like. And the Citizens who rebel appear to do so with no warning. There is no pattern to it." He sighed, catching up his glass and taking a deep swallow. Replacing it. He faced Petronella's bed with one hand drumming his thigh, seeking a blade that he was not wearing. Petronella's eyes met his, full of understanding. "The roads will be all but closed by now," she said. "Winter is harsh north of Bearbank. Surely, the rebels will cease their activities whilst the snow is upon us. We must instruct our captains to recruit more soldiers loyal to our cause. Increase their training whilst we have the time." Joran's eyebrows raised in acknowledgement of her words, his mind turning already to the pile of reports and requests for funds littering his desk. The scarcity of news from the grim northern province of Traitor's Reach. "I will call a council meeting in the morning," he muttered. "By the Gods, I have no wish to raise our taxes yet again. 'Tis only making matters worse." About to reply, Petronella's sombre expression brightened at the quicksilver of childish voices approaching from the anteroom. Fortuna crossed to the door, opening it even as Little Bird raised her hand to knock. Ushered by the young nursemaid, the royal children, Ranulf and Theda, erupted into the quiet room. Ranulf leapt like a greyhound into his father's waiting arms whilst Theda took her time. Her clear blue gaze was a study of concentration as it flickered between her parents. "Why you sad?" she demanded, accepting Fortuna's help in swinging her three-year-old self from the floor to the high bed. She snuggled against Petronella and buried her head in the gap between her mother's chin and her shoulder. "You both sad," she said, accusing. "Perhaps we are," Petronella said, 'tis no fun, lying in bed with a broken leg." Theda struggled upwards, her plump, hot little hands tangled in Petronella's hair. "Isn't your leg," she said fiercely. "Balance me, Papa!" Ranulf said, swinging on his father's powerful arm. Joran wrested his giggling son into the air and stood the lad on his shoulders. "Watch me, mama!" Ranulf said, wobbling madly. His arms windmilled as he strove for balance. "By the Gods, Joran, be careful," Petronella said, her hand raised to protect her belly. Joran chuckled, steadying Ranulf as he prepared to launch himself onto the soft mattress. "Go on then, lad. Show us how you do it," he encouraged. Petronella winced as Ranulf crashed beside her, narrowly missing her stomach. "Be careful of your brother," she said. "You nearly trod on his head." "Did I?" Ranulf scrambled around and pressed his ear to her belly. "Nay. He says I missed," he informed her cheerfully, his green eyes aglow in his rosy face. "Welladay, he was lucky," Petronella replied, pulling her son in for a hug. She planted a kiss on his head. Unusually, Ranulf let her. "Little Bird sad," Theda said, spinning her head to glare at her nursemaid. Still watching his children, held in the cradle of their mother's arms as they pinned her to her pillows, Joran glanced at the girl. Little Bird shifted her weight, awkward under his attention. Slightly tongue-tied as ever in the presence of the royal couple, she flushed and dropped her head, studying the thick Argentian carpet with fierce concentration. Her nibbled nails twisted in her apron. "Well, lass, are you sad?" Joran asked, not really expecting an answer. Little Bird looked up at him, her delicate face woe begone under her nursemaid's cap. "'Tis only that there is no news from Falconridge, sire," she muttered. "And my lad is there. Will Dunn. Fighting with Dominic and the others." Joran nodded, exchanging a glance with Petronella over the girl's blonde curls. Petronella nodded. "You'd better contact Dominic tonight," she said. "Master Ash, too. Little Bird is right. It has been much too long since we heard from them." "And you haven't...?" Joran asked, flicking a hand towards her head. "Nay. Dominic thinks it better that I do not use my Blessed telepathy." He nodded, the familiar irritation with his wife's favourite adding to his mental unease. "And, of course, we obey the commands of young Skinner," he said, biting the words out. Petronella all but rolled her eyes. "He's there, my love. On the ground. If he thinks I am in danger, he will tell me," she said. "If you are not using your gifts, how did he tell you?" Joran asked. Even to him, he sounded abrupt. There was another awkward pause. Little Bird cleared her throat and exchanged a glance with Fortuna, who merely shrugged, her fine copper eyes alight with interest. "Through me, sire," Little Bird stammered. "I've been studying my telepathy hard since they left. Dominic, I mean, Sir Skinner, wanted me to tell the Queen." Irritation hardened Joran's words. "You should have requested my permission to speak with her," he said. "You know our sovereign lady is ill and not to be pestered." Little Bird flushed further, her smooth young cheeks suffused an angry red. Her budding bosom heaved under the practical gown she wore to attend to her duties. She flicked a nervous gaze to Petronella, seeking support. "She would have asked you, my lord," Petronella said, her tone mild. "But you were not here to ask." No, not accusing at all. Joran flinched at her complete lack of aggression. She might just as well have shouted at him from across the room, "You are not here for us." He drew himself up, stiffening his shoulders. "Welladay. I will see to the matter tonight." He knew his voice was cold. Caught the slight wince in Petronella's gaunt face. Theda's forbidding scowl blazed at him from her place at her mother's side. Mother and daughter. Alike as two peas. And young Theda, even at three years old, was already too telepathic for her own good. He bowed and turned for the door. "Papa angry," he heard Theda said as he closed it firmly behind him.

CHAPTER 2

DOMINIC, BEATEN DRUM TAVERN, HARTWOOD, 1609

"Dominic, report."

Holed up in the quiet taproom of the Beaten Drum, shivering, weary and hopeless beyond words, Dominic Skinner flinched to a state of anxious alert at the harshness of Joran's mental voice. Heart pounding, he shrunk against the whitewashed wall. His fingers, still stained with Will Dunn's blood, clenched around his tankard. Numbed by the knowledge of failure, it had taken the battered party a whole day and most of the evening to reach Hartwood from Traitor's Reach. The battle and the fight against the bitter weather had exhausted all of them. Right now, he'd give anything not to have to respond.

Across the table, Aldric's tired gaze flickered towards him, then away. The lad stared into his cup of mulled ale as if he didn't know what it was. In the middle of the room, Tom and Guildford held a quiet, tense conversation. Tom had one hand clamped on the wound he'd received in the fighting, his face pinched with pain. Mistress Trevis hovered over Felicia, bearing potions of her own devising.

"Heartsease, that's what I must have," Felicia said, her soft voice somehow still dominating the space.

"I've no heartsease, my lady," the healer said. "We'll get some in the morn. I'll find a market. A supplier. Never fear."

Felicia turned hollow grey eyes on her. The candlelight should flatter. But the golden glow only highlighted the gauntness of her cheeks, the heavy shadows under her crystalline eyes. Shaking her head, Mistress Trevis handed her a platter of rye bread spread thick with rich, yellow butter. Felicia tore into it like a starving hawk.

Cedric, equally tired, equally exasperated with the outcome of their recent foray into the mines at Traitor's Reach, took his temper out on his late brother's staff.

"Is it beyond the ken of man to heat water?" he demanded, his thick black beard bristling. "Get to it. Every barrel we have. I want a hearty supper on the tables as soon as maybe." White-faced, exchanging confused and somewhat terrified glances, the small staff scurried to fulfil their orders.

"Dominic. What is keeping you? Report at once!" Joran's tone grated against his mind. As cold and harsh as the mines themselves.

"My lord," Dominic paused, uncertain as he'd ever been in his life before.

"At last! Well?"

Gathering up the shreds of his mental energy, Dominic sent a fragmented message to the impatient Prince. *"There is no sign of Dupliss in the caves at Traitor's Reach, but my uncle, Terrence Skinner, is dead,"* he managed. He closed his eyes. A last image of his uncle, lying on his back, blood oozing from his chest, swept easily into his mind. They had left him there, much against Dominic's wish. Poor Will Dunn's body was even now lying in a shed in the Beaten Drum stable courtyard, well wrapped in blankets and patrolled by a member of the Hartwood guard. The freezing temperatures would do much to preserve his remains as they transported him further south for burial. Dominic bit his lip at the thought. He had still not told Little Bird of Will's tragic, heroic fate.

Joran's irritated hiss of frustration strafed a shiver down his back, much like the scourge of Sir Dunforde's whip only a few short days before. "

Your mission has failed, then," the Prince said, his assessment as cold as his mental voice.

"You wanted my uncle dead. He is. And we rescued Felicia of Wessendean," Dominic murmured, raising his eyes to the girl as she drained a mug of milk. The faintest hint of colour had returned to her thin cheeks. *"We achieved that much."*

"The retrieval of a traitor's brat?" Joran bit back.

"She's no traitor. Felicia has survived circumstances that might have killed anyone else." Despite his weariness, some spark of defiance yet lingered in Dominic's soul. *"And Guildford fought hard on our behalf,"* he added, his temper rising. Guildford had left Tom and stood with his sister, both her hands clasped easily in one of his, bending close to hear what she said. Dominic closed his eyes, unable to parse the context. Guildford, vivid with ruddy good health. A giant of a man, despite his youth, and Felicia, his twin, a broken sparrow, pecking fiercely for the crumbs of attention he left. Forever unnoticed behind him.

"Aye, mayhap he did," Joran said grudgingly, *"but the fact remains that his stepfather is still at large and fermenting rebellion. On his stepson's behalf, I might add."*

Frustrated, Dominic shook his head, struggling to conserve his magical energy for the length of the conversation. *"He fought who he thought was his stepfather in the mines at Traitor's Reach,"* he said. *"Tom Buttledon did, too."*

Joran's flow of mental energy shifted to confusion. *"Who he thought was his stepfather?"* he repeated. *"Explain yourself. I would have thought at close quarters his identity would be hard to mistake."*

Dominic closed his eyes, scrubbing his hands through his filthy hair. How to explain? The darkness, the tricks that Cerys had played so easily in their vulnerable minds. His gaze returned inexorably to Felicia. His heart's desire. How much he had yearned for her. Searched for her. Wanted her. What had that cost him? His friends? Petronella?

He had lost the Blade of Aequitas to the hands of a dark sorceress with the morals of an alley cat and a heart blacker than the mines that bred her. By all the Gods, how could he have let that happen?

"Answer me, Dominic. By the Gods, what were you doing in there? We should never have let you go. Never." Joran's voice, bitter with righteous anger, scoured him to the bone.

Dominic wrapped both hands over his head. A child at heart, writhing under the beating hands of his own guilt.

"Please, I can't explain. There is more danger here than you can possibly imagine. I need to speak to the Queen," he said.

"You will speak to her when I allow it," Joran said. *"Remain where you are. You will not return to the Castle of Air. The Wessendeans are not welcome here. And while you keep company with them, neither are you. Do you understand me?"*

"What? No... Surely..." Dominic's mental voice faltered into silence. He stared across the homely, fire-lit tavern almost without seeing it and scraped his hand over his bearded cheeks. Felicia's eyes, twin pools of winter grey in her snow-white face, clashed with his, alive with questions Dominic could not answer. *"Please, my lord, you can't mean it,"* his mental voice dropped to a faded whisper. *"Not after we have faced so much."*

Joran's words, almost lost as the last of Dominic's mental energy faded, bred not a smidgeon of hope to light the devastation in his heart.

"You can write a letter," the Prince said.

CHAPTER 3
JORAN

"You have refused Dominic permission to return to the castle?"

Petronella stared at him in frank disbelief from her snow-white pillows. Early morning sunlight slanted pearl-like into her chamber, glancing shyly off polished wood and burnished pewter. The Grayling, guarding her bed, lifted his savage beak and added his own pointed stare. Bustling around the room in her usual industrious fashion, Fortuna shot a glance at them, bobbed a curtsey and took herself off. The door closed behind her with a quiet click that sounded to Joran more like a rebuke.

He shifted his weight, aware of the tightness of his shoulders under his heavy doublet, the pounding of his head. He'd taken refuge in a decanter of the finest Argentian the previous evening. A poor attempt at drowning his many doubts before and after his mental conversation with Dominic Skinner.

"You must see that the Wessendeans are a danger to us," he prompted as Petronella stared at him, apparently lost for words.

Her brow creased. "The Wessendeans, possibly," she acknowledged after a pause. "But not Dominic Skinner. Never him. What are you about, blaming him for all this? What is it about the lad you detest so much?"

Joran sighed, extracting himself from the sapphire skewer of her disapproval by striding to the window and looking out. The distant spike of World's Peak, piercing the southern horizon like the point of a needle, drew his gaze. Home of the Gods, or so legend said. Part of him wished he could take to horse and travel there right now. He looked at his hands clutching the chilly windowsill as he considered his wife's question. Powerful. Skilled with sword and lance and reins. A warrior's hands. Or a mercenary's. He'd been both in his life. Free to roam. He'd rejoiced in the strength of his skill at arms and his Blessed gifts. Used both to bring justice to transgressors at the point of his blade. He rested his head against the paned windows. Frustration and impatience drove hard at his back. As if it would propel him once more into the wider world where he could bring his force to bear.

"I cannot tell you why," he muttered over his shoulder. "I do not trust him. Is that not enough? Or do you not trust my judgement?"

The room brightened around him as Petronella's ring flashed to life. He closed his eyes, aware of her incredible ability to walk into his mind and share his most private emotions, his most shameful memories. Ever conscious of her power, Petronella wandered only so far into his mental landscape, allowing him his privacy, as she always had.

"You must also trust mine," she said, her voice as soft as the feathers that cushioned her fragile shoulders. "And I perceive your fear, my love."

"I am failing," Joran said. His words cut the air with the bitterness of a rusted blade. "I cannot defend our kingdom, and I am trapped here, waiting for an attack that could come from anywhere, at any time."

He turned to meet her gaze as she pushed herself further up against her pillows.

"Then why banish our most powerfully Blessed and loyal subject?" she asked. "Of all people, Dominic Skinner is driven only by the desire to do what is right. By the Mage. By the crown. He is young, to be sure. Still finding his way, but a little mercy…"

Joran scowled. "Mercy," he growled, "will only get you so far. We need men. Troops. Swords. Warriors to take up arms and fight on our behalf. By the Gods, I cannot believe that everything we have strived for means nothing to our people. That they would rather return to the regime of my father. And your former husband." He choked on the words. Memories rose from nowhere to batter his mind. All those days and nights as a parentless child, fighting for scraps in Blade's over-run orphanage. The city scaffolds hung with blackened, bloated bodies like so much rotting fruit. His fists clenched as one vision came into focus.

"Who are they?" his wretched, ten-year-old self had asked, pointing to the gibbet as yet another terrified person struggled for a few more precious seconds of life. And the matron's answer, smug with the knowledge this grisly end would never be hers.

"They're the witches," she'd said. "They use magic. 'Tis evil." He'd winced as she struck him a savage blow across his boyish cheek. "Remember that!" Her onion-scented breath wafted like poison under his recoiling nostrils. "That's what happens to them that use magic."

To this day, Joran remembered his fear as he slunk away from her malodorous presence, praying that his hapless fellow orphans would keep his secret. Because even at the tender age of ten, his Blessed gifts were clamouring to be heard. Keeping the magic down and hidden had taken every particle of his youthful strength.

Shuddering, he tugged at his doublet. Paced the room, conscious of Petronella's concern as she followed his erratic progress.

"I don't want to fail," he blurted suddenly. "But I am. I know I am." He stumbled to his knees at her bedside. She reached for him automatically, her hands steady on his shoulders, the light of her diamond almost dazzling in its brilliance as a ray of sunlight bounced against its surface.

Petronella's soft breath fell on his cheek. "Nay, my love. This is not the man I met years ago," she murmured, running her fingers through the casual tangle of his hair. "Where is my gentle lover? Buried under this mass of doubt, yearning for his sword once more?"

"Gentleness…" He shrugged away from her. "We don't need any gentleness right now," he said. His voice was harsh with tension.

Her lips lifted briefly as she smiled. "Truly, Joran?" she asked, reaching for his hand. "Remember who your mother was. Good Queen Gwyneth of Oceanis." Her gaze clouded momentarily as she looked at him. "My father loved her well, Joran. I saw it just before his death. She was the only one who truly saw him. Mayhap she was the only one who could have saved him."

Joran grunted. "Aye, and look what Darius' twisted idea of love got her. She died in this room. His first kill. Even if he was not the man who did the deed." He sat back on his heels, staring down at her white face. "Your father deserved the end you gave him," he said. "As a ruler, I must show strength to challenge our enemies."

Petronella flinched. Her eyes dropped to his clenched fists and back. He held her gaze, his heart a nest of snakes, writhing with emotions he could not name. She closed her eyes briefly. His mind tingled as her thoughts melded with his own. When she spoke again, it was with a clarity only she could manage. He bowed his head under it.

"True power isn't just in the sword or the crown, Joran. It's in knowing when to wield both with mercy and when to let justice guide your hand. To rule well, you must master yourself first."

"Mayhap. 'Tis easy for you to say."

He raised a finger to touch the Ring of Justice where it lay against her breast. Its light flared, sending a buzz of power from his fingertips straight to his head. He flinched, ducking away. His palm tingled where the sign of the Mage lay. Forever embedded in his soul, seeking a union with the symbol of ultimate power. And beneath that, the faded sigil of the High Priestess. His mother's goddess. It was rare these days that the High Priestess' wisdom shed her light on his darkness.

He shuddered, his throat dry. The Ring of Justice. The force that had destroyed his mother and brought the kingdom to ruin. His once mighty father reduced to a puppet at the mercy of a ruthless foe—his own wife's father. He buried his face against Petronella's stomach, turning her words over. His mother, gentle Gwyneth, had died here. In this room. At his father's hand. Her death was the first of thousands that followed. Grief and rage combined to shake his heart in his chest.

"But you have fought your battles," he said, dragging his eyes to hers. "I cannot trust myself to fight mine."

CHAPTER 4
DOMINIC

Released from Joran's iron command, Dominic slumped in his seat, his head cradled on his filthy sleeves. His Blessed gifts, already at a low ebb, faded entirely, helped on their way by a crushing sense of defeat. He was conscious of the circle of expectant gazes aimed in his direction. Conversation paused as they waited to hear the outcome of this most recent communication.

"We must stay here," he said, his voice muffled. "The Prince commands our obedience. He will not let me speak to the Queen."

"We cannot return to the castle?" Guildford's eyes screwed into slits of rage. The hand clutching his tankard squeezed so hard the pewter creaked in protest. "Prince Joran wants us to wait out the winter here? In the middle of nowhere?"

Cedric cleared his throat. "Hartwood is no shanty town, my lord," he said in mock rebuke. "You besmirch the place of my birth." His attempt at humour fell short. Guildford took another hefty swig of ale and hurled the empty tankard at the wall.

"There are wenches and ale a-plenty here, Guildford," Dominic said. Still reeling from his conversation with the Prince, he had little strength left to deal with the disappointment of his friends.

"But we can't stay here. Surely they need us?" Guildford reached for another cup.

Felicia placed a grubby hand on his arm. "Peace, brother," she said. "The Prince must have his reasons."

Dominic tilted his head and peered in her direction. "His first thought is the protection of the Queen," he mumbled. "He is angry because we failed to track down Dupliss. And he cannot risk our return to the castle since Dupliss is fighting to place you on the throne." He had to tilt his head to an insane angle to meet Guildford's eyes. To his credit, the lad looked shocked at the news.

"Me? But I don't want it. Never even thought about it," he said. "It was only ever my mother and my stepfather plotting. I never took their words seriously. 'Twas a dream they wanted. Nothing real, truly." He hooked a stool towards himself and plumped down at Dominic's table. Dominic winced when the lad poked him on his aching sword arm. "You believe me, don't you?" he asked.

Dominic sighed. "I am not the one you need to convince," he said. His gaze drifted to Felicia. She was tearing the remains of the bread into shreds. An encouraging waft of roasting meat drifted out of the kitchen, and the girl turned her head towards it. Starving. His own stomach growled in response. It seemed a hundred years since he'd last eaten a solid meal.

"His orders included you, Felicia, and me," he said. "There's nothing to stop Tom returning, or Aldric, or Mistress Trevis. They are not under any form of suspicion."

"I'm not leaving you," Tom announced. Seated by the fire, his broad shoulders bare, he flinched minutely as Mistress Trevis tended the savage cut on his upper arm. "Unless the Prince directly orders my presence, I will remain."

Bent over the wound, the healer huffed a sigh. "You can't fight until this heals. Don't even think it," she said. "We should have tended to you sooner. I am concerned about it." She pressed her fingers to the angry swelling around the jagged gash. "Hot," she murmured. "I don't like it."

"Welladay, then. 'Tis agreed. We stay together," Dominic said. Sitting up with an effort, he nudged Aldric. Pale-faced, the lad blinked. "What say you, my friend?" he asked, softening his tone.

"With you, always," Aldric said, although the words came out stilted. Dominic glanced at Mistress Trevis. She shook her head. "I have something for you, lad," she said, tying off Tom's bandage.

Patting the pocket of her gown, she crossed the narrow room and jerked her chin at Dominic. He stumbled to his feet. "You should eat and rest," she said. "All of us need some time to come to terms with our losses on this mission, including this lad." She took Dominic's vacated place and reached into her pocket. "Here," she said, placing a roll of parchment tied by a scruffy blue ribbon in Aldric's hand. Aldric stared at it. They all did. The outer edges were grubby. Much thumbed and sweat-stained. "Take it," Mistress Trevis urged. "Will gave it to me for you, Dominic, two weeks ago, just in case. But I think Aldric should be the one to read it."

Dominic's heart clenched.

"No time to prepare or say goodbye..." Will's deep voice reached out of the recent past like the clasp of a warm hand. Dominic bit the inside of his cheek, forcing himself to a calm he was far from feeling. Felicia shuffled to her feet and limped across to join them. The cool weight of her palm on his shoulder offered a lifeline of comfort. He reached up to clasp it.

"Can you read it?" he asked.

"Aye." Aldric swallowed. His fingers trembled as he unfurled the page. A leather bag containing something small and heavy tumbled out with it. Will's untutored scrawl, thick with blotting and the odd, fierce crossing out, lifted Dominic's lips in a small, sad smile.

"I was just a soldier." Aldric's voice, but Will's words. Sturdy and self-deprecating all at once. "But I was a proud one. Fighting for what I believe in. The Mage and the Queen. So just know if I'm not coming back, it was the right thing, in the end. Tell Bird I love her. And give her this. Look after her, Dominic. And you, Aldric. Promise me. She must be happy. 'Tis all I ever wanted. Will."

Silence. Dominic swallowed, swiping a hand across his blurred eyes. Mistress Trevis nodded once and returned to Tom. Aldric shook his head like a dog emerging from a stream. His face cleared for the first time since Will's tragic passing. "He was a brave fighter and the best of friends," he said, collecting the bag and weighing it in his fist. "Money, I think." He raised his eyes to Dominic's. "But I think we should just give it to Bird. We don't need to know what he left, do we?"

"Will you be alright?" Dominic asked, clasping his friend's arm. Aldric heaved a gigantic sigh, but his fingers were steady as he re-wrapped Will's last bequest and stowed it carefully in his pouch. "With the Empress' blessing, in time, I will," he said. "But what about you? You're the one who must tell Bird."

Dominic stared at him, but it was Will's face he saw. Square-jawed, sun-tanned. Proud. Loyal. He shook his head, dreading the mental conversation that loomed over him. "By the Gods, I wish I didn't have to tell her," he muttered. "And right now, I can't. Mistress Trevis is right. We all need rest."

Felicia's hand slipped into his. "Then let her have one more day of ignorance," she said. "Let her remain a child just a little longer. This world is harsh enough."

CHAPTER 5
JORAN

"Where is the money coming from for these extra troops?" The Lord High Chancellor, Sir Percival Hollingworth, glared at Joran's most senior general across the polished chestnut table that separated them. Dull light, filtered through the thick glass panes of a many-paned window, glanced off his spectacles and threw shifting geometric shadows against the whitewashed walls of the Council Chamber. There was a mound of parchment in front of him. Rows of figures and reports from across the realm. Seated at the head of the table, Joran glanced at the many red-inked entries and gritted his teeth. He shifted restlessly in his seat as the argument ground on. The room was cold. To keep the meetings short, Joran deliberately kept a small fire. To date, his strategy had failed. The councillors in attendance wore thicker robes and droned on anyway. A young scribe, huddled under a cloak, blew on his fingers as he recorded the conversation. His seat was far from the dull crackle of the fire. He shot an impatient glance at Sir Percival, who was prone to long-winded explanations when left unchecked.

"We cannot maintain this army in this weather for much longer. 'Tis clear to see. Not without more money in the treasury." Sir Percival tapped a figure with his ever-present quill. "As for additional troops and training, think again."

Sir Reginald Fellowes glared back, his thick moustaches bristling. "And the consequences?" he bellowed. "Have you thought about that, man? Death and destruction. Fear and famine. Again. I thought we'd proved that Epera, without its magic, will fall. That's what happened last time. Have we learned nothing?" Accustomed to parade ground volume, his voice almost blew the parchment to the floor. Sir Percival slammed down a protective fist and lifted his chin another notch. "If Dupliss gets his way, there will be nothing left to protect, let alone tax," the general added before the chancellor could open his mouth. "I have my own figures. Sixty civilians dead in Temple Bridge, including the temple priest and his brethren. I tell you, it is starting again, this vendetta against the Blessed and those who support the Mage. We must counter it."

"At least our food supplies are in no doubt," Lord Colman interjected from his place at Sir Percival's side. "We may not pay the troops, but at least we can feed them, thanks to the good harvest this year. That was not the case under King Arion." He patted his belly, round under his ermine-trimmed robes.

"If we are not to raise taxes, we must make savings or increase our exports elsewhere," Joran said. "It is imperative that our army remains strong and ready to face the threat of Dupliss."

Sir Percival peered across at him. "More mist than man," he quipped. "People question whether he is real at all."

"Oh, he's real, alright," Sir Reginald sneered. "But he sends his spies out first. Don't think he doesn't. Spreading lies amongst the population of this Shadow Mage. And then what happens?" The table lurched as the general lumbered to his feet. He glared at them all. "The population starts to think all magic is evil and wrong. I tell you, that's how it works. I saw it as a younger man. The threat is real and growing." He leaned over the table, both great fists clenched. "I am a soldier," he rumbled. "And I would defend this realm from every threat, including any that would weaken it from within. Like a rot. A blight." Turning, he spat into the fireplace. Lord Colman stared at Joran, both eyebrows raised, and cleared his throat.

"Thank you, Sir Reginald. I think we understand you. As to spies, I have my own. They keep me informed," Joran said before Lord Colman, famed for his fastidious nature, could call the general to account for his barrack-bred behaviour.

His gaze wandered down the length of the table to the empty chair usually occupied by Petronella. Despite their nightly discussions, he missed her presence in the room. Her quiet confidence and shrewd judgement. A vivid memory of their first proper conversation flashed across his mind. Both of them soaking wet, the icy waters of the Cryfell river rising by the minute and his automatic contempt for her. The queen of the country he hated, a fugitive, running from justice. Even then, her sapphire gaze had pierced his soul with a single look. Had he known then, he wondered? If not in that moment, then certainly over the days and weeks that followed. Steadfast. That's what she was. Determined, intelligent. Fiercely loyal. Brave.

"My lord?" Colman's voice was at his elbow. "What is your will?" Joran shook his head, realising he'd left his seat to pace the room.

"I will see this kingdom safe," he muttered, dragging his thoughts from his injured wife. "Scribe, take a note. I want a message sent to every noble family in the land. They are to increase their defences by Her Majesty's command. The crown will supply additional food stocks to every manor we can reach in compensation, weather permitting. There is a reward of one thousand crowns for the person who brings me Dupliss' head. I do not care if it is attached to his shoulders or not."

"Very good, my lord." The scratching of the scribe's quill across the parchment scoured Joran's senses like an itch as he scribbled.

Sir Percival cleared his throat and exchanged a nervous glance with the Lord Chamberlain, whose mild brown eyes widened in alarm. "We do not have an endless supply of food, my lord," he ventured. "Our granaries are healthy, to be sure, but it is surely unwise to alarm the population unduly with a demand for increased defence."

Joran shrugged. "I am not rationing anyone. King Merlon of Oceanis will help us if we ask him. At least we do not have to contend with a diplomatic crisis as well. It is not like the days of Arion's rule."

"Aye, our relations with our neighbours are good," Sir Percival agreed. "Just yesterday, I had word from my counterpart in Battonia. They wish to increase their trade for tin."

"Well and good. Make the trade and find more," Joran said. "If we can increase exports, we do not have to raise taxes."

The chancellor's face screwed into a frown as he stared at his ledger. Nodding to himself, he gathered his papers. "Aye, it might work," he muttered. "If we divert our copper production... I will talk to my accountants." He sketched a curt bow as he rose from his seat and stumped to the door.

Sir Reginald swallowed the remains of his wine and wiped his moustache with a heavily-scarred hand. "That was a stroke of fortune," he said.

Joran rolled his shoulders under his thick, fur-lined robe. "Aye," he agreed. "But 'tis temporary." He nodded at the scribe. "Leave us, we would be alone," he said. "Have those letters written out and on my desk for my seal at the end of the day. Tell the messengers to prepare for their journeys."

He waited until the door closed behind the shivering secretary and turned to his most trusted councillors.

"Where is he? Everywhere Dupliss is seen, we look and cannot find him. Every troop I send is in the wrong place at the wrong time. Too late. Forever chasing him."

Sir Reginald's creased face crumpled further as he scowled. "I have the same concerns, my lord," he said. "I do not wish to think it, but..."

"I, too." Lord Colman's generous mouth thinned. "Too much time has passed, and chances missed for there to be any doubt."

Joran's fists clenched at his sides. "Then we agree," he said. "I think it must be so. We have a traitor in our midst. But who?"

"Must be in the army, much though it hurts me to say it," the general said. "But there are few of us with Blessed gifts. Mostly, we rely on pigeons and couriers on fast horses."

"But we know Dupliss travels with former members of the Dark Army," Joran said. "I thought the traitor must be Terrence Skinner, but Dominic informed me yesterday the man is dead. Unless he was lying. Perhaps we could set a trap. Test the theory. If we catch Dupliss, then the traitor was Terrence all along. If not, then it is someone else determined to support Dupliss and his attempt to place another on the throne."

He turned to Lord Colman. "I want a list. Every member of the Blessed at Court and across the country, and a report of their abilities," he said.

Lord Colman blanched. "Are you sure, sire?" he questioned. "That smacks very much of the actions of the late King Francis and the command of Darius of Falconridge back in the old days."

Joran glared at him. "But you made a list, didn't you?" he demanded. "There is such a thing. Blessed families, those who have received training. Serfs and nobles and commoners alike. Do you still have it?'

Lord Colman swallowed. His gaze darted to Sir Reginald, who mumbled something inaudible into his cup and glared at the fire.

"I wish you would reconsider, my lord," Colman said. "If any Blessed families discover such a list is still in existence, they will consider the famine years come again. 'Twill breed panic and resentment when we need calm and stability."

Joran drew himself up. A headache beat insistently in his forehead as his own magic built in his blood, demanding an outlet. "But I require the information," he said. Under his steady gaze, he watched as his councillor shuffled his feet, his plump features a world of dismay and mute resistance.

Lord Colman met his icy stare. "The Queen…" he began.

Joran took a step forward. Just one. The Lord Chamberlain jumped like a startled rabbit. "But the Queen is abed. Ill and vulnerable," Joran said. "And I am tasked with protecting the Queen and her people. You will provide the list. Updated. Within the next three days. Do you understand?"

The older man dropped his gaze to the cold flags that the thick Argentian carpet did little to warm. "Aye," he muttered. He remained where he was, thick, be-ringed fingers clutching the edges of his ermine robe. His chain of office glowed dully in the dim light.

"Now," Joran snapped. "'Twill take you some time, I don't doubt. Tell no-one."

Lord Colman stomped to the door and wrenched it open. Joran watched him leave with one eyebrow raised.

"I understand your reasons," Sir Reginald said. He spat once more into the meagre flames. "But I'm sorry, my lord. I think he's right. If word gets out…"

Joran turned an iron-hard stare on his general. "If word gets out, I know who the traitor is, do I not?" he said.

CHAPTER 6
DOMINIC

Despite his weariness, Dominic's need for sleep battled with his dread of the conversation looming before him as he lay abed that night. The inn servants had provided a barrel bath, hot water, and fresh towels. The heat was a welcome relief for the frost that appeared to have settled into his bones. He'd strip-washed first. Grimaced at the grime and dried blood that stained his basin. Will's blood and his uncle's. The mine's dirt. At his side, as ever, Aldric performed the same mechanical actions. They said little. Glancing across at his friend, Dominic noted the shadow of grief that still clouded his eyes. Biting the inside of his cheek until it hurt, he clamped down on his own. The warm bath had soothed some of the tension from his aching muscles. A lingering scent of expensive sandalwood soap still filled their narrow chamber. A reminder of civilisation amidst a nightmare of horror. Propped up against the wall, the blankets pulled under his chin, he stared at the flames crackling in the hearth and shivered. Little Bird. How could he tell her?

The fire gave him no answers. He stared at the flames until they blurred before his exhausted eyes, and he fell asleep to the sound of Aldric's soft snores, his mind a mess of violent and bloody death.

Breakfast was a quiet affair. The inn servants provided porridge and freshly baked bread thick with butter and honey. A wedge of cold bacon. Light, spiced ale. Hungrier than a pack of wolves in winter, the company stripped the table and called for more. Dominic picked at his food, his appetite blunted by the knowledge that today was the day when he would break Little Bird's heart. Only Felicia's light step as she approached the table lifted a faint smile to his face.

"My lady, how did you sleep?" he said, rising to greet Felicia as she nodded to the company, pale as a wraith, her hair a long braid down her back. He frowned at the patched homespun gown she wore. Only slightly better than the filthy rags she had been wearing. Catching his gaze, she smoothed the skirt.

"'Tis Mistress Trevis'," she said, taking a seat and helping herself to bread and ale. "She loaned it to me."

"Would you like to visit the market?" Dominic said, taking her hand as she took a seat beside him. "We can find something more suitable. Certainly warmer."

Felicia's fingers slipped from his. A light frown crossed her face. "You are not buying me clothes," she said.

"Nay, he will not," Guildford interjected. "I am your brother. I will provide the necessary coin." He nodded at them from over the rim of his mug and plunged a hand into the depths of his serge doublet. "Here. Buy what you need. Whatever takes your fancy." Felicia caught the heavy purse he slid down the table to her, a glimmer of a smile on her thin face.

"Has your prowess at the gaming tables improved over the last two years, brother?" she inquired, tossing it from hand to hand.

Guildford smirked at her and glanced across at Dominic. "'Tis yours. Part of your dowry," he explained.

Dominic blinked. "Her dowry?" he said faintly.

"Aye, to be sure. Surely, you didn't think there would be nothing. You two will wed, will you not?" Guildford stated. "'Tis as plain as the rather large nose on your face."

"Excuse me?" Haughty as ever, Felicia took a few coins out of the pouch and tossed the rest back to her brother. "I have not said as much, nor has Dominic asked." She resumed her meal, concentrating her gaze on her platter.

Uncomfortable under Guildford's mischievous taunting, Dominic twisted in his seat and reached miserably for his ale, not daring to look at her.

"That is unfair, Guildford," Tom said. "And much too soon. As ever, you rush in without thinking of the damage your words will cause."

"Bah," Guildford shrugged. "Dominic's done nothing but pine after my sister since he first laid eyes on her. I remember she begged me not to kill him once. He's looked after her hawk as if it was his own all this time." Unrepentant, he raised his tankard in their direction. "Congratulations, you are reunited."

Grabbing a hunk of bread and some cheese, Dominic swung his legs over the bench and threw a scowl across the board. "You've said enough, Guildford," he said. Guildford's chuckle chased him to the door. He paused, blinking at the morning light glinting off the snow. A rush of freezing air scoured his lungs with the scent of winter.

"Running away, Skinner? I never pegged you as a coward in the game of love. 'Tis cold out. Don't forget your cloak."

"By the Gods!" Cheeks burning at the laughter that followed him, Dominic stalked back to his chamber, somehow resisting the urge to beat Guildford over the head with his own tankard.

Aldric, bleary-eyed, his hair on end, looked up as Dominic marched in and slammed the door behind him.

"What's to do?" he questioned, lacing his doublet. "Are we under attack?"

"Only from Guildford. A good night's sleep was all he needed to bring him back to true form." He grabbed his cloak from a hook on the wall where he'd hung it to dry and shook it out. "This is filthy."

Aldric snorted. "Aye. Everything we've got is filthy. Don't worry. At least you're clean underneath. I'm sure Felicia will understand."

Swinging the heavy garment over his shoulders, Dominic favoured Aldric with his best glare. "Have you been speaking to Guildford, perchance?"

Aldric's dark eyes danced. "No need. The lay of the land needs no skilled tracker. Are we to market? You've been lamenting the state of her wardrobe since she gave her first shiver."

Dominic's jaw tightened. "Aye. But she won't let me buy her anything. Guildford just tried to give her a huge purse of coin that he said was part of her dowry. She was not impressed at the idea."

A grin tugged at the edge of Aldric's lips. "Ah. Welladay. I'm sure you'll bring her round. As you are not yet a betrothed couple, do you mind if I join you?"

"Not at all. Come when you are ready. I am going to the stable to see to the horses." He headed for the door, only to be brought up short by Aldric's quiet question.

"Have you told Little Bird?"

Dominic paused. "I've barely recovered my energy," he said, his voice low. "Not enough for a conversation like that."

"But you will tell her, won't you? As soon as you can? You won't put it off?"

Turning, Dominic met Aldric's worried expression with a matching one of his own. "I promise to tell her as soon as I can," he said. "It will break her heart. 'Tis not something I relish. I wish it could wait until I could tell her in person."

"Soonest said, soonest mended," Aldric replied, but there was a question in his voice that echoed Dominic's own doubts.

"This is Little Bird," Dominic said. He scrubbed a hand over his face. "I wouldn't be sure about how long it will take to mend."

Hunched under their cloaks, the trio followed the busy townsfolk to Hartwood's market. Snow crunched under their boots and decorated every flat surface. The icy air brought a flush to Felicia's pale cheeks that almost made her look healthy. Aldric surveyed the surroundings with lively interest, dragging behind Dominic and Felicia as he stopped to stare into the shop windows and fingered his purse. Hartwood bustled with lively energy. In place of carts, horse-drawn sledges scythed through the icy streets, bells jingling. Smoke drifted into the crystal sky from a hundred different chimneys. The snow blanked out the normal town smell of horse dung and offal and offered a vision of pristine clarity. Every fluffy snow-capped shape a delight to the eye.

Once they reached the market, there was no stopping Aldric. He sallied forth, delighted at the array of produce on display, and disappeared into the throng with all the alacrity of a born merchant. The entire place was a cacophony of noise and movement. Shaking his head, Dominic watched him go, lending a steadying elbow to Felicia as she adjusted her tattered hood.

"What first, my lady?" he said. "Lead on."

Somewhat to his surprise, Felicia's fingers curled around his. She stood like a statue, staring at the bustling scene with tears in her eyes.

"Felicia? Are you well?"

She swallowed. "There are so many people. 'Tis so noisy," she whispered. "I had forgotten..."

Biting his lip, Dominic drew his fingers from hers and placed a careful hand around her shoulders, holding her closer to his warmth. "Aye, to be sure. Of course, you are not used to this. Would you like to return to the inn? I can buy anything you need with your instruction," he suggested.

Her gaze flicked to his. For an instant that sent a blaze of happiness shooting through his body, she almost seemed to cling to him. His heart clenched at the trepidation he saw before she looked away. He turned a shoulder to shield her from the press of bodies, tilting his head to hers. "You know I won't let anything happen to you. You are safe now," he said.

"I can't know that, not truly," Felicia replied. She shrugged away from his protection, and his heart sank. Breaching her defences, when his own heart filled fit to burst every time he looked at her, was almost too much to bear. He'd been thinking of her day and night for two years. Had imagined a thousand different scenarios of a joyous reunion. But she seemed as distant now as she had in the early days of their acquaintance. Remote and colder than the moon. Had she never yearned for him? Was he imagining it all? Longing for a more positive connection, he moved closer to hear her over the din of the stallholders. The insistent jauntiness of a bassoon issuing from a raised dais nearby made him scowl.

Felicia raised her chin, squared her shoulders, and took a resolute step away. "You can't keep me safe. My Blessed gift is the last thing I ever wanted. But for whatever reason, the Mage gave it to me." She laughed. The bitterness lodged within it raised the hairs on his neck.

"You can't mean it, not really," he whispered. "Surely you cannot wish to deny the Mage if he finds you worthy?"

Felicia's expression was stony as she turned to face him. "You find it a blessing," she said. "But for me, 'tis more a curse. So now, I need heartsease. That's the first thing. A lot of heartsease." She cast a gaze around, taking stock of the layout, and Dominic followed her as she moved on hesitant feet into the crowd.

"But you are away from Cerys now," he said, dodging around a sturdy matron with a brood of children clutching her skirts. "Surely you don't require heartsease now? We could definitely use your Farsight."

Felicia grimaced. She stopped and placed a hand on his arm. "You were not listening. I can no longer trust that my Farsight serves only the Mage," she said. The coldness dropped from her face, leaving only a wealth of sadness. A horrible vulnerability from which he could not spare her. Little Bird's face would look exactly the same after he had shared his news. He swallowed, caught between his unspoken love for Felicia and his sorrow at the plight of Little Bird. His eyes searched her face, looking for warmth, but found none. "I spent two years in that awful place, fighting off the Shadow Mage," she whispered. "I tried with all my heart to resist it. But it is evil and insidious. It scrapes away at resistance. Reaches into the darkest parts of your soul and rejoices in your weakness. It is the very opposite of everything the Mage teaches. And I..." She frowned, her cloud grey eyes hazed with tears as she lifted them to his. "Dominic, there is such a lot of darkness in my soul for the Shadow Mage to use."

He frowned, wanting to deny her words. Bolster her with a single truth—his love for her. Tell her how strong she was. That the darkness hadn't won. Do whatever it took to close the chasm between them. But the words remained unspoken. Silenced by the pain in her eyes and his sudden understanding that this was a battle for Felicia alone. He reached for her, but once again, she turned away, inserting herself between the mass of shifting bodies, and he scurried in her wake. As ever, trying in vain to catch her. A haunting shadow, forever out of reach.

CHAPTER 7
DOMINIC

"**I**'m going to the stables."

Dominic's voice pitched low over the buzz of conversation at the dinner table that evening. Aldric and Felicia exchanged glances. Felicia put down her glass of Argentish and scanned his face. Firelight cast a golden glow over her skin.

"You are going to talk to Little Bird. Are you sure?" she said.

Dominic allowed himself a single jerky nod. He didn't trust himself to say more. He rose from his seat, leaving his meal congealing on its platter.

Aldric jerked his chin at it. "You should eat that. You need your strength," he said.

Dominic sighed. "Can't. Not 'til I've told her," he said.

Felicia squeezed his hand. "We will be here when you return," she said. "Wrap up."

Conscious of two pairs of eyes boring into his back, Dominic made his way to the door. Every step felt like the ones he'd taken on his march to the whipping post just a few weeks before. Leaden with dread and the anticipation of desperate pain.

Boots crunching on the treacherous path, his breath frosted in the air. The wood of the stable door was icy to his touch as it creaked open. A covered lantern shone a gentle light around the space, filled with dozing horses and the warmth of their malty breath. He inhaled, comforted by the bulk and placid strength of the occupants, but even the weight of familiarity failed to calm the welter of turmoil in his chest. Scenting his presence, Kismet nickered a greeting from her stall. He moved to her like a man in a daze and smoothed her satin coat with his palms. She pushed her face against him, and he leaned into her, wrapped in her trust. His own heart felt as if it was breaking already. The flicker of his telepathic gift vibrated softly within his skull. Not at full strength. But enough. He ran his fingers over his mare's ears. If he could just stay here. For another hour. Another day. His eyes drifted to the door and the comfort of the inn. The desire to turn his back and walk away had never been stronger. But no. This was Bird. She had to know. And he had to face it.

He sank to the fresh, fragrant straw, his back against the wall, and pulled his cloak further around his shoulders against the stray drafts that chased his skin. Kismet returned to her manger and munched hay. Solid. Real. It was time. Even so, he delayed. Images of Little Bird slid into his mind without him trying. Her mischief. Her laughter. Her tears. Even her unexpected worldliness and wisdom, bred from a childhood on the dirty streets of Blade. By the Gods, how he wished he didn't have to tell her. He scrubbed at his face with his hands, struggling to marshal his thoughts and his depleted energy. Perhaps she would deal with it. His mind jeered back at him for that slim hope. It was time, and it fell to him to tear her open.

Dropping his head to his knees, he opened his channels and searched for Little Bird's familiar light as air energy.

It didn't take long.

"Dominic! You're there! Where have you been? I keep telling you we need news. What's happening? How is Will?"

He swallowed. No matter how much he'd tried, he was unprepared for this moment. He paused, his own grief rising to swamp him, and he struggled for control. The last thing Bird needed was the weight of his emotions, as well as her own. He was too late, and she had studied her craft well. She caught it. The hesitation. His sorrow.

"Oh no. No, no, no." The rising wail of despair screeched into his ears like the blast of the bitterest winter storm. It tore into him with its own blade of steel, slicing his heart in two. He buried his head in his hands, panting for breath, almost knocked down by the force of her mental anguish.

"Bird... Bird... Listen, please listen..."

The wailing continued. Deep, gut-wrenching sobs that squeezed his soul in a grip of iron and didn't let go. Gritting his teeth, he held onto the connection, resisting her attempts to close down. To shut him out. He inhaled, struggling through his own emotions to push peace towards her. He reached out for her despite the miles between them. Once before, he'd held her in the shelter of his arms. They'd been in a stable, much like this one. He'd told her not to worry.

He met nothing but resistance. What a fool he had been.

"You told me he would be alright. You promised. You lied to me!" Her girlish voice echoed down their connection, harsh with accusation.

He winced. *"Bird... I didn't promise. I said I'd try..."*

"You did. You know you did. And I told you. I said I didn't want him to go. And now he's..."

She couldn't even say the word.

"Little Bird, I'm sorry. So sorry. He was a hero. And he loved you so much. Please..."

His voice tailed away. He wasn't even sure what he was asking for. Understanding. Forgiveness. His own nightmares returned to jeer at him from the shadows. *Not worthy*, they said. A chorus of accusations from his childhood that he had never fully left behind.

Bird's sobs died off enough for her to ask a single question.

"How?" she said in a voice colder than a snowdrift. Her tone struck at him like a hammer against an anvil. Heavy with the weight of disappointment.

He told her as best he could. Casting his words into a dull, sullen silence that hurt more than her sadness. He recounted the fight in the

mines. Aldric's attempt to bring down Dominic's assailant, fractionally too late. Will's mad, impetuous rage, such a characteristic aspect of
his fighting style. He could feel her walls go up. Stone by stone. Word
by empty word. A fortress against more pain.

*"He didn't even think. Or wait. He just attacked with no thought of
his own safety. He saved my life..."*

His mental voice faded, and he waited for her response, his fingers
twisting uselessly in the heavy wool of his cloak. Her reply chilled him
to the bone.

"He gave his life to save you?"

"I didn't want him to. I was ready to die if I had to." It was defensive,
and he knew it. He felt her withdrawal, almost as if she was present
and drawing up her skirts away from a pool of vomit suddenly revealed
beneath her feet.

*"Bird, I'm sorry. You must believe me. It happened so fast. I would
have saved him if I could. All of us would. We loved him."*

He waited. Followed the churn of her thoughts as they whirled,
blizzard-like, through her mental landscape. He wanted to tell her it
wasn't his fault. That there was nothing he could have done. But the
sentiment felt hollow. He wasn't so sure anymore. Suddenly, he longed
for Petronella's ability. To mind-walk into a storm of emotion and
bring peace.

"You need to tell the Queen." He knew that without a fraction of a
doubt. *"She can help you, Bird. And she will. Please tell her what has
happened."*

Bird paused. *"You tell her,"* she said. Ice tinged every syllable. *"Tell
her that you lied. Her favourite courtier. Darling Dominic. Tell her
what you did. She's ill. Did you know that? She's pregnant and getting weaker every day. You've woken something that should have stayed
asleep. The Prince is beside himself. It's all going wrong. And it's your
fault."*

"Bird, please..."

"No. You betrayed me. I will never forgive you. Never."

Silence settled between them. Deeper than a well and just as dark. He searched his heart for something to say. Something of comfort. Of hope. He could feel Little Bird waiting for it. A magic hand to pluck her from her darkness and draw her back to a world where the worst that could happen to her had not happened.

There were no words. Nothing he could say.

Just ice.

She cut the connection so quickly that it made him dizzy. He stumbled somehow to his feet and fell against his horse. The warmth was comforting, but that was all. There was no one to turn to. It was as he had feared. He'd let everyone down. Betrayed his queen's trust in him by chasing after Felicia. So wrapped up in his own desires he couldn't keep his mind on what really mattered. Over and over, his mind returned to Joran's deep mistrust. The Queen's fragile health. Cerys. Everything went back to her. But he'd lost the Blade of Aequitas. And Cerys was free to cause as much damage as she liked. All because he'd failed. And now Little Bird, too.

Shoulders shaking, he threw both arms around his horse's neck. Kismet stood like a rock when the tears came. He clutched at her, the only tether to a collapsing world, and wept his guilt and grief into her ebony mane.

CHAPTER 8
JORAN

"You told Lord Colman to do what?" Petronella's startled response shattered the evening peace of her chamber. The Grayling's head snapped from his doze as he bated on his perch. Eyes ablaze, Petronella glared at Joran from her pillows, struggling to sit upright. She threw off her blankets. Her attempt at rising caused both Joran and Fortuna to lunge forward at the same time.

"Nay, nay, my lady, do not move," Fortuna pleaded, "the bone is only just knit. You will damage yourself!" She placed both hands on Petronella's shoulders. The Queen shook her off.

"I will move, and you will help me! Too long have I lain abed!"

"My love...please." Joran shunted Fortuna aside, lifting his fragile wife easily in his arms and standing her carefully on her feet. Petronella bit her lip, her face white with the effort. Fortuna steadied her on the injured side, allowing the Queen to use her as a crutch.

"You will recall your request of Lord Colman," Petronella said, raising stormy eyes to his. "We cannot and will not return to the days of my former husband's reign. I will not allow it."

"But I am acting on your behalf." Joran stared her down, hands on his hips. "Did you not hear what I said? We have a traitor in our midst. A treacherous viper, feeding information to Dupliss and his forces. I must find him, and I need some clue to start the search. A list will..."

"You will make no such list." Petronella's diamond ring blazed to life, lancing light straight into Joran's eyes. He winced, shielding his face from the glare.

"The Ring of Mercy," Petronella said. She raised her hand, forcing his gaze to the pulse of the diamond's pure light. "Do you deny its power in this kingdom?"

Joran scowled. "The Ring of Justice," he said. His lips thinned, and he waved his hand at the jewel dangling from the fine silver chain encircling Petronella's fragile throat. "Both are important. My role is to protect you and our kingdom. Give it to me. I will wear it now and wield justice as I think fit."

Petronella stood her ground, wincing at the pain. "You have yet to don this ring, Joran. Until you prove to me you are worthy of its gifts, I will continue to guard it."

He took a heavy step forward. Intent on taking it from her. She halted him with a single, dismissive look. He blinked, aware of her formidable presence in his mind as he had not felt it before.

"Don't, Petronella..."

"I can help you, if you will only let me. Do not become the man your brother was, Joran. I know you are stronger than that." Her voice in his thoughts was soft but implacable. He could feel the beleaguered, terrified child in him running from its single-minded purpose. Seeking shelter from its all-seeing eye. Hiding.

"But I am not Arion," he said out loud. He reached out to her, longing for her gentle touch. Her understanding. "I am your true and loving husband. I wish only to protect you and our people. Do you not trust me?"

Petronella sighed. "'Tis not a matter of trust," she said, barely above a whisper. "'Tis a matter of judgement. I cannot hand you a weapon more deadly than any have known before. Try to understand." Her face was bleak. Her eyes clouded with sadness. Joran's fists clenched at his sides. Searching her expression, he saw the one he most dreaded. Disappointment. Anger rose in response.

"I have a right to exert justice in defence of this realm," he snapped.

Petronella met his anger with her own. She raised her chin, her expression glacial. "As did your father. He and my father made lists as well. Many of them. You know how that ended."

"I am not them!" Joran snapped, his temper flaring. "Do you believe me so weak, so foolish, that I would repeat the mistakes of the past?"

"It is not weakness I fear," Petronella said, her voice quiet but unshakable. "It is what such power can do to a good man when he is angry and afraid."

Joran's eyes widened, the words striking a nerve. He turned away from her, pacing to the far side of the room, his hands clenching and unclenching as he tried to steady himself. "The people need protection. I must find the traitor before more lives, precious Blessed lives, are lost. This...this hesitation will only lead to more death."

Petronella's gaze followed him, her hand clutching Fortuna for support. "And how many will you sacrifice to this search, Joran? What kind of kingdom will you leave behind if you divide our people into the Blessed and the Unblessed once again?"

"I would never..." Joran's protest died on his lips as he turned and caught the look in her eyes, a look that spoke of battles already fought, wounds already suffered. This wasn't just about the traitor. It was about the ghosts of her past, the horrors she had lived through under Arion's rule. Her own father's bitter role in the nation's ruin.

"You think me incapable of wielding justice. I wish to do so on your behalf. I know what you have suffered." His voice was softer now, wounded. "Do you truly believe I am unable to do that?"

Petronella's features softened as she attempted a step, wincing as she shifted her weight onto her unsteady leg. "No, Joran. I believe you are more capable than you know. But you must not let fear guide your hand. Justice is not something you seize; it is something you earn."

They stared at each other across the divide of the plush Argentian rug, searching for answers in each other's eyes. Petronella swayed on her feet, and Fortuna tightened her hold, steadying her.

Joran dredged his tired brain for the words that would break the deadlock and sadness that thrummed between them. He stared at her, yearning for her approval. All he saw in her eyes was pain.

His fists clenched tighter, the weight of her disappointment settling over him like a shroud. His heart hammered in his chest. He wanted to reach for her and pull her close. Convince her of his love, his loyalty. The divide between them felt far too wide. The Ring of Justice gleamed against her heart, a reminder of the power she withheld from him, the power he could wield if only she would let him.

"I am not my father!" he repeated, his voice trembling with a mix of anger and desperation. "I know what he did. The damage he wrought. But I will not follow in his footsteps. I am your husband, Petronella, not your enemy. Do you truly think me so blind?"

Petronella's gaze did not waver. "It is not your sight that worries me, Joran. It is your heart." She paused, her fingers reaching for the support of her bedstead. "You are not Francis. But power...fear...they twist even the best of men if they do not guard against it."

He felt the sting of her words, and for a moment, his resolve wavered. He wanted to lash out, to demand that she see him as the man he was. Strong. Determined. Capable of protecting their kingdom. But all he could see in her eyes was a reflection of his own doubt, the one that gnawed at him in the quiet moments of the night.

"How can I protect you," he whispered, his voice barely audible, "if you will not let me?"

Her eyes softened, and for a fleeting moment, he thought he saw her wavering. But then her hand moved to the chain at her neck, and the gleam of the Ring of Justice flickered between them. A bright white barrier he could not cross. She wavered where she stood, and her breath hitched as Fortuna helped her back into bed. Her body trembled with the effort, but her gaze never wavered from Joran. Even now, weakened and pale, her presence filled the room in a way that his power could not.

"You are already my protector, Joran," she said, her voice steady despite her frailty. "But do not seek justice through fear. That path will lead you only to ruin."

They watched each other in silence. Wary as strangers. Petronella's breath was shallow. Shadows crawled beneath her eyes. Joran's gaze flickered between her face and the ring, desperate for the words that would bridge the gap between them. He searched her face for something, some sign that she understood him, that she trusted him. But all he saw in her eyes was that same cool resolve, the same determination that had always kept her just out of reach. She was strong; he knew that. Stronger than most. But there was a distance between them now, a divide that his words seemed unable to bridge. And it terrified him more than he was willing to admit.

Yearning to say something that would close the yawning chasm between them, he scowled as a soft knock echoed through the chamber, followed by the hesitant shuffle of feet. Little Bird appeared in the doorway, the children trailing behind her. Their presence, which usually brought a welcome warmth to the room, felt jarring amid such tension. Their bright, expectant faces a flare of light against the sudden darkness clutching his heart. He swallowed, his throat dry. If anything happened to them...

"Your Majesty, the children are here for their visit," Little Bird said, her voice barely audible.

Petronella turned, her drawn face brightening at the sight of her children. Something in Little Bird's demeanour gave her pause.

Still too lost in his own turmoil to notice the girl, Joran waved a hand dismissively. "Not now," he muttered. "We are discussing matters of state."

Petronella frowned, her eyes narrowing as she glanced from her husband to the maid. "What is it, Little Bird?" she asked. Grave with concern, Fortuna glanced at the girl, but she said nothing as she handed the Queen a draft of willow bark tea to ease the pain.

Little Bird hesitated, her hands twisting nervously in front of her. "It's...Will Dunn, Your Majesty," she whispered, her voice cracking. "There's been...bad news."

"Come, sit down," Petronella urged, patting the bed. "Tell me what's happened."

Impatience twisting through him, Joran cut in before Little Bird could speak, his voice sharp with impatience. "We don't have time for this now," he said. Still locked in their previous argument, his gaze flicked back to his wife. "There are more important matters at hand."

Petronella turned on him, her eyes blazing with anger. "What could be more important than the life of one of our own?"

Joran's face hardened, his embarrassment at being contradicted in front of Little Bird and the children fuelling his frustration. "Justice, my lady," he bit out. "Finding the traitor who would see us all dead."

"And what justice is this," she said, her voice low but searing, "if it blinds you to the suffering of those who stand before you?" Her words cut through him like a blade, and for a moment, Joran had no response. Petronella did not need to raise her voice to make him feel small.

Standing awkwardly on the threshold of the room, agitated fingers twisting the ringlets escaping from her cap, Little Bird shrank under the tension she sensed. "Nay, 'tis of no matter," she murmured, bobbing a curtsey. "I will leave the children with you and return later." She backed away, her girlish, tear-stained face schooled to impassivity.

Fortuna patted Petronella's hand, and the Queen nodded at her. "Go with her," she murmured. "Make sure she is well. I will see her later."

"Aye, my lady," said Fortuna. She hurried across the room, chivvying Little Bird in front of her. Bird paused in the doorway, glancing over her shoulder at Joran. For a brief second, their eyes met, and Joran saw the question in her gaze; an unspoken plea for acknowledgement. But the moment passed, and she turned, retreating into the shadows, leaving behind the weight of his silence. His heart lurched, but it was too late. Too late to soften the words he'd thrown at her. Too late, as always, to repair the damage that had already been done. He watched her retreat, her narrow frame swallowed by the shadows in the corridor, and a familiar, gnawing hollowness settled in his chest. How many others had he turned away over the last few years, blinded by the weight of duty, the need for justice? A fleeting memory of the task he had demanded of Dominic Skinner flitted ghoulishly through his mind. The lad's haunted eyes, the way he'd stood there, waiting for encouragement that never came. Joran had as good as accused him of betrayal, stripping away whatever trust Dominic might still have held for him. He had pushed too hard, too soon. And now, the cracks were showing. He dropped his gaze from Petronella lest she read the guilty thoughts that circled there. He'd driven young Dominic away. Perhaps Petronella was right.

Stooping, he gathered Theda and Ranulf into his embrace, holding them close to his heart. Giggling, they clung to him as he picked them up, carrying them to Petronella's side. He deposited them on the bed and bent to brush a gentle kiss on Petronella's soft lips. She glanced up at him; her gaze was soft once more. His daughter's hot blue stare pierced his very soul. Her childish questions were clear to read in her small, accusing face. He ducked his head. For a moment, her resemblance to Mistress Eglion, her great-grandmother and name-sake, was too much to bear. She, too, had looked at him in just such a way once, long ago.

Not trusting himself to speak, he took his leave. Alone in the corridor, he leaned against the panelled wall, allowing it to cool his heated thoughts. The sounds of his children's laughter teased his ears, muffled behind the closed door. He should have felt comforted by the sight of them nestled in Petronella's arms, safe and content. But all he could think about was how far he had drifted from them, how much the crown had taken from him. His mind, as it always did, turned to the traitor. He would find him—he had to. The thought burned through his veins, a necessity now, not only to protect the realm but to give purpose to the sacrifices he had made. Before it was too late, for him and for them all.

CHAPTER 9
DOMINIC

Snow was falling as Dominic left the musky damp of the stables. He latched the door carefully against the weather and stood for a moment in the quiet, frost-wrapped courtyard, his breath misting around him. Muffled conversation trickled to him from the narrow-paned tavern windows. He watched the outlines of his companions through the bubbled glass, crossing and recrossing his line of sight. Their silhouettes appeared as blurred shadows against the golden firelight. Creatures he couldn't reach. The cheerful clink of glass, and the tang of hops crept to his nostrils. He glanced up at the sky, measuring the passage of the moon. He'd been gone at least a half candle measure. Maybe more. The cold had penetrated so far into his heart that it felt like part of him. A frozen, solid centre. His thoughts turned like boulders across his mind. He felt the weight of their stately passage. Immense, impenetrable. At odds with the icy gusts of wind playing with the snowflakes.

A flicker of rushlight drew his gaze to the ramshackle store shed hard against the courtyard wall. Someone had lit torches at its entrance. A wreath of winterberries and ivy, tied with a blue ribbon, hung from the rough wood planks. For Will. His frozen corpse lay within, awaiting burial. A shiver racked his body as the wind rose and pressed against him. Dominic wandered towards the building like a sleepwalker and leaned his head against the door.

"I told her, Will." He whispered the words to his former companion. "I tried my best to tell her how it was. How brave you were. How selfless. I know she hates me now. But I will look after her. I absolutely promise you that. I hope you can hear me…"

Silence. His whisper tailed away, absorbed by the wood. If Will's shade was watching him from his place at the Mage's side, the lad gave no sign. Dominic's strength left him. He slumped to the ground, almost welcoming the snow's icy embrace. The call of an owl came to him, haunting and lonely on the wind. Snowflakes brushed his cheeks. Or was it the gentle touch of a feathered wing? The stroking hand of a more powerful presence? Hard to tell. Held in the moment, he drifted. No longer cold. Floating. Called to the depths of the ancient sky, beckoned by the flute of the owl.

The crunch of boots across the snow came to him dimly. Voices arguing, a piping flute, somewhere far away. Tired to the bone, he stayed where he was as snow sifted over him. Perhaps the footsteps belonged to Will. Any moment now, Will's ghost would come for him. Maybe they would meet the Mage together. Instead, his fading vision snared on Aldric and Felicia as they hurried towards him. Aldric's hand on his cheek burned like fire.

Aldric shot one telling glance at Felicia and grabbed his sleeve. "I told you we should have come out earlier," he said. "He's freezing to death."

"I'm not cold, I'm tired. Let me sleep," Dominic insisted. His thoughts felt sluggish.

"You've gone beyond cold, you complete idiot." Felicia's voice, sharp and determined, cut through his senses. "Get up. Come on. Cedric said this wind is building into a blizzard."

She hooked her arm through his and heaved, but her fragile strength made no impression. Frustrated, she stood back, hands on hips.

"Don't look at me. I can't carry him. Fetch Guildford," Aldric said. "And make the biggest fire you can in our chamber. Don't burn down the inn." He loomed over Dominic and shook him. "Don't go to sleep. Wake up!"

"She hates me, Aldric. Hates me."

"She doesn't. Stop blaming yourself. 'Twill do no good."

Felicia skidded across the ice-crusted cobbles, yelling her brother's name as she went. Aldric doffed his own cloak and wrapped it around Dominic's body. "Dominic, stay awake. We have work to do. 'Tis not time for you to leave us yet," he said. Eyes almost shut, Dominic's head lolled as Aldric shook him out of his stupor. "Come on. You can't let Cerys win." The lad kept up a barrage of words, brushing the snow away from Dominic's skin. "By the Gods, where is that great oaf?" he murmured to himself. He was shivering without his cloak. Dominic could feel the tremble in the lad's fierce grip on his shoulders.

"Probably wenching," Dominic muttered. His words came out as slurred as if he was drunk.

"You're talking. Good. What did Bird say? Tell me."

Too much. Dominic turned his head away. "Ah." Aldric's face softened. "Welladay, the poor lass," he said.

"Mind the path, Aldric," Guildford's ruddy voice, loud in the hushed atmosphere, rich with wine and vivid with life, broke the strange spell that hung over them. He crouched and swung Dominic over his shoulder. "What are you up to now?" he grunted as he braced his legs to rise. "I spend more time carrying you than anyone else. And I'll have you know I just left a willing maid warming my pallet."

Despite his concern, Aldric chuckled as Dominic's head jounced unsteadily against Guildford's shoulder blades. "By the Gods, he's stiff as a block of wood," Guildford said, kicking the tavern door open. The blaze of light and warmth enveloped them.

"You can put me down," Dominic said, his voice muffled by Guildford's hastily donned doublet.

"I'll take you to your chamber," Guildford returned. "You can get up when you've recovered."

He took the stairs at a jog, shouldered the door of Dominic's room, and tipped his burden onto the mattress with no ceremony whatsoever. Felicia grabbed Aldric's blankets from the neighbouring cot. The fire in the hearth was already roaring.

"By the Gods, what were you doing out there?" Staring down at him, Guildford's voice was rough with unaccustomed concern.

"He was telling Little Bird that we lost Will Dunn," Felicia said before Dominic could speak. "'Tis not a simple thing, telepathy. It takes a lot of energy, and if you love the person you are talking to, sometimes you can experience their emotions, as well as your own. I think that's what just happened."

"Is that right?"

Dominic managed a shrug before Felicia smothered him with the blankets and tossed her own cloak over the lot for good measure. His teeth were chattering.

"You continue to amaze me," Guildford said. He shook his head. "I've never known a person like you. So bloody intent on doing the right thing, you're willing to die for it."

"Aye, well," was all Dominic could manage. Tremors were shaking him from head to foot. Felicia's new cloak smelled of heartsease and woodruff. Soothing.

Felicia gave her brother a shove. "Go on back to your conquest," she said. "Leave the nursing for those more qualified. He'll be better on the morrow when we've warmed him up."

Guildford chuckled. "Aye, I know my worth around here. They should call me your cart-horse."

"We call you much worse things than that," Aldric said.

Guildford's rich laughter filled the room as he opened the door. "Excuse me, Mistress Trevis," he said as the healer entered beneath his arm, laden with a clinking tray of vials and potions.

"My thanks," she muttered. "Out of the way, lad. Let's see about Sir Skinner. Again."

Chapter 10
JORAN

L ate-night silence gripped the Castle of Air. Seated at his desk,
Joran's mouth was a stern line as he affixed the seal of Epera to
each carefully penned letter. There was a pile to his left, ready to be
sent to the many outlying estates across the nation. His blood chilled
the longer he sat there, despite the comforting warmth of a cheerful
fire and the glass of Oceanis wine at his elbow. Propping his head
on his hands, he stared moodily at the flames. More troops. Stronger
defences. He knew well what this news would mean to the wider population. A call to arms against a sporadic but deadly force, built of the
disaffected, fanned by the residual resentment that still lingered in the
minds and hearts of the people. Led by the arch-commander, Count
Dupliss. Once Darius of Falconridge's most able adviser. Now, a man
determined to replace the powerfully Blessed Queen with Guildford
of Wessendean. A Citizen. Famed within their ranks for his strength,
his wenching, and his prowess with weapons. A king for the people.
Of the people. Not some distant, Blessed goddess armed with magic
and shrouded in mystery.

His heart ached for his wife. So many of the population distrusted
her still. They despised her failure to bear a child for her former husband, Arion, and their subsequent starvation. Blamed her for every
perceived infraction of their freedom. The Blessed bore the terrible
scars in their family lines and judged her for her inability to quell Arion's persecution of the magically gifted. Her reign carried the legacy of

the terrible events of nearly forty years before. No-one had forgotten, still less, forgiven. He did his best to keep it from her. But she knew. He saw the burden she carried. Had borne alone for so long. No surprise that she was weakening now.

Scrubbing his hands across his bearded cheeks, he lowered his eyes to the last message. "...by the Queen's command," it finished. With space for his signature and seal. They already complained about their taxes. Now, this additional request. He reached automatically for his glass, hating himself. A vision of her lying in bed, faded and pale, flashed through his mind. The Queen's command... Not likely. If they only knew her as he did.

They hated her. And it was his fault now, as it had been his father's before him. Francis was to blame for everything. His fatal weakness and misjudgement had allowed Darius of Falconridge's manipulative fingers to grasp the fragile edge of power and climb. Joran's fingers tightened on the fragile stem of the Oceanian crystal.

Locked in a welter of doubt, at first, he didn't hear the soft rap of knuckles against wood. The noise came again, permeating the haze of alcohol provided by the rich blue wine.

"Come! Gods blast you!"

His guard poked a head around the door. A stocky figure, crowned with a helmet decorated with a flamboyant blue cockatrice. It was slightly too big for him. Tilted at a ridiculous angle. In another mood, Joran would have smiled.

"Have you been asleep? Straighten your cap, man," he snapped.

The soldier reddened under his tanned cheeks, righting his head-gear. "I'm to give you this, my lord," he said, holding out a slim, cylindrical object. His hand shook slightly. Joran threw him a glare and reached over his desk to take it.

"A message, my lord," the guard offered, helpfully. "The master of the dovecote delivered it just now. Said it was urgent. Pigeon's half dead. Storm's coming."

"I recognise a message canister when I see one," Joran grunted. He waved the hapless man away. "Dismissed. You may sleep. I need no further guard tonight."

His heart sinking, the heavy pulse of his magic building in his brow, Joran waited until the door closed before he eased open the leather case. A slim roll of finest parchment spiralled within its confines. He tapped it out and moved nearer to the lamp to read what it had to say. It was brief. Hastily penned and utterly confounding.

"Falconridge under attack. They want the book. Guard the Queen. Ash."

His blood ran colder than the Cryfell in winter. "By the Gods, what's this? Falconridge? What book?" Joran stared at it. Turned the page over. Peered into the canister in case he'd missed something. There was nothing else. He pressed a fist against his chest. His heartbeat was heavy with incipient panic, the crushing weight of dread. How strong was this army to attack Falconridge, already fortified by Sir Dunforde and his troops? Why had he heard nothing from Sir Dunforde himself?

A lifetime of caution warred with the need to open his mental channels. Even now, he pre-judged himself every time he used telepathy to communicate. Mouth dry, he avoided his wine glass and reached instead for a glass of crystal-clear water drawn from the pristine springs high in the northern mountains and kept specifically for the Court of Air. A luxury few could afford. The draft swept his body like a walk in the rain. Pure, honest.

He opened his channels, scanning his mental landscape for the chirpy energy of Falconridge's old steward.

"Master Ash, I have your message."

Nothing.

"Master Ash, 'tis Joran of Weir. Please answer me."

There. A quiver of something that felt like relief. But faint. Too faint. *"My lord…"*

"Master Ash, speak to me. What has happened? What book?"

"Tis too late." The old man's mental voice wavered in his head. Joran ducked his own, aware, suddenly, of the weight of his own body. The touch of death in the room. The uneven beat of his heart. Or perhaps that was Petronella's fiercest childhood champion, projecting his thoughts and fears as best he could. His mouth twisted. He'd heard such stories about cheerful Master Ash and his unsung role in Petronella's youth.

"The black Book of Shadows. That's what they seek. But they must not find it. You must..."

"Please, Master, explain. We must understand..."

"They have my lady Briana's diaries. Tell the Queen. She must guard the black Book of Shadows with her life. They have the Blade of Aequitas. The book is all they need. All she needs... Safe from her..."

The steward's mental voice came at a rush. As if he was marshalling every drop of his strength to convey his message. Even so, it trailed away. Joran's face screwed into bafflement. Mistress Eglion had shared much of her knowledge over the years, but he'd never heard of this. The black Book of Shadows... A memory of Petronella's battle against the might of the Dark Army years before flashed to the front of his mind. Her father had held a small black book on that fateful day. Used it to command his forces. Is that what Master Ash meant? But what could it matter now? Darius was dead. *"Blade of Aequitas? By the Gods, what is that? Whose book? Tell me!"*

The steward's last words drifted to him, faint and weary, dry as autumn leaves across an unswept floor.

"Dominic... Tell..."

"Please..." Joran stumbled somehow to his feet. His hands reached out to empty air as if to grasp Master Ash and hold him in the world for a few moments more. A need to cradle the faithful soul as he left. To thank him for his service. His heart hollowed as Master Ash departed. Locked in mental communication, the man's gentle, merry

soul drifted soundlessly into the ether. Joran blinked moisture from his eyes. Raised his head to ground himself once more in his familiar study. The portrait of Petronella and himself hung over the hearth was the first splash of colour that caught his eye. Ranulf, yet a toddler, was caught in the tender circle of his mother's arms. All of them smiling.

He turned in a frustrated circle, his mind whirling with strategies. The sinking sensation of events sweeping him out of control, like that doomed boat trip down the flooding Cryfell River so many years ago. Frustrated energy propelled him to pace the length of the narrow room and back. He slammed a fist on the wood of his desk. The force of the blow made his quills jump in their ink pots. He reached for the comfort of his decanter.

Dominic. Again. So many times, it came back to that young man. What did Dominic know that he hadn't revealed?

But you won't let him reveal it, will you, the judge of his mind reminded him. Its voice came to him as it always did. A sly whisper creeping under his defences. Digging holes in his self-worth. *You don't want to. You're afraid. Afraid. Admit it, why don't you? You're as afraid of magic as Darius of Falconridge, who wanted to bring it under his control. As scared as your brother when he realised he didn't have it and would never become the respected king he longed to be. As terrified as your father when he realised he had abused the Mage's greatest gifts and lost them for good. Say it. Go on, say it.*

"Shut up," he said out loud to no-one.

Say it, say it... The voice in his mind blurred. Became a chorus of accusation. Like a circle of Blade's orphans gathered together, chanting. "We know. We know what you are. And we are going to tell. And then you will DIE!"

"I am not afraid! You will not say it!" He tossed another mouthful down. The wine failed to soften the edges of his waking nightmare. He slumped into his seat. Opened his channels to their fullest extent. Something that he rarely did.

"Dominic. Dupliss' army has attacked Falconridge. Master Ash is dead. They are seeking the black Book of Shadows. You must get there. Help us. Please."

He pitched his mental voice at a shout. Loud enough to almost wake the dead. One such as Dominic, so attuned to his gift, couldn't fail to hear it. He grimaced, turning the fragile glass in his fingers as he waited for the young man to reply. Dominic probably wasn't the only one who could hear it. His own telepathic gift was formidable. He'd probably broadcasted his desperation to the entire telepathic population if they wished to receive it.

He strained his senses, expecting Dominic's response at any moment. Minutes passed, marked only by the shifting of logs in the grate. He tried again, scanning his mental landscape for a sign of Dominic's fizzing mental energy. There was nothing. He closed his eyes. Something was wrong. There had to be. Or he'd been correct. Pushed too hard; Dominic had closed his mind. No longer trusted him enough to obey even a heartfelt request.

There was only one avenue left. He grabbed a quill and scrawled a hasty message on the back of Master Ash's last communication. Reaching for his cloak, Joran left his office at a run, propelled by the need to do something, anything, to relieve the panic in his heart. Leaving his channels open, he sprinted down palatial walkways and decorated galleries, ducked beneath a tapestry, and found the fastest way to the cluster of service yards via the narrow, shadowed passageways inhabited by servants and mice. Winter crept under ill-fitting window embrasures and warped doors. He stifled a shiver as he quickened his pace.

Freezing wind spiralled around him as he shoved open the low, thickly panelled door that led to the courtyard. The storm was building. Snow in the air. The ice crusted under his feet forced a slower pace. It took him a minute to locate the dovecote in the quiet corner of the yard. A curious cat eyed him from its perch on a nearby dung heap, keeping warm despite the snow dusting its fur. But the cat and the dim silhouettes of the castle guards patrolling the battlements were the only signs of activity. He glanced around at the heavy walls. Ancient, built to withstand a siege. The Castle of Air was a fortress; everyone knew that. So why was he suddenly so terrified? So vulnerable? Pulling his cloak more closely around him, his gaze drifted upwards to a lone candle in a tiny window high in his wife's wing. He'd kept his channels open. If he hadn't, he'd never have heard it. A bleak girl's voice, her grief aching in the night, tugging at his senses. *"Will, oh, Will. Meridan. Don't leave me. Please don't leave me..."*

His heart clenched. Little Bird. Alone in the world. Lost. Just like him. Overtaken by events beyond her control. His heart went out to her. *"Peace, Little Bird..."* He sent the thought to her as he entered the malodorous environment of the dovecote and its dozing inhabitants. A faintly sweet aroma of grain and bird shit. He caught the last thought just before he closed his channels.

"Is that you, Dominic?" she whispered into the night. He frowned, bemused that she might have confused their mental signatures, but there was no time to dwell on it. Squinting in the dim light, he located the pigeons from Hartwood. Plucked a fragile, sleeping bird from the safety of her shelter and tied his desperate message to her leg. The wind was building as he latched the dovecote door and tossed her into the incoming storm.

"Godspeed, little bird," he whispered.

CHAPTER 11
DOMINIC

The blizzard broke over Hartwood with a ferocity that had even Cedric's beetling brows rising in his leathered forehead. Dominic spent the first night of his brush with the northern winter shivering under his blankets. Lightheaded and feverish, his thoughts as thick as mud. Felicia and Aldric watched over him like hens with one chick. Their arguments as to his proper care were many and frequent. He caught their tangled words in glimpses between the tremors that wracked him from head to toe. Mistress Trevis drifted in and out of the room, her expression wry as she overheard Felicia and Aldric battle it out for control of their patient. In a brilliant moment of clarity, in the late morning of the second day, Dominic caught her eye as she entered. She said nothing, but her penetrating gaze, locked on Aldric, contained a singular satisfaction. "Healer," she mouthed at Dominic as she retreated, closing the door gently behind her.

His strength came back over the course of the second day. He watched the storm's anger from his narrow bed. The weight of ice pushing against his windows, the howl of the wind as it battered the small town. By midday, the storm abated. Hungrier than a bear, he ignored the advice of both his nurses.

"I'm getting up, and you are not stopping me," he said.

"Do you need help?" Felicia said as he struggled to unwrap himself from the cocoon of blankets. She turned from the fireplace, a steaming brew of heartsease in her hand. The green, herbal scent filled the small chamber. He pushed the final cover from his naked body aside, and stood up. Aldric shot an alarmed glance at him and fled the room. Felicia's eyes widened. A faint blush suffused her pale cheeks. She swallowed.

"I can see you don't need help," she murmured.

"Oh, I do," Dominic said. He crossed the room in two strides and plucked the flask from her fingers, placing it carefully on a rough-hewed bench. "I need lots of help."

The familiar, earthy scent of heartsease surrounded them, sweet and sharp, like Felicia herself. Captivating and elusive all at once. His gaze locked on hers, searching for something beneath that careful composure she wore so well.

Felicia stilled, her fingers twitching as if she wasn't sure whether to reach for him or retreat. Her lips parted slightly, but no words came. The room felt smaller, the distance between them almost unbearable.

"You're stronger than you think," she said, her voice quieter than usual, as though she was trying to convince herself as much as him.

Dominic shook his head, his eyes never leaving her face. "I don't need strength right now," he murmured, his voice low. Urgent. "What I need is you."

Felicia's breath caught. Her hand hovered near his naked chest, hesitating just before making contact. Dominic took her wrist gently, guiding it the rest of the way until her palm pressed against his heartbeat. Her cool touch lit a fire in his blood.

"Dominic, we shouldn't..."

But the protest was faint, her resolve already wavering. He leaned in, close enough that he could feel the warmth of her breath on his cheek, his mouth just a whisper away from hers. Her scent, the heartsease tea, the rain-soaked moss and mountain heather he always associated with her, clouded his senses.

"I'm not asking for promises," Dominic whispered. His thumb grazed the soft skin of her wrist. "Just this."

His lips brushed hers. Soft at first, testing the waters. But when Felicia didn't pull away, the kiss deepened, a slow burn igniting between them. She responded, tentative but unable to resist the pull. For a moment, he forgot everything—the storm outside, the weight of their responsibilities, the threat to the kingdom. Here, it was only the two of them in the quiet room, drawn together by something unspoken and powerful. His arms tightened around her, holding her close against his pounding heart.

But then, just as quickly, Felicia pulled back. Her breath came fast, her fingers trembling as she pressed them to her lips. The flush on her cheeks deepened, but not just from their kiss. There was something else in her eyes. Fear, or maybe guilt.

"I can't," she whispered, stepping away, the distance between them suddenly vast. "Dominic, I can't."

Dominic blinked, trying to read the emotion flickering behind her guarded expression. His body still thrummed with the nearness of her, but she was already retreating, that wall of cool composure sliding back into place.

"Felicia..." he began, but she shook her head.

"Not now," she said softly, a shadow passing over her face. "Maybe we will, one day. But please, just...not now."

Bewildered, fiery blood still thundering through his body, he could only watch as she caught up the flask and headed for the door. He took a step forward.

"Felicia, I don't understand... Why...?"

She paused, half out of the door. The turmoil behind her eyes chilled him almost as much as the draft from the unheated corridor. *Winter*, Dominic thought bleakly. Always, with Felicia, ice before the fire. He dropped his gaze. Turned away. The soft click of the door told her she was gone.

About to offer some sort of merry quip, Aldric's grin faded at the frustration in Dominic's expression as he entered the narrow taproom. Felicia had joined Mistress Trevis by the hearth. Together, they bent over Tom's arm. Pale-faced and sweating, he sat on the edge of a settle, trying to shrug off the blanket the healer had placed over his bare shoulders.

"By the Gods, keep that on." Mistress Trevis's voice held an unaccustomed note of alarm mixed with exasperation. Felicia kept her back to Dominic as he glanced their way. He grimaced. Tom did not look well.

Forced indoors by the storm, the group had made the deserted taproom into a common room of sorts. Cedric's staff were busy ferrying empty tankards back to the kitchen and returning with laden trays. Cedric was counting barrels and chivvying the servants. Aldric busied himself cleaning tack. Dominic patted his purse as he wandered across the room. It was lighter now than it had been weeks ago when he set out. They would have to ensure they settled their debts with Cedric. He cast an eye at the lowering sky. It had stopped snowing, at last. The townsfolk were abroad, their heavily cloaked forms visible through the clouded panes as they sought supplies.

In the absence of a squire, Guildford was polishing his own sword, pausing at intervals to admire his work. The deadly blade gleamed under his industry.

"How now, better?" he said as Dominic brushed past him.

"Aye. My thanks for your help."

Guildford shrugged, his powerful shoulders straining at the seams of his cambric shirt. "'Twas nothing. Look at this. Who needs a squire, anyway?" He held his sword up for inspection.

"Very good." Despite his frustration, Dominic's mood lightened slightly. After all, Felicia had kissed him. It was a start. "One day, you'll even learn how to use it."

"I'll use it on you if you don't take that back."

Chuckling, Dominic took a seat and reached for a flagon of small ale. Aldric shoved the remains of a tray of bread and cheese towards him. Kismet's bridle took up most of the space. Aldric was cleaning it with tallow, buffing it to a shine with a wad of cloth.

"What happened?" he asked. "Thought you'd take much longer than that. All night, in fact."

A sigh escaped him as he reached for the heel of the loaf Aldric had left.

"Nothing," he said.

"She wouldn't have you? That's a surprise, after all she said while you were abed..." He stopped abruptly as Dominic glanced up.

"What did she say?"

Aldric squirmed in his seat. "'Twas nothing..." he hazarded.

"By the Gods, Aldric, if you know something, you'd better tell me. I thought she felt something for me just now. But then she pulled back, just when things were getting...interesting." He cast a wistful glance across the room as he felt Felicia staring at him. Just as quickly, she looked away, but not before he saw the rosy blush stain her cheeks.

"She's not indifferent. That means something, I suppose," he continued.

Aldric huffed a laugh. "Far from it, the way she fussed over you, I would say," he said. "We nearly came to blows at one point. Something about the relative merits of chamomile over feverfew and willowbark."

"Yes, I think I remember that," Dominic replied. He stretched his arms overhead, surveying the tobacco-stained plaster ceiling, suddenly overcome with delight. She had feelings for him. Even if she couldn't admit it. "Tom doesn't look well," he said, changing the subject before Aldric could interrogate him any further.

Aldric's face clouded. "He's not. Mistress Trevis is worried about him. His arm is not healing," he said. "And she's run out of some things."

Dominic slid his legs over the trestle. "I'll go," he said. "'Twould do me good to be up and about."

"I need to visit the fletchers for more arrows," Aldric said. "I've re-fletched all that I have, but I need more supplies as well."

"Welladay, we'll all go. Mayhap Felicia would like a stroll." His face wreathed in his most charming smile, Dominic strode over to the tense figures at the fireside. Perspiration coated Tom's swarthy cheeks. Dark shadows clung beneath his eyes. "By the Gods, Tom, what's this?" Dominic said.

Tom managed a frayed smile. "Not you, too," he said. "I wish everyone would stop fussing. 'Tis just a scratch."

Mistress Trevis snorted. "You need to let me tend you," she said, peering into her satchel. "But I've run out of garlic and yarrow."

"I'll go to the market for you," Dominic offered. "Would you walk with me, Felicia?" he added.

His would-be paramour rolled her eyes. "Very subtle, Sir Skinner," she said.

Dominic half shrugged. "I wish to spend time with you. Call me an idiot," he returned.

A smile tugged at her mouth. "I often do."

"So, you'll come with me, then? Before we lose the light?"

Felicia sighed. "Aye. If I must."

"Try not to sound too enthusiastic." Despite his words, he was almost skipping as he raced to fetch her cloak. Even Aldric and Guildford's uproarious laughter as they observed his swagger failed to dent his high spirits.

The bitter wind had dropped to a sigh as they left the shelter of the Beaten Drum, nodding a greeting to the passersby. Everywhere Dominic looked, the townsfolk were busy shovelling snow from their doors. It looked to his inexpert eyes as if they must have started the minute the storm subsided. Already, narrow pathways, scattered with dark ashes and straw, crisscrossed the more essential routes. Stoic oxen sweated under their loads as they heaved piles of snow from the heart of the town.

Aldric's eyes darted everywhere, fascinated. "I've never seen snow this deep. 'Tis amazing," he remarked. "Where are they taking it all?"

"Out of the town to the nearest river, I suppose," Dominic guessed. "I'm not sure where that is. It can't be far."

"Look, the fletchers is open," Aldric said. "I'll see you both at supper." He hurried off. Somewhat loath to see him go, Dominic glanced at Felicia. She kept her gaze lowered to the ice-wrapped street, although their path was relatively clear. Dominic drew the folds of his cloak more closely around his body. The weak sunlight was already slipping from the sullen sky. "We'd best hasten," he remarked, "before the market closes."

Felicia gave him her elbow readily enough, and together, they traversed the frozen streets. The winter air, already sharp with frost, caught the back of Dominic's throat. Lads clutching flaming tapers were setting the town's lanterns alight. The lamps cast a golden hue over the scene. His nose twitching at the inviting scent of roasting chestnuts, Dominic drew Felicia to a halt in front of a stand at the market entrance. The rosy-cheeked woman behind the rough counter gave him a gap-toothed grin.

"Chestnuts, fine sir, and good lady," she invited, giving the nuts a shake over the hot coals of her brazier and removing a fresh batch. "Half a penny a dozen."

"We need some of these," he said, fishing a copper from his purse.

Felicia smiled. "'Tis a favourite of mine," she said. "I haven't had roasted chestnuts for such a long time."

The nut vendor scooped their purchases into a twist of cloth and handed it over.

"My thanks, mistress," Dominic said. He handed the savoury parcel to Felicia. "Warm your hands on that."

Felicia's nimble fingers made quick work of peeling the chestnuts. "Here, you take yours," she said, with her mouth full.

"My thanks. Drink?" Dominic suggested as they walked on, munching their snack. The market was winding down for the day, the industrious crowds thinning.

"We'd better find Mistress Trevis' supplies first," Felicia said. "Up ahead. Quick, before she shuts up shop."

Unlike the friendly chestnut vendor, the owner of the herb stall gave them both short shrift. "I'm closed," she snapped. "'Tis a freezing afternoon already, as you must agree. I must be away." She stood her ground with her hands on her ample hips, blocking their access to her goods. Dominic felt some sympathy with her. It was late in the day.

Felicia scanned the rows of dried herbs still suspended from the rough frame with an expert eye. "You still have yarrow and garlic. 'Tis all we need," she said in her most reasonable voice. "I see you have some there." She pointed.

"But I'm closed," the stallholder rejoined.

"'Tis for a soldier injured in the line of duty," Felicia said mildly enough. "Surely you would not deny him aid?"

"Depends, doesn't it?" the woman said, glowering. "On what side he's on?"

Dominic and Felicia exchanged glances.

"Does it matter?" Dominic asked.

The woman drew herself up and favoured them with a beady-eyed glare. "If it's for one of them Blessed devils, it does," she declared. "One of them witches who came here and set fire to our mill. Or one of those others who travel with them."

Dominic's brow lifted. "Oh, for sure. No. 'Tis one of the Queen's guard, sent to help you," he explained.

The woman relaxed. "Well then, of course. I am open. What else do you need?"

"Heartsease," Felicia said immediately. "As much as you can spare."

Dominic glanced across at her. "Don't you already have a supply of that?" he murmured.

Felicia shot him a look, her eyes sharp but laced with unease. "I don't intend to run out," she said, her tone clipped. "Not now."

Dominic frowned, puzzled. "You still need more?"

"Heartsease, is it?" The stall holder's sharp voice cut the air. Her eyes narrowed as she leaned against the counter, her breath enveloping them in clouds of frost. "Strange for a lady like you to need so much of it, wouldn't you say? Weren't you here the other day?"

Felicia stiffened, her fingers tightening around her cloak. Dominic felt a prickle of tension between them, his gaze flicking from Felicia to the woman. There was a weight in the air, the kind that suggested secrets were teetering on the edge of exposure.

"What do you mean by that?" Dominic asked, his voice casual but edged with warning.

The stallholder leaned closer, her eyes darting to the side as if checking whether anyone else was listening. "I know what heartsease is good for," she said in a lowered voice. "It calms the mind, yes...but it also weakens the magic. Keeps those...*witches* from losing control, don't it? The likes of them have bought from me before. I remember him. The old one. Tall. With a scar at his throat." Her work-worn hand traced the sign of the Mage for protection in front of her.

Dominic's heart skipped a beat. The woman fixed her beady-eyed glare on Felicia, her earlier suspicion resurfacing.

"You wouldn't be one of them, would you?" the stallholder asked Felicia, her voice dripping with disdain. "One of those Blessed devils who've brought nothing but ruin to this town?"

Felicia's face remained a mask of calm, but Dominic could feel the tension radiating off her. She kept her voice level, though there was a sharpness to it.

"I am no devil," she said, meeting the woman's gaze head-on. "I buy heartsease because it helps me. That's all you need to know."

Dominic stepped forward, angling his body between the stallholder and Felicia, his tone firm. "Whatever rumours you've heard, this lady is no threat. We're only here to help. Now, will you sell us what we need or not?"

The stallholder sniffed, clearly weighing her options. "If it's for one of the Queen's guards, as you say, I'll sell what I have," she muttered, still eyeing Felicia with distrust. "But mark my words, we keep watch around here. We won't be caught off-guard again. And I won't deal with any of them black-garbed devils. Not anymore. I don't care what threats they come with."

She reached for the yarrow and garlic, tossing them onto the counter with a practised hand, but her gaze lingered on Felicia, her suspicion palpable, as she handed over a hefty package of heartsease.

Dominic shot a glance at Felicia as he collected their purchases. She held herself rigid, but he saw the flicker of emotion in her eyes. A flash of apprehension as she avoided his gaze.

He kept his voice low as they turned from the stall.

"You shouldn't let people like her get under your skin. She doesn't know the truth about you. What you've been through."

Felicia's mouth twisted beneath the weight of her thoughts. "Doesn't she? They're right to be wary. What happened before..." She trailed off, biting her lip. "I don't blame them."

Dominic was about to argue when the sound of hurried footsteps reached them. One of Cedric's staff, out of breath and frantic. His patched woollen tunic offered little protection from the late afternoon chill as he weaved through the dwindling crowd.

"Sir Skinner!" he called, his voice urgent.

Dominic's heart sank. He exchanged a quick, grim look with Felicia.

"A message for you," the boy panted. "Master Cedric sent me to find you. I believe 'tis urgent."

He placed the slim coil of parchment in Dominic's hand.

Felicia slipped the lad a coin. "Our thanks. Get on back before you freeze," she said.

The lad thumbed his forelock and scampered away on coltish legs, skidding on every second step. "What is it?" Felicia placed an urgent hand on Dominic's arm.

Staring at the words, Dominic felt the chill in the frigid air as if it had reached in to squeeze his soul with its iron fist.

He held the parchment out to her. She scanned his face before she held the parchment closer to the dim lantern light percolating from a nearby stall.

"Falconridge attacked?" she said. "But aren't Sir Dunforde and the rest of the troop still there? How can this be?"

Dominic nodded, his mind already racing. "'Tis from Master Ash, the steward," he said. "I have to go there. Cerys has the Blade of Aequitas. But she needs that book to make it work. If she travelled light. Got ahead of the storm... She tried to steal Briana's diaries once before."

The parchment creased between them as he clutched her chilly hands. They stared at each other, seeing the fear reflected in each other's eyes.

"By the Gods. we have lost too much time. We should have gone straight to Falconridge. Not stayed to rest," Dominic said. Frustration swept over him as he headed for the inn. His stride quickened and then slowed as he realised Felicia hadn't followed him.

"My love?" he said, "what's wrong?"

He turned. Felicia was still staring at the parchment, her face white. He could see the glimmer of tears on her cheeks as he drew closer. The slender hand clutching the parchment shook.

"Felicia?" He touched a hand to her smooth cheek. For just a second, she leaned against his palm, pressed a gentle kiss on the sign of the mage that bloomed under his skin. The hairs on the back of his neck rose in response as his magic blazed to life at her touch.

"May all the Gods bless him," she said. Her voice seemed to come from a place far distant.

"Felicia, are you alright? Is it your Farsight?" Dominic whispered. He turned her chin up so he could see her eyes in the lantern light. No gold flare blazed there to tell him she was using her gift. Just familiar grey crystal. Pebbles sparkling in a mountain stream of tears as they trickled down her face. She shook her head and turned away.

"I need no Farsight to understand what my heart tells me. She is the cruellest of women, and she takes advantage of every opportunity," she said. "I fear Master Ash is already dead."

Chapter 12
Joran

Unable to sleep, the echo of Joran's footsteps hounded him as he pounded the endless corridors of Epera's ancient stronghold.

His restless progress passed ornate suits of armour, rows upon rows of ranked weaponry hung upon the cold stone walls. Weary guards bowed to him as he roamed, the murmurs of their concern whispered at his back. The empty silence pressed an accusing finger into the painful mass of his doubt. Almost in a daze, hardly daring to think, he shoved open the doors of the magnificent throne room.

Decorated with the sign of the mage, the massive carved oak doors felt rough under his fingers as he entered. Vacated of the court, the chamber dwarfed him. Fitful moonlight filtering through the new stained glass windows showed him the long approach to the royal dais. Two beaten silver thrones. One large, one much smaller, drew the gaze. Petronella's silver and blue standard rippled against a stray draft behind them. Embroidered falcons flexed their wings as if about to take flight into the stormy night. The hearth was cold. The air chill. Few had gathered here in the last weeks since Petronella's accident.

Lost in memories, he retraced the steps he'd first taken years before when King Arion had sprawled, arrogant and powerful on the larger throne. Back then, Joran had attended the Court of Skies as an emissary of King Merlon, with his orders clear in his mind. Firstly, to offer a revised trade deal to starving Epera. Second, to spy out the lay of the land and, if at all possible, to return to Oceanis with Princess

Alice. King Merlon's daughter. He'd despised Petronella then. The pale, over-decorated wife of a tyrannical monarch, intent on crushing the magic in his kingdom under his booted foot.

Arion had refused his every offer and held the young Princess captive, intent on forcing Merlon to do his will. And Petronella had risked her life to defy her husband. Escaped the castle with the Princess herself. His eyes drifted to the smaller silver throne that had once been hers and slid reluctantly across the taller, more ornate throne at its side. Petronella sat there now. She'd proved herself. Saved her kingdom. Earned his love. His respect. His mouth twisted. What was he? Still an emissary. A supplicant at her feet, dependent on her approval. Disappointing her at every turn.

Wandering to the dais, he slumped on the step. In this very spot, Arion had asked his wife for the gift of death. A surcease from the agonising pain he suffered every day. And over there, by the door, he'd watched the Grayling battle through a maelstrom of evil. Propelled by pure faith and desperation, clutching the Ring of Justice in his beak while Petronella lay as death in front of him and her father tightened his hold on the nation's fate.

Even now, his heart still pounded at the memory. Almost dead, Petronella had leapt into the freedom of her namesake, her beloved Grayling. She'd offered Joran the Ring of Justice, and what had he done? Literally thrown it back at her. His mind twisted. She'd thought him worthy of it then. Why not now?

Agonised, he ground a fist into the headache that twisted between his brows. Someone was trying to reach him telepathically. He didn't dare open his channels once more to discover who it was. He'd already done enough damage to last a lifetime. Perhaps several.

"Papa?" His daughter's voice was tiny in the vast gulf of the throne room. He raised his eyes and squinted the length of the chamber as she squeezed her narrow frame through the slim gap between the two heavy doors.

Scrambling to his feet, he reached out. "Theda? By the Gods, what are you doing?"

His daughter broke into a run, bare feet pattering the cold tiles, holding the tails of her nightgown from the floor. He met her halfway down the room, sliding to a halt as her hands crept around his thighs. He bent. Hoisted her into his arms, holding her close. She buried her feverish head against his neck.

"Is Mama dead?" she whispered, against his throat. Joran's blood turned to complete ice.

"What? No!" he blurted. "Why would you say that? She's ill, that's all."

"But she nearly died, didn't she?" Theda pointed at the door. "Here. In this room. I saw it."

Joran's eyes snapped to full attention. "Was that you, just then?" he asked.

She leaned her head back to stare at him, her wide blue eyes owlishly crossed as she sought to focus on his own. "You saw it," she said. "So I saw it."

"By the Gods." His hold on her tightened. He pressed his head against hers, rocking her gently. "My sweet girl," he whispered into her ebony curls. "My poor, sweet girl. 'Tis too soon for you, all this power you have."

"Did I do wrong?" Theda asked. He could feel the dampness of her tears on his neck. "Am I in trouble? Will Mama be angry with me?"

"Nay, oh nay. Never, my sweetling." He bit his lip, fighting through his own fear to offer reassurance. "Let's go to Mama together," he suggested. "She will likely be asleep, but you can see her. Will that comfort you?"

He felt her nod, her head heavy against his shoulder. "Well then." He shifted her to a more comfortable position in his arms and strode to the door, humming a lullaby he didn't even remember knowing into her ear as he went.

The guard at Petronella's door saluted him as he approached. "My lord," he said, standing back and lowering his pike. Joran nodded his approval. The young man was well chosen. Alert and ready, even at this dead hour of the night.

"Well done, man," he said. "My daughter wishes to see the Queen."

"By all means." The soldier opened the door. Joran slid Theda to the floor. He put his finger to his lips. "Ssh. We don't want to wake her," he warned. He emphasised his tiptoe as they crept across the carpet. Theda stifled a giggle against the back of her hand as they inched to the inner chamber. The ornate oak door, inlaid in silver with a pattern of dolphins and eagles, opened to reveal a room locked in slumber. Petronella lay flat on her back, her face gilded by the dim light of a night lantern, and the slow burn of the dampened fire in the grate. Sheltered on the south side by the ferocious storm battering the castle from the north, the room offered a warmth and softness lacking from much of the enormous keep.

Alerted to intruders, the Grayling's head jerked from his doze. The bird lunged from his perch, bating, until he recognised them. Unusually, Petronella barely moved. Joran saw her head shift restlessly on her shoulders. A light murmur of complaint issued between her dry lips. He bent his head to his daughter. She'd stuck a thumb in her mouth, staring at her mother as if she'd never seen her before.

"There, you see," Joran whispered. He crouched at Theda's side and put his arm around her. "She's alright. Recovering from her broken leg."

Theda nodded slowly, her piercing sapphire gaze drifting around the chamber. She raised her stubby finger and pointed at the corner, where the densest shadows extinguished the glow of the lamp.

"Then who is that?" she asked.

Joran's mouth turned dry. His sharp gaze snatched to the corner. Abandoning his daughter, he strode forward, his hand on his dagger. Expecting an assailant. The traitor. Someone.

There was no-one there.

Panic beat in his chest like the fluttering wings of a trapped bird. He clenched his jaw, his gaze sweeping the familiar, shadowed room, but Petronella slept peacefully on. The Grayling cocked his head, waiting patiently for them to leave. Joran's skin crawled as he returned to Theda and captured her chilled little fingers in his fist, murmuring reassurance.

"Come, 'tis time for bed. I will guard her, I promise," he said, guiding her across the room. The falcon's fierce gaze followed them to the door. But he caught a glimpse as he drew it carefully shut. The bird had turned his head, watching the same corner with quiet, dreadful intensity.

CHAPTER 13
DOMINIC

Felicia's hand clutched firmly in his own, Dominic broke the quiet industry of the Beaten Drum like a blizzard wind with the force of his entrance.

"Cerys has attacked Falconridge," he blurted as soon as the door slammed shut. Aldric's eyes widened in alarm. Mistress Trevis left off fussing over her patient and caught the package of herbs Felicia tossed to her.

"We must set off as soon as possible. Cerys is in front of us, and she's looking for that book," Dominic said, glancing around. Guildford jumped to his feet, sliding his sword into its sheath. "Action, at last," he said. "When do we leave?"

"What has happened?" Tom croaked from his seat by the fire. He pulled himself to standing, his cheeks ashen. "Are we to march?"

Mistress Trevis placed a heavy hand on his good shoulder and pressed him to his seat. "You are marching nowhere if it's not to your palette," she said.

"Leave off, Leora. I will go." Tom's jaw jutted under his beard.

"You will not."

The two stared at each other. Locked in a battle of wills.

Wrenching his eyes away, Dominic marched across the room. "We will leave at first light. Travel as fast as possible. 'Tis only a couple of days away," he said. His blood fizzed with renewed energy. He felt it tingling through his veins to the very soles of his feet.

Cedric cleared his throat. "My apologies, I cannot come," he said, slowly gazing around at them. His cheeks reddened. "In the absence of Sir Jon, I am the senior voice at Hartwood."

Guildford strode across the flags and punched the older man's shoulder. "So far up the pecking order. You never said," he remarked, only half-joking.

Cedric kept his eyes fixed on Dominic, ignoring Guildford's jibe with steadfast good humour.

"He's my older brother," he muttered. "In his absence, the governance and defence of Hartwood falls to me. But I will keep you abreast of events here. Muster the townsfolk in the Queen's defence if I need to."

"Welladay, then you must stay. Tom must stay, too." Dominic glared across the room, where Mistress Trevis was still arguing with Tom in a low monotone that went unheard. "Mistress Trevis, you will remain with Tom." Tom took a pace forward. Dominic stopped him in his tracks, using the lightest touch of his gift to block his way. "I mean it. I know you want to help, but you are wounded. You need to bide here, at least for the time being," he said.

"Let me go, young Skinner..." Tom said, his lips thinning as he tried to throw off the edge of Dominic's will. "How dare you use your magic on me?"

"Nay, Skinner's right," Guildford broke in. "We will need every sword arm on this trip. Dominic can lead."

Aldric exchanged a shocked glance with Dominic. "By the Gods," he said. "Never thought I'd hear you say that."

Guildford shrugged. "He's the best we've got," he said. "Even I can see that, much though it grieves me." He took up a wooden tankard and raised it in Dominic's direction. "Your good health," he said, tossing it down his throat.

Felicia rolled her eyes. "Any excuse for another drink," she muttered under her breath.

"If you were well enough to come, Tom, then by all means," Dominic said. He dropped his hand, releasing his hold. "But we leave in the morn at first light. If you are not well enough to hold a sword, you will stay here." He turned to Cedric. "If you are willing, I would ask you for your help to prepare us for the trip."

Cedric scowled and waved an airy hand. "Of course. Whatever you require. Sledges, supplies. We will provide it."

"My thanks." Dominic stopped as Aldric jerked his sleeve.

"We must remember Will," Aldric said. "Little Bird will never forgive us if we do not do the right thing by him."

Dominic nodded. "Aye, of course. Although I am not sure how we will manage it."

Cedric chuckled. "There are ways to bury our dead in the frozen north," he said. "We will make a space for him in our temple grounds. I will instruct the gravediggers to prepare a brazier."

He chuckled at Dominic's confusion. "Fire, lad. We light a brazier over the spot to soften the earth enough to dig. Many folks die of the cold up here. Sickness, Wolf attacks, and the like. 'Tis not uncommon."

"Then I thank you," Dominic said, his brow clearing. He stared around at the group. "We need to make ready. Eat well. Rest. Tomorrow, we bid Will Dunn godspeed. And then, we ride."

He left the group to prepare, snatching a bowl of thick mutton stew for his own supper on his way to the stairs.

Cedric's staff had freshened the chamber he shared with Aldric in his absence, the vast mountain of additional blankets neatly folded and placed on the window seat. A fresh jug of water in his ewer. Thankful for these ministrations, he threw himself onto his narrow mattress and closed his eyes. Opened his channels.

"Master Ash, 'tis Dominic Skinner. I got your message."

He waited, sifting through the myriad of mental signals that tickled his mental senses. A small frown crossed his face as he noted how many of them there were close by. Surely more than the area around Blade, far to the south. His lips tightened. It made sense. Traitor's Reach had become the dreaded final destination of so many of the Blessed from Epera's capital over the years. He wondered how many of them alive were still loyal to Petronella. How many the Shadow Mage still owned. He traced the sign of the Mage over his heart reflectively, still scanning for Master Ash's lively energy. Nothing.

"Master Ash..." Still nothing. He bit his lip. Felicia was right, as she was about so many things. Only emptiness echoed in the space where Master Ash's signal once flourished. Sorrow flooded him. The tiny old man stood like a giant in his recent memory. Loyal to the last. Guarding Briana's treasure with his every breath. "He said he'd hide it again before we left. But did they find it?" he wondered out loud. "And if they did, I couldn't see anything that might help them. And by the Gods, where is Sir Dunforde?"

His pondering brought no fresh insight. About to dip a wooden spoon into his bowl, Joran's familiar, impatient voice echoed like the clang of a temple bell deep in his mind. Heart lurching with trepidation, he placed his supper on the hearth where it would remain warm and slumped to the floor. He buried his head in his arms.

"Dominic, report."

His jaw clenched. Every time the Prince communicated with him, it was with the same brusque tone. It immediately sent his hackles up and made him bare his teeth like a snarling dog chained to a kennel.

"Aye," his reply was just as short.

"Dupliss' forces attacked Falconridge."

"Aye. I know. We just received a pigeon from Master Ash. We are preparing to ride out on the morrow."

Joran paused. Dominic could feel the Prince's hesitation.

"He...died last night."

The confirmation screwed Dominic's hands into fists. *"How do you know?"* he asked. The question tasted like acid on his tongue.

"I also received a pigeon and then a mental communication with him. He passed into the Mage's grace as we were talking."

"Ah. I am sorry." Silence between them. *"What did he tell you?"* Dominic inquired, his heart in his mouth. Joran's confusion trickled to him out of the ether. *"Something about the Blade of Aequitas and some Book of Shadows. 'Twas nonsense."*

Something deep in the Prince's psychic field told Dominic that this last was more a hope than a fact.

"You know it wasn't," he said quietly. *"I tried to tell you before. You would not listen. There is far more at stake here than Dupliss' attempts to forge a coup."*

Joran sighed. *"I know now,"* he said, his mental voice dropping to a mere whisper in Dominic's skull. *"Petronella is weakening by the day. Her leg is mending, but something is draining her energy. And Theda, little Theda..."* His voice strengthened. *"You need to tell me what you know,"* he said. *"I will listen this time. I promise."*

"Aye, I'll tell you. But then we must stop communicating like this. You will understand why I told the Queen to close her channels," Dominic said. His heart pounded as he related the bones of his story. Everything he knew about Cerys, her birth, her obsessive desire to rise to power, and her formidable psychic gifts. He could feel Joran's alarm growing with every sentence. Something in him almost rejoiced at unburdening himself to Joran after all this time. To know that this time, the Prince was taking him seriously.

"By the Gods," Joran said at the end of his tale. *"She's Petronella's half-sister? This is even worse than I believed possible. Does the Queen know?"*

"I don't think so," Dominic said. *"I will go to Falconridge. Find Sir Dunforde. Find out what was taken, secure the building and the estate, if I can. But you must be on the lookout, my lord. Cerys is evil beyond belief, and she can impersonate anyone she chooses. Anyone at all. She can influence a person's thoughts, create illusions. She has the Blade*

of Aequitas. How she plans to use it, I do not know. But she needs the information contained in Darius' Book of Shadows. That is what she seeks."

All Dominic's senses tightened as Joran registered his words.

"What is it?" Dominic asked. *"My lord, what is it?"*

"Little Theda," Joran choked out. *"By the Gods, could she get to Theda?"*

Dominic hesitated, feeling the tension in Joran's voice as if it were his own. *"Theda is strong,"* he said, choosing his words with care. Picking carefully through the thorny ground of Joran's mental landscape. *"She's your daughter. But she'll need you to keep her protected from whatever Cerys is planning."*

A pause followed. Dominic could sense Joran's guarded scepticism through the mental link.

"How?" Joran's voice came to him clipped, a mixture of frustration and impatience. *"Cerys is playing a game I can't even see, let alone control. If she's already in Theda's mind..."* His words trailed off, but Dominic could still feel the undercurrent of mistrust beneath the horror.

"We've been through this before," Dominic replied. He struggled to keep his tone neutral. *"You all need to close your channels. Block her out. You've done it with others. You can do it with Theda."*

Joran's presence flared with restrained anger. *"I know how to protect my daughter."* There was a coldness in his voice now, an unspoken reminder of his authority. Dominic rolled his eyes. He'd expected resistance, but it still grated on him.

"Of course," Dominic said, tamping down his frustration. *"But Cerys is no ordinary threat. She can manipulate thoughts."*

"And what do you think I'm doing here, Skinner?" Joran interrupted, his mental voice sharp, cutting through Dominic's explanation like a blade. *"You're not the only one who's been fighting this war. Don't presume to tell me what I already know."*

Dominic clenched his fists, his jaw tightening. *"I'm not presuming anything,"* he replied, forcing his voice to stay calm. *"But we need to be cautious. Cerys isn't after just Falconridge. She wants everything. Petronella, Theda, the kingdom. She'll find any crack in our defences and use it."*

Another pause, but this time, Dominic felt Joran's hesitation more clearly. The Prince might not have trusted him fully, but the warning had hit its mark.

"The heartsease tea..." Dominic began cautiously.

"I know about the heartsease," Joran snapped. *"But she's just a child. I won't drug her unless I have no other choice."*

Dominic bit back his response. Pushing Joran further would only deepen the divide between them. *"Understood,"* he said instead. *"But if it comes to that, I trust you'll do what's necessary."*

Joran's mental presence surged with frustration, but it wasn't directed solely at Dominic. There was something deeper. Self-doubt, perhaps, or fear, quickly masked by a show of strength.

"My lord," Dominic continued, his tone more measured. *"I'm not trying to tell you what to do. I'll focus on Falconridge. But if Theda's in danger, you'll need to stay vigilant. We both know now Cerys won't stop until she gets what she wants."*

A heavy silence settled between them, charged with the unresolved tension that always lingered when they spoke. Joran's next words were quieter, less confident than before. *"You're right. I'll deal with it."*

Dominic raised his eyebrows in surprise at the admission, though it came laced with reluctance. Joran's pride wasn't easily set aside. But the mistrust between them remained, hanging like a cloud over their conversation.

"I'll keep you updated," Dominic said, stepping carefully around the tension. *"But I think it's best we limit these communications. Cerys could exploit them."*

"*Agreed.*" Joran's voice was crisp again, more distant. "*Just handle your side, and I'll handle mine. We'll use pigeons or trusted messengers to communicate when the ways are clear.*"

Dominic nodded, even though Joran couldn't see him. "*Very well.*"

Joran hesitated. "*Then we have an agreement,*" he replied at last, his voice tinged with frustration. "*But, Dominic...*"

"*Aye?*"

"*Keep your eyes open at Falconridge. There's something else at play here. I don't trust everyone around us.*"

A prickle of doubt crawled up Dominic's spine. "*You think there's a spy?*"

"*I don't know,*" Joran said, his thoughts guarded. "*But I have heard nothing from Sir Dunforde of this attack. All our attempts to capture Dupliss fail. Just...be on your guard.*"

Dominic clenched his fists, feeling the conversation slipping into uncertainty again.

"*I will,*" he said.

Doubt clouded his mind as the Prince broke their connection. A spy. A traitor. Working with Cerys, moving against the Queen. Someone close enough to obtain military information and pass it on. But who? His mind roved, assessing and discounting the possibilities. Like Joran before him, nobody sprang to mind. The puzzle kept him pacing, even as his companions sought their pallets, their voices fading behind the banging of doors.

Later, after the inn had quieted and the preparations for the journey gave way to slumber, Dominic stood before Felicia's door. His body hummed with the remnants of his exchange with Joran, the tension in his muscles seeking an outlet. He knocked softly, unsure whether he wanted comfort, answers, or just her company.

The door cracked ajar, the warm light from inside spilling into the corridor.

"Dominic?" Felicia's voice was soft, her expression unreadable as she stepped back to let him in. "How did it go? Did you speak to Master Ash?"

He entered, the warmth of the room immediately enveloping him. Felicia's fire crackled quietly in the hearth, casting long shadows on the walls. She was already in her nightgown, a pale blue thing that clung to her form, though she kept her arms crossed over herself as if shielding her body from his view.

"I spoke to Joran. May I sit?" Dominic began. At her nod, he settled into the chair by the fire. The flames claimed his despondent gaze with their hypnotic dance. "You were right about Master Ash. He is dead. Joran is worried about Petronella and Theda. Cerys has been trying to reach the girl, though she doesn't seem to realise it. And Joran thinks there is a spy in the camp."

Felicia turned away, busying herself with something on the small table, though he could sense her tension. "That poor child," she murmured. "She's so young."

Dominic nodded, his attention flitting to her as she puttered about the room, making it tidy. "We spoke about limiting our mental communication. I warned him...but, Gods, this whole situation feels like it's slipping through our fingers."

Felicia's back remained turned to him as she shook out her new cloak and hung it carefully on a peg driven into the whitewashed wall. "You're doing everything you can, Dominic."

Her distance unsettled him. He leaned forward, resting his arms on his knees. "Felicia, look at me."

She stiffened but slowly turned to face him. The firelight danced across her features, highlighting the tension in her jaw and the wary look in her eyes.

"I don't want either of us to go through this alone," he said. "We're about to be thrown into chaos, and I... I need you with me. Not just in battle. But...with me."

For a moment, her eyes softened, and Dominic felt a flicker of hope. He stood, crossing the room to her and reached for her hand, drawing her close.

But just as he thought she might yield to him, she pulled away, turning her back once more.

"I can't, Dominic," she whispered, her voice thick with emotion. "Not now."

His hand dropped to his side, the sting of rejection cutting deeper than he'd expected. "Felicia..."

"I'm sorry," she said, her voice barely audible. "I just... I can't. Not like this."

A beat of silence passed between them, heavy with words unspoken. Dominic's shoulders twitched beneath his unlaced doublet. The very air was thick with secrets.

He swallowed, his throat tight. "Whatever is troubling you, you must know you can tell me. You don't have to be alone, Felicia."

Her lips trembled, but she shook her head. "It's not about being alone, Dominic. There are things...things you don't know. Things I can't...let you see."

He stepped forward, wanting to close the distance, but something in her posture stopped him. She was building walls again. A fortress of stone he couldn't break through.

"All right," he said, his voice low, filled with the weight of unspoken frustration. "But know this, Felicia... Whatever it is, I won't turn away."

She didn't respond, her gaze fixed firmly on the fire, her face illuminated by the flickering glow. Dominic hesitated, then nodded to himself, accepting the rejection with as much grace as he could muster.

"I'll see you in the morning," he said, stepping toward the door.

"Good night, Dominic," she whispered, her voice barely reaching him as he closed it behind him.

Shaking his head, he marched back to his room. Aldric lay abed, sprawled across his narrow mattress. His soft, familiar snuffle filled the air. Dominic shrugged off his outer clothes and curled into a ball under his own blankets. Unease claimed his mind. The gentle oblivion of slumber was elusive as a moorland mist. Images of Cerys, tiny Theda, and Joran danced across his inner vision in some sort of horrific galliard designed by a madman. Biting his lip, he closed down his mental channels, using every trick he had learned over the years to guard his mind from intrusion. The resulting silence unsettled him further. Exhausted, on the verge of dreams, his subconscious conjured an image of a blind man he'd once seen, shuffling crabwise down the street, tracing his hand over the texture of walls and the position of empty doorways. Without his gift, Dominic felt as blind as he. Cut off and isolated from the source of his magic.

Felicia, he whispered into the darkness, knowing she could not hear him. *This is awful. It feels so wrong. How do you do it? How do you live without your magic? I don't understand you. Why would you even want to?*

His tired mind provided few answers. All that remained, as fatigue finally advanced to claim him, was the prickle of apprehension deep in his gut. A nagging sense of unseen fingers playing with them all. Placing them fastidiously on an unseen chessboard. "Some knight," he murmured, on the edge of slumber. "Just a pawn. A puppet. She holds the strings. I must find her."

CHAPTER 14
JORAN

"Are you awake, Mistress?"

Caught mid-toilette, Fortuna de Winter jumped as Joran pounded through her door at first light the next morning. Startled at his unannounced entrance, her own maid dropped into an instant curtsey, scattering hairpins.

Caught up in a panic made entirely worse by lack of sleep, Joran waved an impatient hand. "Dismissed," he said. The girl handed her mistress the hairbrush and bobbed another curtsey, shooting a curious glance between them before she left.

"My lord!" Fortuna protested. She glared at him from her seat, dark hair a mass of ebony, still twisted in curl paper, her everyday gown half unlaced. "You intrude! What do you mean by it?"

"My apologies, Mistress. 'Tis Theda and Petronella. Please, you must accompany me," Joran said.

"By the Gods," Fortuna muttered. "You invade my chamber at this hour in the morning. Dismiss my maid. Do you realise what type of gossip you have just started?"

"I don't care," Joran said. "'Tis not important."

Fortuna stood, turning her back to him. "Well, at least lace my gown."

Grim-faced, Joran performed the honours while Fortuna ripped the curl papers out of her hair. The resulting ringlets danced around her copper skin. She didn't bother brushing it out.

"What is it? What has happened?" she demanded as he harried her down the broad corridor.

Joran jerked his chin at the fresh guard on Petronella's door. "Double the guard here from now on," he instructed the man as they entered. "No-one in or out. By my command."

"What?" Fortuna said. "Not even me? You must explain."

"I will. But Petronella needs to know what is happening. Theda saw someone in here last night."

"Theda saw someone? What was she doing out of bed? I will have Little Bird's hide," Fortuna said. The angry words died on her lips as Joran threw Petronella's door open. The Grayling was all but dancing on his perch. His angry chatter dominated the scene.

"Send the guard for Thurgil," Joran muttered. "That bird needs some exercise and some decent food. He's been too long in here."

Fortuna nodded, hastening back to the door.

Turning to his wife's bed, Joran's breath left him in a rush. She lay as he'd left her. Flat on her back, her eyes open but staring at the canopy above her head, unblinking. "Petronella, my love..." He was at her side in an instant. Patting her hand, her alabaster cheek. "Petronella! Wake up. Please, my love..."

He pressed his ear to her chest. Her heartbeat was faint. Too slow. "Fortuna! Get in here!" he roared, uncaring of the panic in his shout, protocol forgotten.

Skirts flying, Fortuna dropped at his side, bending over the Queen. "By the Gods," she breathed. "What is this? She was fine last night. Just tired." Agonised, Joran watched as she checked her patient, examining her breath, her nails. "No poison, no fresh injuries," she muttered. Tossing the bedcovers aside, she unwrapped the binding on Petronella's leg. It was still swollen, the bruising around the broken bone a fading memory. Shaking her head, she scrambled to her feet, scanning the array of medical supplies laid neatly on Petronella's dressing table.

"What is it? What is wrong with her?" Joran demanded. Fortuna stared at him, her copper eyes clouded with anxiety. Her mouth twisted. "I don't know, my lord. Nothing physical that I can see. But she has been weakening over the last few days. 'Tis odd when her leg has mended so well. I'll send for Master Mortlake. We will discuss it."

"You'll discuss it?" Joran roared, the last shreds of his self-control thrown to the winds. The Grayling lunged in response at his angry words. He strained from his perch, and Joran winced at the savage peck he received. "Bastard!" he exclaimed, clapping a hand to the bite wound on his neck. Rolling her eyes, her lips pursed with disapproval, Fortuna soaked a fresh linen with a selection of brews from her collection and handed it over.

"I believe the Grayling is trying to tell you to take a better tone," she bit out.

Joran threw a glare her way, wincing as the acrid lotion penetrated the cut. The Grayling calmed down, regarding his pacing with his head on one side. Joran clenched his fists. Frustration and fear kept time with his own heartbeat. He came to a halt at his wife's side once more, plucking her hand from where it lay against her heart. "Fortuna, what about the babe?" he whispered, pressing a frantic kiss on his wife's motionless fingers.

"Our Queen yet lives," Fortuna said, her voice soft. "She has not miscarried, so your new son does, too." She crossed the room and placed a warm hand on his shoulder. He inhaled Fortuna's familiar scent, Relaxed fractionally beneath the comfort of her presence. "I promise, by my Goddess, the Empress, I will do all in my power to keep your lady and your children safe," she murmured.

"I know you will. My apologies," he muttered.

"'Tis of no matter," Fortuna returned. "You need to rest, my lord. Have you slept at all?"

"I cannot." Aware of his own exhaustion, Joran slumped to the floor, his wife's hand still cradled in his own. It took him a moment for his mind to recognise what it was seeing. "By the Gods!" he said. Fear clutched at his belly.

"My lord?"

"Her ring, Fortuna. Look."

He spread his fingers. Fortuna's copper cheeks turned pale. "Where has the light gone?" she asked.

"It cannot be." Mouth dry, Joran placed a hesitant finger on the heavy diamond. The familiar flare of connection that so often ignited at his touch had no effect. The stone lay dull and inert. "This was how it was before," he whispered. "Years ago, when we first met." Suspicion corkscrewed across his forehead, slanting his eyebrows in a heavy scowl. He glared at Fortuna. "Have you been giving her heartsease?" he demanded.

"By the Gods, not I!" Fortuna said. "Why would you think such a thing?" She left Petronella's side, sliding potions and bottles aside. The gentle clink and rattle set Joran's teeth on edge.

"Who has done this?" he demanded, "Without my knowledge or permission?"

Fortuna's nimble fingers scurried through her stores, naming each dried herb as she ticked it off. Alarm clouded her gaze as she glanced across at him.

"My store of heartsease is gone," she confirmed.

Joran leapt to his feet. "No-one should have done this without permission," he said again. Fortuna's expression creased into fear as he paced the carpet, rage in every line of him.

"My lord," she murmured, "perhaps it is for the best..."

"For the best? For the Queen to lose her magical bond to the land when our entire nation lies under threat?" Joran stared at her, uncomprehending. "And look at her, lying there so vulnerable. I tell you someone was in here last night. Theda saw a shadow. A shape... And Dominic says... He says..."

He couldn't go on. Fortuna's gaze drifted from Petronella to the Grayling before it clashed with his. She sighed, plucked a small pouch of dried herbs from her store, and waved him away from the hearth.

"What?" Joran grunted. "We stand here with all this going on, and your answer is to make tea?"

"By the Gods, you are a stubborn man," Fortuna muttered. She bent to the fireplace and swung her brazier over the coals. "I will prepare you an infusion of chamomile and valerian," she said. 'Twill calm you and give you rest."

"I don't want rest. I want answers," Joran replied, retracing his steps to his wife's bedside.

A tap on the inner door had them both turning at the same time. Joran advanced, his face grim. His long, ornate dagger appeared like magic in his hand. Fortuna took a wary step back.

The guard poked his head around the frame, eyeing the lethal point aimed at his heart with righteous trepidation. 'Tis Thurgil, from the falconry, my lord," he stuttered through dry lips. "And Little Bird."

Joran took a defensive position at his wife's side. "Let them in. Stay back," he added to Fortuna.

Wide-eyed under his outdoor tan, grizzled Thurgil approached on cautious feet. "My lord, what is your will?" he asked.

Joran glared at him. Dominic's warning still blazed across his brain. Who could he trust? What if this was Cerys? His gaze locked on Little Bird. Tiredness that matched his own drew shadows in the hollows of her features. But was she actually the lively young nursery maid who so delighted his children? How could he tell? His hand tightened on his blade.

"My lord?" Thurgil said again. He scrubbed at the greasy curls under his falconer's cap, his patient, watchful gaze taking in the scene. The tension between Fortuna and Joran. The still figure of the Queen, pale as snow against her pillows. He cleared his throat. "They told me the Grayling requires attention. Is he ill?" His dark eyes searched

Joran's face for answers, noting the fresh wound on his neck. "The Grayling did that?" he moved forward without permission, ignoring the point of Joran's dagger.

"Be careful, man," Joran said. "He is in a vicious mood this morn."

"Nay, he is not," Little Bird's soft treble turned all eyes to her. She blushed faintly, one scuffed leather shoe rubbing the carpet. "He's protecting her," she said, raising cornflower eyes to Joran.

"What? Did any give you permission to voice your opinion, young lady?" Joran demanded.

Little Bird swallowed, her golden curls wafting against her pale cheeks.

"I just know," she muttered. "He's been different for days now. Not eating. I suppose he is hungry. He must be by now." She held out a hand to Thurgil. "Have you anything for him?" she asked.

"Little Bird, do not," Fortuna interjected. "Look what he's done to the Prince."

Little Bird raised her eyebrows. Despite his anger, Joran flinched internally at the accusation he found in her face as his gaze slid over her.

"He won't hurt me," she said. "I know he won't."

Thurgil shrugged his thick shoulders. "Welladay, miss," he said. "You take the risk. He bit me twice a couple of days back. Mind your eyes, now." He scrabbled in his pouch and came up with a handful of raw meat. Little Bird took it.

Heart in his mouth, Joran watched as she held her hand in front of her. The Grayling's golden eyes locked on the offering. He rose to his full height on the perch, his wings batting the air. Little Bird's fine curls twisted in the breeze he created.

"Here," Little Bird's voice was soft, her step unwavering. "You must eat. We will guard the Queen while you do."

Disbelief twisted through Joran as the bird settled, folding his wings. Little Bird stepped into his strike zone and deposited the food in his tray. The Grayling favoured Joran with a glare that sparked a trickle of unexplained guilt through his mind. Hunching over his meal, he tore into it with a savage intensity that was matched only by the complete surprise on the faces of the adults.

"By the Gods," Fortuna said as Little Bird stepped back, the faintest of smiles on a mouth made for merriment.

"That was well done," Thurgil said, rich approval in his voice. "You can work for me anytime with skills like that."

Joran's gaze snapped to Little Bird. "You have been in contact with Dominic recently, have you not?" he inquired.

Little Bird's eyes narrowed. "Aye," she said shortly.

Fortuna glanced at Joran. "Not about Will. Perhaps before that?" she suggested gently.

Little Bird raised her chin. "He told me the Queen was in danger," she said. "And you were not listening."

Joran advanced. He towered over her, this strange, fey child of sunshine and showers. Little Bird stayed where she was, meeting his challenge with one of her own.

"Aye," she said. "I did it. I gave her heartsease. You can kill me if you like. I don't care anymore."

Joran's hand tightened on his dagger, the frayed edges of his temper already untangling to release his ever-present rage.

"You? How dare you?" His shout blasted around the room, only to be smothered by the wealth of soft furnishings. The mound of bedclothes. The embroidered curtains.

Little Bird shrugged. "The Queen knew," she said. "She agreed to it."

Silence. The Grayling raised his bloodstained beak from his breakfast and glared at him from his perch. Joran's gaze snapped to Petronella, still motionless in her bed.

"This is what she agreed to?" he demanded. "To lie there, completely vulnerable? Cut off from her gift?" His eyes narrowed. "I don't believe you," he said. He lunged towards her, grabbing the slender circumference of her upper arm in a deadly grip. Fortuna took a step forward.

"My lord!" she said, "she's but a child!"

"Aye," Joran sneered. "A child, is she? I say she's a witch, tainted by evil." Fear broke in a wave across Little Bird's face. She struggled against him. Anger beating through him, Joran ignored her protests. Raised his dagger.

Fortuna gasped. "Nay!" She sprang forward. "My lord, think! This is Little Bird, no witch!"

She got no further. The Grayling screeched like a banshee, raising the hairs on the back of Joran's neck. He launched himself from his perch to the length of his leash, his wings a blur of protest, talons extended. Joran ducked automatically away from his snapping beak.

Little Bird backed off to the safety of the bird's strike range, nursing her bruised arm. The expression she raised towards him cut through the mask of his rage. Contempt and defiance mixed in equal measure.

Joran's eyes darted across the room at the aghast faces of the company. Fortuna's copper skin was pale, her disappointment and alarm easy to see. Thurgil stared at him as if he'd seen a monster.

Joran closed his eyes. "Get out of my sight," he said. "All of you. Leave us."

Exchanging glances, the group tiptoed out. They left behind a tense silence, broken only by the bubbling of chamomile tea on the hearth and Joran's stifled moan of distress as he buried his face in his hands.

CHAPTER 15
DOMINIC

D awn broke over Hartwood in a glorious song of pink and purple. The storm clouds cleared, leaving the prick of fading starlight in the western sky as the sun topped the mountains and turned the snow-covered slopes to gold. Clustered in the ancient temple yard in the town centre, Dominic stood with Felicia's hand in his. Aldric flanked him on the other side. Tom, Guildford, and Mistress Trevis ranged themselves on the opposite side of the grave. Cedric stood at its foot. Waiting on the temple steps, the priests formed a single, solemn row of temporal authority. Their white robes blended with the ice-crusted environment. Their scarlet surcoats were too thin for the weather. But they maintained their composure, their faces sombre as a mark of deepest respect for the fallen warrior. Their leader carried a long baton crowned with the sign of the mage. His acolytes carried variously a chalice, a dish carved in the shape of a pentacle, and a silver sword. Their collective breath wreathed in the frosty morning, broken by the waking cries of birds. Will's shrouded remains waited on a platform at the temple entrance, surrounded on all four corners by the airy peppermint and heather incense favoured by the Eperan Blessed.

Deep in silent communion with the Mage, the High Priest of Hartwood lifted his eyes and his baton to the rising sun. It was time. He nodded to Dominic, who raised his own hands. Gentle, steady power trickled from his palms to cradle his friend and carry him to his last rest. He bit his lip, fighting through his sorrow, determined to comport himself with dignity. Aldric's shoulders heaved on a single sob that nearly undid him. He swallowed, concentrating his mind. Remembering Will as he had known him at the first. Sturdy and protective. A grubby boy with a soldier's heart. His heart clenched at the thought of Little Bird and the love they had for each other. She should be here. To stand as witness to a brave and selfless soul. To honour his sacrifice. Tears burned his eyes and scoured the back of his throat as he lowered his hands.

Will descended slowly, with delicate precision, into the sheltering embrace of the earth. His shoulders shaking, Aldric felt in his pocket for a pair of dice. He tossed them gently into the grave. A gift to his friend in remembrance of the time they had shared. Cedric placed an offering of bread and honey. Felicia, a simple garland of winter heather, tied with a blue ribbon. Guildford, a cup of mead. Tom and Mistress Trevis stepped forward together to place Will's sword on his chest. Finally, his heart aching, Dominic lowered a feather from the wing of a Peregrine falcon. Petronella's symbol, twisted about with a silver ribbon, embroidered with the sign of the Mage.

"In the Mage's grace, we send you." The soft chorus of the time-worn prayer wove their thoughts into a tapestry of gratitude and grief, echoed by the calls of the birds soaring high above. "To the Mage's heart, we commend you."

A lone flautist sounded the notes of the warrior's farewell as they bent their heads again. "From the Mage to the Mage," the Head Priest said when the last notes drifted into the freshening day. "And in his soul, we rest. Now and always. By the God's grace."

"By the God's grace," they responded. Each made the sign of the Mage at their own heart.

It was over. Dazed by the finality of it, the small group blinked at each other as the priests performed one more respectful obeisance before returning to the sanctuary of the temple. Aldric was still sobbing.

Felicia swapped glances with Dominic and put both arms around him. Aldric's head had to bend at an uncomfortable angle to lie on her shoulder.

"That was well done, Dominic," Guildford said, stepping respectfully around the mound of half-frozen soil waiting to entomb their friend. Something about his robust tone jolted Dominic from the semi-trance he'd fallen into as they prayed. He shook his head, returning to the world with some difficulty.

"Little Bird should have been here," he said.

"Probably better that she wasn't," Guildford remarked with rare understanding. "She would probably have jumped in with him."

Aghast at the macabre chuckle that huffed from his lips, Dominic gestured at Tom Buttledon, who was leaning heavily on Mistress Trevis. White-faced and sweating.

"Let's hope the temple yard doesn't claim another before the week is out," he said.

"Aye. He'll not be making this trip, I agree," Guildford said. "Will you tell him, or shall I?"

Dominic sighed. "If Mistress Trevis doesn't, I will. Come, gather our company. We have done all we can for poor Will. 'Tis time to depart."

Grim-faced, Guildford nodded, and together, the small group returned to the inn, each lost in their own thoughts.

Cedric had been busy long before daybreak. Three sledges laden with supplies awaited them at the Beaten Drum. Saddled and bridled, their mounts pranced impatiently on the icy cobbles, each wearing a rug against the cold. "I told them to split the supplies between each sledge," Cedric said as the group collected in the tavern yard, fortified by steaming mulled cider and oatcakes. "If you lose one, you won't lose everything."

Dominic nodded, encouraged by his foresight. "I'm sending some able lads with thee," Cedric said. "They know the territory well, from here to Falconridge and beyond, to Thorncastle. And they're loyal. My own kinsmen, so mind you look after them." He waved a gloved hand at the sledge drivers, well wrapped against the cold, their faces barely visible. "That's Silas, then Kendrick, and Miles," he said. "Follow their lead. They'll not send you wrong. Horses will need more feed than usual. More water. 'Twill be rough on them. Make sure they're warm. I've put heavy blankets in with their feed. Got the smith up last night to shoe them all for the weather. There's food. Blankets. Even tents, but I hope you won't need 'em."

Dominic's shoulders relaxed. He hadn't realised how much he'd dreaded making the return trip south with so little experience of the conditions. He pounded Cedric's arm with a rough fist. "My thanks to you," he said. "You have been naught but kind."

Cedric's bearded cheeks reddened at Dominic's remark. "Aye, well," he said. "I could have wished for Oswin to show you a better face. He half killed you and left you for dead. This is my way of making it up to thee. And before you ask," he added, as Dominic fumbled for his purse through the thick layers of oilskin and fur, "you'll not be paying for it. My tavern'll be heaving for weeks to come, waiting for news of you. I'll get my outlay back and more. Don't worry about that. Just keep the pigeons flying and the kingdom safe from that witch, Cerys Tinterdorn. 'Tis all I ask."

Dominic blinked, astonished at his comrade's generosity. "You are a true guardian of the North," he muttered. "I will tell the Queen. You will have her thanks. I will see to it."

"Aye, well," Cedric said. Arms crossed, he stepped back. "'Tis time you were away whilst the weather is kind. Keep warm. Stop for rest and let my kinfolk guide you. They know the routes in all weathers."

Nodding, Dominic turned away, squinting into the tavern through the partly opened door to where Tom and Mistress Trevis stood nose to nose, still immersed in their own argument. He rolled his eyes and strode in, unfastening his oilskin.

"I'm telling you, Leonora, I am fit to travel," Tom insisted. "The kingdom needs me. I can't just sit here, like an old man, while the youngsters have all the fun and glory."

Mistress Trevis planted both hands on her hips. "You will sit there if I have to sit on you," she said. "Please listen to me, Tom. You are days away from losing that arm. I will not have you risk yourself further. I can't."

Something in her tone gave Dominic pause. He halted, turning aside to the broad central table and taking a slice of bread and pork he didn't really want.

"Leonora..."

"Tom. I cannot lose you." The healer's voice was low, urgent. Dominic heard her sigh from across the room. Caught up in their private battle, neither of them had noticed him. Unwilling to eavesdrop but aware any further movement might shatter an important moment, Dominic froze in place. He sent a tiny prick of power to Felicia as she appeared at the door leading upstairs, her arms laden with packages. Just the slightest touch was enough to pin her in place before she could interrupt. Eyes wide, her expression drifted from confusion to understanding as she followed his gaze across the room. Both of them waited.

"What do you mean?" Tom's voice was blurred with exhaustion.

"You must know by now," Mistress Trevis said, an unaccustomed tremble creeping under her words. "All these weeks of toil and battle. Duty." She crept closer to him, laid a hand against his whiskered cheek. "If I don't tell you now, I may never have the chance," she said. "I know I am a couple of years older than you. But not too old, Tom."

"Not too old," Tom echoed. There was astonishment in his voice but not discouragement. He stepped closer to her. Bent his head. "I had no idea," he said.

"Why would you?" Mistress Trevis said, capturing his hand in hers. "You see your young lasses. Your mistresses and maidens, and wonder why they last but minutes, or days, in your esteem and affection."

"I saw you. You have the most beautiful eyes I have ever seen," Tom protested, "but I never thought you would be interested in me. I'm a rake. A libertine."

Mistress Trevis laughed. Low and sultry. The unusual sound broke some of the frost in Dominic's chilled and disappointed heart. He raised a pointed gaze in Felicia's direction. She lifted her chin and glowered at him, one eyebrow arched as if daring him to make a comparison.

Biting his lip, Dominic waved Felicia back. He crept out as silently as possible to the bustling courtyard, clutching his bread and meat.

Swinging easily into Kismet's saddle, he chewed his late breakfast, waiting impatiently for the rest of the party to gather themselves to leave. Felicia took a seat next to one of the sledge drivers. Still weak from her long confinement, she was not fit enough to ride. Swathed in furs and oil skins, she huddled close to his bulk, taking advantage of the shelter. The young man budged up a little to make room for her, earning a rare, dazzling smile. Catching a glimpse, Dominic turned Kismet in her usual frolicking circle, wishing Felicia had chosen him to aim it at.

Bickering as usual, Guildford emerged with Aldric, throwing a kiss at the comely young maid who had been keeping him company. She watched his departure with a wealth of pride shining in her grass-green eyes. Something in her appearance reminded Dominic of Cerys when she masqueraded as Celia and caught Guildford's roving eye. A chill prickled across his shoulders.

Arm in arm, Mistress Trevis and Tom emerged from the inn. He, pale and exhausted. Mistress Trevis, smiling through her trepidation. "God's speed," she called from the shelter of the porch. "Look after each other."

"I'll see you soon," Tom said. "You'll not be rid of me that easily. Ride easy. Take care. We want news, Dominic. Lots of it."

"You will have it, my friends," Dominic said. He exchanged a glance with Felicia. "Ready?"

"Aye."

He nodded. Turned his face to the south gate through which he'd entered days previously. Raised his arm.

"Then we ride."

CHAPTER 16
JORAN

Alone in Petronella's chamber with just her comatose form and a watchful falcon for company, Joran fought the need for sleep. Everything conspired against him. The suffocating warmth of the chamber. The subtle aroma of chamomile and valerian released into the air from the bubbling pot on the fireplace. His wife's slow breathing as her fragile chest rose and fell. So slowly. The Ring of Justice winked at him from the safety of her breast. Its light, at least, remained. A subtle reminder that his own latent power lingered. Available. His fingers twitched with the urge to remove it from her while she lay there. Once, he even raised his hand in her direction, only to be brought up short by the Grayling, the sharp edge of his beak in profile as he twisted his head around and shuffled closer to the bed.

He's tethered to that perch. I could move him. The thought came through loud and clear. The Grayling raised on his perch, his wings a blur of frantic activity. Joran scowled. It was as if the creature could hear him. Could read his thoughts as they trickled into his mind. He shook his head. Turned his shoulder. 'Twas impossible.

"I will tell Thurgil to move you," he said under his breath. "And then we will see. I must have more power to counter the threat to our kingdom. To my daughter."

The Grayling responded with an angry chatter that ground like glass across his frayed nerves.

"No? Well then, what do you want me to do?" Joran stumbled to his feet, pacing the room. He was too tired to consider why he was struggling to justify himself to his wife's falcon. The sound of his own voice jarred against his ears. But there was no-one else he could talk to. None who would understand the pain in his heart as well as Petronella. Perhaps she couldn't hear him. But he had to unburden himself or run mad. The Grayling observed his erratic progress with his handsome feathered head held on one side. His golden eyes followed Joran as he paced the length of the room and back.

"I don't understand, my love," he murmured, coming to a brief stop at the end of her bed. "Why have you left me alone with this? The nation needs you. I need you." His voice cracked on the admission. "Cerys was here last night, so Theda says. Our daughter, Petronella. She's in danger. And you cannot protect her any more than I can."

Was it his imagination, or did the glimmer of a frown ripple across his wife's snow-white forehead? "Aye," he continued, his voice stronger, praying that the accusation in his voice would reach her sleeping mind. Spur her back to life. "That is what you have run from, my love. Deserted us. Left your kingdom once again ripe for the taking."

It was working. Leaning over the mattress, he saw the contraction in her features at the fierceness of his words.

The Grayling's soft chatter interrupted the dense silence. He glanced up. "Damn you, be silent," he hissed. "Unless you want to find yourself locked in the falconry with the others." The bird glared at him, raising one vicious talon.

Ashamed of his own temper, Joran scrubbed his hands over his face and moved to the fireplace to retrieve the herbal infusion that was about to boil dry. The acrid aroma pricked the back of his throat as he turned the pot away from the flames. Sleep. The idea was tempting. It seemed as if he'd been awake forever. Cursed by some noisome witch to pace the shadowed corridors of the ancient keep into eternity. Forever keeping watch.

"You must rest," the thought sang through his weary mind. Immediately suspicious, he whirled on the spot, but there was no-one else in the room with them.

Petronella's falcon stood like a sentinel on his perch, erect and alert. Their gazes clashed. The thought came again, brushing through his mind with the delicate whisper of lace on silk. It was Petronella. It had to be her, but how? If she'd taken so much heartsease...

He was too tired to force his thoughts to a logical conclusion. Instead, he raised the heavy brew to his lips and sipped. The valerian and chamomile tasted equally of meadow grass and flowers. He swore softly as it burned his tongue. The Grayling continued to regard him. Taking another sip, Joran could see the bird's watchful stance softening, bit by bit. He took a step to the vast feather bed. Then another. The comfort of his wife's familiar form gave his mind ease as he edged carefully onto the mattress beside her. Curling around her. Shielding her with the strength of his body. The curve of his broad shoulders. If Cerys wanted to kill her, she'd have to do it through him.

The thought gave him some comfort. *There's a double guard on the door*, he reminded himself.

"Sleep, my love." There it was again.

At a loss, exhausted, Joran turned his head to his wife's unconscious shoulder and tumbled into dreams.

The room was dark when he woke, struggling from a feverish nightmare in which he was drowning in quicksand, clutching at weeds, the world around him a rocking sea of mud and freezing water. A memory, he realised as his sleep-fogged mind cleared. That long ago day, when

Alice of Oceanis had conjured her Gods-blessed power to sink Arion's boat and wrecked their own at the same time. He groaned as he levered himself upwards from the comforting embrace of his wife's pillows. She lay as he had left her, her lips parched. Still staring at nothing.

The fire had burned down to embers, and the frost at the window reached sly fingers to decorate the cold stone of the window embrasures. Shivering, Joran rolled off the mattress. His mouth was dry, and his stomach growled for food. After arranging the blankets more closely around Petronella's shoulders, he crept across the moonstruck carpet to the abandoned fireplace, urged the fire back to life, and lit candles to chase away the gloom. The Grayling drowsed on his perch, but somehow, the bird still had one eye open.

"Your turn to rest," Joran said softly. "I will watch her now."

Encouraged, the Grayling tucked his head under his wing. Glancing around the shadowed chamber, Joran checked each corner, even bent to check under the bed. They were alone, as he had instructed. Rubbing his hands together, he strode to the outer door. The watch had changed. On his command, two stalwart members of the Queen's guard held their pikes against intrusion.

"Fetch Mistress De Winter and Little Bird," Joran instructed. "And tell them to bring food and a jug of Argentish."

"Aye, Sire."

The junior guard set off down the cold corridor at a military clip, his boots loud against the stone. Joran returned to his wife's outer chamber, where she had spent most of her days before her accident. His mouth twisted as he gazed around, noting the padded chairs arranged companionably around the hearth. Her desk, strewn with books and paperwork. Toys for the children. A rag doll. A toy sword, a primer, printed untidily by his son. Petronella's scent lingered here. Captured by the shawl she often wore around her shoulders, now draped across her trunk, where she kept her most valuable items. He was standing right next to it. The cool crispness of silver leaf softened by the deep warmth of winter lilies. It heated his blood as it always did. He bit his lip at the discomfort of that thought. Weeks it had been since last they lay together. Too long. Yearning, his gaze crept to her bedchamber door. He heaved a sigh, clamping down on his urge to shake her to awareness.

Waiting impatiently for Fortuna and Little Bird, he folded his long form into the high wooden chair behind her desk, tracing his fingers across the page of elegant, flowing script. Something she'd been writing so many weeks ago.

The Prophecy of the Sword
"In shadows deep where whispers weep,
A blade of fate lies cast,
Aequitas, the soul's eclipse,
A curse from love's lost past.
A token turned to fate's cruel hand,
To sever bonds unseen,
Beware the heart that wields this blade,
For night and day convene.
Aequitas, the knife that cuts both ways,
In balance, true, its power sways,
A whisper dark, a beacon bright,
It holds the realm's own fragile light.
Prophecy in ancient lore,
Foretells of times to come,
When kingdoms rise, or kingdoms fall, beneath the blade's cruel hum.
The bearer walks a path unknown,
Through shadows, thick and thin,
For light and dark both mark the path,
Where destinies begin.
Aequitas, the knife that cuts both ways,
In balance, true, its power sways,

A whisper dark, a beacon bright,

It holds the realm's own fragile light.

To wield this blade of fateful edge,

A heart must find its peace,

For good or ill, its secrets spill

And bring the world release.

The runes that bind both kind and cruel,

Hold truth within their lines,

In hands of those who understand,

Its power intertwines.

Aequitas, the knife that cuts both ways,

In balance, true, its power sways,

A whisper dark, a beacon bright,

It holds the realm's own fragile light."

Brow quirking, he read the words through again. Aequitas. Master Ash had mentioned this elusive weapon as well. As had Dominic. Where had Petronella found this? Why copy it?

The parchment lay atop a large, heavy book. Bound in ancient leather, once water stained and cracked with age, now regularly polished with beeswax to a supple shine. His lips twisted in a reluctant smile as he stroked the cover, his fingers drifting across the pattern chased deep into its surface. Petronella's own Book of Shadows, passed down to her by Mistress Eglion. How often had she sat here, leafing through its crackling pages, a tiny frown of concentration between her brows? Petronella's staff leaned against the edge of her desk. Joran's brow contracted in thought. Both items had been Mistress Eglion's once. And before her, a long line of Seers. All had contributed to Epera's magical lore through the ages. He pulled the book towards him, aware of the pulse of magical energy tingling against his fingertips. A subtle questioning of his intentions and his right to the contents.

The cover was heavy as he lifted it. He turned to the first page, squinting at the ancient handwriting, blotted and faded. "Of Ye House of Ye Eagle in ye Kyngdom of Epera". He frowned. Turned a few more pages, his lips pursed with confusion. This was a history book. No magical tome, packed with enchantments and mystical lore. Yet, it must hold something. Some knowledge. It had never left his wife's side in all the time he'd known her.

"Is this it?" he wondered out loud. "Is this the book that evil enchantress needs to find?" But no. Dominic had mentioned Darius' black Book of Shadows. This was not black. Its cover was deep red. Like burnished blood. It closed with a dull thud as he let it go. A mouth snapping shut.

"Aye, I understand," Joran murmured. "You're keeping your secrets close." Shaking his head, he stared into space, his fertile brain worrying at the new information. Dredging his frustrated thoughts for answers. Sometimes, a Seer's enchantments worked all too well.

"Petronella's book? You'll not find anything useful in that. She's the only one who can read it." Fortuna's amusement broke through his reverie as she strode through the door, accompanied by a welcome aroma of roast meat and ale. Little Bird followed behind on cautious feet, clutching a large decanter and several clean goblets close to her narrow chest. She slanted a look at him from under her long lashes. Like her namesake, perfectly poised between curiosity and wariness.

Joran sighed. "'Tis well, Little Bird. I have slept, and I am now safe to be around. But I still do not understand why you took it upon yourself to defy my orders. I should have you arrested."

Her cheeks pinked. She cast her gaze to the floor and placed her offering on his desk, arranging the goblets in a neat line despite the tremble in her fingers. "I am sorry, my lord. How is the Queen?" she whispered.

"Just the same. I am worried about her," Joran said. "She should not be sleeping like this." The note of accusation hovered in the air between them.

"I will tend her needs." Casting him a warning glare, Fortuna deposited the meal on his desk with brief ceremony and rustled into Petronella's chamber. Evidence of her industry trickled through the partly open door. The gentle glugging of fresh water. The clink of earthenware and the faint smell of lavender. Comforted by the homely atmosphere, Joran plunged into his supper and poured a glass of Argentish. The heavy wine tasted like heaven on his tongue. He waved his glass at Little Bird. She'd retreated to the hearth, warming her fingers.

"Have you eaten?" Joran asked her.

She glanced over her shoulder. "Aye, my lord. Thank ye," she said.

"Do you know of this verse? This 'Prophecy of the Sword'?" Joran asked, scanning the parchment once again. The content intrigued him. Had he heard this once before? A long time ago? A half-memory tugged at his senses, only to vanish as he reached for it.

"Nay, my lord. What is it?" Her periwinkle eyes sparkled in the dim light cast by the lamps. He shrugged. "Something my lady was working on. It seems to have caught her eye," he mumbled. "'Tis a verse. Mayhap a song. I know not."

"If 'tis a song, Master Torry will know it," Little Bird said. "He knows all the songs. I ask him to play for the children sometimes. Shall I fetch him?"

Joran studied her more closely, a new frown clenching his forehead. "Nay, not now, child," he said. "The words are in front of me." She nodded and returned her gaze to the fire, shoulders slumping.

"Thank you for thinking of it," Joran added. Little Bird gave him a fleeting smile.

"That was better done," Fortuna said, wiping her hands on a rough cloth as she returned from Petronella's chamber. She glanced at Little Bird, her expression softening. "The lass is nought but a child trying to do her best. We cannot blame her." She draped her cloth atop the nearest chair. "I am glad you found some rest at last," she said. "You needed it."

Joran grunted and pushed a glass towards her. "Help yourself," he said, nodding to the decanter. "Sometimes excellent wine is the only remedy."

Fortuna raised her eyebrows and poured herself a token measure. "Speak for yourself," she returned mildly. They sipped in silence, lost in their own thoughts.

"Did you discuss our lady with Master Mortlake?" Joran asked, emptying his glass and returning to his meat.

"Aye. 'Tis not of physical origin, we feel," Fortuna said. She jerked her head at Little Bird, who was staring into the flames as if reading her future there. The firelight cast an aura of gold around her blonde curls.

"Heartsease would block my lady's magical gifts, for sure. Especially in quantity. But this other. This waking sleep... We are not sure if 'tis something she has conjured for herself or if 'tis the result of another's power. That is a deeper concern."

Joran's heart sank, his blood chilling. "Then we cannot wake her?" he whispered. "She is to remain stuck like that? Hovering betwixt life and death? How long can she survive like that?"

Fortuna sighed, turning her glass in her hands. "I am blessed by my goddess, the Empress," she murmured. "She came to me on my sixteenth birthday with her offer; to join her in her temple and give up my life in pursuit of the healing path. I denied her. Back then, I preferred a worldly life to a spiritual one." Her copper eyes were bleak as she stared at him. "Perhaps, if I had placed my feet on that road, I might be of more help now," she said. "I could protect her better." Her voice was low, full of regret. "As it is, I can tend our Queen's needs, strengthen her a little. But that is all, my lord. I am sorry."

"Protection," Little Bird said suddenly. The two adults glanced at each other and followed the maid's progress as she withdrew her attention from the fire and stumbled to her feet. Eyes wide, she wandered round to Joran's side of the desk and placed one delicate hand on Petronella's finely carved wooden staff. Crowned with the shape of the Mage Tree, it towered over her head.

"Bird! What are you doing? You must not touch that!" Fortuna hissed. She reached to take the symbol of the Seer's power from the girl. Little Bird said nothing more. She dodged Fortuna's questing hand. Mouth clasped in a firm, straight line, she placed the staff like a pilgrim's stick over her shoulder and marched determinedly into Petronella's chamber.

Joran abandoned his supper and strode in her wake. "Little Bird, what are you about? Leave that at once," he ordered.

"Nay, she lies here in the Mage's grace," Little Bird said. "And he must protect her if we cannot."

She levered the staff from her shoulder and placed it carefully along the length of Petronella's body, folding her mistress' chilly hands firmly around the glowing satin wood. The Grayling observed her with a sleepy eye. Unmoving. His piercing gaze took in the gaping adults in the doorway and then twisted towards his mistress. Joran strode to the bedside, a harsh rebuke ready on his lips, intent on returning the staff to its place at Petronella's desk.

He halted in mid-stride, scrubbed his hands across his eyes, just in case he was dreaming. Petronella had not moved.

But she was smiling.

CHAPTER 17
DOMINIC

Hartwood's town gates creaked open, shouldered as wide as they would go under the combined efforts of two puffing gate guards. A narrow, well-trodden cart track twisted outside the walls and downwards to the left. Scattered with ash, straw, and liberally sprinkled with dung, Dominic guessed this was the path taken by the wagon drivers heading to the river with their loads of snow. Squinting to the south, his eyes widened at the incline stretching before them. No-one had attempted this route since the blizzard. The world around them was an ocean of rippling white, topped off on the horizon by a thick band of grey cloud, and the mountain ranges closing in from east and west. He could see nothing of the roadside shrine to the Mage he and Aldric had passed on their way to Hartwood. The familiar, distant shape of a motionless windmill was all that remained to give some perspective to the scene. Hungry birds cast zig-zag silhouettes against the lowering sky.

"By the Gods." At his side, Aldric shuddered. "I am not sure I like snow in this quantity. How are we going to haul this lot up there?"

The three sledge drivers jumped from their seats, convening just outside the main gates. One of them, Dominic thought, could be Silas, although he couldn't be sure, kicked the snow, testing it out with his boot. The three put their heads together. Dominic threw Kismet's reins to Aldric and dismounted, steadying himself on the ice with one hand on his mount's neck.

"Are we stranded before we've even left?" he asked as he approached them.

Silas, the oldest member of the group, scratched at the wiry curls peeking from beneath his hood. "Nay, my lord," he said. "We just have to decide how best to make this slope. Once we are on the flat of the ridge, 'twill be easier. But first, we must get up there."

"See here, we can tread it down," the second driver said. 'Tis firm, this snow. We could use the sledges to push it down. They're heavy enough."

"Aye, but you'll wear out the horses," Silas said. "And they need all the strength they can get."

"Walk it, then? Tread it down ourselves?"

Silas rolled his eyes. "If we're going to do that, might as well unload and get the townsfolk out. 'Twill take most of the day." He grimaced. "Haven't had a blizzard like this in years."

"Is there a timber yard in town?" Dominic asked, scanning the length of the slope.

"Aye, of course."

"Good. We need a log. Something smooth and heavy. And some rope."

Silas's heavy brow wrinkled. "Why?"

Dominic grinned. "We're going to make a path," he said. He tramped back to Guildford, who had tired of the wait and was chatting with Felicia, his mount's reins dangling from his hands. Exchanging dubious glances, the drivers followed him.

"You know how we use you like a packhorse?" he said as he drew level.

Guildford's eyes narrowed. "Aye?" he growled. "What do you want of me this time, stripling?"

"Fetch a log. We need to create a road up that slope, and this is the quickest way I can think to do it." He turned to survey the drivers. "Which of you is the strongest?" he asked.

"That'll be my brother, Miles," Silas said. "He's our anchor man. Strong as a rock." He jerked his thumb at the stockiest member of the group. Miles glanced at him, then away, one foot tracing delicate patterns in the snow. "He never says much, but he's the one who always wins in a fight," Silas continued. He reached out and slapped his brother on the back. Even standing with most of his weight on one foot, Miles hardly moved.

Dominic laughed. "Impressive," he said. "We'll wait for you."

Grumbling under his breath, Guildford handed the reins of his enormous horse over to Dominic. "You owe me," he said as he trudged off.

Watching his retreat, Dominic locked a mischievous gaze on Felicia. "He's yet to find out what he'll be doing with that log when he returns," he said. "Then I really will owe him."

Felicia laughed. The cold air turned their breath to soft clouds between them. Taking advantage of the driver's absence, he scooted next to her, glad to remove his booted feet from the icy earth, and put a sturdy arm around her shoulders. Driven by the cold, she leaned against him. Feeling her slight weight, Dominic let himself relax, the tension of their coming journey dimming a little.

Aldric eyed them with some frustration. "I'm off to make a new friend," he said, tossing Kismet's reins to Felicia. "Here. You hold him."

Chuckling under his breath, Dominic rested his chin on Felicia's hooded head. Aldric jumped down from Hamil's back and joined the two drivers, stamping his feet to keep warm. Stolid Hamil stayed where he was, dropping his head to mouth at the snow.

"Warm enough, my lady?" Dominic murmured. He felt Felicia nod her head, her fragile cheek pillowed on his shoulder. Of a sudden, the world seemed a pleasant place. Were it not for the beat of urgency low in his belly, prompting haste, he would be content to stay at her side all day. Breathing her scent, fresh, clean air in his lungs. The sigh of the winter wind against his cheeks.

"Are you going to hang on to that all day?" he asked her, tapping the package of heartsease she held on her lap under her cloak. "I can think of other things to occupy your hands."

Felicia lifted her chin to meet his gaze, the tiniest smile playing on her lips. "Just as well I'm keeping hold of this then, isn't it?" she replied.

"Seriously, you don't want to put it in with the rest of our supplies?" Dominic said. "We can do it now if you like."

"Nay. I'd rather look after it." Her voice was soft, watching Hamil as he nosed through the snow to the crusty grass beneath. "If push comes to shove, I'll eat it like a horse and not bother brewing it." His arms tightened around her in response, disturbed by the grim finality weighing her words.

"I wish it didn't have to be that way for you," he murmured. "I'd do anything to drive your fears away." He plucked one delicate hand from beneath her cloak and pinched the glove from her fingers. Slowly. She kept her face turned away. He could feel the slight tremor in her body as she rested against him, poised for flight. "Nay, my lady. Do not run from me," he whispered. He captured her palm against his mouth, smoothing it across the silk of his bearded cheeks. Gently, gently. The smallest of sighs escaped her.

"Dominic..." Her protest faded and died as he rolled his shoulder, tipping her head into the strength of his arm. Her eyes shone into his, dark with desire. Hot blood swept his body under the thick layers of winter clothing.

"By the Gods, Felicia," he breathed, "what you do. What you do to me." He closed the distance between them, aching for the touch of her lips. The world seemed to halt around them. The bustle of the town behind them, even the harsh croaking of the midnight crows circling the ramparts, faded to nothing. He put his heart into his kiss.

In his blood, his magic sang to life, exalting when she responded with a wondering hunger that matched his own.

Lost in the world they had created between them, the kisses growing wilder, more urgent, both of them jumped at the sound of Guildford's chuckle and the spray of icy snow that enveloped them as he tossed his burden down next to the cart.

"Which log do you have the most use for, Dominic?" he said, with no pretence at delicacy.

Dominic lifted his head, a growl of frustration on his lips. Felicia's hand drifted from his chest, a flicker of laughter under the warmth of her expression. She rolled her eyes. A reluctant answering grin spread foolishly across Dominic's face.

He tossed a mock glare in Guildford's direction. "Your timing leaves much to be desired," he said.

Guildford smirked. "Nothing wrong with my timing," he declared. "Ask any maiden you choose. They'll all say the same thing." He winked. The hearty slap to Dominic's shoulder nearly batted Felicia off the cart into the nearest snowdrift.

Felicia steadied herself and added her glare to Dominic's as she straightened her clothing. "My long-lost brother," she said, deepest sarcasm sharpening her tone. "How much I have missed your vibrant wit."

Unabashed, Guildford threw his head back. His gust of laughter swept the pristine slopes. "Come, lovebirds," he said, "the day is wasting. I thought we had work to do."

"Aye, we do." Dominic slid from the warmth of Felicia's slight form with a regretful sigh. "And you are about to pay for your untimely interruption," he pointed at the slope and chuckled as the merriment left his companion's face. "You and Miles are going to haul that log from here to the top. I will flatten the drifts and make a trail for the sledges to follow."

Guildford stared at him. "Me?" he demanded. "You want me to do the work of an ox?"

"Why not?" Felicia rejoined cooly. "You act like one half of the time."

Guildford straightened his shoulders. "I do not," he said.

"Aye, you do," Aldric cut in. His shrewd gaze took in the scene as he slithered across the snow to join them. "'Twill work. And Dominic will use his gifts to help." He prodded Dominic's ribs. "Won't you?"

"Aye," Dominic said, relented as he noted the true resistance in Guildford's alarmed expression. "Of course. You and Miles are not doing all the work. I will help. I just need you to keep in a straight line and manage the log between you."

Eyes narrowed, Guildford regarded him with his hands on his narrow hips. "If any ever find out about this, I'll have your hide," he rumbled.

"Won't be the first time," Dominic said, shrugging. "Come. Let's get to work. We have already lost too much daylight. If either of you tires, Silas or Kendrick will take over."

Guildford sighed and stooped to pick up the log. Dominic exchanged glances with Aldric. Despite his teasing, Guildford's sheer strength always amazed him. He shouldered his burden like a man carrying a half-stuffed pillow.

"Where do you want it?" Guildford said.

"Over there. Fetch the ropes, Aldric," Dominic said, pointing to a relatively flat portion of snow directly in line with the gates. "And then fetch some blankets for the horses. I don't want them standing around in the cold. Lead them out of the way, just in case something goes wrong. The sledges, too."

Together, the group fashioned a harness. Guildford was still grumbling as he draped the rough rope over his shoulders and took the strain. Miles, on the other end of the log, formed a comical contrast. Short and stocky.

"Guildford, shorten your stride to match Miles," Dominic remarked as he flexed his fingers. Mage power gathered in his palms. "The log will twist, else. I will try not to push you harder than you can walk. Ready?"

"Aye," Guildford grunted, stabbing at the packed snow at his feet, testing the weight of the log tugging at his chest. Miles said nothing. Stoic and patient as an ox himself. He turned his face to the top of the slope. Matched his stance with his partner.

"By the Gods, then. Let's go."

Energy flickered through his fingertips. His breathing slowed as he aligned himself with his power. "Slow, steady," he reminded himself. Together, Guildford and Miles took the strain. Digging in their feet. Bit by bit, the log moved behind them, compacting the drifts. Dominic helped it along. Kept it steady. Spreading his power in equal amounts as the two hauliers puffed ever forward. Encouraged by the success of his plan, Dominic used some of his energy to push the heaviest drifts to one side, trying to smooth the way for the two men when they struggled for footing. Slowly, slowly, the group battled up the slope. Halfway up, Miles threw up a hand. His breath came in short pants as he bent double, gasping with the effort. Dominic signalled to one of the other drivers. "Replacement!" he yelled.

Not bothering to see which of the other two drivers responded, he crossed the short distance to where Guildford was taking a breather. Sweat cascaded from the young man's freckled brow, but his grey eyes glistened with enjoyment, his cheeks red under his soldier's tan. He clapped his hands to his thighs. "By the Gods," he boomed as Dominic joined them. "They should add log dragging to our training at the castle."

"Don't encourage it," Dominic said, turning his attention to Miles. "Are you well, my friend?" he inquired, bending so he could make out Mile's features beneath his woollen cap and beard. The man's face was scarlet. Steam wafted from his greasy scalp as he snatched his cap from his head.

"Aye." Still panting, Miles waved him away.

"'Tis hard work, but see what you've done," Dominic said. He threw a hand behind him. The newly formed track cut a neat swathe between the drifts. Distant shapes in the shelter of Hartwood's walls, Felicia and Aldric were tending the horses. Some of the townsfolk, alerted by the activity, stood in the open gateway, watching their progress. Closer to him, Kendrick strode up the slope, out of breath.

"I'll take over," he said, nudging the smaller man aside.

Miles cast a sour look in Guildford's direction. "He's not even half-winded," he muttered, rearranging the rope around his chest. "If he can do this. So can I."

Kendrick slapped him on the shoulder. "If you're sure," he said. He turned to Dominic. The ghost of a wink flitted across his weathered face. "Most he's said for months," he muttered, standing back. "Can't bear to be beaten."

Dominic arched an eyebrow and cast his gaze forward. The rest of the incline loomed before them. A wilderness of white, steeper towards the top. "Stay with me," he ordered, stretching his fingers once more. "Just in case."

"'Tis fascinating, seeing how your magic works," Kendrick rejoined. "We have a Blessed population in Hartwood, but they keep to themselves, mostly. Especially after the raid." He kept pace with Dominic as Guildford and Miles took up the slack once more and bent themselves to the tiring task ahead.

Dominic nodded, dropping into the well of his power. Playing with it. Today, the Mage was kind. Or perhaps it was the knowledge that Felicia returned his feelings. That beneath her frosty exterior beat a heart hot with desire. The match of his own. He forced his mind away from her with an effort. Concentrating on the task at hand as they progressed. Observing the two men, he bit his lip. Despite his brave words, Miles was tiring. Lagging behind Guildford's mighty effort.

"Pride won't win this race," Dominic murmured. Even as the words left his lips, Miles stumbled. He fell face down, bashing his head on the icy ground. The log twisted. Dominic sent a quick burst of energy to it as the sudden imbalance caused Guildford to slip as well. The weight of the log dragged the two men down the slope, struggling to keep their feet. In danger of being crushed by the very burden they hauled. Lurching around, Dominic's boots skidded beneath him. He landed on his backside, battling to collect his concentration enough to control them all. Perspiration dotted his forehead as he flung his hands out. Braced his mind under the weight of the men and their burden. The world slowed. Halted. He had them. Safe. Guildford's face, turned towards him, wore a complex expression balanced equally between amazement and gratitude. Reaching across the space, he hauled Miles to his feet. Dazed, the shorter man wobbled, swiping at the blood pouring from his nose. Swallowing hard, Dominic pushed his power around them as they gathered themselves to resume. He could feel his energy breaking down just a little. The unexpected call upon it was greater than he had expected. At his side, Kendrick watched him like a spectator at a play, starved of entertainment. Hungry for more. Of a sudden, Dominic disliked him. He turned his shoulder.

"Are you well, Guildford?"

"Aye, my thanks," Guildford responded gruffly. He dusted snow from his breeches and rolled his shoulders, eyeing the last length of slope with determination written large on his freckled face. "'It's not beating me," he said.

"Your turn, Kendrick," Dominic said, giving the man beside him an encouraged pat that held a slight note of vengeful glee hidden deep within it. The driver shot him a surprised look. Dominic shook his head, impatient to have this first hurdle behind them. The sun was halfway to its zenith. There was a way to go before they could make some sort of shelter at the edge of Falconridge lands, protected by its forest. He had no time to play favourites with this magic-struck Citizen.

"Miles is in no fit state. Get to it," he said. "There is but a few feet to go."

Reluctance in his step, Kendrick threw him a reproachful look and shuffled away. Miles surrendered his place with ill grace.

Harnessed once more, Kendrick and Guildford sweated their way up the last steep incline. The wind blew wild and cold across the plateau of the ridge, tossing snow at their faces so hard it stung. Guildford rolled out of his ropes and dropped his steaming face into the nearest drift, his shoulders heaving, panting for breath.

Dominic waved at the sledge party, already moving to angle their sledges at the base of the slope. The result of their efforts stretched before him. A long, clean line cut through the drifts. He huffed a quiet sigh, relieved his plan had worked. Tired himself, the drain on his power sucking at his reserves, Dominic half-walked, half-skidded down the hill to meet them. Miles and Kendrick followed. Their one-sided conversation drifted in the quiet air. Kendrick's awestruck gabble contrasted oddly with Mile's monosyllabic grunts. Guildford trudged along beside him, a broad grin on his face. A cheer went up from the group of citizens clustered at the gate. It echoed to him like the distant sigh of the wind on the ridge.

"Thought you'd roll down and crush us like a couple of barrels at an alehouse." Aldric clapped Guildford on the shoulder as he approached.

"Nearly," Dominic said. "We got lucky." He yawned, almost ready to sleep. But no. There was still too much to do.

"Well done." Felicia's quiet, rare praise raised a prickle of pride within him. "That took a lot more than physical effort."

Dominic gave her a half smile. "My thanks," he murmured. "A moment's rest, and then we must be away. The weather is closing in again up there." He nodded to the distant plateau, where darker clouds were already gathering. Anxiety clawed at him as Miles and Kendrick removed rugs from their mounts and took their places on the laden sledges, ready to depart.

"Our compliments and godspeed." Dominic turned in surprise at the voice behind him. The chestnut vendor tramped across the crusted ground and tossed well-wrapped packets of hot roasted nuts to every member of the party. Guildford's latest conquest followed in her wake with a tray of mugs and a heavy jug of mulled ale. Apple-scented steam wafted from its ill-fitting lid.

Behind them, a long chain of citizens scurried past them, onwards up the hill, weighed down with packs of straw. Pails of ash. Sipping his ale, warming his frozen hands on the mug, Dominic watched them tramping the fresh path, making it firmer. Lending the horses added grip for their forthcoming travail.

"You have helped us dig out," the girl with the sparkling green eyes said. She stood at Guildford's side, one hand on his arm. "We thank you. 'Twould have taken us a week without you."

Guildford bent and placed a smacking kiss on the girl's lips. Eyes dancing, he caught Dominic's amused stare over the top of her head.

"Aye, I'm a hero," he said. "I'll take all my thanks like this. Kiss away, lass. Kiss away."

CHAPTER 18
JORAN

"A word, my maid."

His mind ablaze with questions, Joran gestured Little Bird out of Petronella's chamber. Little Bird glanced at him as she sidled past, a small, secretive smile playing around her lips.

It lingered just long enough to spark Fortuna's ire. She grabbed Little Bird by the elbow and gave her a shake that made her teeth rattle. "By the Gods, girl. You stole from me and drugged the Queen. And now take it upon yourself to do what you wish with her most precious possessions. What do you mean by it?" Hands on her hips, rare anger shining in her copper brown eyes, she loomed over the Little Bird. A mighty oak over a tender sapling. Joran leaned against Petronella's desk and tore off a slice of ham. It tasted like ash on his tongue as he chewed, striving for control over his desire to lash out. Feigning a calm he did not feel.

"I talked with the Queen last night," Little Bird said, her voice flat with weariness. "We spoke of Dominic and my Will. And about the shadow woman I saw two years ago. Under the Mage's temple in Blade." She raised stormy eyes to Joran, alert to his movement, as he dropped his hand to the dagger at his narrow hip.

"We were never sure, me and Dominic," she continued, wary as a sparrow, watching his every movement, "who it was. We didn't know if it was a ghost. We both thought it was the Queen. She looked so like."

Joran exchanged glances with Fortuna. "Like the Queen?"

"Aye, tall, slender. Black hair. But her eyes... Her eyes were different," Little Bird said. "She's got black eyes. Like coal." A shudder swept through her as she said the words. "Dominic thinks she's a telepath. Like us." Her hand traced a delicate circle between herself, Joran and the motionless Queen. "And so, we thought... The Queen agreed..." Her voice trailed away, lost in uncertainty as she moved to place a defensive distance between herself and Joran. Her throat worked as she swallowed. "We thought, mayhap, it would be better for the Queen to damp her magic right back. So that the woman couldn't get to her through her mind. Or in her dreams while she slept."

"By the Gods," Joran breathed. He closed his eyes. One hand reached behind him to clutch the edge of the desk, wrestling with the urge to strike the girl down where she stood.

"Dominic said to tell Fortuna to go to the restricted section and find what she could about a special knife." She nodded at Petronella's Book of Shadows. "That Blade of Aequitas. He seems to think it's important." Her face was white with anxiety as she twisted in Fortuna's direction. "I didn't tell you that..." she whispered. "I should have. But the Queen was so tired, and the children so lively... And then Will..." She hung her head. "I forgot. I'm sorry."

"But heartsease would block her magic, not make her sleep," Fortuna argued. She pressed a hand against her lips. "Did you give her anything else? Add another herb to the mix, mayhap?"

"Nay. Just the heartsease." Little Bird's lips trembled. "I swear it on my life."

Fortuna sighed. She turned in a circle, staring around the room like a woman seeking a lost purse, and threw up her hands in defeat. "Then I am at a loss," she said. "This is something else entirely."

"The restricted section," Joran ordered, "go there now and find out anything you can. Bring all the references back here." He fixed a piercing stare on Little Bird. "You go with her. Help her carry them."

Bird's throat jerked as she swallowed. "What about the children?" she whispered.

Joran scowled at her. "I will watch them. What do you think?" he said. "You may have taken Petronella away as a target, but thanks to you and young Skinner, Theda is now vulnerable. And she cannot block her channels."

Little Bird gaped at him, the blood draining from her cheeks. "Theda?" she stuttered. "No, but she's too young. Surely…"

"Aye, Theda." Joran's voice dropped dangerously. "Her grandmother was a Seer of rare talent, blessed with Farsight. Petronella can walk minds. And I know not what other gifts Theda may possess." His hand drifted to his dagger, and Little Bird took a tentative step toward the door, her fingers clutching her skirts, ready to flee.

"It falls to me to keep our daughter safe," he mumbled, struggling with the weight of his fear and anger. "And I will do it if I have to eliminate everyone around her. Including you. Do I make myself clear?"

Fortuna needed no further urging. Face grim, she herded Little Bird in front of her and gave her a shove for good measure. "You foolish, foolish girl," she muttered. "You and young Skinner are meddling in forces way beyond your comprehension."

Little Bird said nothing more. The door shut behind them, the guards' faces a stoic mask of calm.

Joran let out a slow, rattling breath, pushing away from the desk. His eyes flicked to the nursery suite, judging the distance. His gaze returned to Petronella's room, now shrouded in quiet, the fading light casting shadows of gold and black across her face. The Grayling edged closer to her along his perch, tawny eyes watchful.

"I suppose you'll scream if anything happens," he muttered, half to himself. "Watch her for me. I'll be but a moment."

A sleepy-eyed maid, younger than Little Bird, greeted him as he entered the outer chamber of his children's domain. Rich oak panelling ended halfway up the stone walls. Two low-slung beds strewn with blankets, sleeves, and bodices showed that it also doubled as the maid's bedchamber. The girl gaped at him and bobbed into a curtsey. "My lord," she gasped, turning a gap-toothed smile in his direction.

He nodded impatiently at her. "Where are the other maids?" he demanded, turning to the door of his children's bed chamber.

"Little Bird is with you, is she not?" Her tone was pert. He scowled. In no mood for games.

"And there are no others? Who are you?" She blanched, caught up in the force of the ferocious stare he turned upon her. "Maria, Sire," she whispered, bobbing another curtsey.

"Maria." He looked her over thoughtfully. Committing her face to memory. She blushed slightly under his intense scrutiny, her hands twisting in her apron. "Well, Maria, go to the door and shout for the guard. Shout loudly."

She frowned. He raised an eyebrow.

"Aye." Her serge skirt swished as she hurried past him, giving him a wide berth and a look that bespoke her certainty that he belonged in the nearest asylum.

"Guard!" she shrieked, her treble voice bouncing off the hard walls. Her alarm triggered a burst of thundering feet. Satisfied, Joran watched as two more members of the Queen's guard ground to a halt, pikes raised.

"Good," he said. "But I need more of you in the future. "Double the guard on this corridor. I want you to watch over the children when they are here."

The senior guard gave him a cautious nod. "Aye, Sire, we already do that on your order," he muttered.

"I want two of you at this door at all times from now on," Joran said. "Not halfway down the passage. Understand?"

"Aye." The man jerked his head in response, waving his hand at two of his companions. Grim-faced, they took up a defensive position.

"Better," Joran muttered. He waved Maria to a low seat by the fire.

"They are abed, Sire," she assured him. "I settled them myself after supper."

"Hmm."

Softening his step, Joran cracked open the door to the inner chamber. The room smelled of hot milk and cinnamon. Squinting in the glow of a single lamp, he could make out the blockish shapes of sturdy oak chests on the walls, the shadowy rectangles of tapestries warming the walls where the panelling ended. Heavy curtains blocked the draft from the windows. Head cocked, he listened to Ranulf's soft breathing nearest him. The lad's sleeping face was a picture of youthful innocence, crowned with a riot of honey-brown curls. He slept with one hand flung out to clutch the adventure of life before him, his blankets crowded with tin soldiers and scattered with sugar crumbs. Comforted, Joran leaned against the sturdy post of his son's bed. No nightmares stalked the boyish prince's dreams. Joran passed a tired hand across his face. To date, Ranulf showed an appetite for adventure, a slim talent for telepathy, and much of his late grandmother's empathic nature. If he had other Blessed gifts, they were yet to make themselves known.

Smothering a yawn, he turned to the opposite side of the room. Theda's bed space, shrouded with curtains, was a strange study in neatness, in direct contrast to her brother's. He drew her curtains back, fully expecting to see a slumbering child. His blood chilled as Theda turned her small face towards him. She was sitting cross-legged atop her bed, her back straight as a beam, hands folded in front of her.

He swallowed at the shock of it. The stare she turned on him was fully adult. Aware. He blinked, startled. Rubbed his hand across his eyes. For a second, just a second before she saw him and smiled, he could have sworn her eyes were black.

"My Theda, what keeps you up like a little soldier?" he whispered, crouching to kneel beside her. Her hand was icy in his, but she did not seem to notice.

"I must keep watch," she whispered, leaning closer to breathe in his ear. Her breath clouded in the air. He frowned, flicking his eyes to the glowing hearth, banked for the night behind the fireguard.

"Nay, my love, sleep," he returned. Reaching for a tiny shawl, he wound it around her shoulders. "There are lots of guards at the door. And Maria is just outside."

She shook her head. "I must watch her." She tugged her fingers from his and pointed at a shadowed corner.

His skin crawled. "Theda?" he said, more sharply than he wanted. "Are you dreaming?"

"Nay. Can't you see her, Papa? She's over there."

Joran closed his mouth on the frantic denial that threatened to burst from his lips. There were no words to describe the complete horror that gripped his belly as he followed the line of her gaze. Every hair on his neck prickled as her tiny forefinger traced a wavering line closer and closer to the bed. "Here," Theda's voice was the merest whisper against his ear. "She's looking for Mama. She says Mama is hiding. But she doesn't mind."

His powerful arms closed about his daughter, squashing her against his heart. "She doesn't mind?" he echoed.

She shook her head against his chest. "She says she'll find her soon," she said.

CHAPTER 19

DOMINIC

D riven to fury through the mountain passes on the ridge above Hartwood, the north wind howled like a wolf at their backs. The blizzard had blunted all the hard edges of the rocky terrain. Around them, the landscape undulated in icy shades of white and grey. The horizon blurred into the cloud-wrapped sky, softened by the wisps of snow dusted into the air by the gale. Sledges to the fore, the riders moved in single file, following the narrow path carved by their passage. The chill penetrated Dominic's clothing even through the insulating layers of fur. He rode with hunched shoulders. Kismet tossed her head, fighting the bit. Her energy was hard to contain. Rested from her time in the stable, she was desperate to move faster. She picked up her legs, prancing across the snow. Dominic moved easily with her gait, allowing her the extra energy. "I know, my lady," he said. "'Tis cold. You want to move." He patted her neck, his own hand already half numb. Kismet's ears flickered at the sound of his voice. "But we have a way to go yet," Dominic continued. "So you'll need all your energy." He sat back a little in the saddle. Kismet tossed her head once more, settling under his calm control as she matched her pace to that of the sledges.

Dominic twisted in his saddle to check on Aldric and Guildford's progress. His companions faced much of the same conditions. Sturdy Hamil trudged along. Aldric didn't even need to guide him. He'd tied Hamil's reins in a loose knot and rode with both hands wrapped around his body inside his cloak. Further behind, Guildford whistled a tuneless ditty. The wind snatched the notes away. If the young giant was cold, he didn't show it. His horse, a magnificent charger, plodded onward like a battleship on a rough sea. Ponderous and majestic, both.

Satisfied they were well, Dominic's eyes drifted forward. He could just about see beyond the rich dark blue of Felicia's hood, peeking from behind her layers of fur. She sat next to Silas, close at his side on the second sledge. In the front, Miles took the lead. Kendrick drove the third sledge. Cheered, he turned his gaze further south towards Falconridge. If they could keep up this pace, they would at least reach the magnificent forests at the edge of Falconridge land and find shelter amidst the trees for the night. But first, they would have to stop. Water the horses. Eat. Where was the stream he and Aldric had stopped by on their way here? By his reckoning, it should be close.

Nudging Kismet with his heels, he urged her into a trot on the packed snow, chasing Silas' sledge. Despite the weather and the urgency of their journey, a smile edged the corners of his lips, delighted at the sense of onward progression. Kismet drew him level with Silas' sledge, and he slowed her to a walk, leaning across and grazing Felicia's cheek with a gloved hand. She cast him a tight smile through chattering teeth.

"Are you well, my lady?" he asked.

"Aye, cold." Felicia's lips were pale.

"We'll find you an extra blanket when we stop for food," Dominic said, frowning as he took in her pallor. "Can you wait that long, or should we stop now?"

"I will do," she replied, making a grab for the cloth-wrapped parcel of heartsease as it slid from her lap.

Dominic's lips tightened. "We'll put that in the sledge when we stop," he muttered. "No sense you trying to hang on to it all the way to Falconridge."

Felicia lifted her chin. "I want to keep hold of it," she said. "There's little heartsease to find this time of year."

Dominic rolled his eyes. "Have it your way," he said, grinning. "Will we stop to rest the horses?" he said, over her head, to Silas. "There's a stream around here somewhere, I think."

"Aye." Silas raised his whip, pointing to a stand of frost-decked trees in the distance. "'Tis there. A good place to stop," he said. "But not for long. This wind is building again." His thick black brows twisted as he turned his head to the magnificent mountain tops. "'Tis hard to believe this weather, so early in the season," he muttered. "Haven't known it like this for years. 'Tis strange. I mislike it."

A frown creased Dominic's forehead as the driver made the sign of the Mage over his heart. "How long ago was it like this?" he questioned, bending close to hear what the man had to say. Silas glanced at him, then at Felicia. Was it Dominic's imagination, or did he move slightly away from her?

"'Twere bad before the Queen came to the throne, proper," Silas said. "And now, here it is again. 'Tis odd. That's all."

"Odd," Dominic echoed. His gaze clashed with Felicia's before she dropped it to the package in her lap, holding it close against her belly. Despite himself, his lips thinned. Something about that movement was off. Furtive. Almost guilty. "Are you well?" he said. His voice came out harsher than he'd thought.

She scowled at the question. "Aye," she said again. "I said so." She turned her face away, huddling her chin close to her neck against the wind.

"We'll stop soon. Warm up a little," Dominic said. His practised gaze swept her narrow form, noting the tremble in her shoulders. The tension on her face. Nodding to Silas, he dropped back to his place in the train, his thoughts suddenly a whirl of unease that he could not put a name to.

At the stream, the party drew the horses to a halt. Subdued sunlight was already fading from the sky as Dominic stumbled from Kismet's back. His legs and feet had all but lost their feeling. He stomped to the nearest sleigh, burrowing like a mole into its unfamiliar load in search of blankets for the horses. Aldric prepared their teams, and Silas took a hefty ice pick to the frozen stream, making space for the horses to drink their fill. Felicia left her parcel on the seat and joined Guildford in a further foray for food and wine. The group spoke but little. Tending their needs took away the need for conversation. Icy wind still harried powdered snow across the landscape, building by the hour.

Mouth full of cured ham and cheese, Dominic picked up Kismet's feet, using the edge of his blade to prise ice from her hooves. Kismet nickered and dripped freezing water down his back.

"Thanks for that," he mumbled through his mouthful, moving around to her hindquarters, out of target range. "We've still a way to go," he said, lifting his head to peer south. "We'll not reach Falconridge today. Not in these conditions."

"Aye," Silas rumbled. His breath wreathed the air as he gulped small ale from a wooden tankard. "There's a likely spot on the edge of Falconridge's estates. Sheltered from the wind. We'll aim for that. Make camp. 'Twill be a cold rest, though."

"Cedric thought of everything," Aldric said. Ever curious, he removed his head from beneath the oilskin covering Mile's sledge. "There's kindling in the sleighs. Three tents. Even some oil lamps and a spare flint box. And look what I found!" He skidded across the small patch of flat ground, nearly losing the closely wrapped package clamped in his fist. "Marchpane!" His eyes glowed. "Anyone?"

Guildford rolled his eyes at the thought. "A woman's treat," he scoffed. "Find me a fletch of salted bacon and a barrel of mead. That would make me happy."

Aldric tossed the package to Felicia and swept a ball of snow from the ground. "Have that instead, then," he said, aiming it squarely at Guildford's face.

"Bastard," Guildford said, but his eyes were bright with amusement as he wiped his chin. "There are many drifts to plunge you into between here and Falconridge," he rumbled. "Don't imagine I will forget such insolence."

Dominic grinned. Even Felicia lost her pinched look as she dipped her fingers into the twist of cloth.

"It's good," she said through a mouthful. "Here, Aldric. You found it." She re-wrapped it and gave it back to him. "Enjoy while you can. And be aware that Guildford was not joking just then." Dominic's spirits lifted further at the sight of her smile as it tugged at the edges of her lips.

"Come," he said, drawing his hood closer around his bearded cheeks. "The sun is lowering. We must away. Have you all eaten your fill?"

"Aye," Silas said. "Hoy!" He jerked his thumb at his fellow drivers, clustered together and deep in conversation. Still muttering, they gathered themselves for the onward journey. Removing Kismet's nosebag, Dominic's brow quirked at the wary glances they were throwing in Felicia's direction. Silas definitely slid away from her on the seat as she took her place beside him. His lips thinned. She would be cold without the warmth from his body, but he could not burden Kismet with a double weight in the weather. He tugged a blanket free from the sleigh bed and spread it carefully around Felicia's shoulders. "Stand up, get this under you," he said. She did as he instructed, pulling the heavy wool around her shoulders. His nose wrinkled at the stink of lanolin. "By the Gods," he said as he turned to mount. "It might keep you warmer, but you'll smell like a sheep by the end of the day,"

"Bah, I will not," Felicia said, her lips curving on the small joke.

Chuckling, Dominic vaulted onto Kismet's back. Turning her against the wind, the party set off into the lowering afternoon, striking across the deserted ridge for the downhill ride to the Falconridge estates.

Mid-afternoon brought no respite from the cold. The hazy sun disappeared beneath a thick bank of clouds, and the weather closed. Everyone's shoulders bore a light mantle of additional snow. It frosted their cheeks and numbed their fingers. The horses trudged stoically onwards. Shivering, Dominic followed the line of sledges like a man half hypnotised, his vision a blur of snowflakes. Dizzy with tiredness.

At first, he couldn't make out what fell from the second sledge. So suddenly did it happen, his sluggish brain failed to catch up. One moment, the small package lay dark against the snow. The next, the runners of Kendrick's sledge shredded the fragile cloth. The wind caught the contents in an instant, adding a drift of dried heartsease to the wild winter storm. He had a second to process it and then forgot it as Felicia followed the package headfirst into the snow. Kendrick cursed and hauled on the reins lest he run over her. Dominic leapt from Kismet's back, forcing his frozen limbs to a sprint.

"By the Gods, by the Gods!" He didn't even recognise the panicked voice as his own. Felicia's lips were blue with cold. She opened her eyes and stared at him, confused and momentarily so vulnerable his heart seemed to stop in his chest. He clutched her close, throwing his own cloak over her chilled form, and threw a narrow glare at Silas. "She's freezing to death, and you refuse to sit closer?" he demanded, his voice harsh. Silas bit his lip, hung his head. "'Twas when I heard about the heartsease..." he muttered into his beard. "My aunt's the herbalist in the market. She told me what it's for. Who needs it..."

"By the Gods, Silas! This is Felicia of Wessendean, the late king's own daughter. She's no witch!" He didn't care if he was raising his voice.

"What's he done?" Guildford's roar eclipsed his own. He dismounted and strode across the intervening space with one hand on his sword. The genial giant disappeared in an instant, replaced by a mountain of muscle with flashing grey eyes and a temper to match. Silas quailed, reading his own death in the princeling's hard stare.

"Nay, nay," he stuttered, holding out his hands in supplication. "I never meant..."

"You never meant!" Guildford roared. He shoved Dominic aside with a single thrust of his boot and swept his sister from the frozen snow with one arm. Her head lolled against his massive chest.

"How far are we from a place to camp?" Dominic regained his feet and threw Guildford a stormy look of his own. Guildford looked momentarily shamefaced at his outburst. "Apologies," he said, although he still glowered at Silas.

"A mile, maybe," Silas said. He threw a hopeful hand south, where the edges of the trees threw a shadow across the gloomy snowfields.

"Lead on then," Dominic said. "The sooner we set up camp and make a fire, the better. Make haste."

"She can ride with me," Guildford said, reading the indecision on Dominic's face as he glanced at Kismet. Almost out of strength, his valiant horse's head drooped. As tired as her rider. "My mount can carry us both. He's sturdy and can make the distance."

"My thanks." Exhausted, Dominic hauled himself shivering onto Kismet's back. He raised his arm. "Come, then. The day is nearly done, and we've a camp to set and a girl to warm up."

"Never been a problem for either of you in the past," Aldric remarked as the party lurched onward, the wind a hound at their backs.

CHAPTER 20
JORAN

Joran's breath fogged in the cold air that curled around him as he squatted at Theda's side, holding her close against his heart. She clutched at him but didn't remove her steadfast gaze from where it had landed, at a spot close to her pillow on the other side of the bed. Squinting in the same direction, Joran frowned. Whatever his daughter could see, he did not share her vision. A tremble racked Theda's frame. "Nay," she whispered. "Nay. Keep back. I won't let you."

His throat dry, Joran picked Theda up, one hand on his dagger, his entire body stiff with tension. The back of his neck crawled in the chill atmosphere. He backed out of the room to the antechamber, where Maria, in the absence of anything better to do, was folding shifts and bodices and stowing them away.

"Sire." She glanced up at him as he entered, a light frown crossing her face as she saw Theda with him. "What's to do? Is she ill?"

"You will sleep in the nursery with Ranulf tonight," Joran said. "Use Theda's bed. Any disturbance, call a guard, send for me, and I will come at a run. Understand?"

Maria's frown deepened. "Disturbance?" her dark eyes turned to the nursery door. "Is my lord Prince ill as well?"

Joran shook his head. "Nay. I don't think so. I hope not. Ranulf is well. I pray he remains so." He shifted Theda higher in his arms. A small whimper escaped her as she battled between sleep and terror.

"Theda will come with me," he said. "I will sleep in the Queen's solar tonight, with Theda at my side. Your job is to watch the princeling. Can you do that?"

She curtsied automatically, her eyes travelling to the young princess drooping in Joran's embrace. Biting her lip, she crossed the room and knelt at a trunk, her fingers skipping through the contents.

"Then take this, Sire," she said, handing him a rag doll, a heavy blanket, and a corked earthenware bottle.

"What's this?" he said, immediately suspicious.

"Just valerian," Maria said. "She's been finding it hard to settle at night lately."

Joran's lips thinned. "Aye. No wonder," he muttered. Nodding his thanks, he caught Maria's offerings over his arm and retreated to the relative sanctuary of Petronella's rooms.

Her head nodding at the even pace of his stride, Theda wound her arms around his neck. "Papa, are you angry with me?" she asked.

"Nay, little one, but there is only one of me, and I need to watch over both of you," he whispered into her ebony curls. "So you can sleep with me tonight. Will that comfort you?"

"Aye," her voice was small, even though her mouth was close against his ear. "But she might follow, Papa. What will we do then?"

Ever perceptive, Joran thought wryly. The girl was so in tune with the doubts of his own mind it was uncanny.

"I am not sure yet, my heart," he returned, wishing he could give her a better answer. His mind was racing as he nodded to the guards outside Petronella's door. They saluted stiffly, pushing the door aside so he could enter. "Send for a pallet, pillows, and blankets," Joran instructed. "I will sleep in here tonight."

"Aye, my lord."

If the soldiers resented his rare interference with their nighttime routine, they gave no sign. "Lady de Winter brought some books," the first guard said as his companion departed. "She's gone back for more."

"My thanks."

Heart in his mouth, Joran deposited Theda in a padded armchair by the fire and wrapped a blanket around her. She stared up at him with bleary eyes, her exhaustion clear in the violet shadows that clung beneath them. Joran tucked her doll into her blankets. Her tiny digits clutched it against her chest. "Are you comfortable?" he asked.

"Aye."

"They will bring a pillow for you. Try to sleep." He stood with his hands on his narrow hips, staring down at her as if he'd never seen her before. His own eyes clouded. She was so like her mother. Hair so black it dissolved into the shadows. Dark blue eyes, deep enough to drown in. Petronella's generous mouth, her broad white brow. Twins. They could be twins. He turned from her sharply before she could see the sudden fear that sparked to life within him at the thought. *By the Gods, what if she's another mind-walker? What then? How do I protect you from this evil? How?*

Brow twisted, his mind racing, he paced the carpet to Petronella's chamber. The Grayling's head snapped up as he approached, but the bird was calm. Petronella lay as he had left her, her staff still clasped between her pale hands. Joran bent to the fire and added another log. Scraping his hand across his bearded cheeks, he closed his eyes. Sent a brief prayer to the Mage for strength. Leaning, he pressed a kiss against Petronella's dry mouth. About to turn, his attention snared on her ring, and his brow contracted. Was it some trick of the light? His heart pounded like a war drum in his chest as he caught her hand in his and turned it gently to the light of the oil lamp burning on the mantle. The diamond reflected the warm glow. He peered more closely at it, watching the sparkle in the depths of the ancient stone flaring just a little as he touched it. "By the Gods, my love," he whispered. "What magic is this? Are you returning to us? Is that it?" He pressed his lips to the stone. "Gods will it so," he urged. "Bring her back to me. To us." Heartened by the sight, he replaced her hand around her staff and left the room.

Fortuna's foray into the restricted section had already produced a daunting wealth of ancient magical lore. Petronella's desk was a clutter of books and scrolls. Joran chewed his lip as he took it in. Books. Just the sight of them swept him back to the chilly schoolroom in Blade's orphanage. During Arion's reign, the inhabitants had squabbled over the one story book it possessed. Waited their turn for the battered primer. Scrawled their letters on cracked slates, fingers dry with chalk. His lips thinned. Learning. One of the first things Petronella had made manifest in her years on the throne. Face wry, he took his seat at her desk and dragged the first book towards him. His beautiful, studious wife would have made quick work of this task. These days, Joran was more at home with lists and letters than the philosophical musings of sages long dead. He leaned forward, squinting into the shadows of his wife's bedchamber. She hadn't moved.

Stifling a sigh, he turned a page and reached for a dry quill. Skimmed the close text for anything that might help him. Heartsease, Shadow Mage, mind-walking. Protection. Banishment. Soul bonds. The Blade of Aequitas. Legends. Prophecies. Anything.

Nothing. He dropped the tome to the floor and pulled the next one towards him.

The barest threads of information trickled to him from the minds of the past as he laboured. Whispers and meanderings. Theories and gossip. So many arguments. Counterarguments and opposing views. Yes, heartsease could help. No, it couldn't. The Blade of Aequitas didn't exist. It was a song, not a prophecy. No-one had ever seen it. The Shadow Mage did not exist. Yes, it did.

By the end of the fifth book, even skimming, Joran's mind whirled even more than it had at the start.

By the Gods, he thought, shoving the thing aside and causing an avalanche of abandoned scrolls to roll to the floor. *I'm a soldier, not a scholar. How does anyone have the patience to make sense of this?*

His frantic gaze roamed across the swirl of ancient script, panic rising to claim him. Of a sudden, his palms were clammy with sweat. A brief vision of the King of Epera's crown flashed to the front of his mind. Last seen on his dead brother's head. "Did you feel this too, brother?" he muttered to no-one. "I wager you did. 'Tis a bitter weight to carry. I understand it now."

Steeling himself to try again, he rubbed his forehead and pulled the next book forward. His head jerked up almost immediately at the light knock on the door. Fortuna staggered through it, laden with more books, her arms bowing with their combined weight. Little Bird followed at her rear, clinging fiercely to a pile of flaking parchment.

"Have you brought the entire contents of the restricted section?" Joran demanded, rising to relieve Fortuna of her burden.

She huffed a tired laugh. "Not even close," she said, retrieving a lace kerchief and using it to wipe the dust from her cheeks. "This was what seemed most likely." Her copper-eyed gaze travelled to the mess Joran had made on the desk, the random pile of books and scrolls littering the carpet. "I see you have made a start."

Joran scowled. "'Tis all but beyond me. An army of scholars could parse it for a twelve-month and find nothing," he said. The words were sour on his tongue. His gaze drifted to young Theda, who had drifted into a deep sleep in her chair, one cheek propped uncomfortably against the heavy scrollwork of the unpadded arm.

"She says she can see the shade of this woman, Cerys, who is looking for Petronella," Joran said. "I know not what it means. If 'tis a vision, or a prophecy. A ghost or a projection. But I believe Petronella's magic might be returning. Her ring is aglow."

Fortuna's eyes widened. She scurried into Petronella's chamber and bent over the Queen, much as Joran had done minutes before.

"You may be right," she agreed as she returned. She frowned, her eyes dropping to the wealth of ancient information in front of them. "I cannot tell what this means," she continued. "Perhaps the drug is wearing off. That is always a possibility. But is she safe from this Cerys if it does?"

Joran dragged his hand through his hair and waved an impatient hand at the mountain of paperwork. "I have found nothing here so far. To involve our students and scholars would open the doorway to untold panic. I cannot risk it." He sighed, reaching for a half-empty decanter of wine. "Here," he said, pouring three glasses. "Rest a while. And then help me, if you will."

Little Bird blinked as he held one out to her. "For me?" she said.

"By the Gods, girl, you may as well," Joran said. "Our path is dark, and I must involve you now, but I bid you say nothing to anyone else. On your honour."

"To be sure," Little Bird mumbled. Her fingers trembled as she accepted the offering. Her dainty nose wrinkled as she inhaled the aroma and took her first sip. Joran chuckled as her eyes widened. "Why, 'tis good," she said.

He managed a tired smile. "You have only taken small beer in the past?" he asked.

"Aye. 'Twas all Fortuna and Dominic would permit," Little Bird said. She raised the glass again.

"Then I bid you caution," Joran said, watching her. "One small glass will do for a maid like you, lest it unwind your tongue."

Little Bird frowned. "Unwind my tongue?" she said.

"Aye," Joran said. "We believe there is a traitor in our ranks somewhere. I am placing you in a position of trust, Little Bird. It is a heavy responsibility. The penalty for breaching my trust is fatal. I hope you understand this." He took a step forward. Little Bird took one more cautious sip and then handed the glass back to him.

Her eyes narrowed. "Then I do not wish for wine," she said. "But on the soul of my dearest Will Dunn, I trust my tongue, even if you do not."

"Well said, Little Bird," Fortuna remarked. She waved a capable hand at the library of information they had gathered. "We will organise this a little, and I will help you," she said. "I am still at a loss to account for our lady's condition. But Little Bird mixed all the heartsease I had. It should have been enough to last for six weeks of normal use. Without it, I have to assume her magic will return at some point."

"Then we must find more heartsease," Joran said. His heart felt like a lead weight in his chest as his eyes travelled the short distance between his wife and daughter. "'Tis the only weapon we have to keep them both safe."

"I will travel to Blade myself on the morrow," Fortuna murmured, helping herself to a couple of likely looking scrolls from the random pile on the floor. She glanced up at him. "There may not be much, though," she warned. "We harvest heartsease in the summer. And it is a scarce herb at the best of times."

"Get what you can. As much as you can," Joran replied. "Dominic told me this Cerys Tinterdorn is Darius of Falconridge's daughter. The living embodiment of the Shadow Mage, with her entire being focused on Petronella's crown. Whether shadow, or sage, phantom or witch. We must stop her. We must."

CHAPTER 21
DOMINIC

Daylight faded quickly as the party crossed the shrub-draped boundary between moor and forest. Beneath the thick interlacing of denuded branches, a slim moon rose, stripped of clouds as the wind chased the storm further south.

Grateful for the shelter from the wind, Dominic's head twisted with every new sound as they pushed cautiously onward, following the well-trodden track to Falconridge he and Aldric had travelled just a two weeks before. Somewhere close, a hunting owl called. The forest was almost silent, apart from the song of the wind through its rattling canopy and the distant soft clomp of snow falling from overladen branches.

"Stay close," Dominic hissed at Aldric. "We don't know what has befallen Falconridge or where the attackers are. Even Cerys could be here somewhere. Stay alert."

"Aye." His friend's voice was dull with fatigue. Dominic glanced behind to where Guildford ploughed steadily onwards, cradling his sister before him. Fitful moonlight cast crystal from his pale eyes as he nodded. "I have her safe," he mumbled. "She's sleeping."

Dominic nodded, spurring Kismet to a faster pace. The horse responded, barely. At the end of her strength.

"Where is the camp spot?" Dominic demanded, drawing close beside Silas in the lead.

"There, by the stream." The driver pointed with his whip and hauled on his team, taking a narrow sloping path. The sledge cut a wavering pathway through the tangle of bracken and brambles, tearing through the frozen vegetation. A faint smell of moss and rotting leaves rose in its wake.

Sheltered in a hollow, a stream trickled peacefully in a slim fissure left by the ice-crusted edges. Silas had chosen the spot well. He waved his arm at his fellow drivers, and they drew their sledges to a practised halt in a semi-circle facing the stream, with gaps for the tents left between. Dominic slid from Kismet's side and dug in his pack for his oil lamp. His fingers fumbled as he struck the flint and hung the light on a nearby branch. The resulting pale yellow glow cast a sickly glaze over the foreground and threw a mantle of blackness over the surrounding forest. He glanced at it, a shudder chasing between his shoulders. He'd have to set a watch tonight, no matter how tired they all were.

"Come, let's get to it," he said. "Aldric, can you set a good fire? I'll help with the tents."

"You'd better help me with Felicia first," Guildford muttered, drawing his mount close to the stream. "She's dead to the world."

"Aye, of course." Standing close, Dominic held his hands out to catch her.

Guildford shrugged his sister awake. "Come away, lass," he said. "We need to make camp for the night." Felicia grumbled her disagreement, burrowing closer to her brother's warmth. Guildford sighed and prised her clutching hands away, lowering her steadily into Dominic's embrace. He rocked her against his chest, and she responded by throwing both arms around his neck. He smiled against her hood, revelling in his ability to offer her the comfort she so often refused. Guildford dismounted and led his horse to the stream. The great white charger plunged his head into the freezing water and drank before Guildford had the chance to remove his bridle. Guildford let him, shaking his head. "Even the General wouldn't have made it much further," he said, looking around as the drivers rummaged for more lights and hauled the heavy oilskins that comprised the tents from the sledges.

"There's dry kindling in here, Master Haligon," Kendrick said. "That'll help ye." He heaved a sack out and threw it across to Aldric, who was scowling at the frozen branches available as he stamped a rough circle into the snow.

"Thank the Gods," Aldric returned gruffly. "Wasn't looking forward to that at all."

Dominic laid Felicia across the seat of the nearest sledge and covered her with her blanket. Before long, the group had pitched their rough shelters and were variously advising Aldric on the best way to lay a fire with half-frozen wood. Rolling his eyes, Dominic left them to it and hurried to tend to his horse. Kismet's noble head drooped heavily to his shoulder as he piled her nose bag with grain. He curried her with a handful of dried straw filched from Aldric's sack of kindling and bundled her into the warmest blanket he could find, whispering his gratitude. Kismet only just had the energy to whicker a response.

"Felicia, wake up," he whispered when the group had finally coaxed the campfire to life and hauled a couple of logs around it to serve as seats. "Come, my love, you must wake and eat. The fire is ready." Felicia rose with Dominic's aid, blinking slowly at the crackling firelight and the scent of warming food. "We have bread," he said. "Bacon. Cheese. Come on, or Guildford will eat it all."

She accepted his help to the ground, clutching her blanket fiercely around her against the damp chill of the forest night.

"Where are we?" she asked, taking a seat by the fire and accepting a loaded plate from Aldric.

"Edge of Falconridge lands. We will set out early in the morn. Be there by midday, I reckon," Dominic said. He helped himself to a mug of mulled ale from the pot Aldric had hung over the fire. The thick, autumnal warmth of it glowed like fire in his belly. "By the Gods, this is good," he said, gulping another mouthful. "What other wonders did Cedric bury in his sledges? Is there a group of minstrels in there, perchance? Some dancing girls? A performing monkey?"

Aldric grinned around a mouthful of his marchpane. "No dancing girls," he said. "But if you want to perform, I could do with a good laugh."

"'Tis true. I'm not much of a one for dancing," Dominic admitted as Guildford chuckled. "That's Little Bird's territory. Or Fortuna's."

"Aye," Guildford said suddenly. "I wonder how they do back there at the castle."

The two knights exchanged glances over Felicia's pale head. Dominic read the question in the younger man's eyes. He shook his head. "I dare not, Guildford," he said. "We have agreed to limit the use of our telepathy. The Prince has shut his channels, as has the Queen, on my advice. And Little Bird..." His voice trailed off. "I don't think she wants to, even if the Prince would allow it," he finished on a sigh. "I miss her."

Aldric huffed a laugh. "We all do," he said. "There's only one Bird."

Dominic hid his trepidation in his mug before he lifted it. "To those at the castle then," he said, raising it to his friends. "The Mage's blessing and good fortune to them."

The two men lifted their mugs. Felicia, seated beside him and patting her cloak, peering around the tidy campsite, did not.

"Where's my heartsease?" she demanded as the toast finished, and they refilled their plates.

Dominic flinched, a slice of cold bacon halfway to his mouth. Felicia's voice held a wealth of terror as she stumbled to her feet and shook out her blanket. "Where is it? Have you taken it? Where is it?" On the other side of the campfire, the group of drivers, huddled over their ale and taking little part in the conversation, glanced up. As one, they crossed their hearts with the sign of the Mage.

"Felicia…"

"Where is it, Dominic? I need it. Tell me!"

Dominic glanced at his companions. Guildford and Aldric were staring at Felicia as if she'd taken leave of her senses. "Felicia, please, my love…"

"You still need heartsease?" Guildford's broad face was a study in confusion. Aldric wore a look of such pure fear at her sudden outburst that Dominic's mouth dried in response.

"Come," he said. Standing up, he grasped Felicia's wrist, stalking away from the security of the campfire. He gave her a little shake as he drew her to a halt, both hands on her shoulders. "Steady yourself," he said fiercely. "We are in dire straits enough without you adding to it."

"You don't understand." Under the moonlight, her icy eyes pierced his soul. "I was not joking. I need it, Dominic. Tell me where it is." She twisted away from his grasp and dragged her cloak around her.

"It's gone," Dominic said. "It fell from your lap into the snow way up there, on the ridge." He waved an impatient hand north. "And you fell after it. Kendrick's sledge went over it, and the wind took it. I'm sorry, Felicia."

"By the Gods." Her voice dropped to an appalled whisper. She stared at him with her hand clamped across her mouth. Unease churned Dominic's stomach. The ale and bacon made an uneasy combination.

"What?" he ground out, suddenly angry at the evasions and half-truths. "What is it that so concerns you? You must tell me!"

"Cerys!" Even quiet, Felicia's voice clashed against his fear with the weight of solid steel. "What do you think, Dominic? You think me so strong, don't you? So brave to resist her after all that time!" The words tumbled from her lips. A dam breaking under a flood.

"You are strong! I know you are!" He flung his hands up as if to push the words back. To wish them unsaid.

She grabbed hold of his arms, forcing them to his sides. "Look at me, Dominic," she breathed, thrusting her face close to him. "Really look at me."

Shaking his head, confused, he stared at her. The familiar grey crystal eyes he so loved shining in the spare lantern light sparkled back. Ice and storm. Felicia. His love. His heart.

"I see you," he whispered. "Only you. Always you, Felicia. What else is there?"

"When the heartsease wears off, you won't see that anymore, Dominic," she said. "Sometimes you will see my Farsight."

He nodded. "I've seen it before, glowing like gold in your eyes," he said. "I don't understand. What are you saying?"

She turned from him, the weight of tears trickling down her cheeks. "That won't be all you might see next time," she whispered, her voice breaking. "Next time, you might see the Shadow Mage."

CHAPTER 22
JORAN

JORAN

Heartened by the possibility of Petronella's return to life, Joran worked through the night. Little Bird curled up on another chair, swamped by a quilt, her face rosy in the glow of the banked curls. Little Theda slept on, her thumb in her mouth, whimpering under her breath from time to time. Sometime after midnight, Joran waved Fortuna to her chamber, anxious she should sleep before her journey to Blade. He carried on, his eyes gritty with fatigue, fortified on the one hand with a decanter of wine and on the other with a flagon of fresh water.

All to no avail. Some things he found appeared to be fact. The scholars agreed the Blade of Aequitas was a prophecy more than a song. Heartsease would dampen magic to a great degree in high dosages, but all agreed the drug wore off and was a temporary measure. Of the Shadow Mage, the references were still obscure. Many ancient scribes cited the great power offered by the Shadow Mage. His face grim as he traced the ancient text with the tip of his quill, Joran read of souls lost. Of great magic twisted beyond recognition. Of madness and delusion, and the strength of character a person would have to exhibit to remain immune to its temptation for any length of time. His mind skipped from memory to memory, matching what he knew of Darius of Falconridge with this new information. His jaw flexed. He could see it now. A powerful Citizen, exposed to the dark heart of the Shadow Mage in the shadows of the deepest crevices of the Iron Mountains. And his daughter, Cerys, born there. He came across a few more modern references to the Tinterdorns. A powerful merchant family with a talent for creating arms and weapons, and in particular, the unique power of Juliana Tinterdorn to imbue her runes with magical power. Died in the mines of Traitor's Reach in 15xx. His jaw tensed. Cerys' mother. She must have been. The meticulous lists he discovered were a long roll call of the Blessed of Epera. Family names with ancient histories, their ranks now decimated. Their magic dulled. Forever lost.

A growing fury possessed him as he dragged his eyes down the even rows. This impersonal record of lives lost and powers extinguished. A swirled signature at the bottom of one list caused him to thrust the thing away as if it scalded him. *By his hand, Darius of Falconridge, 1602.*

Belly roiling, he stumbled from the desk and rushed to the window, where dawn poked a sullen finger of daylight through the narrow gap of the curtains. He yanked it open, heaving his lungs full of fresh air. Tasted snow on the wind. Clamped his hand on his belly as he fought the need to vomit.

"My lord, are you well?" He all but jumped out of his skin at the sound of Fortuna's voice, so immersed in the past he'd lost track of where he was. He spun on his heel with one hand on his dagger. Alarm sparked in Fortuna's gaze as she took a couple of quick steps back, nearly tripping on the edge of her fur-lined travelling cloak. She held up her hands. "My lord, Joran, 'tis I, Fortuna," she said, eyeing the wicked edge of his blade with righteous caution. "Be at peace, I but came to let you know I will set off for Blade. Is there anything else you wish?"

Joran shook his head. A headache lanced through his skull. Sheathing his knife, he marched to Petronella's desk and threw the remains of the water down his parched throat.

"Will you tend our lady before you leave?" he asked. "I would see her comfortable."

"Aye, of course," Fortuna murmured. "I wish she would wake. She has not eaten in days. I will see if I can wet her lips a little."

"Her ring has not changed," Joran said, lifting a weary hand towards Petronella's bedchamber. "But she is still sleeping. 'Tis unnatural."

Fortuna inclined her head, her steady gaze turning to the pile of books, now stacked neatly on the floor. Bookmarks jutted out at various angles where Joran had discovered pertinent information. She pursed her lips and regarded him more closely. Joran took no notice of her intense perusal. His gaze drifted north, to Falconridge, and beyond, to Traitor's Reach.

"It all started with him," he said. "Darius of Falconridge. The Shadow Mage possessed him when he was just a young man. Up there somewhere." He crossed to the window, leaning his aching brow on the chilly iron frame. "He didn't even know, I believe." His voice was quiet. The fatigue was almost overwhelming. "He was a mere Citizen. With no magical senses fine-tuned enough to register the Shadow Mage's presence in his mind. But there it sat. Feeding on him. Amplifying every unworthy urge he had. Ambition, cruelty. Envy. Revenge."

He rolled his head to look at his wife's friend. Fortuna stood square on the carpet, her shrewd gaze fixed on his. He breathed the honey scent of her. Relaxed fractionally in the solidity of her presence. Her gentle fortitude. "You are a marvel," he said. "I give thanks to the Mage for your presence in our lives."

Fortuna inclined her head. "I thank you for the words, but I am your friend," she said. "'Tis what we do in times of need." She paused, her eyes wandering from his to little Theda, restless in her chair, on the verge of waking. "Let Little Bird look after Theda when they both wake," she said. "I will be as quick as I can."

Joran jerked his head in response. "They are safe with me," he said. "I will watch over them all, as best I may."

"You must rest as well. Little Bird is a sensitive, natural telepath. She will rouse you if there is a need."

He closed his eyes. "I cannot leave my wife and child in the care of a youngling like her. You've seen how impetuous she is."

"She has a good heart," Fortuna said. "And you have given her your trust. I think 'tis time you trusted yourself with your own judgement."

"And yet my wife mistrusts that. If you remember." He favoured his friend with a spare smile that did not meet his eyes. "I would take my ring from around her neck before I go, were I you."

"Nay, I won't," Fortuna said stoutly. "That decision is not mine to make, no matter that Little Bird considers herself free to do as she wills with the Queen's possessions." She favoured him with her wide smile, curtsied, and took herself into Petronella's chamber. Joran poked his head into the corridor to request a breakfast and firewood from the nearest guard.

"Papa..." Theda's face, pale with anxiety, peeped at him from the depths of her blanket. He crossed to her side in an instant, dropping on one knee to place his head on a level with hers as she knelt up on the seat. "Mama," she said, her eyes a turbulent sea of emotion in her small face.

"She is still asleep, my little one," Joran said, smoothing a tangle from her clammy forehead. "Do you wish to see her?"

His daughter nodded. "Bad dream," she said as he unwrapped her from the cocoon of the blanket. Her tender cheek was red from the pressure of the chair arm. Joran stroked it. The servants had neglected to bring her a pillow despite his request.

"You had a dream?" Theda nodded, sliding to the carpet and holding out her hand. He took it, disturbed by the tears collecting in her azure gaze.

"By the Gods," Fortuna's voice, coming from his wife's bedside, sent a whirlwind spike of fear through his blood. "Joran, come quick." Her raised voice roused Little Bird from her slumber. The young woman shoved her quilt aside and leapt from her chair, her face a blur of anxiety.

"I had a dream," she choked, darting past Joran to the chamber.

Together, they crowded around Petronella's bed. Fortuna's hand slipped from the Queen's. Joran swallowed. Petronella's hand slumped to her side.

"She has hardly a pulse," Fortuna said, her face pale. "By the Gods, what is this?"

On his perch, the Grayling cried his alarm, his screech overwhelming in the small space. For an instant, Joran considered throttling him until Little Bird threw him a disgusted look and slipped by to stroke the bird's feathers with a hand that trembled. The Grayling calmed a little, pacing the length of his leash and back. His face flashed to his mistress and then at the window, his wings thrusting against his restraint.

"Ssh," Little Bird said, still stroking him. "You will hurt yourself... Rest... Be calm..."

"My lord." It was another voice, tinged with urgency, coming from the threshold of the room. Despairing, his haunted gaze darting from Petronella to his crying daughter to the Grayling's alarm, Joran turned slowly, dreading what he might find.

His guard's face was grey with concern. The man shifted his weight from foot to foot, his dark, curious eyes shifting to the mass of bodies crowded around the Queen. "My lord," he repeated. He thrust a grubby letter into Joran's hand. "Just come, my lord, from a bird up Bearbank way."

Dazed, Joran took the fragile parchment from him like a man in a trance. Read the sparse sentence. "Folly Hall fallen. Dupliss in control. No sign of D. Terril Corn."

The paper fluttered unheeded to the floor.

"Dismissed," his voice wavered.

The guard stood his ground. "My lord?" he said, dumbfounded. "What are your orders?"

Joran stood stock still, his shoulders hunched. Fists clenched at his sides.

"Dismissed," he repeated, clinging to the one word as a man clutching a rockface in the teeth of a storm. In front of him, Fortuna patted the Queen's cheek and reached for her potions. Theda stood like a statue at his side, her thumb still in her mouth. He took her hand automatically. It was cold in his grip. Colder than ice. Blinking, he looked down at her. She looked up. Her eyes were a blaze of gold in a face turned whiter than snow.

"Blood," she said.

CHAPTER 23
DOMINIC

C hilled and hungry, Dominic's small group arrived at the gates of Falconridge Manor by midday the following day. The storm had reached the Falconridge estates and churned south overnight. The manor lay serene against a crisp blue sky, surrounded by dark, skeletal forest and the ever-searching northern breeze. Brow twisted in a forbidding scowl, Dominic dismounted and led Kismet to the battered gate. It hung open, dangling from one hinge. Unbrushed snow piled in drifts in the courtyard, stained in places with the blood of the fallen buried beneath it. A clutch of crows sounded the alarm of their arrival, their harsh, insistent calls echoing from the quiet stone. Dominic's gaze swept the courtyard. Travelled to Falconridge's maze of rooftops. Not a trickle of smoke from its many chimneys. No sign of life. Head cocked on one side, he strained his ears and widened his senses as much as he dared without fully opening his channels. Nothing. His grim gaze clashed with Aldric, who reached for his bow. The sledge drivers urged their horses into the courtyard as far as they could without disturbing the entombed souls and peered around. Exchanged glances full of dread. As one, they turned to look at Felicia, who raised her chin and glowered back.

"Where are they? Where is Sir Dunforde?" Aldric said. He slid from Hamil's back, leading the horse behind him.

The sigh of Guildford's heavy sword as he removed it from its sheath foretold death and danger. "There must be someone still here," he rumbled. Handing control of The General's reins to his sister, he strode to the stairs leading to Falconridge's normally hospitable interior.

"Be careful," Dominic said. "We will follow." He took a cautious step across the ice towards Felicia, offering her his arm as she slid from the General's giant back. She accepted his help without a word of thanks, her face a mask of indifference. Dominic's soul shrank from it. She'd hardly said a word since their fatal argument the following evening. Refused his every offer of comfort or support. Locked herself away. Tense and remote. Her head half-cocked, listening for something only she could hear. He'd heard her overnight, rummaging through her belongings, searching fruitlessly for a last drop of heart-sease. Caught her sob as she thrust the bag from her with a murmur of distress. His searching gaze roamed the many-paned windows and decorated chimneys. There would be a stillroom here, somewhere. Perhaps a supply of the herb that might offer Felicia some relief from her soul-crushing fear. They would look.

"Silas, stay here and watch the horses. Kendrick and Miles, search the outhouses and stables for anyone still alive. Stay alert. Shout for aid if you need us. If it looks safe, see to our mounts. We will search the interior and return if it's safe." He wound his arm around Felicia, holding her close to his side despite her protests. "You will stay with me," he said. "Where I can protect you." Aldric had already drawn his bow, creeping forward in Guildford's wake.

The drivers accepted his command with better grace than Dominic had expected. He watched them for a moment as they discussed his orders, gesticulating to the archway that led under the upper storey of the manor to the service yards beyond. Clearly, they were no strangers to the place. His mouth twisted. In days gone by, there would have been much travel between Hartwood and here. Trade and company. Gossip and the warmth of a near royal welcome, headed up by the cheerful energy of Master Ash. His hand on Felicia's elbow tightened.

The old steward lay here, somewhere. His lively intellect and good humour lost forever. A sigh drifted from him, shifting his clouded breath with the breeze. A tingle of magical energy pricked his fingertips, ready to rise to their defence.

"Come," he said to Felicia. "Let's see if we can work out what has happened here." She bowed her head, walking reluctantly by his side, her gaze fixed on her boots as if she dreaded what she would see if she looked around.

Shrouded in gloom, cloaked in shadows, the wide passageway opened in front of them as they entered. Guildford's huge, damp footprints glistened momentarily in the daylight, showing his progress through the ground floor. Smaller and lighter, Aldric's footprints led upwards to the magnificent staircase rising to the first floor. Their breath rose in front of their faces. Dominic's gaze roamed the vaulted ceiling and the dull metal edges of the many shields and ancient weapons decorating the walls. Cautiously, bit by bit, he opened his telepathic channels, stretching his abilities for mental activity. There was nothing. Not a voice or a shout from the servants. No swish of cloak or skirt marred the dreadful, watchful silence. His Blessed telekinetic gift powered through his body, resting in his palms. Ready. Felicia was watching him, her gaze as intent as a hunting bird, a small, sad smile at the tight edges of her lips. As if she already knew what they would find. Uncomfortable in her presence for the first time, he glanced at her and then away. Alerted by a hint of primaeval fear at the absence of expression on her mobile features. Her air of waiting. He shuddered away the pinprick of doubt that inched spiderlike across his shoulder blades and took a step back. Drew his sword. To protect her? To defend himself against her? He wasn't sure.

"Aldric?" he yelled. His voice bounced back at him. Almost as if the doomed mansion had no use for the voices of the living.

"Here… Look…" Leaving Felicia to follow as she would, Dominic took the stairs two at a time. He blundered down a further corridor and skidded to a halt on the threshold of the room he and Aldric had occupied days before. The chamber was all but torn apart. His bed was a tangle of shredded linen and wool. Trunks rifled through, their worthless contents spilt untidily across the rush-covered floorboards.

Aldric was staring at the ruin of oak-panelled wall at the head of Dominic's bed.

"See," he said, over his shoulder, as Dominic entered. "They found the books." He moved out of the way. Dominic's forehead creased with concern as he took in the jagged edges of torn wood. It looked as if someone had taken a blade to it. Or more like an axe. He'd kept Briana's diaries there for ease of access during their brief stay.

"Nay," he said, shaking his head. "I asked Master Ash to hide them before we came away. Surely, he would have found a more worthy spot?" He bit his lips as he stared around. Entering behind him, Felicia surveyed the wreckage with her hands on her hips and stirred the mess on the floor with a dainty foot.

"There's no-one alive downstairs." Guildford's voice from the passageway made them jump. "Cook's dead with a ladle in his hand. They were hungry, for sure, whoever they were. Ransacked the kitchen. A couple of servants with him, but that's all. I took them all out to the kitchen courtyard.

"My thanks," Dominic said. Guildford's face was a study in rough sympathy and distaste for his self-appointed task. He wiped his hands on his cloak. "Good thing 'tis so cold," he remarked more quietly. "Not as bad as it could have been. We should bury them, though. 'Tis only fitting."

"But where did everyone else go?" Aldric asked. "Did you see any sign of Sir Dunforde?"

Guildford shrugged. "Nothing. His office is empty. Cleared out properly."

Dominic's eyes narrowed. "Cleared out?"

"Aye. Mayhap..." Guildford scowled, running a nervous hand around his softly bearded lips. "By the Gods, I pray 'tis not so..." he added, as he caught the cynical look Dominic threw at him.

"Sir Dunforde has no great love for the Blessed," Dominic murmured, his tone flat. His back prickled at the memory of Sir Dunforde's heavy hand with a lash. "We all know that."

"Could he have turned? Gone over to Dupliss' side?" The young knight's expression was heavy with menace.

Aldric dragged his eyes from the chaotic mess and threw his shoulders back, his fingers tense on his bowstring. "He's the traitor?" he demanded. "All this time?"

Dominic shrugged. "I don't know. Are there no soldiers amongst the fallen?"

Guildford shook his head, his grey eyes troubled. "All servants, so far," he said. "I can check the poor souls in the courtyard."

"By the Gods. An attack from without and within..." Aldric slumped to the torn mattress across Dominic's bed, raising a fluff of feathers into the chilly air.

The yawning gap in the panelling claimed Dominic's attention again. He wandered across to it, tracing the rough edges with his fingers. "Last time, Cerys came here, in disguise, looking for these books, did she not?"

"What books are you talking about?" Guildford asked, confusion once more in full rein.

"Lady Briana's old diaries. Master Ash gave them to me. We think they must hold knowledge for Cerys. Either something she needs or something she does not want us to find."

Guildford's eyes sharpened in alarm. "Is one of them the book Cerys is looking for?"

"I cannot tell. I read as much as I could in our time here, but there seemed nothing likely within them. 'Tis a mystery," Dominic admitted. "But mayhap I missed something. I did not open every single one."

"Aye, and so?" Guildford said.

"Last time, she knew where to look. But Aldric disturbed her. Sir Dunforde never knew about Briana's diaries and wouldn't have cared if he did." His lips thinned as he followed the thought to its logical conclusion. "So, that means either this is an attack from outside, perhaps the work of a member of Dupliss' forces acting on information gathered from Cerys. Or, it was Cerys herself, trying again."

He paused, his gaze travelling around the small group. Aldric's dawning realisation, Guildford's confusion, and the mute resistance on Felicia's face. "But that still leaves us with another question. An older one."

Aldric finished the thought for him. "How did Cerys know where to look in the first place?"

An uneasy silence fell between them, crowded with words left unspoken. Dominic dragged his hands through his hair, his thoughts as muddled as the detritus on the chamber floor, each demanding attention. "We need to find Master Ash," he said. His eyes dropped on Felicia and sprung away. Unwilling to land on her. She held her hands crossed in front of her. Tension in every slight line of her body. Her breath came light and quick. Almost a pant.

"There is no-one here. Why not find the stillroom and seek some heartsease?" he said, striving to keep his tone even. Her pale grey gaze slanted at him from beneath curving brown lashes.

"Why not, indeed," she said dryly. A ghost of mischief twinkled in the depths of her pupils as she turned for the corridor. Dominic flinched to see it there. It felt inappropriate under the circumstances. At odds with the silent watchfulness of the day. Her light footsteps receded, taking some of the tension in the room with them.

He rubbed the back of his neck and gestured to his companions. "We need to find Master Ash," he repeated quietly. "I cannot believe a man of his wit would have left something of such value to be discovered so easily. There must be something more to this."

"I will check the courtyard," Guildford said. "Mayhap the poor man lies there."

"As you will. I will go to the temple," Dominic said. "That's where the diaries were hidden after Lady Briana died. Aldric, check Sir Dunforde's quarters. See if he left anything that might aid us."

"Aye."

They dispersed. Dominic ran on silent feet, flitting through the shadows, avoiding the lower corridors where the stillroom would be situated. He did not want to see Felicia. The thought flashed across his mind. He let it go. He had no desire to chase it. A brace of maidservants lay tangled together in a narrow hallway, knife wounds in their chests, staring in silent shock. Uttering a blessing, he passed them by, his skin crawling at the reek of blood and the residual terror in the sullen atmosphere.

By contrast, the interior courtyard looked much as he'd left it a sennight ago. The temple graced the far corner, crowned with the ever-present images of the falcons entwined within the sign of the Mage. His head tilted, admiring its pale sweeping lines etched crisply against the brilliant sky. A snowy white owl perched motionless on the tip of its delicate steeple observed his progress with a sleepy, almost benign gaze. Dominic paused in admiration. Fascinated by the bird's steadfast stare. The owl tilted his head downwards to the thick, ancient doorway to this most sacred of spaces. Squaring his shoulders, Dominic drew his sword. Crept onward. Wary as a fox.

The door cracked open. It moved inwards on a grind of hinges as if reluctant to give up its secrets. He inhaled the familiar twist of Eperan incense, a frown crossing his face as his eyes adjusted to the relative gloom after the brightness of the courtyard. The heavy tapestry draped on the far wall behind the altar drew his eye as it had the first time he saw it. His heart contracted at the sight of the house priest, still clad in his scarlet and white robes, lying on the icy floor in a crumple of blood-strewn fabric. He crossed his chest with the Mage's symbol without even thinking about it and swept onward, aware of the eyes of the carved stone falcons as they watched his progress. There was another body lying in front of the altar. Small. Rotund. His plump fists clenched, holding on to life as long as he could.

Master Ash.

In death, the old man's face was a faint, mottled blue. His eyes were clouded but open and turned to the sky. Scanning his body, Dominic could see no sign of injury. His brow creased in sorrow as he traced a gentle hand over the former steward's cold, bony fingers. He'd felt the looming of the old man's death himself, here on this very spot. Master Ash had known he had little time left. Perhaps this latest shock had been one too many.

"In the Mage's grace," Dominic whispered, exerting gentle pressure with his gift to close Master Ash's eyelids.

He waited in silence for a few minutes, honouring all the fallen of Falconridge with his thoughts. Lost in contemplation, it took a while before he realised what felt off about the space. The smell of incense. So much stronger than it should be in the absence of a priest to replace it. Nose wrinkling, he raised his gaze, the skin on the back of his neck prickling with dread. A slim coil of fragrant smoke drifted from the two sacrificial cups on each side of the altar. Such a commonplace item that he'd failed to pick up on its import before. He jumped to his feet, power surging through his palms.

"Who's there? Show yourself!"

He held his breath, every sense straining. There was someone there. Watching him. Hiding. Slowly, he raised his palms, sending a surge of power to the weighty tapestry. The embroidered figure of the Mage shifted. Undulated, as if he had come to life to bless the unfortunate dead himself. Lips set, his face grim, Dominic increased his energy, gathering the piece in a series of folds, pushing it up, away from the floor.

The man crouched behind the altar shivered like an aspen in a mountain breeze, his face thick with dirt. Encrusted with blood.

"By all the Gods." Shock almost made Dominic lose control of the altar centrepiece. Grinding his teeth, he supported it with one hand and batted the man out of hiding with the other. "Clem. By all that is holy. What are you doing here?" he demanded.

"Sir Skinner, thank all the Gods. We hoped you would come." The young soldier stumbled to his feet, smudging more dirt across his grimy cheeks. His eyes dropped to the chilled, motionless bodies. "There was nothing I could do," he said. "Master Ash said someone had to remain. Someone loyal. For when you arrived. He had faith you would."

"What happened here?" Dominic's tone was harsh. "Where is Sir Dunforde?"

Clem's bearded mouth twisted. "Gone with them," he spat between clenched teeth. "Dupliss' men. They were here. And her. The witch." His broad shoulders trembled with the force of his inner rage. "Carnage," he said, raising his eyes. "They killed everyone. Master Ash and I, we hid behind there." He jerked his thumb at the slim space between the tapestry and the cold temple wall. "Master Ash said he'd left something for you. He went to get it, but then..." His gaze wandered to the old steward's body. "He were a kindly soul," he whispered. "Said you'd know where to look..."

"Ah." Dominic's lips thinned. "How steady are you?" he demanded. "Can you guard the door a while?"

"I'm powerfully hungry," Clem said. "But aye, I can do that."

"Good. Let no-one in. There's something I have to do."

Clem nodded, striding down the aisle, blessing himself as he passed the body of the unfortunate manor priest.

Biting his lips, Dominic closed his telepathic channels before turning to the ancient flags. A pull of power from his Blessed energy teased the heavy stone from its bed. He slid it gently out of the way and reached with his gift deep into the hollow beneath it. There was something there. For an instant, his spirits lifted with the idea that this might be the book Cerys sought. But it was almost weightless. Insubstantial as a cloud. Heart sinking as he gathered it to him, he registered a dainty volume, unbound. He'd hardly noticed it before. Distracted by the more substantial items Lady Briana had left behind. That precious pile was gone. Vanished for good if Master Ash had not found another place for them. Frowning, he glanced down the narrow aisle to where Clem leaned against the door, humming a haunting, tuneful melody fitted to the mood. So why this? Master Ash had hidden this and guarded it with his life. But not the rest.

His fingers shook a little as he peeled the document open, slanting it to the cool blue light filtered by the stained-glass windows.

In shadows deep, the truth lies hidden,
Silent, 'til his heart is bidden.
Blood of blood, and son of kings,
Together, they must bind the rings.
One must break, so one may rise,
A falcon's flight to pierce the skies.
And when the shrouded crown is riven,
The light, once lost, shall be forgiven.

He blinked. A prophecy, etched in a sure, scholarly hand. And signed.

Theda Eglion, of the Owls. Her name seemed to whisper to him, etched as deeply into his bones as into the parchment.

His eyes dropped to Master Ash. "You left this here for me," he murmured. "And you were waiting for me before. Is this it? Is this what I must do?" He stretched his senses, desperate for confirmation, but Master Ash was gone. Received already into the waiting embrace of the Mage. There was one other document, curled with age, added to over time by different hands and varied inks.

A family tree. His blurred vision traced the Eglion bloodline through Theda and beyond. To Briana. And Petronella. He swiped tears from his eyes as his grubby finger traced a wavering line backwards. From Theda Eglion and to her uncle. Another Robert. A Skinner. His mind froze. Theda Eglion, born a Skinner? Like him?

His blood chilled. Petronella's grandmother. He had but a distant memory of her. A remote figure swathed in pipe smoke. He'd seen her only once, at a distance from his humble place as a newly arrived stable boy. Throat dry, he swallowed, his tremulous gaze drifting to Master Ash as he lay there. Loyal to the last. What had he said the last time they stood together on this spot? *"She said a young man would come, distant kin to the Queen herself."*

Disbelieving, he traced the faded script with his thumb. Was it true? Was the enigmatic, powerful Seer of his distant youth really a Skinner by birth? Could he truly share kinship with the Queen? His soul sang at the knowledge. Petronella. His first moonstruck calf-love. His first telepathic contact. Exalting, his thoughts leapt to her without him trying. It was a few seconds before he could gather himself to slam his channels shut, but the slim time they were open filled him with terror. The Queen lay somewhere desolate. Pale and silent. Surrounded by darkness. Just a flicker of her brilliant light remaining somewhere close by her motionless figure. Stumbling to his knees, he pressed his palm to Master Ash's motionless chest. "You were ever her guardian," he whispered, hoping that somewhere, Master Ash's watchful shade could hear him. "'Tis my turn to save her now." He turned his head, certain he heard a sigh somewhere nearby. His hair lifted, and his skin prickled with awareness. She was there again. Lady Briana. Her presence was stronger this time. Heavy with portent. *"Find all the books, boy,"* she whispered deep in his heart. *"That witch will not have them."* He shot to his feet, instinctive fear propelling him away. Clutching the fragile parchment close against his chest, he left the haunted altar at a run, grabbing Clem's dusty sleeve. "You will come with us, Clem," he said as he sprinted back to the silent house. "You have done all you can here. The Queen is in mortal danger. We must return to the castle."

Harsh sunlight all but blinded him as he slithered across the snow-crusted courtyard, watched by the carved falcons clinging to the chapel walls and the snowy white owl. The majestic bird took flight, almost as if he'd been but part of the finely carved frescos, now free to soar. The almost silent beat of his wings followed Dominic to the house, blending with Dominic's shadow on the ground. Leading him on.

"I will reach you in time, Petronella," Dominic vowed as he panted through the corridors, yelling Aldric's name. "I swear it. On my honour."

CHAPTER 24
JORAN

"Theda!" He gave her shoulders a light shake, terrified at the sudden change. Fortuna jerked round at the sound of his voice, her own eyes wide with alarm as they registered the golden glaze of Farsight gleaming in the child's eyes.

"By the Gods," she said, her hands trembling as she crouched at Theda's side. "This should be impossible. Theda, can you hear me? Come back to us." She patted the girl's cheek. Her entire body shaking, Theda stared straight through her. Her breath came light and rapid. Locked in a world neither of them could see, she made no response to Fortuna's entreaties. Tears trickled down her dainty face. The sight tore Joran's heart to pieces. Caught in a turmoil of guilt, he dabbed her cheeks with his kerchief. First, Petronella, now, Theda. Should they even be in the same room? His shoulders slumped. Despair clawed at him. His family was slipping away from him, and he had never felt so powerless to help them.

"By the Gods, Fortuna, what is happening?" His voice was hoarse, cracked with exhaustion.

Fortuna's expression hardened, her mouth set in a stern line. "We need that heartsease for them both," she said. "This is too much for a child her age. The visions she sees will send her mad without knowledge and training."

Joran's fists clenched in an instinctive denial. He had to close his mouth on the urge to challenge her. On the bed, Petronella lay silent, her face like marble, her lips paler than parchment.

"By all that's sacred... I can't think..." He turned in a frustrated circle, watched by his wife's bird. The falcon's majestic head turned to the shrouded window. He lunged from his perch, only to be brought up short by the length of his leash. His angry chirrup dragged Joran's attention. "That blasted bird, again," he muttered. "Now he wants to fly." The Grayling snapped his beak. Despite Joran's irritation, something about the falcon's insistence bred a trickle of apprehension in his overwhelmed mind. Something important but unspoken. He stared at the bird for a moment, trying to decipher his mood. The Grayling stared coldly back. At Joran's side, little Theda's hand crept into his, although she remained locked in the grip of her Farsight. Travelling somewhere in her mind, far away from the tense chamber and the panic beating through Joran's heart.

"My lord, look..." Fortuna's sudden grip on his forearm nearly unbalanced him. "Look at the Queen's ring."

Dreading what he might see, he dropped his eyes to Petronella's diamond. The faintest of lights was glistening from its heart.

"What does it mean?" he breathed. "Does she yet live?"

"'Tis her magic returning," Fortuna said. "She has been too long without the heartsease. One as powerful as her requires an equally potent dose to hold it back." Her brows contracted in a frown as she felt for the Queen's pulse once more. She sighed. "Still not waking, but her magic is stirring." The look she gave Joran filled him with unease. "On the surface, her magic returning is a good sign, but not when she cannot wield it. It leaves her vulnerable to whatever this black witch has planned."

His jaw tightened, and his eyes swept the room, wondering if Cerys Tinterdorn even now hovered in the shadows, watching them.

You won't win, witch, he thought. *You will not take my wife and daughter. Not while I live and breathe.* Fortuna's copper eyes locked with his. Pleading with him to see sense. He bowed his head. "Send for the herb then," he said, his voice thick with reluctance. "But don't leave us now, Fortuna." He gripped her sleeve. "Please don't go yourself. Send as many servants as you need to as many suppliers as you can. With all speed."

Her broad brow creased. She patted his hand before prying his clutching fingers away. "Nay. I'll not leave you, my lord," she said, her voice hushed. The crisp rustle of her long skirts across the carpet accompanied her light step to the guarded door. Her voice was sharp and urgent as she relayed his command to the guard. Joran twisted in place, shifting from foot to foot, torn between the needs of his wife and the strange, wide-eyed, tearful trance exhibited by his daughter.

"Well?" he snapped at Little Bird. "What do you make of this? Now we are watching the Queen as still as death, her magic under threat. And my daughter is driven mad by visions of the future beyond her understanding. Are you satisfied now?"

Her wary gaze flitted from monarch to child and then back to the Grayling, who was regarding the window with an intensity he normally reserved for recently dead mice. His unwavering attention drew a frown across Joran's already creased forehead. Little Bird tightened her lips and drew herself up to her full height.

"Nay, my lord, this does not satisfy me," she said, her voice so low he had to stoop to hear her. "No more than you."

Anger whirled through him. Cold fury. Volatile as a storm wind and just as unpredictable. He had to turn from her. Force his hands away from his dagger lest he use it against her.

"You need to leave the room," he said, his voice ragged and breaking. "Before I forget myself and prove to the world I am an unfit king."

He waited for the brush of her feet. A stirring of the air that would tell him she had gone. Little Bird had not moved. Instead, her voice broke the silence, low and laced with concern as Theda's sweaty hand slid from his. His gaze lowered to his daughter, crumpled at his feet like a rag doll. Little Bird dropped to her knees and gathered the tiny princess in her arms.

"The visions have passed," Little Bird said. The periwinkle gaze she raised to him from her humble position on the floor played havoc with the anger crowding his senses. Her voice was soft as she smoothed the child's curls, rocking her gently in her fragile arms, whispering reassurance. Joran stared at her, anger still roiling deep in his belly, but unable to deny the tenderness of her care towards his tiny daughter. Raised a hand to press against the headache skewering between his brows. Fortuna's bleak expression as she brushed past him mirrored his own.

"Little Bird is a child as well, Joran," Fortuna said as she returned to the Queen's bedside and reached for more valerian. "Try to remember she is on our side before you do something you will forever regret."

His jaw clenched. "By the Gods, woman, you go too far," he blurted.

"Aye, mayhap I do." Fortuna faced him with her hands on her curving hips. "But it is nowhere near as far as you are likely to go in your present mood, is it?" She raised a challenging stare, her copper eyes implacable and determined. He glared at her, the need for action pumping like acid through his veins, tearing at his resolve. The atmosphere was a savage twist of ire laced with frustration. About to reply, a knock on the door brought him up short.

"By the Gods, not now!" he snapped, snatching the parchment held out to him by his trembling secretary. The man bowed and backed out, head lowered. Fortuna tossed a glare Joran's way and rummaged through her many potions, searching for something to aid the sobbing princess.

Leaving them to it, Joran strode to Petronella's desk and helped himself to a draft of wine he did not really want. The alcohol warmed his belly, and he crossed to the window where the light was better.

Bearbank under Dupliss control. Send reinforcements. Captain Dumond.

It was the last message he wanted to see. He stared at the slanting script, unable to believe his eyes. "What is this? Fighting in the heart of winter?" he said aloud, smudging his hands across his face and trying to force his tired brain into action. Gritting his teeth, he marched to the door. "Send for Sir Fellowes," he instructed. "And bring us food and wine. Food for the Grayling." The soldier took one look at the forbidding expression on Joran's face and leapt into action like a hound after a fox.

"Aye, lord."

Joran slammed the door on the soldier's drumming feet and twisted on the spot, overcome by a need for action so great he could barely contain it. Ever before, he'd felt free to run and race his horses. A legend in a joust. A fiend on the battlefield. And now, here he was, trapped in the role of protector, relying on others to lead the charge on the kingdom's behalf.

"By the Gods, Dominic," he muttered aloud, pressing his face so hard into the nearby wall the panelling pressed a ridge into his aching forehead. "You had better not let me down."

CHAPTER 25
DOMINIC

Despite the need for haste, the group lingered long enough to see Falconridge's fallen laid to rest in the frigid manor burial ground. Borrowing Cedric's trick, they piled a large enough area with braziers and hacked at the half-frozen soil like men possessed, taking it in turns to move the earth and pile it to one side. Felicia observed them from the temple steps, restless hands picking at the herbs for remembrance required for the committal. Her face remained remote and watchful, her actions almost mechanical as she stripped the dried herbs from their fragile stems. Dominic tried countless times to catch her eye, but she refused to meet his gaze. Saddened by her silence, he'd checked the manor stillroom for heartsease himself but came away empty-handed. Judging by Felicia's tense features, he guessed she had, too.

One by one, they roamed the manor, collecting the battered bodies of the servants and binding them with herb-scented layers of coarse linen or rough serge. Whatever they could find. In the absence of a priest, as the fragile winter sun sank in the west, Dominic murmured the prayers for the dead, lowering each to their last rest. Sorrow pierced through him. Sharper than steel.

At his side, Guildford's mighty fists clenched and unclenched on the handle of the spade he held. His freckled face was stern with outrage. Catching a glimpse out of the corner of his eye, the look struck Dominic with an awareness he had not expected. A grim measure of fierce resolve and iron-plated will. It boded well for the man Guildford would become. A half smile flitted across Dominic's mouth. *Ah, Joran,* he thought. *If you could but see him, you would not doubt him. I do not.*

Clem's rich, tuneful tenor took up the notes of the warrior's farewell. He'd filled his cheeks with leftovers from Falconridge's denuded pantries and clucked at the broken strings of his battered lute. Now mended, his skilful fingers coaxed gentle peace into the crystal air, his breath weaving like incense over the gravesite. The melody wrapped around them as it had days before, filled with thanksgiving and gentle release.

Gathering in the shadows of the after the brief service, they checked their supplies, preparing for the long journey ahead. Firelight flickered in the hastily piled hearth. A crock of pottage shed a hearty aroma into the subdued atmosphere. On the hunt for food, Aldric had found an unbreached barrel of small ale in an abandoned storeroom. Guildford sipped with his eyebrows raised, bemoaning the lack of good Argentish.

"After all that heavy labour," he grumbled, shaking mud from his cloak, "the least we deserve is decent wine."

"We will bide here tonight," Dominic said, raising a quelling eyebrow. "But we must press on back to Thorncastle on the morrow. Joran told me there could be aid for us there. The journey further south will be rough going, I don't doubt."

His glance took in the three sledge drivers clustered in a defensive knot around the fireplace. "Silas, a word," he requested.

Silas heaved himself from the three-legged stool he squatted on and sauntered over, a hunk of leftover bacon clenched in his fist.

"Aye?" he said. His eyes ran over Felicia's narrow figure and then jumped away as she glared back.

"We must move south," Dominic said. "Would you come with us, at least as far as Thorncastle?"

The man scratched his beard as he surveyed the group. "Aye," he muttered. "If we must. I gave my promise to Cedric, and that is my bond." He cleared his throat and placed his thumbs in the low-slung belt at his hips. "But I have no wish to share a sledge with your woman," he said, squaring his broad shoulders. "Nor do the others. We trust her not."

"As you wish," Dominic said. He cut his glance for the hundredth time to Felicia, who had all but stopped speaking to any but Aldric. "I could say that she is not the dark-hearted wretch you so dread, but I doubt my words hold much authority with you."

The sledge driver shrugged. "It is as it is, but you won't need us after Thorncastle," he said, helping himself to more ale. "You can catch a riverboat from there. The weather is less harsh once you get down past Bearbank. If the Cryfell is flowing, 'twill take you near to the castle. Quicker than a sledge or your mounts can go in this weather." He paused, gulping his drink. "Won't be kind on the horses, and this time of year, the river has its own hazards, but still. If speed is your aim, 'tis mayhap worth the risk."

"I thank you," Dominic said. He dipped his spoon into his pottage, his mind wandering over the route between the castle and this harsh, northern landscape. The possibilities offered by the river route. At a cough from Silas, he glanced up from his plate. Trepidation filled the driver's kindly eyes.

"Are you so sure she's not a witch?" he hissed, nodding at Felicia. "My aunt talked of her before. Seeking heartsease. Either her or the old man. Always after it, they were."

Dominic's stool tipped with a clatter to the damp rushes of the floor as he stood, his jaw clenched with tension. Mage power flared at his fingers, demanding release. He clamped down on the urge to let it rip. Aldric swapped an alarmed glance with Guildford.

"By the Gods, Silas. For the last time. She is not a witch." Dominic's voice rang to the dusty rafters. Felicia raised her head. Was it his imagination, or did he see a sneer disfiguring her rosebud mouth be-fore her face resumed its quiet watchfulness? A shiver prickled across his shoulders. Half of him wanted to run from her. The other half clung desperately to his boyish, distant worship and the heat of her kiss, unable to let go. Taking advantage of Dominic's rare hesitation, Guildford rose from his seat, towering over Silas, his hand on his eating knife. "What would you like to say about my sister?" he asked, teeth bared behind a mirthless smile. Silas paused. Blanched. "Nothing, my lord," he stammered, taking several steps back to the warmth of the hearth and the dubious security of his kinfolk. "But I'd trust you afore I would trust her. That's all I'm saying." He yelped as Guildford flung his knife. It left his hand in a dizzying blur. Cartwheeling through the tense atmosphere, it tore through Silas's rough sleeve, momentarily pinning him to the panelling at his back. Silas prised himself free, a scowl on his rugged face.

"That's better," Guildford said quietly, surveying the disgruntled group with ill-disguised threat. He lunged forward to retrieve his blade. Silas took a careful step back, his hands before him held out in supplication. "Make sure you do not mention her in that light again. Your continued good health depends upon it." Guildford favoured Silas with a baleful glare and wandered over to his sister, handing her a glass of ale. Protecting her. She raised an eyebrow and said precisely nothing.

"Well said, Guildford. Now we all know where we stand," Aldric remarked, glancing at Dominic, who was struggling to keep a grip on the overwhelming power racing through his veins. "Just think your-selves lucky that was only Guildford's rebuke and not his." He jerked his head at Dominic. The three kinsmen drew together. Kendrick looked almost eager to see what might happen should Dominic lose control of his gift.

By the Mage, Dominic thought, favouring the entire party with a glare that bounced off indifferent Felicia and only caused a smirk on Guildford's sparsely bearded lips. *If I can't hold this lot together before we even set off, this mission is like to fail as well.* The unbidden thought startled through his senses like a hare snared by an eagle. His lips thinned. He threw his cloak around his shoulders and placed one powerful hand on his sword. Drew himself up to his full height. "We will rest while we can. Be ready to set out at dawn."

CHAPTER 26
JORAN

Joran's general, Sir Fellows, entered Petronella's outer chamber like a storm wind, his creased face fixed in a frown of forbidding proportions. "Wondered when you would send for me," he rumbled with brief ceremony. "I received a message about Folly Hall and the news that the rebellion is spreading further south. Judging by the scowl on your face, you did, too."

"Aye. And more than that. Bearbank has fallen." Distracted by the sound of Theda's sobs and the older women's attempts to comfort her, Joran crossed to the door of his wife's inner sanctum. Little Bird and Fortuna formed a close knot around his daughter, their heads bent. The Grayling stood sentinel on his perch, his gaze shifting from the Queen to the window and back. Alerted by Joran's soft footsteps, his golden gaze snapped around. He shifted on his perch. Someone, probably Little Bird, had released his leash. The loose ends dangled, the bells decorating the carved leather sang a delicate chime as they danced in the warm air. Something about the falcon's quiet vigilance sent a shiver down Joran's spine. *Aye, you protect them. I cannot,* he thought. *You will probably do a much better job than I. But do not presume to judge me. Only my wife and Queen has the right of that.* He closed the door on the ever-watchful falcon and turned to Sir Fellows, wondering what Petronella would say if she could see him now. Would she understand his doubts or just raise an eyebrow at his erratic temper? Close her fingers protectively around the Ring of

Justice to prevent him from claiming it? Shaking his head free of the thought, he forced his tired mind to the task at hand. At least strategy was something he could grasp. Perhaps alter the odds in their favour. Crossing the room, he poured the older man a draft of fine wine and leaned against his wife's desk.

"I see you've been busy. How does the Queen?" Sir Fellows said sourly as he accepted the offering. His stern grey eyes drifted across the litter of books and parchment, the tangle of blankets that had covered Little Bird and Theda overnight. Joran sighed, scrubbing both hands through his beard, hardly knowing where to start. He clamped his mouth shut on the desire to burden his practical general with the deeper, more sinister invasion of his daughter's mind. A sturdy Citizen, Sir Fellows lived in a world of strategy and steel and would have little help to offer against this unseen, looming presence.

"You don't want to know," he said, fighting the dread that twisted inside him, begging for freedom. "She is too ill to be involved in our battle. I wish it were not so." Dragging his mind away from Petronella, he focused his attention on his general. "Tell me everything you know about what we now face. I understand now 'tis a joint effort. 'Tis clear Cerys Tinterdorn, the bastard daughter of Darius of Falconridge, is intent on moving against us. Against the Queen."

"Cerys Tinterdorn? Who is this?" Sir Fellows' brow creased. "What has she to do with Dupliss and his actions?"

"I was going to tell you. Too much has happened," Joran said. "And you will likely not believe half of it." He launched into the story, his spirits sinking at the frank disbelief spreading across his general's whiskered cheeks.

"Darius' get? A witch?" he blurted. Joran's lips thinned, watching the older man as he fumbled for another glass of wine. "And you have proof of this?"

"Aye. I wish I did not," Joran admitted. "They are working together, Dupliss and Cerys Tinterdorn. For the moment, at least. Sir Skinner tells me her power is formidable."

The general slumped in his chair and shook his head. "Blasted magic," he muttered. "Just when we thought 'twas over, and the Queen sound on her throne."

"My thoughts entirely," Joran agreed.

"Aye. But warfare in this weather. When travel is hard, and the conditions harsh. 'Tis uncountenanced." Sir Fellows hawked phlegm in his throat, prepared to spit into the hearth, and then sat back, realising in whose chamber he sat. He swallowed a mouthful of wine instead and cleared his throat. "I cannot comment on this Cerys, but we must consider Dupliss receives more support than we had hoped," he continued. His once mighty shoulders slumped in a sigh that trembled his thick grey beard. "I have heard more from my sources at Temple Bridge since we spoke last. Dupliss sent his civilian allies before him. Seems they started some rumour about the Blessed priests of their local temple. How they were under the power of the Shadow Mage. Under cover of night, some violence occurred. Dupliss' forces targeted the mills and granaries. The combination was enough to spread discontent and unrest across the town. The Citizens received Dupliss with open arms when he appeared as their saviour and 'drove the witches out'. Then, he promised them that Guildford would take the throne. The lad is popular. That's what happened there. I can only assume Dupliss is replicating his success at every strategic location he can think of. The traitor in our midst ensures he does not strike where our forces could oppose him."

Joran's eyebrows raised. "Clever," he mused, glancing at the closed door. "That would work indeed. Ensuring the local guards remain alert for any magical activity. Recruiting likely lads to his army."

Sir Fellows cut a glare at him. "Aye. Dupliss' forces do not always have to commit bloodshed, although I'm sure they instigate it. Instead, they stir the pot and allow fear and suspicion to complete their dastardly work. Turning our citizens against one another. 'Tis only what I said before. The question is, how do we counter it? Everywhere the man goes, dissent and death follow, sure as fate, and the Queen's position weakens. Even her followers are questioning her right to the throne."

Joran sighed, fisting a hand through his hair. "We are in a stalemate," he agreed. "The only way to counter this is the capture or killing of both Dupliss and Cerys. I cannot leave the castle whilst the Queen lies defenceless. And there are other threats here. Cerys is a dark witch indeed. Dominic Skinner has experienced her force." He frowned, glancing towards his wife's chamber. "'Tis strange," he said. "She shares many Blessed gifts with Petronella."

Sir Fellows snorted. "How now? You misspeak, surely. Our Queen, and this black-hearted, misbegotten wench?" He slammed down his goblet, spilling red wind over his fist. Joran's gaze tracked it as it oozed across the man's skin. Thick and ruby rich. Like blood.

"They are half-sisters," Joran said, treading carefully lest he detonate panic in his general's rigidly defended world view. "But Cerys was born into the realm of the Shadow Mage. Her Blessed gifts warped and turned to evil. A dark queen, determined to rise."

The general's thick, greying eyebrows twisted. "But Dupliss is promising Guildford as their king," he protested.

Joran huffed a bitter laugh. "What, you don't think Cerys will turn on him at the earliest opportunity? 'Tis what a black-hearted wench would do, is it not? Use and then abuse. Divide and then conquer." Unable to remain still, he took his favoured path through the cluttered office, from desk to window. Sir Fellows tracked his restless pacing over the rim of his glass.

"'Tis a sorry turn of events," the older man agreed. "Hard to know how we can challenge a person's belief. We could send messengers to warn our people of Dupliss' strategy, mayhap. Try to bolster their resolve in the face of his manipulation. Try to bolster the Queen's reputation…" He stretched out his hand, observing the strength of his fingers. The callouses on his palms from a lifetime of wielding a sword. "This is what I know," he said, his rough voice a growl in his barrel chest. "I know warfare. Hand to hand. Fist against fist. Eye to eye." He shook his head. Took another sip. "But our might is useless. No matter how many troops we have, we cannot counter gossip. Whispers in the wind. Shadow magic. Fear, soul deep."

"We don't have enough messengers or pigeons to reach every town under threat," Joran said. "The thought is good. Our resources are insufficient. Even if we did, I cannot guarantee removing Dupliss and Cerys would be enough to return us to peace. Not now. Nay." Joran turned at the window, sending his gaze across the distant vista to the World's Peak, conscious of the claustrophobic weight of the castle walls pressing against him from all sides. "We need her." He nodded to the inner chamber. "We need the Queen. She's the only one strong enough to combat the Shadow Mage. She did it once before. Beat him down. Forced him back. Killed her own father when, under the influence of its control, he would not stop."

"Aye. She's a wise and powerful woman," Fellows agreed. "But what about you?" He tossed down the remains of his drink and strode towards Joran, one hand on his sword belt. "That ring she wears, so close to her heart. That is yours, is it not?" He paused, measuring his words against Joran's frown. Laid a heavy arm across his tense shoulders. "You are our rightful King, my lord, not Guildford," he said. "You have a right to that jewel and the power it brings."

Joran's heart contracted. He scowled at his comrade-in-arms and crossed his hands across his chest. Clenched his fists. Little Bird's face flashed to his mind's eye. Fearful. Wary. Petronella's challenging his ability to rule fairly, her eyes fierce and watchful. Even the Grayling. He raised one hand to massage his neck, still sore from the falcon's savage peck, and shook free of his general's grasp. His need for action.

"I cannot use it," he said through gritted teeth. "I am so full of rage and sorrow, I nearly killed a young girl, a Blessed telepath whose only crime is to care for the welfare of the Queen." His mouth twisted on the words. The wine in his stomach burned like fire at the memory of Little Bird's terrified face. Her shock at the alteration in him. "So I dare not, lest the Mage strips me of my own magical gifts, and I lead our realm once more into ruin. Do not expect it."

"Yet we need leadership, my lord," Sir Fellows said. Glancing toward him, Joran read the same disappointment in his piercing gaze as in his wife's. It seemed Sir Fellows harboured equal doubt about Joran's ability to take control of the situation. "Indecision costs us dear. Every moment is precious. And the traitor is still abroad. We have yet to find him despite my many attempts in the last few days."

"Aye, the traitor. I had not forgotten," Joran said. "I know my role in this, Sir Fellows; do not doubt me. But you do not yet know the full weight of what we face. 'Tis not merely a secular matter. Perhaps it never was." His gaze turned once more to the closed door. "My daughter is using Farsight. Sees images of Cerys Tinterdorn in every dark corner. 'Tis too much for her. My wife lies under some sort of sleep. Her magic is returning, but she cannot wield it unless she awakens. And meanwhile, Cerys is creeping closer. I can feel her eyes on us. Watching." His eyes flicked to Petronella's chamber, where little Theda suffered for her visions. His memory served him the point of her tiny finger, tracing the line of Cerys' invisible path across her fire-lit chamber. He shuddered. Tried to hide it. Failed.

"Bah. You sound like the doddering old women crowded around a village well," Sir Fellows said, his tone rough. He paced back to the hearth and helped himself to a fistful of nuts. "She cannot have reached us yet unless her Shadow Mage lends her wings to fly. 'Tis a long journey between Traitor's Reach and here. Give me leave, and I will take some soldiers. We will throw a ring around the castle. Question every person who approaches."

"You may do that if you will." Joran forced the words out through a dry mouth. "But be aware, the one power Cerys possesses that no-one else does. She is a shape-shifter. A powerful illusionist. She could assume the guise of a fellow soldier. A peasant, a courtier..."

Sir Fellows snorted his disbelief. "Shape-shifting," he repeated, rolling the word like a bitter pill. "I thought that was but a myth. If it were true...aye, it would explain much of her success. But Gods above, how do you fight what you cannot see?" He shook his head, his eyes flickering as they processed the information.

"There is but one chink in her armour. Sir Skinner assures me Cerys cannot access a person's memories, even if she borrows their appearance," Joran said. "Therefore, we deny access to any strangers we have not met before. And those familiar to us, we should question more closely about shared events in the past. 'Tis the only weapon we have against her."

Sir Fellows chewed, his face thoughtful. "I will relay these orders, and we will do our best," he said.

"We must do more than our best. Epera's future depends on it." Joran let the words hang. Long enough that Sir Fellows arched a grizzled brow and narrowed his eyes. "So, I bid you..." he placed his hand on his general's shoulder, encouraging him toward the door, "guard us as you wish. Question as you may. You have my leave. But trust no-one. No-one at all."

Sir Fellows nodded, his ruddy face gaunt in the light of the new information. "I will do what I can, then," he said. "As I described. We will watch every road. Every valley. No-one will approach unless by the Queen's Guard. We will question everyone. I pledge my soul in the Queen's service and to yours, my lord." He offered Joran a rare, stiff bow. Joran took his arm. A warrior's salute.

"Warn our men well," Joran said, his voice quiet in the wavering light from the guttering oil lamps as they burned down. "On the

Queen's life, I charge you. We must all play our parts, even if the outcome remains wrapped in darkness."

"Aye."

Alone, Joran turned back to the window as Sir Fellows departed. The silence closed around him like a shroud. He flexed his hands, scarred from battles he understood, battles he had won. But this... This was a war of shadows. And in the deepening dark, he could not be certain whether the light would break.

CHAPTER 27
DOMINIC

The dull light of dawn matched the mood of the group as they packed up and prepared to move out of Falconridge. Frost nipping his fingers, Dominic saddled Kismet with his jaw clenched and his shoulders prickling, convinced someone was observing him from the shadows. Rested, the mare nudged him. He pressed his face against her flat, warm cheek in response. Ruffled her ebony mane.

"'Twill be a long, hard journey," he whispered to her. "I pray to the Gods they keep us all safe. I wish I could inform the Queen." He bit his lip at the last thought. A foray into Falconridge's dovecote minutes before had revealed a dozen pigeons lying in a miserable heap of flattened feathers on the grimy floor, their necks broken. The pitiful sight had angered him to the core, but it highlighted the cold-hearted foresight displayed by their enemies. Reducing their ability to communicate, except by telepathy, which a skilled telepath could intercept. He shook his head, rubbing Kismet's silken nose as she searched the flat of his spare hand for a slice of dried apple. "We're on our own, lady," he said. "That much, we know."

One by one, they gathered in the courtyard. Light snow had fallen overnight to dust the hollows left by the fallen. Falconridge lay wrapped in silence, stone cold and still. Desolate. Crows called from the distant forest. Guildford disappeared to the blacksmith's hut, searching for a hammer and nails. Felicia led the General into the yard and glanced round for a mounting block. Clem shifted the weight of his lute more equally across his shoulders and fingered his sword, his thoughtful gaze already scanning the forest.

"Felicia can take turns riding with us all," Dominic said as Guildford approached, tools in hand. "'Twill be better for the horses not to carry double weight for long." He bent and cupped his hands for Felicia, expecting her to use his help in mounting Guildford's enormous horse. She nodded, a more haughty lady than ever. Of a sudden, he was catapulted back in time to his days as a young stable boy. A featureless mobile mounting block for the gentry. His gaze narrowed as he boosted her upwards, lingering to lay a hand on her slender calf. She stared down at him and nodded her thanks. But there was no warmth in her smile, and her eyes held nothing but trepidation and sadness. He lifted his hand to her but quickly drew it back before turning to her brother, who thankfully offered much more in the way of congeniality.

"She weighs but little," he said. "But you are probably right. I have no wish to deprive you of her company."

Dominic raised his brows. He'd said precisely two words to Felicia since the communal burial. Her hands were trembling on the General's reins. He opened his mouth to say something. Closed it again. Unsure what he could say to cross the distance between them. A thorny path trod by a hopeful man on unshod feet. Dangerous. Painful.

Gritting his teeth, he led the way through the battered gates. As a last gesture, he used some of the pent-up magical power tingling in his palms to heave the heavy oak doors back in place. Guildford performed a rough repair, his shoulders bunching as he pounded nails through the hinges into the frozen wood. The blows rang through the silent forest, sending a startle of birds into the morning sky.

"'Twill hold," Guildford said, giving the last nail a hefty whack. He deposited the hammer on the nearest sledge and leapt to his saddle, slinging a casual arm around Felicia as he took the reins.

"All set," he said cheerfully.

Dominic glanced across at Aldric lounging in Hamil's broad saddle, his shrewd brown eyes watchful, his bow ready. "Are you fit, Aldric?" he asked.

"Aye. ready," Aldric murmured in response, but he didn't remove his gaze from the surrounding forest. "There are tracks over there," he said, pointing. "Left by those who came before us, creeping through the trees. Look. You can see where they disturbed the snow from the undergrowth."

He urged Hamil forward to investigate. "Plenty of folk," he reported after a minute. "Spread out, they were. Some on foot, some mounted." He twisted in his saddle, scanning the space in front of the gate. "No sign of a battering ram. They broke down the gate," he said as he rejoined them, "but no battering ram. You know what that means?"

Dominic's face hardened. "Aye," he muttered. "There is a tele-mantist amongst them. Like me." He gathered his cloak around him, nodding his thanks to Aldric. "I'll be ready. Stay alert, everyone. They could still be here on Falconridge lands." He paused for a moment, taking in the pale, pinched faces of his companions bunched together as they waited for his order to move out. "This will be a hard journey," he said. "We must press on with all speed. Cerys and Dupliss are ahead of us. But we must catch them."

They rode out in single file, as before. The sledges in front, pulled by their sturdy mounts, scythed a path for those following behind. Every noise seemed heightened in the ice-wrapped forest. The sun rose in the east and cast a dazzle of rainbows from each frozen branch. The world seemed suddenly filled with enchantment. Hushed and frosted with the brilliant colours of winter. Aldric rode with one hand on Hamil's reins, his face awestruck at the silent beauty surrounding them on all sides. Guildford dropped his head to his sister, muttering encouragement as she fought to maintain her seat. Dominic tried not to look at her. Her silence cut like a knife through his weary heart. He turned his gaze instead to the snow-laden shrubbery, alert for danger, all his senses on edge.

Compared to the heavy going of their previous journey, the long march through Falconridge's substantial forests proved uneventful. Aldric had them stop every so often, dismounting and snuffing through the ground like a hungry boar searching for acorns. There was little to report. The marauding forces had swept through Falconridge, gathered hardened new recruits in the shape of Sir Dunforde's troop, and carried on.

"By my reckoning, they are two days in front of us," Aldric said when they finally stopped to break their fast beside an ice-crusted stream, the bank thick with trees. "We must have arrived at Falconridge almost on their heels. We would have caught them by now if we had not stopped to honour Falconridge's victims."

Dominic's shoulders stiffened. "We should be glad they only left Clem behind," he said, glancing at the young minstrel-turned-soldier as he loosened his mount's bridle and led it to the water. "At least we know whose side he's on. Master Ash chose him well."

"I'd still monitor him," Guildford grunted under his breath as he handed Felicia down, steadying her on a patch of ice. "Just because he stayed behind does not make him an innocent in all this."

"You surely jest," Aldric said. "The man's a soldier with the soul of a poet and the voice of an angel. You've heard him. Missed his calling, from what I can see." He cut his wide-eyed glance towards Clem. True to form, the young man abandoned his steed, dusted a log free of snow, and took out his lute. The song he sang sent a chill of remembrance straight through Dominic's veins. It was the strange, haunting melody that had so savaged his heart and accompanied him on his journey. The song of Aequitas.

Hearing it again out of doors, surrounded by ice and crystal, sent every magical sense into overdrive. He closed his eyes, suddenly overwhelmed by it.

"By the Mage, Clem, play another tune," he said.

Clem clamped a hand over the strings. The song died mid-chord. Dominic breathed a sigh of relief. That God's-blasted melody always seemed to want something from him he could not give. Asking a million questions for which he had no answers.

"Play 'Where the Robin Roves'," Guildford ordered with a grin. "That'll cheer us all up."

"Cheer you up, mayhap," Aldric jibed. "Not sure how you're managing so long without access to ale and wenches."

Guildford reached out a long arm and gave Aldric a mild-mannered shove that sent him head over heels into the nearest bush. He emerged, furious, spitting snow. Clem grinned. His smile lit his eyes, pale blue and limpid. "Oops," he said.

"I warned you," Guildford said, relenting somewhat and hauling Aldric out by the neck of his tunic. "And I am a man of my word." He gave Aldric another shove, this time in Clem's direction. The musician had to abandon his precious lute and steady Aldric as he teetered on a patch of black ice. "Whoops again," he said, brushing Aldric's cloak free of ice. "Mind how you go, there."

Watching the horseplay, Dominic hid his smile behind Kismet's neck as he led her to the stream, where, half hidden by a stand of reeds, Felicia had stooped to refill their water skins.

She crouched stock still, staring out across the stream, freezing water dripping from her fingers.

"Felicia?" Leaving Kismet to sort herself out, he strode across the couple of feet that separated them. Felicia's fingers were turning blue with cold. She didn't move a muscle. Panic rose within him. All his previous doubts vanished as he glimpsed her eyes. Glowing gold. Farsight.

"By the Gods, Felicia. Felicia!"

His panicked shout brought the others at a run. "'Tis her magic. The heartsease has worn off," Dominic murmured, plucking the water skins from her unresponsive grip and handing them over to Aldric. Frantic, he gathered her chilled hands in his own, warming them against his chest. "Felicia, come back to us. Please, my love."

"What's to do?" Silas sauntered towards them, with the other sledge drivers filing behind. "Has she fallen in?" His tone showed it was nothing to him if she had.

Something fierce rose in Dominic's blood at the man's obvious indifference.

His eyes narrowed. "'Tis her magic, rising," he stated. He gained a guilty primaeval enjoyment at the sight of the blood draining from Silas's whiskered cheeks. "Who knows what it might lead to?" He left the last words hanging in the crisp air, challenge in his glare, suddenly utterly fed-up of their dumb suspicion—the typical, uneducated superstition the Citizens bore towards the Blessed.

"Her magic?" Silas stuttered. He glanced across at Felicia, whom Guildford had picked up, wrapping her carefully in his own cloak. Guildford bared his teeth, equally irritated.

"Aye," he said. "Her magic. Would you like to test it?"

Speechless, Silas exchanged terrified glances with Miles. Both of them backed off several paces, crossing their chests for protection, bumping into each other as they retreated. Kendrick, entranced, watched Felicia with hungry eyes. "What's her magic?" he asked, stepping closer to have a look.

"You'll not touch her," Aldric said baldly. He swept his bow from his back and strung an arrow so quickly his fingers blurred. Kendrick gaped at him. The tall young squire, skinny as a sapling, stared him down through the length of his arrow, eyes full of thunder.

The driver swallowed, stepped away, and raised his hands. "I'm only interested," he protested.

"Be interested from a greater distance," Aldric advised.

At first, Dominic thought Felicia's teeth were chattering. He swept his cloak from his shoulders, intent on keeping her warm. It was only when he draped it around her he realised she was talking. Gabbling. Her eyes were still full of golden light, dazzling in their brilliance against the icy trees. He started when she clutched at his arm.

Her eyes were wide but unseeing. "Remember, Dominic. He who holds the Grayling holds the crown. Holds the crown."

Skin crawling, he stared at her. The same prophecy. One he'd first heard years ago in a whore's chamber on the back streets of Blade. He blinked, his mind churning. He'd thought the prophecy was fulfilled two years ago when he rescued the Grayling from Arabella of Wessendean. Returned him to Petronella. Her falcon. The wild, magnificent bird Dominic had nearly died to save. Surely, his part in all of that was done? He shivered. The sun vanished behind a bank of grey clouds. Denied its light, the encroaching forest presented a more ominous face. More wasteland than wonderland. A creeping mist twisted silently in the undergrowth, stretching to claim the trees for its own.

Felicia's golden gaze was fixed on him. Still repeating the words. "Remember, Dominic, he who holds the Grayling holds the crown." Beneath his confusion and his own unspoken denial, the prophecy stirred something deep within him. A bitter sadness. Something tender and unresolved but dreadful in its immensity. It was waiting to claim them. Waiting for them all. He knew it to the depths of his soul.

Appalled, he tore his eyes from hers at a shout from further away. He looked up in time to see two of their sledges vanishing into the forest, the horses whipped to a frenzy by their terrified drivers. Their flight disturbed flocks of birds from their chilled slumber. The flurry of their wings, as they took to the sullen sky, dragged his eyes upwards.

"Nay! Wait!" He leapt after the sledges, skidding in their wake across the hard-packed ground, but he was much too slow. His chest clenched with the sudden activity in the icy air. Dominic gritted his teeth and pounded a fist on his thigh as they disappeared into the mist. That was two-thirds of their supplies and the driver's knowledge of the terrain. Grim-faced, he returned to his companions.

"Blast it." Still clutching his lute, Clem aimed a kick at his pack. "'Twas my fault," he said. "I shouldn't have sung that song. 'Tis a powerful thing, I know. There's magic in those words. Always was. But it felt right. Like something I needed to do..."

"It wasn't all your fault. We baited them," Dominic muttered. The silence of the forest returned to surround them in its icy embrace. A chill warning that the worst was yet to come.

He strode towards Guildford, who was rocking Felicia in his mighty arms as one might shelter a newborn babe. The concern in his bright grey eyes mirrored the dread clutching Dominic's ribs in a vice of steel as their gazes clashed over her hood. She stopped speaking when he touched her fingers. The flare of Farsight faded from her eyes. Her head rolled back against Guildford's arm, a sob trembling at her lips. Completely at a loss, he pressed a kiss to the back of her shaking hand.

"How is the lady?" Clem asked. Stepping to them, he touched a gentle, string-calloused finger to Felicia's finely drawn cheek. Strangely, Aldric made no move to stop him. He lowered his bow, his dark eyes wide. "You are no Citizen," he whispered. "This is a different Blessing." Almost in a trance, the lad caught Clem's hand in his own. Turned it over. The musician clenched his fingers, but not before Dominic caught a glimpse. Mage light burned deep within Clem's palm.

The young soldier dropped his head. "Aye," he muttered. "I don't tell many. Keep it close, like. 'Tis better so."

"That's why you stayed with Master Ash," Dominic murmured.

"Aye, it's also why we can do nothing but listen when he sings," Aldric said. "That song... It triggered Felicia's vision. I'm sure of it."

Clem raised his eyebrows in acknowledgement. "I didn't mean it so," he said. "But aye, it can happen. Doesn't work on the Citizens all the time, though. I tried. Played the most patriotic tunes I know." His fragile jaw jutted. "Once Dupliss and his forces arrived, it took Sir Dunforde but a moment to turn. And the rest of them with him. They want you, my lord." He nodded at Guildford. "That's what Dupliss is promising them. Those loyal to our Blessed Queen..." He paused, his eyes clouded with sadness. "They just cut them down where they stood."

"By the Gods." Guildford's eyes blazed with fury as he slid his sister to her feet. "Must I fight the entire army to prove my loyalty to our Queen?" His challenge rang amongst the trees like the blare of battle trumpets.

Dominic caught Felicia to him as her legs wobbled. Eyelids fluttering as she recovered, she clung to him, her breath coming light and fast against his cheek. He clasped her closer, his breath warming the frost clinging to her hair. "'Tis alright, Felicia. You are safe. We have you," he whispered. "Do you remember what you saw? What you said?"

Her fingers locked on his wrist, her trembling lips brushing his ear as she spoke. "We must move," she murmured. "No matter what Dupliss thinks, Cerys has her own plan. I could see it plain, and time is slipping away." She drew a shuddering breath. "There is but one chance left."

Around them, the forest seemed to hold its breath. Snow-covered branches creaked under their icy burden. Somewhere in the distance, an early owl called, its cry swallowed by the undulating mist. Dominic glanced toward the shadows where the sledges had vanished, unease prickling at his spine. The mist thickened around them, swallowing the forest in a grey shroud. The weight of Felicia's words pressed against his chest. Somewhere close, a branch snapped. A small sound, but it fractured the stillness like the crack of a whip. Bidding them hurry. Driving them on.

"Come, mount up," he said. "Kendrick, you must show us the shortest way to Thorncastle. Our Queen needs us. There is no time to rest."

Chapter 28
Joran

"**M**y lord, my lord?"

Dragged from slumber by Fortuna's hand tugging at his sleeve, Joran sprang half-awake with a snarl on his lips, tipping Theda off his chest and onto the thin pallet that cushioned them on the floor. Theda opened bleary eyes, glowered at them, and returned to sleep with her thumb in her mouth.

"By the Empress." Face pale under her nightcap, Fortuna glared at him. "'Tis I, my lord, not the Shadow Mage," she hissed.

"What hour is it? How is my lady?" Joran grunted, removing the point of his blade from her throat and re-sheathing it in one fluid motion. He tucked a corner of the blanket further around his daughter, taking a moment to smooth her tumbled curls from her forehead.

"Just before dawn. I am expecting the first of the servants to arrive with heartsease for us if they found any," Fortuna said. She moved past him to light another candle. "Petronella's ring is growing brighter. I thought I felt her stir in the night. Mayhap she will wake today." Her lips lifted briefly at the thought, but she stifled a yawn as she folded a discarded blanket with an impatient snap of her wrist.

"Your turn to go without rest?" Joran said.

Fortuna shrugged, "Aye," she said shortly. "And I do even worse without sleep than you, so expect little patience from me today." Turning to the cluttered table, she grimaced at the mess of empty platters and drained decanters. "I will have a servant freshen the chamber," she muttered, crossing to the window. "'Tis worse than a pigsty."

"Nay. We will do it ourselves," Joran countered. "Time is moving on. Cerys Tinterdorn could be here already. We must not trust even the most familiar faces."

"You are feinting at shadows," Fortuna said, opening the window a crack. The icy breeze stirred the papers on the desk and sent the candle flames into an erratic dance. "The witch cannot be here yet," she said, leaning out. "She has not had time enough to travel so far."

"Aye, mayhap," Joran said, his chest tightening around the thought.

He joined Fortuna at the window, scouring the courtyards and battlements spread around them. Faded torchlight glowed from the walls. The sky was lightening in the east, the pale shapes of the snow-covered mountains showing dusty grey against the haze of starlight. The sight of the soldiers manning the battlements heartened him, but only by a small degree. "She's out there," he said, his voice low. "And creeping closer. Sir Fellows will order as many troops as he can spare to surround the castle. He will question everyone who approaches."

"If the woman can imitate anyone she chooses, how will he know the difference?" Fortuna asked.

"Cerys has a weakness," Joran said. "Her illusions are only on the surface. Careful questioning would expose her as a fraud. I have commanded Sir Fellows to pass this information on to our soldiers." He sighed, massaging the tension in his shoulders.

"Dominic will find her," Fortuna said, turning her hand to catch a single, fragile snowflake as it drifted in the wind.

Joran frowned, glancing across at her. "Are you really so confident?" he demanded.

"Of Dominic Skinner? Of course." Her dark eyes were bright in the candlelight as she looked up at him. "Petronella is right to trust him," she murmured. "I wish you could do so as well. Of all your subjects, he is the least likely to give up in the face of great odds. Surely, he has proved that to you by now?"

Unable to bear his friend's intense scrutiny, Joran turned his shoulder. "I see myself in him," he said, his whisper harsh in the quiet room. "All that bright hope and brilliance. And now, when I need it, my self-belief lies in tatters." He paced the length of the room and back, snatching his goblet and draining the contents. Slammed it down. "I have demanded too much of him. As harsh a ruler as my half-brother, Arion. And my temper…" He rounded on her suddenly, hardly seeing the reflexive pace she took away from him. "Just recently, I hardly recognise myself. I do not know what has happened. Ever since the last rebellion, when Dominic brought the Grayling back, I have carried this anger inside me." Reaching past her, he yanked the window closed so hard the panes of glass rattled in their frames. Fortuna jumped. "'Tis like a disease. It is not who I am." He stuttered to a halt, clutching his temples. His jaw clenched so tightly against the need to shout it hurt. Fortuna stared at him, her dark eyes wide. From Petronella's room, the Grayling shrilled an alarm. The noise stirred Joran's senses to high alert. The candles guttered again as a draft from the chilly corridor trickled into the room.

"The Shadow Mage." Little Bird's voice, soft in the tense silence, snapped both their heads around. She'd entered the room so quietly neither of them heard her. Fortuna slammed her hand against her chest, and Joran strode towards the girl, a forbidding scowl twisted across his face.

"What are you doing in here? I have given you no leave," he snapped.

"I have the heartsease you sent for," Little Bird said, scowling back. She held out a slim package as evidence. "'Tis all they could find so late in Blade," she said.

Joran grabbed her arm. "And what transgressions of courtesy have you crossed in the last three days?" he demanded.

"More than I have time to tell you," Little Bird snapped back. "Where should I start?"

"By the Gods, Joran, how many times must we remind you?" Fortuna's tone left no room for doubt. She marched towards him with genuine rage in her face. "Raise your hands against someone your equal, not a child! I am glad Petronella cannot see you like this. It does you no honour. The sight would bring her nothing but pain." She took the package from the girl. A shadow crossed her face as she weighed the contents in her hand.

"He cannot help it. 'Tis not him, Fortuna," Little Bird said more softly. "'Tis the Shadow Mage's presence here, in this room. Can you not feel it? The doubt and the darkness?"

Joran stared at her, his mind a swirl of shifting thoughts. "The Shadow Mage, here?" he echoed, gripped with a terror in his soul so great his bladder ached. His mind leapt back to the day of Petronella's awe-inspiring battle against her father and his Dark Army. The crushing weight of their evil force smothering his gifts, defeating his purpose as he and Domita struggled to fight free and come to her aid. Even Domita's flames and fury could not ignite against it. And he, barely healed from an almost fatal wound, weakened by the long journey from Oceanis, had no strength left to fight it. His heart plummeted to his boots. Had he ever regained that strength?

Hollow-eyed, Little Bird met his gaze, but her expression shifted as she read the deepest fear in him, softened by a rare compassion. "Aye, the Shadow Mage," she said. "His presence was there, under the temple, the night Dominic rescued the Grayling. Just as Cerys was. We all felt it. The despair. 'Tis like your worst nightmares, rising to smite you all at once. He is here now. Those are his thoughts in your mind, my lord. Do not trust them."

Joran released his punishing grip on her arm and stared at his fingers as if he could not believe they belonged to him.

"I have food for the Grayling, my lord. May I give it to him?" Little Bird asked. She glanced between Fortuna and Joran, twisting her fingers in her apron, obviously afraid she'd gone too far.

"Aye, lass," Joran managed. Little Bird bobbed a quick curtsey and retreated. He could hear her murmuring to the Grayling as she approached and the bird's chatter of welcome as he spied his breakfast. Ordinary sounds. But still, the crushing dread remained, growing stronger. Little Theda whimpered in her sleep, shifting restlessly as she emerged from slumber. Fortuna knelt by her side as she came to, snuggling the little girl to her warm bosom. Still whimpering, Theda buried her head in her neck. Fortuna rose smoothly to her feet. She dangled the package of herbs in front of him. "We have a problem."

"Another one? Tell on," he said. He took a stale heel of bread from a denuded platter and chewed mechanically, struggling with the implications of Little Bird's quiet statement. The Shadow Mage, reaching its clutching fingers for control of his own soul. He shuddered. The bread he swallowed formed a lump in his throat. He reached for wine to force it down.

"This heartsease. There is not enough for two doses. We have one large one here. Enough to tamp down one person's magic."

He stared at her. "Only enough for one?"

"Aye. The Queen's magic is returning. If she wakens enough to use it, all could be well. However, we cannot know she will wake. If she does not, her magic could return, but her channels would be open and unguarded. This is a risk. Theda," she paused, rocking the girl against her, "little Theda is still at the mercy of her uncontrolled magic. She is too young to control her gifts. You can see already the toll this is taking on her. And on you, my lord."

"By the Gods." Over Fortuna's shoulder, Joran's gaze crept to his wife, where she lay, still motionless under her heavy covers. The Grayling lifted his head from his breakfast and regarded him with a baleful eye. Little Bird crossed his line of vision, bearing a tray containing a bowl and a cloth. She paused at the Queen's bedside and bathed her face, careful not to spill water on her blankets.

Joran's heart twisted in his breast. "'Tis rare to see such devotion in one so young," he murmured.

"Aye. Less Little Bird and more mother hen," Fortuna quipped. "'Twas a lucky day for your children when that young maid joined your employ. I don't think I have ever seen one so apt. 'Tis a great gift, she has, for making others happy."

Joran grimaced. "She also has an equally outstanding talent to annoy," he remarked. He stretched his hands out for his daughter. Unusually, Theda struggled from his grasp, pushing his hands away.

"Thirsty, Papa," she said. A small frown crossing his face, Joran poured some water for her. Fortuna watched him with her hands on her hips. "You must decide, my lord," she warned him. "Petronella or Theda. We are running out of time."

"I know, woman. Let me think." Pricked by her demand, Joran returned to his seat at Petronella's desk and attempted to bring order to the mess of books and paperwork.

A frown denting her brow, Fortuna busied herself at the hearth. Pots rattled as she readied the heartsease for steeping. Revived, Theda retrieved her rag doll. She sat cross-legged by the fire, humming a lullaby to it, her dark head bent. For a moment, with the morning light gradually rising and the subtle aroma of heartsease spilling its promise of calm into the air, Joran almost allowed himself to relax in everyday tranquillity. It could be any morning of the last few weeks, with no grim decisions demanding his attention. Theda finished her lullaby and began another song. Alerted by the tune, Joran glanced up as he stacked a pile of parchment together. That melody... Something about it wasn't right. Where did that cold, atonal song come from?

Still humming, Theda danced her doll across her knees. Turning it in a circle, standing it upside down so its skirts tumbled over its head. She stopped humming. In its place, a chilling giggle erupted from her lips. "Let's go for a walk, Theda," she said. He frowned, confused by the compelling, crystal clarity of the voice. His eyes clashed with Fortuna's as she looked around, removing her brew from the heat.

Theda scrambled to her feet. "Where shall we go, Cerys?"

Every single hair on the back of his neck stood up. He shot to his feet, ice crawling down his spine. Fortuna winced as she jerked to attention, spilling hot liquid over her fingers.

"Nay," she breathed. Joran swallowed, already moving to block his daughter's progress to Petronella's room. The Grayling launched himself at the window, battering it with his beak, wings flailing. The screech of his insistent alarm call pierced Joran's ears, adding to the monstrous panic that spiked his blood. Petronella moaned, shifting her weight against her mattress. On the verge of waking.

"Theda," Joran said, his throat dry, his palms sweating, "sweetling, look at me. Come to Papa."

Another giggle. Theda danced around him, the doll dangling by her fingers, her expression wild with delirious glee. Unable to escape, the Grayling was soaring like a whirlwind around Petronella's room, agitated and afraid. Joran glanced at the bird and then away as Theda attempted to sidestep him.

"Theda!" He took a step towards her.

She paused where she was, her dark hair dangling in front of her face, both hands clutching her rag doll, her knuckles white. "Nay, I won't do it. I won't! Papa, help me! She's here, she's here!"

Her head lifted, and she looked up at him with such desperate need, his heart clenched in his chest. Her eyes, her beautiful eyes, so like Petronella's, a deep, aching blue. Even as he reached for her, they changed. Ink black. Soul dark.

"By the Gods." Fortuna swept towards him, tipping the remains of their flagon of water over her brew to cool it as she approached. "Hold her," she said. Face grim, she pinched the girl's nostrils shut and massaged her throat as she administered the drink in as gentle a stream as she could manage. Theda choked and flailed, batting fruitlessly at Joran's hands, struggling against him. Hating himself, he held her still. There was no choice now. She had to swallow. Tears pooled down his cheeks as her struggles abated. Her curly head drooped as the wild fury departed.

Fortuna bit her lip as she laid down the empty glass and checked Theda's eyes. "Blue, thank all the Gods," she breathed, her voice an appalled whisper. Even Fortuna's fingers shook as she grazed Theda's cheek. "I'm sorry, Joran. I had to do it," she said.

Joran sagged, pressing his lips to his daughter's hair. "Aye, I know." Their gazes clashed over the child's head, each looking for reassurance.

"Papa," Theda wound her arms around his neck. Regret and sorrow writhing within him, he rocked her, holding her close to his heart.

"I am so sorry, my poppet," he whispered to her. "We had to help you."

Her curls tickled his chin as she shook her head. "Nay, look."

Fresh dread swept through him as she pointed at Petronella's room. His wife lay as they had left her, but the light from her ring was dimming, flickering like a dying flame.

"By all the Gods." Fear lancing through him, he crossed the short distance to the bed. Even as he watched, Petronella's heavy diamond darkened. He swallowed, sensing the shadows in the room yawning closer, already at war with the sunlight rising on the eastern horizon. A freshening breeze at his cheek drew his gaze to the window, where Little Bird leaned, standing on tiptoe to draw it softly closed. He was suddenly aware of the silence. A terrible absence over and above his dawning horror. The young girl's face was paler than he'd ever seen it. Drawn and guilty. And the Grayling...

The Grayling was gone.

CHAPTER 29
DOMINIC

Challenged by the lack of supplies and the thick, cloying mist that clung to their every shadow, Dominic's small group reached Thorncastle's gates two cold, weary days later.

Thick snow had gradually given way to sleet somewhere along the way. It had seeped through their cloaks into their bones. Every new breath, every extra step, was an effort. Their horses wore a thick coat of crusted mud. Hamil was lame. Aldric had alternated between riding the sledge with Felicia and Kendrick and slogging through the sodden paths next to his downcast mount, cursing his frozen feet. Kismet plodded gamely on, her head hanging. Exhausted and hungry, they formed a sorry, ragged line in front of Thorncastle's heavy gates. A far cry from the triumphant band of flags and steel that had reached Thorncastle's southern gate just a few weeks before.

"Ho!" Dominic's hoarse shout gained the attention of the nearest motley-clad guard.

"What do you want?" The man looked down his nose at him. "If you're messengers here to tell us the Queen's dead, you're too late. We already know."

"What?" The guard's terse words startled Dominic out of his self-absorption. His empty stomach lurched as if he'd taken a blow. The Queen...dead? The man's words echoed in his skull. He stared speechlessly at the guard, lost for words. Aldric gasped, clamping his hand to his mouth.

Panic surging in his blood, Dominic glanced at Felicia. Her face was a mask of stoicism. She gripped the edges of her sledge seat with white knuckles, head erect. Something about her fixed expression reminded him of a person bound for execution, determined to defy the noose. He shook his head to dispel the impression. Guildford urged the General closer to the wall and shoved his hood back, an impatient scowl plastered across his broad face.

"I am Guildford of Wessendean, son of the late King Arion," he roared. "No messenger. Explain yourself. And let us in. We need food and rest."

"Guildford of Wessendean!" The gate guard's surly demeanour changed in an instant. He snatched off his own hood, bowed, and gestured furiously to his fellows. "'Tis him, Guildford. Dupliss said he would come. Open the gates, quick!"

"By the Gods, news travels fast," Clem hissed, pulling his own hood down over his eyes. "Sir Dunforde has got here before us."

Guildford swapped an amazed glance at Dominic. "Fastest anyone's ever opened up for me," he said, stifling a tired grin. "And that's saying something."

Dominic scowled back. The guard's bald statement echoed in his mind, loud enough to drown out the clash of chains as the guards prepared to open the gates. "Did you not hear him? What does he mean, the Queen's dead?" he demanded, in a furious undertone. "Surely she's not? She can't be."

"Nay, she's not." Felicia's voice was quiet by his side. "'Tis just what Dupliss wants them to think. Be wary here, Dominic. His spies will be everywhere." She raised a booted foot and gave Guildford a nudge. "You too, King-in-waiting," she said. "Don't get carried away by the welcome they are like to give you."

"Hah. If their welcome comes with ale and good company, bring it on," Guildford said, turning his shoulder.

"What if they also want to use you? What if some here do not want you? Did you not consider that before you opened your mouth?" Felicia demanded. Her voice held a sarcastic edge that penetrated even her brother's thick skin. He turned a reproachful look on her. "That's what I have you for," he said with exaggerated impatience. "You are my guard dog, are you not? Ever ready to warn me when before I need it?"

"By the Gods, I wish it were not so," Felicia muttered through thin lips. She said the words to herself. Dominic stared at her. That hadn't sounded like a jest. Before he had time to consider her further, the gates ground open. Kismet threw her head up, snorting at the noise. The bustle and scent of the town billowed out to meet them. Despite his fatigue, Dominic's shoulders relaxed. There would be food here. Warmth and comfort. Possible aid if Joran's words were true. They could restock, rest, and be on their way. Surely, even Dupliss and Cerys Tinterdorn had needed to rest as well?

Gathering Kismet's reins in his frozen fingers, he led them in, careful to keep his hood lowered and his eyes down.

"Trouble is," Aldric muttered as they took their first, hesitant steps within the town walls, inhaling the aroma of dung and stale hops from the slush-filled streets, "no matter what Dupliss says about our King Guildford, Sir Dunforde knows he's with us. Better be on your guard, Dom."

"Aye. They had little use for us as the Queen's men last time we were here." Dominic's hand slid to his sword. He rode with one hand on its hilt, Mage power collecting in his fingers. Ready to use at a second's notice. Even Felicia fumbled at her hip for her slender eating dagger, ensuring its readiness, the edge a silver sliver at her side.

Thorncastle remained much as he had last seen it. A jumble of low-level buildings clustered around the market square. The southern route led over steep cliffs. His gaze narrowed as he followed the narrow road rising in the far distance. He knew the state of that path already. Had nearly died traversing it on their way north. That narrow, crumbling cliff face. With ice and snow in every direction, it was likely impassable. Cedric had been correct. The river was the only way out.

Heaving a sigh, he rolled his eyes at the sight of Guildford, riding with his head high, basking in the admiration of the local towns-folk. Some of the more forward maidens paced alongside the General, reaching out to touch Guildford's muddy, booted foot. Guildford played his part well, revelling in the adoration, but Dominic caught the flicker of hesitation in his pebble-eyed smile, the slight doubt. This wasn't just a hero's welcome. It was a test. The lad's fingers were tight on the General's reins whilst he raised his hand in greeting with the other.

"Guildford, the King is come!" The whisper seemed to ignite on the chilly wind, twisting along broader streets and the mean back alleys along with the mist that still dogged their footsteps. The few people turned to a score and then a four score, crowding their path. Kismet's ears flickered. She threw up her head, annoyed by the pressing of strangers. Even tired, Dominic had to ride steadily to keep her facing forward. But not everyone's greeting was as warm. Dominic's skin pricked as he scanned the crowd from beneath his hood. His careful gaze noted one tall fellow skittering away into the mist. A passing matron clutched her child closer as if she sensed a threat, not promised salvation. He didn't miss the watchful eyes lurking at the edges of the crowd, nor the hurried whispers that died when he glanced their way. Thorncastle was no haven. Instead, it bore a conflicted face, where emotions ran high, and the future was unpredictable.

"We need shelter," he said, his shoulders stiff with rising tension. "Where shall we head?"

Guildford shrugged. "I know not," he said. "These people are like to lead us straight to Dupliss, and that's the last thing we want."

"If he's even here," Aldric interjected. "He could be gone by now. Sir Dunforde and his troop with him."

Felicia nodded her agreement. "If Cerys commands them, she'll move them on. That's her nature. She won't care how much rest they need or how hard they drive their horses." Her cool grey eyes scanned the crowded streets. "Dupliss promised them a king," she said, slowly. "Perhaps it's best if we give them one for now." She turned to her brother, a grudging smile lighting her drawn face. "Keep it up," she said. "Be a king. But don't take your hand off your sword."

Guildford hesitated, his broad shoulders tense. "A king for now," he muttered, bestowing a charming smile on the nearest besotted maid he saw.

"There," Aldric said, pointing to a modest inn tucked between two larger buildings some way off. Its shutters were closed against the mist, but the glow of firelight seeped through the cracks. A painted sign hanging from a rusted iron hook bore a faded image, hard to pick out in the uncertain light. Seven swords. Four lying horizontally, three pointing up, formed a crosshatch of possibilities. "What about that one?"

"Aye." Felicia's voice lowered. Dominic's brow creased as he glanced across at her. She blinked at the unprepossessing building like someone waking from a dream. "There. We must go there."

Kendrick snapped to attention at the sound of Felicia's voice. Something about his expectant, fox-like features had Dominic's fingers tensing on his sword. He averted his gaze before Kendrick could read the suspicion in his eyes. They pressed on to the inn. Uncomfortably aware of their heightened visibility. The clutching hands. The charged atmosphere.

"I don't like this," Guildford hissed. "Despite this welcome, it's too quiet. Where are the local dignitaries? If Dupliss has been here, shouldn't they be falling over themselves to buy my favour?"

"Perhaps they're afraid," Dominic replied. His voice was low, but it carried enough steel to make Guildford glance his way. "Let's find out which."

Glancing around, his eyes caught the troubled stare of a young woman huddled at the curb with her basket clutched to her chest like a shield. Her gaze darted from the crowd to Guildford, thick with unease.

"How now, mistress," Dominic said, leaning out of his saddle. "What kind of welcome can we expect in yonder hostelry?"

"You'll find the inn warm enough, my lord," she said, bobbing a quick curtsey.

"And what of the people inside?" Dominic asked, his voice quiet but firm.

The woman hesitated, glancing over her shoulder at the shuttered windows. "Some of us are loyal to the Queen, still," she murmured. "But others..." She glanced back at him, her wide green eyes sharp with warning. "Be on your guard, sir. This is a troubled town full of strangers. More so since the fall of Falconridge."

Dominic dropped a coin into her basket. "My thanks for your warning, mistress," he said.

He glanced at his companions. Kendrick avoided his gaze. The young man had said little since the abrupt departure of his fellow drivers, keeping to himself. But Dominic was aware of his attention. The covert glances. His particular interest in Felicia. His gaze hardened. "What do you think?" he murmured under the noise of the crushing crowd. "Do we risk it?"

Felicia caught his eye. "'Tis important, that place. I have seen that sign before. In a vision," she murmured.

"Visions or not, I think we must," Aldric said. "We cannot go much further without rest. The horses need attention. We need to take stock of our supplies, find someone willing to put a boat on the river."

"Guildford?"

"Ale," Guildford said simply. He was already dismounting, leading his weary horse behind him as he crossed to the small hostelry. "Please, Gods, this place has a worthy stable."

Dominic huffed a sigh, sending up a silent prayer to the Mage for protection. The people quieted as he followed in Guildford's wake, parting silently for the passing of their remaining sledge, then reforming. Dominic felt the weight of their avid stares at his back. Far from the warmth of welcome, they felt more like the prick of swords. All aimed at his heart.

CHAPTER 30
JORAN

"What have you done?" Fear had dried Joran's voice. The words emerged as a harsh croak, stained with a blood-red rage. Striding to the window, he flung it open. The Grayling's piercing cry was faint against the wind. His beating wings blurred. A vanishing silhouette against the stormy sky, wheeling north. Joran watched his progress with a crick in his neck, straining to see the bird as he changed direction. He swallowed, conscious suddenly of a crushing loneliness. The terror of a tiny child abandoned and alone. Primaeval anger rose in response.

Theda's clinging hands at his throat were damp with perspiration. Her small body heaved as she sobbed. For an instant, only an instant, Joran's mouth twisted. Her arms twined around him like vines, clinging. Demanding. Suffocating. Little Bird stared up at him. She hadn't moved from her position at the window. Her breath came in small pants, her eyes watchful, following the movement of his free hand to his dagger. Reading death in his expression, she wrapped both arms protectively around her chest.

"He wanted to go. He was hurting himself," she said, shrinking against the panelling. Her eyes darted, seeking an exit.

Joran had to close his eyes to blot out the sight of her face. His fist closed on his deadly weapon, almost without his knowledge. Like a bird breaking free, his heart pounded a mad tattoo within his chest as his anger soared. "The Queen's staff, and now her falcon. What else will you take from me and make free with?" he demanded. "What about Theda and Ranulf? Would you take them? Take her crown? Would you?"

"He wanted to leave. I had to let him go," Little Bird repeated. Her small fists clenched, although her body still trembled. "I had to free him. No-one else would."

His shadow loomed over her as she spoke. Terrified into immobility, trapped by the window seat and the narrow corner, Little Bird could only gasp as he removed the knife from its elaborate sheath. She raised both arms and turned her face, her whole body resisting.

"No!" Fortuna threw herself across the room between them and planted her feet. Immovable as solid rock. Her ferocious grip on his forearm contained surprising strength. "Joran!" Fortuna's voice cracked through the storm of his mind, a whip of steel and fire. "This is not justice. This is despair, feeding on your soul. Fight it. Fight him."

Joran shook her off. "I will rule this kingdom," he hissed. "You will not stand in the way of justice."

"Papa!" Theda's thin, treble wail scythed his senses. "She's found Mama. She's fighting her. Look, look..." Locked in the cage of his panic, Joran almost didn't hear her. The words bounced off his skull without penetrating. Theda gripped two fistfuls of his hair and wrenched his attention from Little Bird. The unexpected pain dragged him back from the precipice of madness yawning before him. Blinking, appalled at his own behaviour, he thrust Theda into Fortuna's arms and stumbled away from his maid, his mind a swirl of hazy images that refused to come into focus. There was anger there, somewhere deep in the past. Helplessness and pain. Was it his? He couldn't tell.

His erratic progress took him to his wife's bed. He glared at her, his thumb caressing the hilt of his dagger. The familiar weight of it in his hand should have been a source of strength. Instead, it seemed slippery in his grasp. As if intent on following a bloody path of its own devising. Shuddering, he slid it away. Wiped his perspiring hands on his doublet. Totally vulnerable, Petronella lay with a frown etched between her delicate brows, her long, graceful fingers clutching the staff Little Bird had placed there as if it was an anchor in a storm. The Ring of Justice rested on her breastbone, unchanged. Crossing his arms around his chest, he stared at it. The temptation to place it on his finger and access its power was almost unbearable. His fingers twitched. Petronella's bleak words of a few days ago struck him with startling intensity even as he reached for it. Bleak as a winter morning. Clear as Oceanian crystal, ringing in his mind. "'Tis what power will do to a good man when he is angry and afraid…"

Exhausted by the barrage of emotion, he sank to his knees and laid his head on her blankets. He could not, would not, succumb to his fear. "I will not, Petronella," he breathed into the comfort of wool and lavender-scented linen. Saying the words out loud, he raised his voice a little. Made them true. "I will not take the ring from you. I promise." He would have given anything for the touch of her hand on his head in response to his vow. Her blessing. His beloved wife had no answer for him. At his back, Fortuna murmured reassurance as she ushered Little Bird and Theda from the room.

"You must come with us, my lord," she said, pausing behind him. She laid a warm hand on his shoulder. "The Queen's ring is darkening. Little Bird is right. Cerys has left Theda and attacked her. The Shadow Mage is with us now. The longer you stay here, the more he will battle your highest nature for control of your soul. At least that much I know from our reading."

Joran screwed his head around and peered up at her. Fortuna's copper skin was pale. She looked as shaken and troubled as he had ever seen her. A frown creased between her brows. "We must take some time to decide how to protect our lady as best we can," she whispered. Her eyes darted around the room, searching the shadowed corners. "Petronella has her staff. We must hope it will help her, but if she wakens…"

She tugged at his sleeve, urging him to his feet. He rose stiffly, his knees creaking. He frowned. Where had that come from? He was young still. Agile. Not so old his knees would protest a simple action.

"Aye," he said. His gaze dropped to Petronella's ring. Darker now. As if something malign and dreadful had injected it with ink. He jerked his eyes from its muddy, leering light. "I am deeply sorry, Fortuna. You are right. There is something here. Some trick or illusion. But how can I leave her at its mercy? Even the Grayling has flown." His eyes scanned the Grayling's perch, his bloody meal abandoned in his bowl. He strode to the window, hoping to see the bird circling the battlements. There were birds there, to be sure. The castle starlings playing with the thermals as they always had. But no sign of the Grayling. His fists clenched at his sides.

"He wanted to leave. I had to let him go..." Little Bird. His heart contracted in his chest. Even the Grayling had chosen freedom, his wings cutting through the rising wind as if fleeing the chaos Joran carried within. The falcon's cry echoed in his mind, a lament for something lost. What did it say about him that even a creature of loyalty and spirit could no longer stay? How close had he come to crossing that line? To becoming the monster he so feared? What kind of man was he?

His heart breaking, he allowed Fortuna to lead him away. His gaze stayed with Petronella, imprinting her face on his memory. Gaunt and stoic. Locked in her own internal battle with a malevolent, deadly enemy.

I cannot help you, my love. Tears pricked his eyes. He swiped them away, hating the sight of the poison eating into the heart of her diamond. Little by little. Smothering hope.

His feet dragged on the carpet as Fortuna reached past him to close the door. She pushed him to a chair at the fireplace and scanned the table for herbs, her expression grim as she sorted through the contents.

"What are you looking for?"

"If Cerys has truly left Theda for Petronella, we know but one thing," she said. Her voice trembled as she rifled through her supplies. A tiny smile lifted her lips as her fingers closed on a small, close-wrapped package. She opened it, sniffed at the contents, and nodded in approval.

"What?" Joran couldn't think. The events of the morning conspired to twist his mind against itself. A storm-churned battle of silent retribution. He turned to the flicker of the flames. The familiar peace of their snap and crackle soothed his battered soul.

He flinched as Fortuna slammed the lid on her steeping pot, the sharp rattle pulling him from his turbulent thoughts. She brushed past him at the hearth, swinging her pot over the heat. When she spoke, her voice was heavy with foreboding. "If Cerys truly has found a way into her mind," she said, her voice raw with conviction, "we cannot risk Petronella waking. This is Moonveil. 'Twill keep her asleep. Whatever malign force is invading her will remain locked within her." She paused. Joran sighed, noting her hesitation.

"There's a but, isn't there?" he mumbled, too tired to think. "I can hear it."

"Moonveil is erratic," Fortuna said. "'Tis the strongest drug I can give her. But 'tis hard to measure the dose. If I get it wrong..." She gripped his sleeve. Dragged his gaze from the illusive peace of the crackling flames. "If I get it wrong, she could die. So, you must tell me now." He flinched at the question in her eyes. Her voice dropped. "'Tis your choice, Joran," she whispered. "Your risk. But we cannot afford mistakes. Not now. Too much is at stake."

He blinked and levered himself to his feet, his eyes already smarting as the Moonveil cast its pungent scent across the room. He could sense its effect already. A subtle blurring at the edges of his vision.

"Take that pot from the flame," he said. "Give her something else. Something to keep her calm."

Fortuna stared at him. "Are you sure, Joran?" she said. "Are you ready to face what Petronella could become when she finally rises?"

He met her gaze and raised his chin. For the first time in days, he found an iota of certainty in his conflicted heart. Something he could cling to. However small and desperate. "In all the time I have known her, Petronella has been strong," he said. "So, I must trust her now. As I would want her to trust me." He turned to the closed door, where Petronella lay locked in her own battle. Bowed his head. "I serve the Queen and the Mage. Always," he said.

CHAPTER 31
DOMINIC

T he fusty Seven Swords tavern failed to live up to the grandeur of its name. Following in Guildford's sweeping wake, Dominic's senses prickled with tension as the exhausted group crossed its grubby threshold. Rushlights strived to enliven the scene, fighting a hopeless battle against the coil of pipe smoke and the acrid plumes blowing back from a chimney that required sweeping. The tavern keeper's head jerked towards the door as they entered, passing from face to face, an acquisitive gleam in his pale eyes.

"Masters and mistress, how may I serve thee?" he asked, leaving the shelter of his bar and approaching them in the time-honoured fashion of greedy innkeepers everywhere, with much bowing and rubbing of thin, grimy fingers. Dominic felt Felicia's distaste as she shrank closer to his side. He left his hand on his sword. Readied the Mage power in his fist.

"My name is Guildford of Wessendean. We require food and lodging, good man," Guildford boomed, playing the part of King-in-waiting to the hilt.

Fingers tightening on his sword, ready to fight with a second's notice, Dominic held his breath. It was a risky strategy. Accustomed to keeping a low profile, he glanced at the motley patrons from beneath his hood, noting the covert looks and the low, questioning murmur issuing from behind glove-covered mouths. If they'd got this wrong, a rope for each of them seemed a likely outcome. Out of the corner of his eye, he watched as a serving wench slipped away through the back door. Putting distance between them and herself? Or simply to fetch food? She looked familiar somehow. He frowned as the atmosphere stretched. Everyone appeared to be staring at the tavern master, waiting to see which way he jumped.

"To be sure," the inn man said in answer to Guildford's request. "We've some room for ye if you don't mind sharing. Have a seat, masters. We will bring food and ale."

"Make it your best ale," Guildford said. He tossed his cloak aside as he spoke, revealing the weaponry he carried with casual ease about his person. "Our mounts require attention. You have stables, of course?"

The innkeeper stared at the hilt of Guildford's long, silver-chased sword and ran a tongue over his lips, his gaze darting to the broad shoulders of four men taking up residence by the fire. "We, er..." he faltered. Guildford slammed his hands on his hips. "You do not have stables? Then, of course, we must depart."

He waved his arm, turning on his heel. Despite his automatic contempt for the oily innkeeper, Dominic reserved a smidgeon of sympathy for him as the man watched the prospect of a month's takings dissolve in front of his eyes.

"Nay, er, we have stables, to be sure!" he said. His tremulous gaze met the raised eyebrows of the fireside group. They stood as one, their bulk blocking both light and heat. The air sang with the sound of unsheathing blades. Tables scraped across the floor as the patrons dragged them to the walls. Preparing for a fight.

"You were saying?" the leader of the group advanced a pace, the light of battle in his narrowed eyes. "We have paid the stabling fee for our mounts and our beds for the night," he stated with quiet, implacable certitude. "'Tis a chill night, Master Forsyth. I'm sure you would not wish us to make our displeasure known."

"Nay, Master Corn, of course, in other circumstances, but this is Guildford of Wessendean. A future king." High and stuttering, the man's voice put Dominic in the mind of a clucking chicken. He opened his channels, allowing just a thread of his telepathic ability to rise. A mere taste of his normal level. Just as quickly, he shut it down, but not before he'd registered another member of the fireside group and his questing mental signal. He frowned. What was that he'd heard in the instant their signals collided? A single name. *"Joran of Weir."* His eyes darted to the spare, muscled figure. Was it his imagination, or did the man favour him with the briefest of smiles? Could these be the friends Joran had mentioned?

"They're Blessed," he breathed to the others. "The tallest is a telepath."

"Guildford of Wessendean." The leader of the group rolled his tongue around the name. "Now there's a legend if the stories are true. Tell me, good sir," he said, his voice convivial but with an underlying current of menace that sent a spike of unease across Dominic's senses. "Is it true you have turned your back on our Queen? Are you ready to take the throne of Epera?"

Silence. Every eye and ear in the place turned to Guildford. The young would-be-monarch paled. His eyes darted to Dominic, looking for support.

Jaw clenched, Dominic drew his sword. "Who are you to ask?" he demanded. The challenge rang in the fetid air.

"Terril Corn, at your service." The older man's voice was flat. "Who are you?" His eyes took them in, lingering on Dominic, travelling upwards to Guildford, whose head nearly brushed the tobacco-stained ceiling. Drifting to Aldric, tense and tall. Clem, standing ready. Felicia was trembling. Dominic could feel her light shudder against his ribs, where her arm pressed. He glanced at the tallest member of the group. The telepath. The man wore an intricate tattoo. It ran down the side of his left cheek, clear to see. His eyes widened as he recognised the intertwining symbols, the sign of the Mage in a fantastic embrace with the sign of the High Priestess of Oceanis. He'd seen both sigils in

Joran's palm occasionally in the past but never etched so proudly on a man's cheek. Clear to the world.

"Who do you serve?" Dominic demanded.

Terril's dark eyes glinted with amusement. "Ourselves, mostly," he said.

Dominic's fingers tightened on his sword hilt, the metal warming beneath his grip as he measured Terril Corn. The man's casual stance belied the power radiating from him and his group. A coiled spring, ready to strike. "Ourselves, mostly," Terril had said. A dangerous answer, and one that left everything and nothing on the table.

Dominic lowered his blade slightly, though his guard remained raised. "Ourselves, mostly," he repeated, his tone equally non-committal. "That sounds like the words of men who value coin above kings. Or perhaps..." He let his gaze drift to the telepath's tattoo, lingering meaningfully. "...men who have loyalties that run deeper than declarations and thrones. Which is it, Master Corn? Should I sheath my blade? Or prepare to cross it with yours?"

Terril's lips curled into the ghost of a smile. "That depends on your answer, sir. What brings you here with this so-called King of Epera? Are you here to claim a kingdom? Or to burn it down?"

The tension in the room thickened. Guildford's chest swelled, his jaw working, but Dominic cut him off with a subtle shake of his head. This wasn't a fight they could win through bluster. These were men who thrived on certainty, not showmanship.

Dominic stepped forward, his movements deliberate. He sheathed his sword in a single fluid motion and extended his hands, palms outward—a gesture of peace. "We are travellers, nothing more," he said, his voice calm but firm. The tall telepath's eyes sparked as they registered the sign of the Mage in Dominic's palm. "The road is long, the night is cold, and the enemies of Epera grow stronger with every passing moment. If you're looking for loyalty, you've found it. But if you're looking for fools, you've misjudged your quarry."

Terril studied him for a long moment, his expression inscrutable. The tattooed telepath shifted slightly, his head tilting as though catching an unheard whisper. Dominic felt the faintest brush of thought against his mind and immediately fortified his mental shields. The telepath's smile widened, a flicker of acknowledgement passing between them. Dominic did not miss the subtle dip of the chin he directed at the leader.

Apparently satisfied, Terril nodded. "A fine answer, sir. And one worth hearing." He gestured to the seats by the fire. "Sit. Eat. The night is bitter, and we may yet find common cause."

Dominic hesitated, his senses still alert, but he caught the flicker of relief on Guildford's face and the tension easing from Aldric's stance. He glanced at Felicia, her trembling subdued but not gone. Doubt stabbed at him. Had she known this would happen? Or had her vision been incomplete?

"We thank you for your hospitality," Dominic said, inclining his head. "But the night's peace will depend on more than words. Trust is earned, Master Corn. Let's see if you're men worth trusting."

Terril chuckled, his deep voice a rumble. "Fair enough. We could say the same about you."

He raised his eyebrows at the nearest group of revellers. A broad smile swept his cheeks as he relieved them of their rickety table and waved them up. "We require your seats, good sirs," he said cheerfully. "I'm sure you have had your fill tonight?"

Grunting and grudging, the ill-favoured few gave up their seats, casting lowering glances over their shoulders as they shuffled out, deprived of entertainment. Terril deposited the extra table next to his own and arranged the seating to his liking. A dull murmur of conversation resumed, the atmosphere lightening gradually as the innkeeper relaxed and broached a cask of his brew.

"Welladay," Terril said, spreading his legs wide, enjoying the warmth of the fire. "Sit. Tell your tales. I'm sure you have many."

"What about the horses?" Dominic said, staring at the top of Terril's head. Despite the man's apparent congeniality, certain issues were yet to be settled. "They are tired. We must settle them for the night. Elsewhere, if not here..." His gaze roamed, piercing the walls, wondering where he would risk leaving their precious mounts. Not to mention their depleted supplies. The journey ahead was like to be uncomfortable, to say the least.

"Sit, sir." The telepath eyed him with a burning intensity. "There will be room for your mounts. Fabian will see to it. You can trust him. He likes horses." His spare smile lit his lantern jaw.

"I can, can I?" Dominic said, raising a tired eyebrow. "What if he takes it into his head to sell them?"

"I wouldn't." So far, the youngest of the group had taken no part in the conversation. Dominic put him in his mid-twenties. Still wet behind the ears compared to the other men. Still, the dark eyes were watchful, his actions quick and smooth as he helped himself to ale. A knife hilt decorated with gemstones gleamed at his hip. His bow, leaning against his chair, would require magnificent strength to wield with skill.

"We'll go with him." Aldric raised an eyebrow at Fabian. "And see to the horses. Won't we, Clem?"

"If we must," Clem growled, but there was no bite in it. The two had spent much of the last two days bickering, enjoying the cut and thrust of their mutual banter. Dominic's lips curled in a half smile as his men departed, relaxing fractionally as the serving wench returned and thrust a pewter tankard full of apple-scented ale into his grubby hand.

Guildford, never out of sorts for long, was already engaged in conversation with the stern-faced telepath. Felicia raised her brows as the maid insinuated herself between them.

"Seen you afore, I have," she announced casually, slipping into Dominic's lap, agile as a cat. He choked on his brew, conscious of the warm pressing of her buttocks against his starved groin. "Passed through here before, haven't you?"

Felicia glared at him over the top of the maid's braided curls, her expression sharp enough to cut wood. Guildford looked over with surprise flaring in his pale eyes.

He raised an eyebrow. "Really?" he rumbled, glancing sideways at Felicia. "Brave man."

The maid wound a finger in Dominic's hair and snuggled closer. Embarrassment clawed at him. He moved to tip her off his lap, but she tucked her head into his neck.

"Beware, my lord," she breathed. "The man you scalded last time you bided in Thorncastle saw you arrive. He was seen passing messages to Dupliss just a couple of days ago. You scarred him, and he vowed his revenge. It won't stay quiet here for long."

Pressing a light kiss against his cheek, she removed herself from his lap and held out her hand. Dominic pressed a coin into it.

"Don't worry, mistress," the girl said, catching the edge of Felicia's ferocious stare as she tucked the coin into her stays, "your man is safe from me, but he'd better keep his wits about him." Felicia's mouth thinned. Stifling a giggle, the girl took herself off, collecting empty tankards on the way back to the bar. Dominic watched her retreating and flicked a glance at the far corners of the room, noting the subtle shifts among the patrons. A couple of men playing cards exchanged a look before one slid to the door. The informer and his pig-like friend were not in attendance, but that was slim comfort.

Terril regarded the exchange with a gleam in his eye. "A likely lass, to be sure," he remarked. "Seen her before, eh?"

"She tried to stop a fight when we arrived here a sennight back," Dominic said, ignoring Felicia's glare with difficulty. He shifted uncomfortably under his heavy cloak, pushing it from his shoulders as the warmth from the hearth spread heat through his exhausted body.

Terril sat back, nursing his tankard. The firelight threw shifting shadows on his craggy features. His eyes ran over the group, taking in their travel-stained garments, their tired faces. "You've come a long distance, by the look of ye," he muttered. "The roads are no safer than they used to be, eh? I've heard there's trouble from the north. Armies stirring, allies turning. What brings you here with a would-be-King in tow?"

Dominic shrugged. "The same trouble that stirs us all. Allies may turn, but the right ones always find their way back." His stare met Terril's over the edge of his own cup. The older man's head dipped in recognition. He reached into the folds of his cloak and withdrew a slim roll of parchment.

Dominic raised an eyebrow as Terril unrolled it on the table between them. The sullen candlelight cast a red glow over Joran's familiar signature. His breath hitched. The Prince's mark was instantly recognisable. As emphatic and impatient as the man himself. Terril watched his face as he read the few spare words. "Dominic Skinner, travelling south. Give aid." He exhaled his relief, his heart racing as he scanned Terril's broad, inscrutable features. Aid he may have found. Trust would have to wait. Under the table, he reached for Felicia's shaking fingers. Squeezed them between his own with quiet reassurance. She returned the caress, but tension claimed her face and stretched her skin thin across her fine, drawn features. As delicate as a vase about to break.

"Aye, lad," Terril said, his voice a harsh whisper. "You've found us. Joran's old crew. We'll get you down that river. But she's a treacherous mistress, running fast. And the enemy's close. The price may not all be in coin."

Chapter 32
Joran

A tableful of reproachful faces greeted Joran later the same day as he entered the Council Chamber for their weekly meeting. Taking brief pity on his' pinched expressions, Joran ordered more fuel for the fire and slumped into his chair. Outside, pristine snow had given way to heavy rain that sent tendrils of dampness through every crack and crevice. It filled the air with a chill that seemed to seep into bones and souls alike.

Lord Colman sneezed, his flaccid cheeks red with fever. Sir Hollingworth perched spritely as a carrion bird over his ledgers, sharpening his quills with meticulous fervour. Sir Fellowes poured himself a glass of wine, his movements heavy with the fatalistic air of a man enduring a long, thankless sentence. None of them were talking to each other, Joran noticed, peering at them over the rim of his goblet. The secretary shifted in his seat and dipped his quill into ink, poised and waiting.

"Welladay, let's get to it," Joran said, forcing a brightness into his tone that he was far from feeling. "Who would like to complain first?"

Sir Fellowes huffed a sour chuckle through his moustache. "Why, Sir Hollingworth," he said dryly. "Let's get the best news over with. You are bursting with joy, I can tell."

The Lord High Chancellor took his time arranging his papers, each movement deliberate, calculated. "Financially, I suppose it could be worse," he announced at last, tracing his quill down a long line of figures. "The Battonians accepted our proposals for increased copper exports. Their consent arrived two days ago. It goes a long way toward balancing our books."

Joran dipped his head in acknowledgement. "How long is the agreement?"

"'Twill take the better part of a year to fulfil." An unfamiliar expression crossed the chancellor's features; a smile, fleeting but present. Joran raised his eyebrows in faint surprise.

"Then my congratulations," he said. "That is good news indeed."

Sir Hollingworth straightened in his seat, his narrow shoulders drawing back with quiet satisfaction. "I had an excellent emissary," he said. "She will go far with the right support."

"Oh, yes? And who did you task with this mission?" Joran asked, already half-guessing the answer. "Not Domita Lombard, by any chance?"

The chancellor's thin lips twitched with rare amusement. "I sent a bird to her," he said. "Lady Lombard agreed without hesitation. Seems she has a mission of her own, and they need the metal. She placed an additional order for swords and light armour on the Lombard family's account. The Gods know what she's doing down there."

"Up to no good, I don't doubt," Joran said, allowing himself the ghost of an inward smile. The Court of Air was a less cheerful place without the spirited warmth of Petronella's best friend and confidante. She had left the castle a year ago in response to a summons from her family, and they'd heard little since. "You've done well, Chancellor. Proof that this council can act with strength, even in times of trouble."

Sir Hollingworth puffed out his chest, a faint smirk curling his lips. "Strength, yes. Though I wonder, my lord, if strength in words alone will suffice."

Joran's brows drew together. "State your meaning plainly, sir," he said, his voice clipped. "I have little patience for riddles."

Hollingworth cleared his throat and waved a hand as though brushing away his own comment. "Only that the court clamours for news of our Queen," he said. "They have not seen her in weeks. They worry for her health. 'Tis unsurprising, under the circumstances..." His voice trailed off, his glance darting to the others as if seeking support. Finding none, he pressed his lips into a tight line.

"You speak out of turn, Chancellor," Joran said, his tone sharp as the rain rattling against the windows. "The Queen's health is no concern of gossipmongers. She is receiving the best of care and is recovering. That is all anyone needs to know."

Sir Fellowes shifted uncomfortably in his seat. Lord Colman sniffled and blew his nose.

"Aye, of course, of course," Hollingworth said quickly, raising a hand in placation. Yet a hint of smugness lingered in his tone, a faint smirk tugging at the corners of his lips. Joran's eyes narrowed as he caught the expression, his irritation sharpening.

"Yet you must see, my lord," Hollingworth pressed, "that appearances matter. The Court of Air wishes to see both their monarchs united and strong. If she could just..."

"Enough!" Joran's voice cracked through the chamber, reverberating against the stone walls. The secretary flinched. His quill slipped from his fingers and splattered ink across his parchment.

The councillors froze, startled into silence as Joran rose to his full height. His gaze swept over them, dark and unyielding. "The Queen's welfare is not up for debate in this chamber," he said, his voice low and dangerous. "If any of you dare to question her strength again, you will answer to me."

The Lord High Chancellor's face was a study in poorly concealed contempt as he ducked his gaze to his ledgers. His fingers fidgeted at his quills and ink pots. Sir Fellowes looked him over and rolled his eyebrows. "You spend too much time with your accounts," he said. "Now is not the time." He glanced around the table and settled his weight more firmly into his chair. Joran crossed his arms to hide their trembling and glowered through the window. Rain lashed at the windows like an angry mob, its rhythm a ceaseless reminder of the storm brewing both within and beyond these walls. Each drop seemed to hammer at his thoughts, demanding answers he could not give.

Sir Fellowes cleared his throat. Joran turned reluctantly. He could already tell from his trusted general's stiff posture that his news was not happy.

"Your report, Sir Reginald?" he requested.

"Aye, latest is that Dupliss was sighted moving down the Cryfell. They are but a seven night away from the castle." The general spat the words out like a mouthful of sour ale. Eager to be rid of them. Joran's spirits contracted. His heart squeezing under his thick serge doublet. "I suppose you are going to tell me that there is unrest in Blade and in the towns nearest to us," he prompted when Sir Fellowes paused, chewing at the ends of his moustache.

The older man sighed. "You have the right of it. We are questioning everyone on the main road to the castle and further abroad. There are no strangers here that we can tell. All can answer our questions and thus pass our tests. The witch is not yet here. For now."

"Always a but," Joran said. "You may as well say the worst out loud. Don't be shy. I am rapidly becoming acquainted with disaster."

"You are correct in your reasoning," Sir Reginald muttered, his voice gruff. "We have encountered more resistance amongst our Citizens. Blade's prison is full of detractors and sympathisers. Much as I loathe to admit it, Sir Hollingworth is correct. The people are worried and becoming more unruly by the day. They need sight of our Queen to steady them."

"My thanks for your vigilance, Sir Fellowes," Joran said quietly. "I wish the Queen were fit enough to show herself to our people. Unfortunately, her health does not permit it."

"Perhaps a proclamation?" Sir Colman suggested. His voice sounded hoarse. "I could draft one to be read in every town square on your command, citing the Queen's goodwill for her people."

Joran raised an eyebrow. "Exactly what are they complaining about?" he asked. "Is it the usual grumble about our taxes or something more?"

"Taxes, yes. But there are more accusations against the Blessed, that they are once more the chosen few, benefitting from the labour of the Citizens. Complaints about the Blessed using their magic unfairly against the Citizens. Even accusations against you, Sire. Some are saying the Queen is dead at your hand. Like father, like son, they say."

"They think I have murdered my wife?" Joran said. His soul stumbled from the thought. He clutched his stomach as it lurched in revulsion at the idea.

Completely oblivious to the reaction his comments stirred in the younger man, Sir Fellowes drained his glass. "Always the same," he mused, tipping the dregs into the fire and watching the coals hiss and spit. "Seen it as a raw soldier. Gossip and scandal. The only thing we have in our favour is that the Queen's Guard are uncommonly loyal these days. I've been searching for the traitor, but he's not here, close to us. I'm sure of it."

He glanced up, blinking at the complete horror clear in Joran's blanched face. "Do not concern yourself," he mumbled awkwardly. "I misspoke. 'Tis gossip. Just gossip..." but his eyes were worried.

Joran drew a deep breath, clenching his fists to remain in control of his emotions. He heard Sir Fellowes' words as if through a veil, the echo of his father's madness lurking in his thoughts. Was this how it had begun for Francis? The whispers of doubt, the fire of betrayal flickering at every turn? No. He was stronger than that. He had to be. An image of Petronella's pale, oval face, still as death, lingered in his mind's eye. He shuddered. Forced his battered mind to concentrate.

His wife's guard was on her side. That was one thing less to worry about.

"These sympathisers, are they all agitating to put Guildford on the throne?" he asked through stiff lips.

"Looks like it. To hear them, you'd think young Guildford was the second coming of the Mage and all his prophets," Sir Fellowes replied. "The Citizen King, they're calling him."

Joran gritted his teeth. "As far as I know, the lad's ambition stretches no further than the next keg of ale or willing wench," he said sourly. "But if he has designs upon Petronella's throne, I will take him to task myself." His fingers dropped to his dagger, caressing the hilt.

"Hmm. My last piece of news," Sir Fellowes said, taking out a slim roll of parchment. "My informant tells me he sighted Dominic Skinner and a small party, including Guildford and Felicia of Wessendean in Thorncastle." He paused, nibbling again at the edge of his beard. "You may not like this," he added.

Joran sighed. "It cannot be worse than the rumour I've murdered my wife. Say on," he encouraged.

"Guildford rode into Thorncastle waving at the crowd. They're calling him the king, my lord. My source confirmed it with his own eyes."

"By wind and storm." Cold fury rippled through him. "He actually called himself that? The King of Epera?" His thoughts twisted through his brain like a blizzard, chilling his heart. "Is that what your spy heard?"

"Nay, nay." His general blundered to his feet and held out a placating hand. "That's what the crowd called him, my lord. Guildford waved back. That is all he reported."

"'Tis what I said," Hollingworth said, taking a prim sip from his glass and wiping a drip of wine from its edge. "The people are crying out for leadership, and not before time."

Joran lunged. His dagger jumped into his hand almost of its own volition. The weight was familiar yet foreign, like a memory dredged up from another life. His breath caught as he saw the blood welling at Hollingworth's throat. A single drop, trembling at the edge of the blade. He could end it. End the whispers, the doubt. But at what cost? Hollingworth shoved his chair back from the table, leaning as far away from the point of Joran's blade as he could, his cold eyes narrowed to slits.

"My lords, my lords!" Colman grabbed Joran's wrist, his feverish grip surprisingly strong. Sir Fellowes, eyes bulging in alarm, leapt across the table in a single, impressive bound and hauled Joran back from the brink.

"Calm yourselves!" he demanded. "Hollingworth, apologise to the Prince Consort."

Glowering, Lord Hollingworth stood, smoothing his robes with hands that trembled. He wiped the blood from his neck with the same care he took in the collation of his rows of accounts. Locked his gaze on Joran. Reached for his books. Breathing heavily, hatred racing in his veins, Joran could only see the rows of names of innocent victims once inscribed with just such fastidious, cold-hearted indifference by Darius of Falconridge. The two men were the same in his view. Lower than reptiles.

"Get out of my sight," he spat. "You may leave your accounts and your chain of office. You are no longer welcome on my council. I relieve you of your position and all your benefits with immediate effect. Send your deputy to me for investiture within the next hour. You will leave my court by first light. Scribe, take the note."

Hollingworth raised a greying eyebrow and one shoulder in an insulting half-shrug. "Your court?" he sneered, throwing caution to the winds. "Perhaps. For now." Snatching the gold chain of office from over his shoulders, he flung it with a clang of metal to the table and departed the narrow chamber. Fighting his rage, Joran watched him go with fiery blood thudding in his temples. He could almost see a ghostly outline of Hollingworth's corpse lying dead in his chair. An alternative end to their argument. The council secretary huddled in his corner, wary as a rabbit. Firelight flickered in his pale northern eyes. The silence Sir Hollingworth left behind was suffocating, broken only by the faint scratching of the secretary's trembling quill. Joran could feel the weight of his remaining councillors' stares. Fearful, calculating. Sir Fellowes regarded him with weary resignation, sloshing wine into his glass with a hand that shook slightly. Lord Colman blew his nose again, his watery eyes lifting toward Joran with a mixture of dismay and pity.

What do they think of me? The question churned in Joran's mind like storm-tossed waves. *That I will not act when the kingdom teeters on the edge of ruin? That I will not face down those who threaten my wife, my children, my people?* Yet even as he sought to justify his outburst, guilt whispered insidiously at the edges of his thoughts.

Rain lashed against the windows, a relentless rhythm that seemed to echo the accusations battering his soul. Each drop felt like a condemnation. He rubbed a trembling hand across his face.

"They will betray you," the voice in his mind murmured, low and poisonous. *"You can trust no-one. No-one."*

Joran shivered, battling the darkness that twisted itself around the recesses of his thoughts. He could almost feel the icy tendrils of his father's madness reaching for him, the weight of Francis' sins pressing down like a hand on his shoulder. *No,* he vowed silently. *I will not fall like he did.*

A sharp knock at the door shattered the suffocating quiet. A guard stepped inside, his face pale and strained. "My lord," he said, his voice tight, "a messenger has arrived. He is wounded. There is fighting just south of here." The words hung in the air, heavy with dread.

Joran's chest tightened. The councillors exchanged uneasy glances, their eyes darting from the guard and back to him. The rain continued its assault against the windows, a reminder that the storms outside and within were far from over. Joran waved his hand. The bitterness in his voice as he spoke surprised even himself. "By all means, send him in," he said.

CHAPTER 33

DOMINIC

Much like the quality of its ale, the Seven Swords provided little overnight comfort to the travel-stained group. Guildford commanded a chamber to himself, daring any to ask why a would-be king would choose such meagre lodgings. Aldric and Clem bunked out of the inn altogether, preferring to set up camp in the stables to guard their horses. Kendrick lingered only long enough to see to their sledge, pulling it against a wall and securing a tarpaulin over its contents. Dominic did not see him go. Unwilling to let Felicia out of his sight, he spent an uncomfortable night in a ramshackle chamber, keeping her warm, miserably aware of the press of her slender thighs against his. She accepted his presence with little scruple. The chill of the night saw to that, but she refused to meet his gaze or answer his increasingly impatient questions.

Shivering in the stable courtyard the following morning, the dawn greeted the group with the sight of rain dripping dismally from gutters, stirring the melting snow to filthy streamlets of ordure and mud.

"Gods rot it," Aldric said, his face pale under his hood as Dominic emerged, towing Felicia behind him like a reluctant mare. "'Tis a full foul day to be setting off down the blasted river."

Felicia's icy gaze rested on him for a moment before flicking away. Dominic glanced at her. Mauve shadows dominated the hollows under her eyes. He wondered whether she had managed any sleep at all. "I need to see if they have heartsease here," she said before he opened his mouth. "I am going to the market. Guildford, you must go with me."

Stifling a yawn, her brother shook his tousled head. "Apparently, I'm a future king. We'd be mobbed or cut down in our prime. Surely Dominic can go with you. You'll be safe with him." He frowned as he looked between them. "What's to do? Have you had another falling out?" he demanded.

Felicia's shoulders twitched. "Nay, he just doesn't know when to stop asking stupid questions," she said, favouring Dominic with a scouring glare that triggered instant irritation.

"I'm trying to help you, and you won't talk to me. It's annoying," he shot back.

"I don't need your help," Felicia flung, tossing her head.

"Except that you do. To keep you warm, and see you fed, and protect you from all harm," Dominic murmured. His heart clenched in his chest, solid as frozen mud under the coldness of her attitude. He took her hand and bent to meet her fierce, icy gaze. "Pax, my lady," he said, for her ears alone. "You have my strong arm and my beating heart. Stop tearing strips from my pride with your fingernails."

Lips curving in a reluctant half smile, she allowed him to squeeze her fingers. "I am sorry," she whispered back. "I spent an ill night."

"I know. We are all tired, and there is still a long way to go." He held out his elbow. "Come, let's scour Thorncastle for heartsease since you require it. Clem and Aldric can see to the horses and our supplies for the journey. I have an errand with the local dovecote. I must inform Joran of our presence here and our loyalty to our queen. He will take it ill, else."

"What ho, travellers, are you ready to board?" Terrill asked, striding towards them from the gloom of the inn with the light of adventure in his gimlet-eyed gaze.

"We have some errands to run first, but aye, in the main," Dominic said. "We will meet you at the river dock when the temple bell strikes the call for morning prayers."

Terrill nodded shortly, settling his cloak more closely over his stocky shoulders. "'Twill do," he said. "Look for our boat, The Eagle. Only three horses and the barest of supplies. But bring blankets, weapons, and food."

"We'll be there."

Nodding his understanding, Terrill gestured to his team, and they melted into the damp mist. Grimacing, Guildford turned back to the inn. "What?" he demanded in response to Aldric's single raised eyebrow. "You want me to break my cover now and help you curry the horses?"

Aldric kicked moodily at the muddy wall. "Of course not, your kingship," he muttered. Tall at his side, Clem nudged him and whispered something in the lad's ear. Aldric's face split into a tired grin. "Aye. Good idea. Why don't you settle our debts?" he said. "That'll give you something useful to do. A king with a conscience. Give the townsfolk something to talk about."

"Good King Guildford," Clem added brightly. "It has a ring to it."

"Hah," Aldric said. "If he's the King, then I'm the Mage reborn."

"I'll thank you to treat me more kindly," Guildford growled, pulling his purse from beneath his doublet. "Or it's the block for both of you when we get back."

"Shut up!" Felicia hissed, rolling her eyes at their chortling. She tugged her hood over her tangled braid. "You don't know who might be watching." Her face tightened, her knuckles tight at her throat. "Come, Dominic, let's go now," she said. "I can feel the visions battering at my mind. There is little I can do to stop them without the herb."

Dominic's face softened. "Aye, love, I understand," he said, glancing at the others. "We'll be travelling light from now on. Transfer our goods from the sledge. Aldric. See if you can find a buyer for what remains. We may as well salvage something from what we have left."

"Aye," Clem tipped a brief salute and turned on his heel. Aldric's eyes sparked at the idea of trade. "I'll get us the best price I can," he said, rubbing his hands as he followed Clem to the stalls.

"Stay with them, Guildford," Dominic said, his gaze ranging upwards to meet Guildford's troubled gaze. "But be on alert for trouble. Not everyone is happy with the idea of you gaining the throne."

"I know it," Guildford said. His voice pitched low. "I have an uneasy feeling. Someone tried my door last night. And it wasn't the tavern wench because she was already in my bed."

"In Gods' truth, do you ever stop?" Felicia demanded, facing him with her hands on her slender hips. "You must indeed be short of company, brother. 'Tis time we found you a wife."

"Hey! I've been traipsing across the wilderness to get here. A willing companion and the comfort of a barrel of ale is the least I need," Guildford said, staring down his nose at her. "Don't thrust your nunnish manners on me, sister."

"Don't call me a nun!" Felicia said through clenched teeth.

"Stop acting like one, then," Guildford snapped back. "I see the way you treat Dominic. 'Tis poor of you, Felicia. Especially when I know you love him."

Felicia took a step back as if he'd struck her. Her eyes flicked to Dominic, full of alarm and guilt.

"Enough, Guildford," Dominic bit the words out, his own frustration warring with his loyalty to Felicia. "'Tis none of your affair."

Guildford glowered. "'Tis what she'll get if she questions my life again," he said, squaring his shoulders. "I'll meet you at the dock." He marched back to the inn, slamming the warped door shut so hard behind him the windows rattled.

Dominic stared after Guildford, his fists tightening at his sides. The man was insufferable, but his words lingered like an echo in a cavern.

When I know you love him. Did she? Dominic wasn't sure what scared him more; the possibility that Guildford was right or that he'd never know for certain.

Felicia's retreating figure disappeared into the misty morning, her cloak whipping behind her like a storm cloud. Muttered curses reached his ears, sharp and bitter. He sighed and started after her, pausing only to glance at the sledge against the wall. A corner of the tarpaulin flapped loose in the wind, exposing a small gap where a crate should have been. He frowned.

"Aldric!" he called over his shoulder. The lad poked his head around the stable door, a curry comb in hand. "What?"

"Check the sledge. See if everything is there," Dominic said. Aldric's brow furrowed, and he shuffled over to inspect the load. Dominic quickened his pace toward the market, his unease growing. The group's supplies were their lifeline. If anything was missing, it would cost them precious time to replace.

He caught up with Felicia just as she reached the edge of the market square. Stalls sprawled before them, their tarps sagging under the weight of rainwater. Vendors huddled under makeshift awnings, their faces pinched against the cold. The air smelled of wet wood and sour vegetables. His magical senses prickled at the sight of pale faces talking behind their hands. The suspicious gazes cast their way from under sodden hoods.

Felicia moved with purpose, her eyes scanning the stalls. Dominic matched her pace, his boots squelching on the muddy cobbles. "You didn't have to run off," he said. "We're in this together, remember?"

Felicia's lips tightened, but she didn't look at him. "I need heartsease, Dominic. That's all."

"And if you don't find it?" he asked, his voice low. Her steps slowed. She turned to him so suddenly that he almost knocked her over.

"On the riverbank that morning," Felicia began, her voice faltering, "I saw a vision. I talked about the Grayling again, didn't I?"

"Aye, you did, what of it?" Hating the fear in her eyes, Dominic touched his fingers to her soft, lowered cheek.

"Dominic, tell me true…" He bent to hear her whisper. His senses clouded with her familiar, elusive scent. "It was just me that time. You didn't see…him…did you?"

"Nay, my love." He put both hands on her face, lifting her gaze from the puddled ground. "I saw only you. The Shadow Mage does not hold you now, Felicia. I wish you could believe it and trust yourself." *Trust me.* His mind whispered his deepest wish. He bit his lips on the urge to say it out loud. "There was no sign of the Shadow Mage," he repeated more robustly. A passing matron threw him an alarmed glance as she brushed past them, signing the Mage's symbol protectively over her matronly bosom.

Felicia swallowed. "No sign of him," she murmured. "But there was once. There was…"

Shivering in the chill mist, Dominic waited, hoping this might be the moment Felicia opened her heart to him. Once more, he watched as she closed down. Clenched her fists. Turned away. "There. We'll try there," she muttered, shaking herself free of his gentle grasp. *I can't trust Felicia.* The thought came to him like a warning. He watched her determined progress, the tail of her cloak twisting through the growing bustle like an adder. Sinuous and evading. Defensive and dangerous. Perspiration prickled the back of his neck. *Please let Sir Dunforde be the traitor,* he prayed in the dark recesses of his mind. *Dunforde or anyone else, but not her. I couldn't bear it.*

"Storm's a-coming," his ears caught the edge of someone's conversation as he followed her. The words sent a shiver through him. He drew his cloak closer to his neck, splashing through stagnant puddles, dodging the odd, bedraggled peasant, the reek of damp wool and sweat in his nostrils. *Storm's a-coming.* Less a warning. More a prophecy.

Desperate for heartsease, Felicia stopped at every likely stall. Her face took on a pinched, haunted quality that grew darker at every shrug of refusal. Dominic followed her progress with half his gaze on her, mindful of the tense, shifting crowd. His shoulders twitched as he marched beside her. The prospect of confrontation was almost more intimidating than the real thing. His hand caressed the hilt of his old dagger under his cloak.

Snatches of conversation reached his ears as they progressed. Much about the prospect of the new King Guildford and what his reign might bring. The people of Thorncastle talked little of Petronella. It didn't surprise him. The Queen's popularity faded the further north in Epera one travelled. That much had become obvious to him over the last few weeks.

"Swept through here like a spring gale with extra men. From Falconridge!" one stalwart member of the town militia said, his voice reaching easily over the bustle of trade. Seated on a bench under a skeletal tree, breaking their fast with a hot pie and mulled ale, Dominic exchanged an alarmed glance with Felicia. She brushed crumbs from her lips. Her shoulders hunched to her ears, and she made to rise. Frowning, Dominic shook his head and lowered his gaze to his wooden tankard, listening for all he was worth. Encouraged by the audience of his fellows, the speaker squared his shoulders and took a mighty gulp of ale. "Count Dupliss," he said, raising his voice slightly in competition with the clanging, metallic din erupting from the blacksmith's shop nearby. "Never thought to meet him. Knows how to order his troops, though. I will say that. Aye, I will. If he says Guildford will rule, we should believe him."

"To Dupliss." The group lifted their tankards in salute. Dominic leaned closer, his grip tightening on the tankard as he forced himself to remain seated. A confrontation here would be foolish, but the urge to defend Joran and the Queen burned in his chest.

"Where are they headed?" one man asked from the edge of the group. His tone was so bland it was impossible to tell which side he favoured. Dominic took a mouthful of pie, fanning his mouth as the gravy scalded his lips.

"South," the speaker muttered, wiping a ring of ale from his bearded upper lip. "To the castle. The entire country is rising. I tell you, 'tis but a matter of time until Dupliss pronounces Guildford as our king. With the Queen dead, who will take the throne but him?"

"Joran of Weir?" the same mild tone, even in dispute, inserted itself like the point of a blade into the older man's argument. Risking a glance over his shoulder, Dominic's eyebrows raised. A tingle of apprehension spiked in his blood. The fourth member of Terrill's group had said nothing the previous evening. Though tall and sturdy, the man appeared to have mastered the art of blending into his environment. Unthreatening. Almost invisible in his ordinariness. Dominic couldn't even remember his name. And here he was. A buzzing fly, gathering information.

"Pah. That wastrel? Spends all his time clinging to the Queen's skirts, playing with his children, and trying on new doublets." Dominic's muscles bunched in automatic protest at the slur. He threw his shoulders back, ready to rise and spring to Joran's defence as a chorus of agreement erupted in the group. Felicia's iron-hard grip on his thigh pinned him to the bench. She jerked her head to the river. Blood boiling, Dominic grimaced and tossed back the last of his drink. He exchanged a glance with Terrill's man. A cynical smile on his lips, the spy melted unnoticed into the crowd.

"By the Mage's balls," Dominic swore as soon as they were out of earshot. "Playing with his children and trying on doublets? The Gods-blasted cheek of the man. I should have put a dagger through his rotten heart."

"Just as well you didn't, or we'd never get out of this rat's nest," Felicia muttered. "Look," she pointed at a rundown stall at the edge of the market. "That's the last one we haven't tried."

Rolling his eyes, glancing around for the fourth member of Terrill's crew, Dominic followed her, his boots splashing through shallow puddles on the cobbled street. The rain had lessened, but the air was thick with moisture, clinging to his skin and seeping into his bones. "Felicia…" he began, but she silenced him with a look.

"I don't want to talk about it," she said flatly. Her pace quickened, her braid bouncing against her back as she wove through the market stalls. Dominic's frustration simmered, but he bit back his retort. Now wasn't the time.

Dragging his feet as Felicia lengthened her stride, Dominic's gaze caught on a group of vendors huddled under a tattered awning. Their whispers carried faintly on the damp air, just loud enough to reach his ears.

"…trader from Hartwood came through at dawn. Sold half his load for a pittance, then vanished."

"Odd, that. Looked like good wares, too. Tools, tents…"

"Hope he's not looking to undercut the guild. Those types bring trouble."

Dominic slowed his stride, the words gnawing at the edges of his thoughts. *A trader from Hartwood? Dawn?* A chill that had nothing to do with the weather crept down his spine. "Felicia, wait," he called, but she didn't stop. With a curse under his breath, he cast one last glance at the murmuring vendors and hurried after her.

By the time he caught up, Felicia was leaning against the edge of a stall, her face pale and drawn. The merchant, a stooped old woman with hands like gnarled roots, shook her head. "No heartsease, love," she said, her voice creaky but kind. "Not this time o' year. You'd have better luck come spring."

Felicia turned away without a word, her shoulders slumping. Dominic reached for her, but she shrugged him off. "Let's go," she said, her voice thin and brittle. "There's nothing here."

"Felicia…"

"I said let's go."

Her tone brooked no argument, and Dominic bit back his protest. He fell into step beside her as they made their way back toward the river docks, his fists clenched. The market square faded behind them, but the tension in his chest only grew, along with a rare fury. *Where's Kendrick?* he wondered. *If he's taken our supplies, how will we make it? And Felicia... I'll have to watch her from now on."* It was a gloomy prospect. Had he been wrong about her all this time?

"I must find a dovecote," he said, squinting at the surrounding buildings bundled close to the busy river. Despite the weather and the time of year, the Cryfell was a lifeline for Thorncastle. Dozens of boats crowded at the busy dock, taking on supplies. He could see their patched sails from here, bobbing and rolling, eager to embrace the wind. The air near here smelled of riverweed and rotting vegetation. "I need to let Joran know what is happening up here. He's running out of time. We all are."

The tolling of the temple bell broke across his words. Its deep chime reverberated through the air. A prickle of sleet stung his eyes. Dominic glanced at Felicia, her face hidden beneath her hood. The sound seemed to weigh on her, her steps faltering for just a moment before she pressed on.

"Storm's coming," a voice muttered from a nearby alleyway. Dominic's head snapped toward the sound, but the speaker was already gone. His grip tightened on his dagger. *You don't say,* he thought grimly, his eyes scanning the street for unseen threats. There was none he could see, but the pounding of boots behind him snapped his attention backwards. Aldric and Clem jogged towards him, their cheeks scarlet in the chill.

"Have you seen Kendrick?" Aldric gasped, heaving air into his lungs.

"He's taken our goods," Felicia said. Her voice was quiet. Flat.

Aldric's mouth closed. He exchanged a quick, surprised glance with Dominic. "Aye. Scoundrel," he panted. "Must've needed the money for the return trip to Hartwood."

"He could have just asked me," Dominic said, his voice tight. "I would have paid him."

"Not as much as what he'd get for our gear."

Dominic grimaced, kicking himself for assuming Kendrick would wait for payment. Amusement and sympathy warred for control of Felicia's expression.

"You knew he would steal from us? Why didn't you say?" Dominic asked, needled into taking her arm. Felicia shrugged. "Because we don't have time to look for him, Dominic. We must hurry," she said.

Hurt at her lack of trust in his judgement, Dominic scowled at her. "You should have told me," he muttered. "We could have done something. Unloaded the sledge..."

Felicia sighed. "You don't understand the first thing about Farsight," she said. "You think a Seer's visions are easy to see? To interpret? The future isn't set, Dominic. It's more tangled and more fragile than anything you can imagine. I see possibilities. Many of them. I can only use my judgement and my intuition to focus on one that is the most likely outcome." Her voice dropped to a whisper. "'Tis tiring. Confusing. Frustrating. I hate it."

Aldric's eyes widened at her words. "So not everything you see will come true?" he asked.

"Exactly. The trick lies in the Seer. The ability to judge wisely, without bias." Felicia's shoulders slumped. She looked exhausted. "I am trying to protect you all as best I can," she muttered.

Dominic raised an eyebrow. "Forgive me for saying it doesn't always feel like that," he said, squeezing her shoulders. He'd said it to lighten the mood. The glare Felicia flung his way told him the small joke had misfired.

"He didn't take everything," Aldric said, filling the awkward gap. "But he took the tent. Some tools. Things he could sell. We have enough for now, Dominic. Truly."

Dominic pinched the bridge of his nose, his mind racing. "Mage take it," he muttered, his voice low. "We're running on scraps as it is."

"Ho, there!" Terrill's deep voice cut across their conversation. He pounded the damp cobbles towards them, snatching at his hat as the breeze threatened to steal it. "What are you about? Where are your goods? Come, we must be away. The weather is turning, and 'twill take some time to balance our load."

"Gods blast it." Dominic gestured to the market. "Aldric, go collect our gear and find Guildford. Drag him out of bed by his hair if you have to. I must send a message to Joran. Let him know what is going on. Warn him, somehow. Gods only know what they must be thinking at the castle."

Aldric frowned. "All is ready," he said. "We but came to tell you about Kendrick."

"Well and good. Felicia, you go with them. Ride Kismet for me." She jerked her head at his brusque command.

"Aye, sir," she said with grim irony.

"Please," he supplied.

"Better."

They parted company, but Dominic's thoughts clung to him like the damp air, heavy and unwelcome. Above him, messenger pigeons wheeled and darted against the iron-grey clouds, their restless flight echoed the turmoil in his mind. Felicia's words lingered. *"I am trying to protect you as best I can."* He wanted to believe her; he needed to, but doubt gnawed at the edges of his resolve. She was his love, his heart, yet her shadows stretched too far for him to ignore. The Shadow Mage. The mines of Traitor's Reach. Two years under Cerys Tinterdorn's hand. Felicia had endured a crucible of torment, her scars hidden but undeniable. Her fear haunted him now, as much as her sporadic use of heartsease. He bit his lip, the splash of his boots against the cobbled street muffled by the weight of his unease. How much of her was still bound to that darkness? Could he trust her with the kingdom's future or with his own heart? Reaching Thorncastle's dovecote, Dominic scribbled his message to Joran with a trembling hand: *"My lord, we are heading your way with TC. Dupliss is closing on the castle. We are loyal. D."* Pricked by doubt, he duplicated the message and sent a second pigeon skywards as security. A bitter realisation settled over him as the birds disappeared into the slate horizon. He didn't truly know Felicia at all. Worst of all, he wasn't sure if he ever would.

Chapter 34
Joran

Joran's fist closed on his dagger as the guard moved from the door, making room for the newcomer. Sir Fellowes rose to his feet, his shadow reaching before him. Leaning heavily on his pike, a dark-haired young man shuffled in. His cloak dripped mud on the ancient flags. Beneath his dented helmet, a crude, bloodstained bandage circled his head. His face was pale beneath his weathered tan. Joran exchanged glances with Sir Fellowes.

"Your name, Pikeman?" the general barked.

Dazed eyes turned upwards to the taller men. *Concussion,* Joran guessed.

"Your name," he commanded, more softly, when the man said nothing. The soldier ran a narrow pink tongue over his parched lips.

"Betts," he murmured. "Betts, they call me. By your leave, sir."

"Pikeman Betts..." Sir Fellowes cocked an eyebrow at the guard. "Do you know this man?" he demanded.

"Aye. He's my wife's brother," the guard said, his brow furrowing.

"Good. Ask him something only you and he would know," Joran said. He waited, tapping his fingers on his thighs, his blood racing through his veins as if it were on fire.

The guard raised an eyebrow. "Surely, Sire," he said, turning to his fellow soldier. "Albert Betts, do you know me?" he asked.

"Aye, of course," Betts responded. His gaze wandered around the chamber, taking in the forbidding expressions of the wealthy lords ranged in front of him.

"What did we eat at our last meal together?"

A slow smile crept across the wounded man's lips. "Our Margaret's ale pie and roasted apples," he said. "I could fair do with some now."

The guard clapped him on the shoulder and jerked his stubbled chin. "Aye, lad, that's right," he said, his tone softening. "What news do you bring to his lordship?"

"Goldfern has turned to the Citizens," Betts said. His tone was dull, the words slow to escape his lips. "There was fighting. Some of Goldfern's Blessed escaped into Oceanis. Captain Lyons wanted someone to tell you in person. He's holding out as best he can. But the Citizens want Guildford, my lord." He scowled as he said the words. "'Tis uncanny," he added, "like a plague sweeping through. So much hatred, all at once. I never knew that before. Mostly, Goldfern's packed with the Blessed, being so close to Oceanis. But now? The Blessed are falling over themselves to leave. The Citizens are celebrating in the streets."

"Like before," Sir Fellowes muttered. "Just as it was before."

A chill ran down Joran's spine. "Take your kinsman to Master Mortlake," he said to his guard. "See to his wounds and let him rest."

"Aye, Sire." The two men shuffled out. Joran paced the room. Frustration bled through his thoughts. "What can we do against this?" he demanded of his two closest councillors. "There is blood on every side. Betrayal. Turmoil."

Sir Fellowes grimaced. "I will send reinforcements to Goldfern," he said. "But we don't have enough loyal troops to contain the unrest in every major town. This is beyond a mild rebellion now. This is civil war."

Joran stared at him. Beyond Sir Fellowes' craggy features, his mind's eye dealt him a vision of bloodied corpses. His muscles ached as they once had on the battlefield. His heart pounded. Almost as though he was fighting still, breathless and outnumbered. Counting down the bodies as they fell under his flashing blade. Through the condensation-smeared window, the sky was black with the oncoming storm. Riding the rising wind, the castle starlings reeled and writhed in the air like tortured souls, folding their wings and taking shelter as they always had within the ancient castle walls.

"We must stay alert," he said, hating himself for the hollowness of his own words. His inability to protect his kingdom. "'Tis all we can do now. I can feel her coming. The black witch and her borrowed army. Her very breath stains the air."

Sir Fellowes placed a bracing hand on his shoulder. "We are not dead yet," he declared. "And we won't be until I say we are. Take heart, my lord."

"I will see to the defence of our granaries," Lord Colman said softly. "We can last a long time in the castle, my lord. Do not despair."

Joran shook his head. "I can feel her," he said. "Closing in. We must question everyone. Trust no-one in the castle. Anyone you do not know, who cannot vouch for their identity, send to the dungeons." Nodding at his councillors, he turned to the door. "I must go to my family," he muttered. "Let me know the minute there is more news."

"My lord..." Colman raised a hand, but Joran didn't wait to hear what his chancellor had to say. He forced his weary body through the castle halls, noting with half his mind the heightened activity. The sense of disorder and confusion amid the castle residents, noblemen and merchants both. The servants pressed themselves against the walls to avoid his fierce gaze, although Joran barely saw them, such was the turmoil within him. His boots pounded through the corridors, anxiety forcing him to a faster pace. Suddenly, he found he was running. Fierce and swift, low to the floor, like a hound following a scent. Closing on an unseen quarry. The strange thought grew in his mind as he reached the long gallery, where the remaining courtiers warmed themselves at the hearth and clustered at the windows, pointing at the incoming storm. He could feel their puzzled glances chasing him as he swept through, a cloud of gossip rising behind him. He ignored their shouted questions. Their requests for his attention. There was something he had to do. Something important.

Panting up two more broad flights of stairs, he juddered to a halt at the doors of the . They stood open, inviting scholars and scribes into their world of books and knowledge. Oil lamps illuminated the long chamber. The air was thick with the smell of ancient parchment and ink. He frowned, confused. The urge to run had left him, but he couldn't imagine why it had led him here. This was Petronella's realm. Never his. There were few knowledge seekers in the chamber today. A scatter of papers littered the desks closest to the door, abandoned by their readers. He supposed dinnertime must be close. The day was so dark it was hard to guess the hour. A muffled voice from deep between the crowded shelves trickled to his ears. Two voices. One deep and rumbling, the other a tinny, familiar treble. His brow contracted. He swept through the room, his cloak stirring a thin film of dust from the floor. The huge librarian's desk, once occupied by Petronella's grandmother, Theda Eglion, stood vacant near the enormous hearth. The current Chief Librarian, Eoghan Cunningham, was nowhere to be seen. His lips thinning, Joran tracked the voices, pacing past the tall, heavy bookshelves, his shadow flickering before him as he crossed and re-crossed the light from the lanterns.

"Theda. What are you doing in here?" Fuelled by his clawing anxiety, Joran's voice thundered down the long line of shelves in the economics section. A slight figure beneath his dull scholar's gown, Master Cunningham jumped. He wheeled around with one narrow hand clutched at his heart. "By all that is holy. Prince Joran, thanks all the Gods," he said. He stood aside. Theda's pale face peeped from behind him, her dark blue gaze innocent as a daisy. Purple shadows highlighted her pinched cheeks. "Hello, Papa," she said.

Alerted by the deep scowl on Joran's face as he closed the distance, Master Cunningham raised a nervous hand to the book trolley at his side. "I just found her here, my lord," he gabbled. "Says she's looking for a book."

"A book?" The thought sent a shiver across his shoulders. Uttering a sigh, Joran bent to his daughter and gathered her in his arms. She snuggled into his embrace. "What book are you looking for, my poppet? Do you not have enough fairy tales in your chambers?" he asked, striving for a normal tone.

Theda leaned away from him, squinting in her familiar way to meet his gaze at close quarters. She shook her head, her tousled curls dancing. She'd clearly just roused from sleep and escaped before her maids could make her tidy. Joran smoothed her hair automatically, taking comfort from the familiar weight of her against his chest. "Hey?" he jogged her, raising a rare smile. "Whose tales do you want to hear? What about Father Bear?"

She shook her head again, enjoying the game. "The Yuletide Fairy?" Another shake. Another giggle. "You must tell me, then," Joran said, running out of titles for books he knew Theda loved.

"We have to find a special book," she breathed, leaning close to whisper against his ear. "'Tis a secret. You mustn't tell."

Joran froze. His gaze darted to Master Cunningham, who had returned to his trolley and was busily re-shelving his precious titles, humming under his breath, oblivious to the dawning scent of danger. Twisting on his heel, he searched the shadows, his heart racing. Was Cerys Tinterdorn here already? Had she found a way past the guards?

"What book is this, my poppet?" His voice was taut. Harsh with suppressed panic.

Her hair brushed his cheek, softer than feathers. "Just a book. The lady said she wants it." Joran closed his eyes, dismally unmanned by the single tear that fell from his eye before he smeared it away. His skin crawled. Was it his imagination, or did he feel a gentle touch on his arm, the subtle stroke of a woman's perfume hanging in the air? A faint, savage whisper. Not a threat. A promise. *"I'm waiting..."* His jaw clenched, every muscle in his tired body tense.

"Can you see her now, my sweetling?" he managed.

"Nay. Not now. But that's what she said before, I remember." Theda twisted in his arms, her feet dangling as she tried to disentangle herself from Joran's clutching hands. "Can we look for it, Papa? Perhaps she'll go away then."

He swallowed, hoisting her up. Hating to use his strength against her will.

"Nay, we can't." He marched out of the library, ignoring her protests. "That lady is nasty," he said as he strode back to the nursery suite. "Whatever she told you. You must not listen. Promise me, Theda. 'Tis important."

"But why, Papa?" Theda's voice rose with protest, choked with sobs. "She said she needed it. She said she'd hurt Mama if I didn't find it."

"Oh, Theda." There were no words in his vocabulary simple enough to explain it. Even dosing her with heartsease couldn't keep Theda's shadows at bay. All his doubts kept time with his thudding feet as he left the room. Marching like the enemy's boots across Epera's soil. Battering his pride. Reaching the nursery door, he threw the door open and walked into the middle of an argument. The two guards snapped to attention. Little Bird and Maria gaped in surprise. Maria dropped into a curtsey. Little Bird bobbed and hurried across the chamber, relief and irritation struggling for supremacy across her face. "You found her! Thank the Gods! We only just found out she was gone."

Joran ignored the accusing look Little Bird threw at her fellow nursery maid. "She was in the library," he said, brushing her aside and marching into his children's bed chamber. Ranulf scattered tin soldiers as he raced across the room and threw himself into Joran's one-armed embrace.

"They won't let me run in the corridors, Papa," he said, "and I want to see Mama. What is happening?"

By the Gods, I wish I could answer that. The thought flashed across his mind and vanished beneath the onslaught of dread coursing through his body.

"Mama is ill," he said. "And you children must stay here. 'Tis not safe to roam the castle alone." He met his son's wide-eyed, confused gaze, forcing himself to remain calm for their sake. "Ranulf, you must promise me. On your honour as a Prince and Knight to protect your sister. Theda... " He unwound her arms and sat on her bed with his daughter on his knee. Ranulf dashed across the chamber and retrieved his small sword. He took a defensive stance, proud to obey his father's command. His expression was a picture of such boyish resolve, Joran's heart clenched in his chest. "That's it, Ranulf," he murmured. "My brave prince." He gave Theda a little shake to get her attention. "You must stay here, my sweetling. Just for now. It won't be for long. I promise. Let Little Bird and Ranulf look after you."

Theda glared at her brother. "Ranulf is stupid," she said.

Ranulf glared back from his station close to the door. "Am not."

"Are."

"Neither of you is stupid," Joran declared, bouncing his daughter onto her bed as he stood. "But you must stay here. I will return later."

Ruffling Ranulf's hair, he left the room, closing the heavy door softly behind him. In the outer chamber, caught in remorseless rage, Little Bird was berating Maria in the low language he remembered from his own childhood, struggling on the back streets of Blade, stealing what little food he could get. Under her verbal onslaught, Maria's flashing eyes wore the dazed expression of a person hit over the head with a hammer. He blinked. Little Bird could have been him as a youth. Scrappy. A survivor. The thought gave him strength somehow. *We both survived*, he thought. *And we will now. No matter what.* Raising his eyebrows at the impressive variety of swear words, he raised an eyebrow at Maria. The maid blanched, reading her fate there.

"You are dismissed," Joran said curtly. "Little Bird, discuss with Fortuna and find an obedient replacement. One who knows her place and will not spend her time flirting with the guards."

Little Bird turned, her face scarlet with embarrassment. Her hand flew to her mouth. "I'm sorry," she gasped. "I didn't hear you."

"By the Mage's hairy bollocks," Joran stated emphatically. His voice rose against a peal of thunder as the storm roared in and the shadows deepened. "If we survive long enough, I give you free permission to teach Ranulf every swear word you know. But before then, you must guard my children with your life. Do you understand?"

Little Bird's eyes hardened, one hand dipping into the pocket of her gown. It came up clutching a knife. The edge of it gleamed in the firelight. The girl handled it easily, with the ease of experience. "Always, my lord," she said.

CHAPTER 35
DOMINIC

B ad weather chased The Eagle down the Cryfell over the next few days. Tired and out of temper, Guildford had arrived at Thorncastle's river dock trailed by a bevy of smitten townsfolk and a local band of pipers playing 'Where the Robin Roves' in a key far stranger than the one in which it was written. An avaricious group of merchants accompanied the crowd, falling over themselves to tempt him with their wares. Flanking him, Aldric rode Hamil, steering the placid gelding easily with his knees, his bow already strung, his dark eyes bright and watchful. Clem brought up the rear, driving a narrow cart loaded with their packs, feed for the horses, and a waterproofed oilskin containing some food and their precious water skins. Surrounded by amateur drink-sodden musicians, he winced every time someone played a wrong note. Felicia rode Kismet, gripping her reins with white knuckles as the bay mare tossed her head and skidded over the slippery cobbles. The triumphant procession arrived at the riverside with Guildford in full king-in-waiting mode, his broad freckled face split with a charming grin, his pale eyes sparkling against his weathered tan. The cheers of Thorncastle's Citizens rang in the misty dampness. "King Guildford! Aid us!" "King Guildford, our Citizen King!" Even the ladies of the night, resident amongst the dockland taverns, were hanging out of their chamber windows to catch a glimpse. Dominic scuffed his feet in the shadows of the dovecote doorway, armed and alert for trouble, a deep scowl contracting his eyebrows under his hood. Aboard the bobbing Eagle, Terrill's men moved with the efficiency born of long experience, casting their eyes over the approaching cargo, moving boxes and crates to make room for the horses.

"Good people of Thorncastle!" Guildford cried as he reached the gangplank. He raised his hands, commanding their attention. "I go to claim a throne and a kingdom! Who will wish me good fortune?" The resulting cheers sent Kismet into a frenzy. Dominic sent a quick blast of energy her way. Felicia's pale eyes sought his as she sensed the invisible barrier blocking her progress. Dominic nodded at her. The last thing they needed was for Felicia to crack her head open on the cobbled stones of the jetty. He rolled his eyes as Guildford slid smoothly from the General's broad back and yanked the nearest maiden to his manly breast. She melted against him, her face rosy, and the crowd cheered some more. Felicia's face was a study of exasperation as she averted her eyes.

"Come on, Guildford," Dominic muttered under his breath. "That's surely enough kingliness to last a lifetime." He shoved away from the cold stone wall at his back and strode forward, holding Kismet's bridle as Felicia dismounted. Clem urged his carthorse towards the riverbank and hurled the tarpaulin aside. Together, they obeyed Terrill's direction, balancing the load according to his brisk instructions. Dominic eyed the rushing river with trepidation. The Cryfell in winter was a wild water rich in salmon. Not the flooded, untamed beast he remembered from his childhood, but a mighty force still, its swift black depths unknowable and menacing. Its rippling surface was an ever-changing study in grey and white under the sullen sky. The air was full of bird cries and the tang of iron-rich water. Felicia's face was white as she took her first hesitant steps aboard the low, broad-beamed vessel. Terrill settled her in the small shelter the boat provided amidships, hemmed by canvas sacks of horse feed and a barrel of small beer. They had to coax the horses aboard. Snorting and nervous, a sweating Hamil required a blindfold before Aldric could lead him onto the boat. Dominic provided a steady boost of power at the horse's rear to urge him forward. They secured their mounts to study iron loops at the rear of the vessel. Kismet's ears flattened in protest, and she refused the nosebag Dominic offered to her. The remaining space was slim. The weather bleak and closing. Beneath their feet, the deck writhed like an eel as the boat rocked at its mooring. Blowing lustily and beating time with their feet, the pipers danced to a wild rhythm of their own devising, their faces wild and feverish. Dominic's shoulders tensed as he took his place, glad for even this small distance between himself and Thorncastle, where the fraught atmosphere grew more strange and dark with every passing second.

"Ready?" Terrill waved them to the rails, taking his place at the tiller. "The day is already wasting, and we have far to go."

Guildford was the last to cross the gangplank, still waving to his adoring crowd. "By all that's holy, let's get going," he muttered to Dominic as Fabian cast off and the northerner hoisted their sail. "I can't stand much more of this. 'Twas a battle just reaching the dock. These people are odd. Overcome..." His forehead creased momentarily. The townsfolk watched. Eyes bright as starlings. Gossipy and alert. Still cavorting. Still cheering.

Dominic raised an eyebrow, his fingers white on the gunwale. "There's something very wrong here," he murmured. "None of these people are in their right minds." Skin crawling with trepidation, he grabbed the gunwale as The Eagle found the current, grateful to put Thorncastle and its manic, maddened atmosphere behind them.

As Terrill had predicted, the weather turned as they set off. They'd spent the last week locked in a miserable test of endurance. Uncomfortable in their damp boots, cursing the water that penetrated through their oilskins. Sick of the smell of pitch and manure. Cramped and miserable, the horses fared no better. Dominic spent as much time as he could with Kismet, offering her slices of dried apple, reassuring her as The Eagle bucked and bucketed down Epera's major watercourse, her single broad sail filled with wind and rain.

Distant squads of militia and soldiers tramped south through the muddy forests, taking advantage of the shelter of the trees. Dominic spotted them from time to time as The Eagle swept ever onward, grateful for the wind at their backs. The sight bred increasing unease through him the further south they travelled. So many troops. And from this distance, it was hard to pick out those loyal to Petronella from those hoping to place a Citizen King on the throne. Guildford observed the same sight, muttering under his breath. Shaking his head. Clenching his fists. "Not in my name," he murmured, thinking himself unheard.

The nights had been the worst. Not daring to disembark, they hauled into the nearest banks, sheltered by overhanging branches, huddled together under a stretched-out tarpaulin, nose to tail, shivering under their cloaks. One of them kept watch, warming their hands on the single oil lamp Terrill permitted. Squabbles broke out during the day for the rickety shelter available. Terrill and his crew eyed them with grim humour. Accustomed to the conditions, they ate sparingly and went about their duties as best they could. Dominic lent a hand whenever required, grateful for something to do. Felicia retreated from him. She didn't eat, turning up her slim nose as the bread grew more stale and the meat more salty. Wrapping her in his arms at night was like hugging a log. She was rigid with tension, the shadows growing darker under her crystalline eyes the further they travelled.

"How now," Terrill said as the light faded on the afternoon of the sixth day. South of them, the sky was taking on an ominous, sickly yellow, edged with deepest black. The harbinger of the storm. "Take heart, you land-loving folk. Thanks to this gale blowing from the north, we've made good time despite your grumbling. If we can keep the horses from kicking the boat to bits, we might just make it in one piece."

Clem and Aldric exchanged glances. The two had become inseparable over the last week, drawn together by a mutual dislike of travel by water and speculation about the groups of soldiers they spotted on the river road. Clem's fingers had grown more calloused. His voice hoarse as he dipped into his Mage's gift to soothe their tempers and calm the jittery horses. Guildford stared grimly ahead, bracing himself against the prow rail as if willing them faster. "I could murder a haunch of venison and a pint of Argentish," he growled at Terrill. "Please tell me we are within striking distance of the castle. If I have another mouthful of sour ale and stale bread, I will not be answerable to the consequences."

"We are nearly there," Terrill assured him. "One more night if the Gods are kind."

"If the Gods are kind," Felicia sneered from the shelter. "The Gods are never kind. Especially our God. We should land here. Go no further tonight." She pointed at the bank, where a coil of smoke curled beyond the treeline.

Dominic blinked at her tone. She glared at him from beneath her hood, putting him in mind of the malevolent gnomes of his childhood. The ones who haunted the shadows beneath toadstools. A shiver prickled the hair on the back of his neck. Felicia's eyes were clear of Farsight. But she'd grown almost completely silent over the last few days, apart from offhand comments like this.

"Why here?" he asked, out of patience with her evasion. "You keep trying to delay us. You've done it every single evening so far without fail."

"Aye, and you keep overriding me," Felicia returned, her voice resigned. "So, like Guildford, I am not answerable to the consequences." Her chin dipped until Dominic could barely see the pale crescent of her forehead. "I have tried to warn you..." her whisper trickled across the deck, claiming the attention of the entire company despite its low volume. "You should stop here for tonight."

Terrill glanced at her and then back at Dominic. "What do you want to do?" he rumbled. "There is still some daylight left. We are making good time." He raised a grubby, black-nailed thumb and jerked it south. "Castle lands yonder," he said. "Nearly there. It's a wild ride through Fortune Gully, but you'll see the battlements in the distance around the next bend."

Biting his chapped lips, Dominic leaned against the rail, rolling with the boat, conscious of the slap of water at its hull. The creaking of the ropes as they shifted and stretched. The wind blew steadily at his left cheek as he scoured the eastern banks. Birds were already drifting to roost in the bare treetops for the evening. His sharp eyes spotted the familiar shape of a peregrine falcon, soaring on the wind, eyeing the territory. Its sharp, wild cry seemed to urge him on, tangling with the rush and tumble of water and the sigh of winter singing through the forest. No buildings presented their familiar landmarks. They could be anywhere or nowhere. The half-edible aroma of rotting vegetation rose and creased his nostrils as they sailed past a patch of weeds, skeletal and tall in a rare eddy.

"Please, Dominic, listen to me." Felicia's hand on his arm made him jump. He hadn't heard her approach. "There is danger ahead. I saw blood and black water..."

He hardly heard her. The falcon wheeled, turning to the castle. *Petronella.* The name crept under the guard he placed on his telepathy, a harsh whisper. Chill as the winter wind. *Petronella.*

"Dominic, please," Felicia repeated. Her fingernails were sharp on his wrist. Sharp as a falcon's talons. *Petronella.* The whisper came again. And with it came a vision. A falcon's lure. The Grayling's jess, silver bells dangling. An empty perch. *Petronella...* He clasped Felicia's chilled fingers, the need for haste warring with the fear in Felicia's whisper. The savage clutch of her hand in his. "Please don't go further tonight..."

"Well? Anchor or continue?" Impatience laced Terrill's voice. "We must decide now. The current will take us to the gully else."

Dominic swallowed, his throat dry, torn between his growing mistrust of Felicia and the crushing certainty that time was running out. "She needs us," he said into the tense silence. "We press on." He heard Felicia's sharp dismay in her choked sob. She snatched her hand from his. Somewhere beneath the vision of his queen, lying still and silent in her carved wooden bed, he heard the ghost of laughter and a dark, acid triumph. His fingers tightened on the wet wood of the railing. Was he wrong? But it was too late to change his mind.

Terrill jerked his chin at his watchful crew and steered the boat once more into the central current. A savage gust of wind filled the sail, stretching it to its maximum. The horses whickered their panic as the vessel surged, soaring down the river on black wings, almost as swift as its namesake.

"By the Mage, Aldric, did you not tie Hamil tighter?" Clem snapped as the gelding threw back his head and lunged, his terrified whinny rending the air. He scrambled past Guildford to fasten Hamil's halter.

"I did," Aldric snapped back. "But he knows how to untie it."

"Blast it, keep those horses quiet," Fabian snarled, dodging a lashing kick as he bent to adjust the sail. "They'll have us all in the water, else."

Dominic avoided Felicia as she crept back to her shelter and dropped her head to her knees. "When it comes, don't say I didn't try..." her voice came to him in a tired whisper as he crossed to Kismet. He frowned. More unsure than ever if he could trust her. Cradling his beloved mare's tossing head, he rubbed her ears, murmuring comfort. She whickered, searching the folds of his cloak for a treat, thrusting her nose against his chest when he failed to provide it.

"I know. You are tired and hungry. I am, too," he whispered to her. "But 'twill soon be over. I promise." He turned his gaze back to the riverbank, scanning the dense, shadowy forest as the fading light played tricks on his weary eyes. The sun emerged, momentarily pale and shy as a bride, sprinkling diamonds across the waves. A sudden glint followed, piercing the gloom under the ancient trees. A sharp flash, unnatural in the dark underbrush. He froze, narrowing his eyes. Sunlight catching on polished steel. A shield? Or armour? The shimmer disappeared as quickly as it had come, swallowed by the shifting shadows as the boat dashed on and the sun retreated. In the distance, the sky was turning black. Ever ready for attack, his lips thinned. His hand crept to his sword.

"There's someone out there," he called, keeping his voice low lest it carry across the water.

"Where?" Aldric followed his gaze, loading his bow automatically and taking a wide stance on the rolling planks.

Dominic pointed. "Can't see it now," he said. "Back there. Close to the bank."

"Mayhap we'll out-run them," the Northerner said, joining them at the rail. "The river narrows just ahead, and the current is fierce. 'Twill bring us out at Fortune Hall. Do you know it?"

Dominic shrugged. "Aye. For a place with so grand a name, 'tis nought but a collection of fishermens' shacks," he said. "They supply the castle."

The Northerner grinned, his tattoo creasing on his cheek. "'Tis why they call it Fortune Hall," he said simply. "Those are a wealthy bunch of fishermen. With some very comfortable shacks." He stretched his back, easing out the kinks of confinement. "Do us good to put our feet on dry land," he continued. "And a fish supper. What say you?"

Dominic's stomach growled at the thought. He'd been trying to keep from thinking about food in the last two days as their supplies dwindled. He clamped his fist to his hollow belly, turning his gaze forward to the steepening banks on either side. "Whoever's out there, those cliffs will slow them down," he said.

"Aye. If they're not already there." Felicia's sarcastic voice at his back pricked his ire. There was no time to argue his case with her. Fortune Gully loomed, its massive cliffs crowded with rocks and scrub. The churning air was a mass of chanting birds approaching their roosts. The aged planks groaned and creaked at the savage current that bore them.

"Drop the sail!" Terrill shouted from his place at the tiller. "This is a fast passage." Fabian leapt to work, his broad shoulders heaving as he strained at the wet ropes. Guildford moved to help him, adding his strength to the task. The sail dropped to the deck in a cloud of canvas. Denied the added impetus of the wind, the boat slowed slightly while the water boomed beneath its broad hull, urging it remorselessly onward.

"Hold tight. Watch those horses. Dominic, you know what to do. Lads, man the oars. Steady away."

"Aye." Breathing deeply, Dominic raised both hands, funnelling his Blessed gifts into a halo of support around the three terrified, white-eyed horses. The boat rocked as it found the midpoint of the racing current, riding the bucking waves' last stretch. The voice of the river roared in his ears.

Green-faced, Aldric and Clem grabbed the gunwales, winding rope around their fists, bracing themselves as the boat plunged. Locked in concentration, Dominic gritted his teeth as Hamil kicked out, taking a chunk out of the worn wooden planking. "Keep steady, lad," he said, "won't be long."

He cast a quick glance at the shelter where Felicia huddled. He couldn't see her from the bow. "Hold on," he shouted.

"No, I'll just slide around and fall overboard like any normal person," Felicia shot back, her sarcasm even more grating than usual. Dominic rolled his eyes. He could tell she was terrified beneath her gallows humour. His heart racing, he sent a tendril of support to her, bracing his feet on the slippery boards. At the oars, Fabian and the Northerner strained every sinew to keep the boat on course as it entered the gloom of the ravine. Little light penetrated the narrow gap, hemmed in by the massive cliff faces on both sides. The shred of grey daylight in the distance glowed like a beacon, pointing the way to safety. The fourth member of the crew leaned over the prow, ready to shout if he spotted a hazard. Despite his terror, Clem was singing, his voice broken in places as the boat jumped and skipped, dangerously close to the rock-strewn shallows dashing the cliffs. The melody wreathed with Dominic's Blessed gift, twisting like smoke. Under its gentle caress, the horses calmed. Dominic exchanged gazes with the Blessed musician, appreciating his skill as their magic blended. Clem nodded back, still singing, his pale eyes turning gratefully to the end of the gully where the landscape flattened, and the river spread its watery arms once more into the surrounding countryside.

The passage narrowed in the last stretch, the jagged cliffs striving to squeeze the boat and all its occupants between them. Eyes wide with terror, soaked to the skin, his boots sliding uselessly across the deck, Dominic could have touched the slippery weed coating the tearing stone. He held his breath, certain the boat would dash itself against the rocks. Terrill gripped his tiller with both arms, a vein popping in his forehead, his dark gaze fierce as he tamed the vessel. Forced it to his will. Denied a victim, the river spat The Eagle out of Fortune Gulley like a cork from a bottle. The sudden flare of departing sunlight dancing off the water after the grim dark of the ravine was blinding. Thunder growled in the distance. Dominic blinked, rubbing his eyes. A grin on his face, Fabian worked his oar as the boat bobbed and turned in the last rush of rapids.

"Welladay. Always fine fun," he said, standing up and turning to look back at the clifftops.

The hush and whine of the approaching arrows took them all by surprise. Fabian staggered, staring in shock at the projectile piercing his left shoulder. For a startled second, no-one moved. Dominic jerked around and threw his hands out automatically, batting away the next volley, a shout of warning on his lips. A snarl twisting across her face, Felicia darted out of her shelter as Fabian's knees folded under him. The glower she threw Dominic's way was pure fury. She hauled at Fabian with surprising strength, dragging his tall body out of the way into the meagre shelter. Another volley of arrows sang in the air. His blood on fire, mouth set in a grim line, Dominic cartwheeled them away.

"Boarders!" The northerner leapt into battle like a demon, his tattooed face dark with concentration as he raised both sword and dagger in their defence. Aldric joined Terrill at the helm, firing arrows at the approaching forces, splashing through the shallows to their boats. Momentarily becalmed, sail down with no-one manning the oars, T

he Eagle was a defenceless bird, unable to fly. Drifting in the current, she wallowed in a random circle, approached on both sides of the river by soldiers in small craft, obviously stolen from the local fishermen.

Hamil's frantic whinny ground in Dominic's ear as a stray arrow breached his defences and pierced his flank. The gelding lunged at his ropes, hooves lashing. The boat shuddered under the onslaught. A jagged hole appeared in the worn planking. The Cryfell rushed in, quick to claim territory. Kismet's powerful whinny blasted the air as she tossed her head, pulling at her restraint, hating the sudden flush of water at her hooves and the smell of blood in the air. At the bow, Guildford fought back-to-back with the Northerner, face grim with purpose. His height and power were a formidable weapon against the swarming enemy. Blood and water stained the deck as his great blade flashed and descended. Guildford's victims floated face down in the water. Unable to attack with his gift, Dominic could only use it to defend, waving away incoming projectiles, trying to hold off the incoming boats. His sword waited at his hip. But there was little room to wield it at the stern without risking Clem or Aldric at close quarters.

The battle took place in surprising silence, broken by the shrieks and grunts of wounded men and the high, youthful, face-pitched wicker of terrified horses. The clang of steel and the stomach-churning noise of tearing flesh scraped prickles of dread down Dominic's spine. Joran's old crew were a formidable force, combining and recombining their blows and blades with the grim efficiency of battle-hardened experience. Barrels and bags rocked as the boat tipped, taking on water at an alarming rate. Risking a glance at the bank, Dominic's icy stare clashed with that of a much older man. Count Dupliss. Tall, thin and armoured in black, he oversaw proceedings with a tight smile on his face. Hands on hips. Sure of victory. "Dupliss is there, Aldric. Take him out!" Dominic hissed, sending a wave of power to fend off another volley of arrows fired from the cliff tops.

"Aye." Aldric whirled, notching his last arrow, his youthful face set and determined as he took aim.

Barely waiting to see if Aldric's shot hit, Dominic inched backwards as the river slopped around his feet and then his ankles. He stretched a hand to Kismet's halter, unwinding the rope with a tug and twist of his power. Freeing her. The boat was going down. He couldn't risk her going down with it. Not with the shore so close. Eyes wheeling, searching the skies for more incoming missiles, he performed the same duty for the other horses. There was a falcon up there, high above the next volley of arrows, circling. His cries excited and piercing as he soared, effortless and free on the chill of the gale. Something about the falcon's cry touched the wildness in Dominic's fragile heart. Spurred him on. A battle cry on his lips, he blasted another wave of arrows away, pulled his sword and leapt into the shipboard battle. His glance clashed with Felicia's as he darted past her shelter. She'd hauled Fabian onto her lap and bandaged his shoulder with grim efficiency. Her icy glare bored into his back as he engaged with one soldier and the next. There were no more arrows falling from above. But there was no time to process Felicia's attitude. Now, the fight was all about saving themselves. He risked a glance at the shore; Dupliss had vanished. The Gods knew where. Out of ammunition, Aldric lowered his bow. Lips pressed tight with determination, he fumbled for his light sword. Panting and red-faced, Clem battled next to him. Plunging his blade with fierce precision through a man's throat as he rose from a rowboat at the rear. The Eagle was tipping stern first. A cry from the bow jerked Dominic's attention to the Northerner. The telepath reeled, clutching his neck, his fingers slick with blood as it pulsed from his veins. Sickened, Dominic leapt to Guildford's side, almost tripping over the Northerner as he fell, eyes blank and staring. His blood flowed with the water boiling over the dark planks. *Blood and black water.* Felicia's vision. Now apparent. Side by side with Guildford, grim-faced, his heartbeat drumming in his ears, he added his weight to the fight. Fewer men approached from the bank. They were winning. Holding their own. His sword arm was tiring. He dodged and weaved in a daze of concentration, expecting any second to feel the deadly slice of a sword thrust. The punch of a blade.

The boat was sinking under them. Barrels and bags caught the current and floated away. Kismet's panic burned in his heart. He risked a glance around at her in time to see Clem's last strike, glancing off a soldier's armour and leaving a vast gap in his defence. Dominic's shout of horror came too late to stop Aldric. The lad raised his sword and blocked the blow that would have taken Clem's life. Dominic threw out his power, slowing the soldier's downward thrust. Even so, his heart contracted as the man's blade made contact, and Aldric stumbled into the water. The horses followed, white-eyed and terrified, heads held high as they paddled. Frantically searching the waves for Aldric, Dominic turned the steeds to shore, urging them onward, his heart in his mouth. There was no sign of Aldric. Abandoning his precious lute, Clem leapt into the freezing river himself, yelling Aldric's name.

There was no more time. At the bow, his boots skidded for purchase, his sword thrusts wavering as he tired. Shivering, Felicia levered herself from her shelter, waist-deep in water, one arm supporting Fabian's head. She'd fastened her travel bag over her shoulders, wrapped in oilskin. Her face wore a mask of sadness. Fabian's face was white.

"How many more of them?" Dominic demanded of her. "You knew this was coming, so you must know that."

"There is help," Felicia muttered. She jerked her head to the shoreline. "Watch."

Heartened by the resilience shown by The Eagle's crew, the inhabitants of Fortune Hall were inching from the shelter of their homes. Dupliss' force was depleted, the banks of the Cryfell draped with fallen soldiers like so many bleached and landed fish. Stealthy and determined, armed to the teeth with fishhooks and gutting knives, the fishermen slid into the water. Slipped beneath it like eels. Emerged like avenging sea monsters to split and gut the remaining soldiers. The Eagle sank with a protesting gurgle and sucked for a last breath of air as she disappeared beneath them. Felicia bobbed at his side, towing Fabian with determination. Brow quirking at her effort on the man's behalf, Dominic paddled madly, circling in the freezing current, spitting water, looking for Aldric. Ahead, the horses made landfall, shaking and bucking in a frenzy of deliverance. Guildford strode to the shore, his clothes soaked and clinging to him. Blood ran freely from a cut on his arm. Another at his waist. He turned and raced away as Clem shouted and pointed at a spot fifty yards further downstream.

Tired to the marrow of his bones, the usual result when his Blessed powers deserted him, Dominic's boots caught on the pebbled shore. He reached an arm automatically for Felicia, helping her closer, but his legs wobbled underneath him as he took most of Fabian's dead weight against his shoulder and forced himself the last few feet to land.

Aching in every muscle, his eyes flicked to Terrill Corn. The man stood with his hands on his hips, staring at the patch of river where his friend had died. The gaze he turned to Dominic was sad but resigned. "'Tweren't your fault, young 'un," he rumbled, reading the devastation and guilt warring on Dominic's face. "They were waiting for us."

"Aye." Dominic's mind was numb. His hand jumped from Felicia's sodden arm to drag her chin up. Weeds tangled in her hair. There were tears in her eyes. Or maybe it was just river water. But it was the expression on her face that made him falter. Made him hate her. Guilt. Pure, undeniable guilt.

"They knew," Dominic said, his voice hollow with disbelief. He stared down at her as if she was a stranger. Someone he'd never known. Could never know. "You're the traitor. You have been all along..."

"Dominic, please..." she held her hand out, her voice a whisper in the dull afternoon. The Cryfell dragged at his feet. Tugging him back to its chill embrace.

He shook his head, glancing down the riverbank to where Guildford returned at a run, carrying a precious cargo in his arms, his broad face clouded with fear. Frantic at his side, Clem herded him onward and pressed Aldric's copper-brown hand to his lips. Anguish in his face.

"If Aldric is dead, I will never forgive you," Dominic said. He could feel his heart shrivelling. A shivering, freezing mass in his chest. "I swear it on my soul." He turned from her. Left her staring after him as he ran to meet Guildford. Above his head, he barely noticed the circling falcon, but he felt its call. The haunted cry of an abandoned soul, naked and raw, pierced the wilderness of his heart. Felicia. His love. His dream. A traitor. Giving away her visions to their enemy. Tears ran freely down his face as he drew level with Guildford. Aldric's head drooped. Water ran from his nose and mouth. "By the Gods, Aldric, Aldric..."

They passed Felicia, still waiting on the riverbank. She'd sunk to her knees in the weeds at the water's edge, her shoulders shaking. For once in his life, he made no move in her direction. Had no desire to comfort her. Even Guildford ignored her. Ducking into the warmth of an unfamiliar cottage, hung about with nets, eyed by a wide-eyed parcel of children, they passed Aldric into the capable care of a matronly woman standing ready with blankets and salves.

Staring at his friend's pale, dripping face, Dominic's chest clenched with anguish and guilt. Clem's unceasing entreaties to the Gods and Guildford's barely concealed rage blistered his ears. But there was a yawning gap where Felicia should be. Missing from his side, but most of all missing from his heart. His gaze drifted through the open doorway where Felicia accepted help from another concerned fisherman. Her tear-stained gaze lifted to his. Dominic averted his eyes. He'd never felt so alone.

Chapter 36
Joran

F ortuna's back was turned to him when Joran entered Petronella's quiet chambers. Her shapely figure outlined in silhouette against an almost black backdrop of scudding clouds. Lightning flickered over the battlements. Thunder rumbled in reply. An ancient call and response. The rising gale rattled the windows in their panes. A draft crept into the chamber, stirring Fortuna's hair, playing with the edges of the paperwork on Petronella's desk.

She jumped at the sound of the door closing and whirled around, one hand pressed to her heart. "Oh, 'tis you. You nearly scared me free of my wit," she said.

"Apologies," Joran muttered, heading for the desk and a fresh flagon of wine. Fortuna had been busy in his absence, tidying the solar. Their blankets lay folded atop Petronella's massive oak chest. The mass of books and paperwork stacked in regimented piles on her desk. A snapping apple log fire blazed in the hearth. The chamber smelled of fresh air and valerian, steam issuing from the jug on by the windowsill where Fortuna had placed it to cool. Its green, herbal scent stung in his nostrils. Joran's lips stretched in a tight smile as he poured a glass, glancing at Petronella's closed door.

"How is she?" he murmured, taking a long drink. The wine slid down his throat like a benediction. Soothing. "Any change?"

Fortuna grimaced. "I hate to say it, but she is becoming more alert," she whispered. "I have given her valerian. Enough to knock out a person your size. I can still hear her talking, but..." Her hands twisted restlessly, playing with the many gold rings adorning her fingers. "I'm afraid," she said hoarsely. Her mouth twisted as the words left her lips. As if the thought of her own fear disgusted her.

"She's talking?" Joran took a stride towards his wife's bedchamber. Snatching her jug, Fortuna darted from the window and laid an urgent hand on his arm. "Don't go in there, my lord," she breathed.

He shook her off. "Why ever not? She's my wife. I must go to her."

Fortuna swallowed. "I'm not sure she is your wife..." she muttered. She hung her head. "I... I've locked the door, Joran."

"What?" He meant to roar. Instead, stifled by an instinctive superstitious fear, his voice emerged as a hoarse whisper. He took another sip of wine to soothe his dry throat, ashamed of the pulse of terror deep in his belly.

Fortuna raised her gaze from the freshly swept carpet, her forehead creased. "I heard two voices," she said after a pause. "Only one of them is our queen's."

Joran ran a tongue over his lips. "What did they say?" he demanded.

Fortuna shrugged. "I couldn't really tell," she admitted. "Sounded like an argument, but I dared not open the door in case..."

"I understand." Joran patted her arm, his mind racing. Fortuna's eyes were sunken in her head. The woman looked exhausted.

"I don't think you do," she muttered. "You are as tired as I am. Too much has happened. Neither of us is prepared for what may come."

He read the doubt of him in her shadowed gaze as clearly as if she'd shouted it from the castle battlements. "You mean I am not prepared," he said icily. He could see the pile of neatly folded blankets from where he stood. The sight of it spiked his anger. The order Fortuna created in marked contrast with the chaos that followed in his wake. Other people picking up the pieces of his failure and indecision. Dying of it. "I don't know why you hold back, woman. Just say what you mean."

Fortuna raised an eyebrow and put her hands on her hips. "You are right, my lord," she said, throwing her head back. "I do not think you are ready. You are tired. Volatile. Liable to commit errors of judgement. There. I've said it."

Errors of judgement... An image of his father flashed across his mind. Standing in that room beyond the locked door. Angry and vengeful. Looming over the dead body of his wife. Joran's mother. His chest tightened at the vision. He shook his head to dispel the image. Surely, it couldn't be his memory. He'd been but a newborn babe, lying red-faced and squalling in a crib by the hearth. Too young to remember. *It could be you...* The thought insinuated itself into his mind like a fly creeping under a milk cloth, tasting victory. His blood crawled. He dropped a hand to his dagger, comforted by its familiar feel within his clammy palm. The handle felt colder somehow. A reminder of all the choices that had led him to this point. Fortuna remained where she was, stoic and determined.

Joran's eyes narrowed. "Rest," he suggested, his jaw clenched. "I will stand guard here."

"Nay, I can't leave you with her," Fortuna said. She chewed her lip, her trepidation clear in the look she gave him. Uneasy. Reluctant. Her rich brown eyes travelled to the silver chased edge of the dagger, ready in his fist. "The Shadow Mage is here, Joran. Whatever is in that chamber with her wants to control her. If it controls you as well, we are lost."

Grabbing at the edges of his reason, he nodded. Drew an unsteady breath. Reining his anger and panic in before it overwhelmed him. Fortuna was right to urge caution. But there were other matters, just as important.

"I just found Theda in the library, looking for a book," he muttered. "She says the woman wants it and will hurt Petronella if she doesn't get it. It must be this Book of Shadows. The witch thinks Petronella knows where it is."

Fortuna's brow cleared, but her unease remained. "And our queen is not telling her." She stood a little straighter, glaring at the bedchamber. "Even so overcome, she is still strong," she said, wonder in her voice.

Joran raised his eyebrows, acknowledging Fortuna's words. His gut twisted at the recognition of his own failure.

"Goldfern has fallen to the Citizens," he murmured, staring into the swirl of the deep red Argentian he held. "Our queen lies here, battling a witch for control of her mind, and I cannot contain a few rebels." His voice was rich with self-loathing. *What am I? Not a King. Not a leader. Just a man afraid to face his own fears.* His fingers clenched on the fragile goblet. Tightening with the weight of doubt in his mind. "They want to place Guildford in Petronella's place. Her rightful Gods-blessed place. Gods blast them. Damn them all." He paced the room. Blood-red wine spilt over his shaking fist. "They don't deserve her. None of them do." He slammed his goblet onto the desk. It broke with a small, ordinary, insignificant clink. Fragile and ominous within the building weight of the storm. Fortuna flinched as he strode to the bed-chamber door, straightening his shoulders, clutching his dagger.

"Nay, Joran. Wait. Don't," Fortuna gasped. She grabbed his sleeve. "You don't know what is in there with her. It will consume you, like your father..." She stopped, trembling for once under the force of his rage.

"Damn him, and damn you as well. You think I'm not strong enough to face it? Is that it?" Joran wrenched his arm away from her. "Gods take it. This is my wife. I will not desert her like all the rest. I will not!"

"Joran, you are *not* ready. This darkness... This isn't just in Petronella. It's in you, too. Please, don't let it swallow you whole. Please!" Thunder deadened Fortuna's plea as he turned his back on her. The roaring of a sky god. Urging him on? Bidding him to wait? He couldn't tell. His heart pounded in rhythm with the storm, every beat another lash of panic. Suffocating. Inescapable. Swearing under his breath, his heart racing, he strode to the door and fumbled at the latch. The heavy black key fought him. Grating in the lock as if it, too, would deny him entrance. The door itself felt cold under his hand. Theda and Ranulf flashed across his mind in the instant before he turned the handle. Their laughter. Their tears. His heart ached for them. If he failed... His jaw jutted.

"Watch my children," he snarled over his shoulder. He took a step. The snick of the door closing behind him felt like the snapping jaws of a trap.

He blinked in the gloom. His breath clouded before him as he shuffled through the darkness to Petronella's bedside. A candle burned on the mantel, its light casting a flickering montage of shadows against the panelled walls. Petronella's fire was lit, but the warmth did nothing to dispel the chill in the air. Just as the single candle only highlighted the darkness. It clung. Oily and thick. To the walls. To the heavy, embroidered hangings surrounding her bed. Anger and rage only took him so far before the hopelessness reached for him. Found his doubt. Wrapped it in its gloating arms. *Here you are*, it seemed to whisper. *I've been waiting for you for so many years.* His breath constricted in his chest. The booming thunder battering the castle echoed the beating of his heart. Her curtains billowed in the draft from the juddering window.

Swallowing hard, he looked at the still figure on the bed. The change in her dragged a shocked gasp from his lips. He swayed on his feet as his world slipped into nightmare. A dark and twisted counterpart to the brightest of his memories. They'd made love here. Held each other. Rocked with laughter. Nursed their children. His mother had died here. An innocent victim of one man's jealousy and rage and another man's weakness. Petronella's father and his own. Joined forever in the annals of history. Darius of Falconridge. Francis of the

Eagles. Even dead, their malign influence lingered. Reaching beyond the sanctity of death to manipulate the puppet strings of the living.

Almost in a trance, he sunk to his knees at her side and reached one trembling hand to hers. Beneath his reluctant gaze, the light from her diamond danced. Ever on the move, shifting from dark to light, quicker than thought. Locked in place, her fingers clutched at her staff. Under her pale blue lids, almost translucent, her eyes moved like someone in a dream. Her lips were flaking, the surrounding skin dry and cracked. The small mound of her pregnant belly jutted obscenely from her fragile hips. Dark shadows under her eyes and the hollow of her cheeks.

"Oh, my love," he whispered, his heart breaking. "My beautiful, beautiful love."

"Joran..." Her soft whisper in the dimness made him jump. He squeezed her hands and then dropped them, afraid he might break her. Conscious of the fragility of her bones in the strength of his grip. Fragile as a bird's. So easy to snap.

"Petronella, my darling. I'm here. Wake up, wake up!" He bit his lip, cursing the tears that tumbled freely from his heavy eyes. He turned, automatically looking for Fortuna. Anticipating her practical good sense. Her arrival with food, or water, or medicine. But he'd shut her out. They were alone with the sneering, watchful darkness.

"Joran..." her voice came again. He had to bend to hear her. Her breath was acrid. A faint, tainted lavender drifted from the linen.

"Aye..." He closed his eyes, yearning for the touch of her. Her wry humour, her quick, assessing mind. "Tell me," he whispered. "Help me save us all."

"Can't." Her voice was so tired. Bleak. Walking a vanishing line between despair and death. "She's strong. Growing closer."

"I know, love." His words matched Petronella's for bleakness. He'd clung to a cliff face once. Clutched desperately at slender, slippery vines, his feet scrabbling for the most shallow of footholds. The two-hundred-foot drop into Goldfern Falls had yawned at his back. Jaws wide, ready to claim him. Petronella had saved him then. Thrown him a hasty lifeline. Dragged him to safety. He realised suddenly that he'd never really thanked her. And now, here he was again. Still expecting her help. He shook his head, rubbing his face against her heavy coverlet. *By the Gods, man. Think of something.* But his brain was gone. As tired as hers. The chill was creeping into his bones. Perhaps they could both die here. Drift into a peaceful oblivion. The thought was comforting.

"Don't give up."

As ever, she read his mind. He blinked in the stuffy, chilly darkness, wondering if he dared open his telepathic channels to her. Just as quickly, he decided against it. Cerys was already here. Too close. Stalking Petronella's very thoughts. Lightning flickered, pale against the windows, and disappeared. Chased by the crack of thunder.

"I won't give up," he assured her.

"Oh, I think you will give up. The question isn't if you'll give in. It's when. You've already lost. I have already won, Joran of Weir. And I have all the time in the world to wait for you to break." Gasping with terror, he jumped from her side. Petronella's voice had changed in a heartbeat. This was stronger. Harsher. The flat croak of the blackest of crows. His hand jumped to his dagger, his skin writhing with disgust. Anger and dread clawed at him.

"Get out!" he shouted. "Get out of her mind, you disgusting parasite!"

"Oh, and how you fear me," Cerys Tinterdorn's voice said. Her tone dropped, smug with satisfaction. "I'd say, judging from your complete failure, victory is mine. Don't you agree? You are half out of your mind now and like to remain so. Weak. Just like your father."

Horror-stuck, Joran backed off, fingering the hilt of his dagger. "You have no right to judge me." His voice panted in the suffocating atmosphere. More like a trapped animal than a powerful monarch.

The thought dragged his gaze to the Ring of Justice resting on Petronella's heart. The stone drew his attention, as it always did. He could just make it out between his wife's tense fingers and her grand-mother's staff.

"I don't have to. You are doing so well, judging yourself." Cerys's withering words taunted him as he waited, frozen in the moment, unable to move either forward or back. "Look at you. Blown this way and that, lost and alone without your precious wife telling you what to do. You make the game too easy, Joran. Has court life and all that automatic deference made you soft? You weren't always like this, were you?"

Joran clapped his hands over his ears. The room swam in front of his eyes. "Stop talking, witch. I won't hear you..."

"All those battles... Remember them? Twirling your sword about, thinking yourself so strong. Look at you now, cowering like a scared puppy. You are weak, Joran. Unfit. You've always known it. I am just waiting for you to prove it to yourself."

"No." The word came out more like a sob.

"Yes. Your father didn't want you, did he? Got rid of you as soon as he could..."

"Please...stop... Please, just die..." He lurched to one side, support-ing himself on the wall. Pressure built in his chest. He couldn't say where it came from. An urge to scream. To wail. Like an angry child. Like a baby howling for its mother. "Don't..." He took a huge breath, forced his eyes open. The Ring of Justice had slipped from Petronella's chest, dangling like a child's toy on a chain. Mouth dry, his fingers twitched, reaching for it.

"Hah. I can see you want that trinket," Cerys sneered. "You are as fit to take it as the lowest peasant. Try it, why don't you? See what your precious Mage thinks of you then." Scrubbing the back of his hand across his mouth, Joran eyed the distance. He could snatch it, perhaps, and then...and then...

Cerys's mocking laughter burned in his ears. "Go on," she hissed. "Use it. I'm here. Inside her. Go on. You could kill me. It would all be over."

The casement behind him creaked open on the force of the storm, the draft cold and damp at his neck. He crept forward, dagger out, his eyes wild and searching the haunting shadows. They seemed to reach for him. Spectral fingers clawed his sleeves, urging him on. "Go on..." Cerys's voice dropped to a guttural hiss. Taunting and devious as the most experienced harlot. "It's the only way you'll save her. If you kill me..." she added when he hesitated. "And I know you want that more than anything. Even more than your precious throne. And your Gods-blessed wife."

Sheer hatred propelled Joran to Petronella's bedside. He loomed over her, his knife in his fist. The ring filled his gaze. He didn't even have to take it. He could just slide it on... No-one would know. They'd think she'd died of illness. Disease. Hunger. He swallowed, his breath as shallow as Petronella's. She was near to death, anyway. If it worked. If he killed Cerys... His throat dry, he watched his own hand slide out, his dagger poised to strike. Petronella's eyes opened. But they weren't hers. These eyes were dark as night. Filled with derision. Waiting. Sure of her victory. A ghoulish smile stretched her dry lips. A trickle of blood followed.

"I'm dying, anyway," she said. "End it. And then you can end yourself." Grimacing at her eyes in Petronella's beloved face, he raised his knife, his shadow blending with the ones climbing over her. Inside her. Inside them both.

A delicate chime sliced the thick atmosphere. The Grayling's jesses, decorated with bells, dangled from his empty perch, tossing and flickering on the breath of the storm. The noise grew louder. More urgent. His head turned reluctantly, following the familiar sound, his mind churning with doubt and dread. He blinked, half hypnotised by the gentle motion of the leather straps. Was the wind and the storm

in the room with him? Or was it in himself? Pushing and pulling.
Demanding.

"Joran, my love." Petronella's voice filled his head, soft and yearning.
A sudden image of her face turned towards him. Her smile, warm and
intimate, meant just for him.

"You never had the strength to lead, did you? You're nothing without her. Just like your father... Just like the man who abandoned
you." Cerys' voice again. Mocking. "Take the ring. Use it. Be the
King she deserves." The Grayling's jesses spiralled in the increasing
breeze. The chink of the bells loud against the storm in his mind.
Petronella's precious falcon. A memory of beating wings floated across
the quagmire of his mind. The Grayling. Flying towards him through
a whirlwind of darkness, the Ring of Justice clutched fiercely in his
beak. The diamond, flashing in the light, tumbling towards him. And
Petronella's voice. "It's yours. Take it. Please take it..."

His heart juddering, he sheathed his dagger. Hugged his hands to
his chest. The damned bells were still ringing. A clarion call, promising freedom. He backed away, footstep by terrified footstep. Forcing
himself against the pressure to act. To raise his knife. Bring it down.
Take the ring. The force of it beat in his skull, shoved at his shoulders,
urging him back to the bed. Tears streaked his cheeks, and he held on,
his feet scrabbling for purchase. "No, I can't, not yet. It's what she
wants."

The door refused to open under his clutching fingers. Panicking,
his palms damp with perspiration, he fought with the handle. Desperate to leave. Desperate to stay.

"You haven't won, Joran of Weir," Cerys taunted him as the door
cracked open, spilling candlelight into the darkness. "I am still here.
Waiting for you."

Joran slammed the door on her words, stumbling on the thick rug,
snatching for his breath. Vomit erupted from his mouth, scalding his
throat as his stomach reeled. Wine and bile spewed blood-like across

the priceless carpet. From somewhere, he heard Fortuna's startled gasp. The rustle of her skirts as she approached with cloth and bowl. Rolling over, he turned his face from the floor. Little Bird, her face pale and delicate as a daffodil in springtime, loomed close to his. Her eyes bright and watchful.

"I nearly did it," he gasped hoarsely. "I would have killed her. My wife. My Petronella..." He clutched at the girl's rough hands like a man on the edge of a cliff, scrabbling with terror at the yawning chasm of madness opening beneath him.

"'Tis alright, my lord, you didn't hurt her," Little Bird murmured, patting his shoulder. "You couldn't."

CHAPTER 37
DOMINIC

"Will he live?"

Dominic's voice sounded harsh above Clem's babbling. The sturdy matron glanced at him from under greying eyebrows, brushing a strand of hair out of her eyes.

"If the Gods will it," she muttered, waving them aside. "Stand away, let me see."

"He has to live. He has to. We've been through so much together." Dominic's fingers shook as he reluctantly stepped back, exchanging a grim glance with Guildford. Aldric's face was so pale, his lips blue. By the Mage, he couldn't lose another precious friend. Teeth chattering, overwhelmed with fatigue, he slumped suddenly on the settle by the fire. A pot bubbled there, but the enticing aroma of fish stew failed to gain his attention. He held his breath as the elderly woman stripped Aldric's shirt and checked him for further injury.

"No cuts. He's just bruised," she reported shortly. She pressed his chest. "Now breathe, lad," she said, setting herself more comfortably at his side.

Fighting his exhaustion and desperation, Dominic watched her as she worked, her hands pumping Aldric's chest. Breathing into his mouth. Clem stood like a statue, his gaze locked on Aldric with the same tenderness in his face he normally revealed when playing his lute. They'd grown close, Dominic realised, dimly, under his own crushing dread. Drawn together by their shared adventure. Clem was praying.

His lips moved without sound. At his side, Guildford stood tall as a pillar, ignoring the blood oozing from his own injuries. He folded his massive arms across his chest, his head hanging like an ox labouring under a heavy load. His face was pale under his tan. Dominic's eyes snapped up as a shadow blocked the open door. Felicia stood on the threshold, her tear-stained face dirty with drying blood and the slime of water weed. He couldn't bear the sight of her for long.

"You shouldn't be here. This is your fault," he snapped. He turned away, back to his friend, hoping for a miracle.

"He's my friend, too," Felicia said on a whisper.

"What do you mean it's her fault?" Guildford glared down at him, his eyes a turmoil of trepidation.

"Get out of here if you're going to fight," the matron cut in, wiping her perspiring cheeks. "Last thing this man needs is to wake up to another scrap."

Dominic gritted his teeth on the urge to continue the argument. He fixed his eyes on Aldric, hands fidgeting, useless without his Blessed gift. *Aldric, you must live,* he thought. *Your life is all your own. Don't give it up. Please don't leave us.*

A violent cough ripped through the air. Aldric lurched to his side, spewing water and mucus in a thick stream across the scrubbed wooden floor. Dominic's breath left him in a rush. He ducked his head to his knees, fighting a wave of dizziness. Clem lurched forward and hauled Aldric to a sitting position.

The elderly matron batted his hands away. "Give him a minute," she ordered, giving Aldric's heaving shoulders a hefty pat. "Let's get the river out of him. And pass me that quilt."

She waved a hand at Dominic. Dazed, he dragged the quilt from the back of the settle and handed it across.

"Our thanks, mistress," he croaked. The woman sighed, sitting back on her knees, her worn hands braced in her lap.

"He's alive. Nothing more I can do," she said, using a corner of the quilt to dab Aldric's face. "Someone help me up." A twisted smile crossed her lips as the three young men converged to lend her aid. "Such swift service. Ah, If I were but two score years younger," she quipped, a twinkle in her bright blue eyes. She patted Guildford's sturdy arm as he helped her to her feet. "Aye, the Gods can laugh."

Hands braced on her hips, she watched Aldric as he continued to cough. "Keep him warm," she said. "The village will feed you tonight. You've been through enough, I'd wager. I'll tell the elders to beg space for you. There's not enough room for you all in my hut." She brushed past Felicia to the door, stretching her hands to her stiff back. "Watch that pot, lass," she said over her shoulder. "Or you'll not be getting fed."

Her eyes narrowing, Felicia stalked across the space and gave the defenceless stew a stir that slopped some of the contents into the coals. An instant reek of burnt fish filled the cottage.

"Mage's balls, Felicia," Guildford said, grabbing the spoon. "Watch what you're doing."

Felicia's eyes burned like coals in her thin face as they locked on Dominic. He glared back. Clem had dropped to his knees on the floor, closing the quilt around Aldric's shuddering body, humming softly under his breath. The lad laid a head on his shoulder. Guildford glowered at his sister. "I see you two need to talk," he said, passing her the spoon. "I'll see to the horses."

Shoulders slumped with fatigue, he ducked out into the lowering afternoon. Felicia and Dominic faced each other across the width of the hearth. Silence fell between them, broken only by the crackling of the flames and Clem's whispered voice, humming a half-forgotten lullaby.

Felicia stared at him, her eyes scanning his face, testing his mood. Trapped by anger, Dominic faced her with his hands on his hips, one eyebrow raised. She swallowed, her tongue running across her lips, and moved the pot away from the fire.

"We have to talk, Dominic," she said.

"Not here." He left the room, his damp cloak twisting between his legs. Felicia sighed and followed him out of the warm cottage to the edge of a roughly fenced vegetable garden nearby. The wind lifted their hair. Played with their damp skin. The moon showed its face briefly between the thrusting clouds. Lightning flickered somewhere against the distant hills. The sun had long vanished. The river remained. Rushing ever onward.

"So talk," Dominic said, folding his hands across his chest. He could feel the anger building within him. It merged with his despair. His loneliness. His guilt. He should have known. Should have guessed. And the northerner would still be alive. Aldric safe. Fabian whole and hearty. "Tell me you're not a traitor. Like your mother."

She flinched. "You don't understand," she began.

"Aye, I never do. And you know why? Because you won't tell me!" Dominic wanted to scream it in her face. "You've been just the same ever since we dragged you out of that Gods-forsaken hole at Traitor's Reach. And I know why now. Cerys let you go. She wanted you to come with us, didn't she?" He grabbed the edges of her dress, dragging her from her feet. "Didn't she?"

"No, yes. I don't know! Dominic, let me go! You're hurting me!" She flailed in his crushing grip, her eyes wide in the scudding moonlight.

"Aye, you should fear me," Domini= said, almost stuttering with rage. He gave her a shake and then a push that sent her to her knees on the stony ground. "You've led me such a merry dance, Felicia. For years. I believed in you. Trusted you. And now this. We could have died. Aldric could have died. Dupliss knew we'd be here. How could he know unless someone told him?"

She scrambled from the wet earth, quailing under his fury. "It wasn't like that... It wasn't..." she protested, raising her arms as he took a furious step towards her. "No, hear me out. Please, Dominic."

His jaw clenched. He wheeled away from her, hating the frustration and rage battling in his heart, the confusion and loss beating at the soul of him.

"I can't do this, Felicia," he ground out, his voice breaking. "I can't do this anymore."

Silence. Broken only by the lonely call of a hunting owl. He clenched his fists around his chest, holding the emotion down as it swelled, demanding release. His eyes burned. The cold twilight sky blurred in his vision. There was a storm out there. But it was nothing to the one that was crushing his soul.

"Dominic, look at me." Her voice. Whispering on the wind. Like cool silk, soft and fragile. "Please, my love. Look at me..."

"I can't, Felicia. You've destroyed us," he murmured, swiping a hand across his eyes. "Everything I've fought for. Believed in. Trusted. All for nothing." He swayed where he stood. Felicia had been his lodestone. His north star. Without her, he was a leaf tossed in the breeze. Aimless and lost. *Where did I go? I knew myself once...* The thought wandered like a nomad across his mind. He was so tired he could hardly see straight.

"Please..."

The owl cried again. Closer this time. He blinked and turned his head. The bird perched on a fence post, watching them. Its snow-white feathers gleamed like a benediction in the black of the night.

He turned. So slowly. Felicia stood before him, trembling from head to foot. Biting his lip, he watched as her hands moved to the ties of her cloak. The laces of her faded dress. His brow creased. He raised his arms to stop her.

She shook her head. "Nay. Let me do this. I must let you see." Biting her lip, still shaking, she kept her gaze on his as she let the folds of clammy fabric drift to the cold ground.

Felicia. Naked. Her hair flowed in a stream across one shoulder. Her small breasts pointed and pimpled with gooseflesh, her legs long and finely muscled. But that wasn't the first thing he saw. He gasped, his heart racing. A shocked, instant denial blurted from his lips before he could stop it.

"No. By all that's holy..." His words caught in his throat as the weight of the truth crashed over him. She wasn't just physically damaged; she had been broken in ways he couldn't have imagined. The tracery of scars covered almost every inch of her. Some thick and ragged, perhaps inflicted by a blunt blade. Some... His skin crawled, thinner. Deep, scoring lines. Caused by what? A sharper blade. Needles? Fingernails? His mind whirled. Her mother, Arabella, had sewn Felicia's mouth shut once. The memory of it revolted him. But some of these scars were newer. Still healing.

She turned, presenting her slender back to him. The same random pattern greeted him. A horrific pattern of abuse scrawled madly across her skin.

"I hate my gift, Dominic," Felicia said. Facing away from him, her voice drifted in the wind. Became part of it. "My mother tried to beat it out of me. Or prevent me from speaking. You saw the lengths she would go to. The fear she had of it."

"Aye, I saw." His words emerged through stiff lips. "She was an evil woman." He didn't know what to think. Could only imagine the pain the woman standing before him had endured. His fists clenched at his sides, struggling to reconcile her betrayal with the pitiful sight in front of his eyes.

"That night in the temple, I truly thought I would die. I was glad to leave if it meant you would survive." Felicia turned, watched him carefully, shivering in the cold night. "But I didn't die. Cerys kept me alive. Nurtured my gift. I was supposed to share it with her. That black-hearted, murdering witch. And I tried not to, Dominic. Your uncle, Terrence. He helped me. We tried to help each other. Finding the heartsease... But you've seen, haven't you? There's never enough. And so, she could hear..."

She paused, grimacing. Raised one hand to rub her eyes. Torn to pieces, Dominic battled with his instinctive need to comfort her. He kept his hands folded across his chest. Raised his chin. Wanting so much to believe her, it hurt.

"She wanted to hear what my Farsight whispered. She's used it. That information she got from me. And I couldn't stop her, Dominic. You must believe me. I tried so hard..." She paused, her chest heaving, her eyes welling with tears.

Dominic stood, rooted to the spot, his eyes still unravelling the patchwork of damage laid before him. A grotesque map carved in flesh. His mind flashed to the telepathic scream he'd heard on Felicia's sixteenth birthday. The day when her gifts became mature. She'd tried to deny it then. Knew what her Farsight would mean for her. He swallowed. All those times in the last few weeks, he'd reached for her, and she'd pushed him away. But the heat of her kiss. That had been real. Surely, he hadn't imagined that...

"Dominic, you must believe me..." she moved closer to him. "Yes, I told her things. But I swear to you, as I'm standing here, there are some things I never told her. No matter what she said or did..." She'd closed the distance between them. His gaze clashed with hers, searching for the truth. Something solid he could grasp. Understand.

"She said she'd ruin me forever in your eyes. And I understand. I'm hideous. Ugly. But I never wanted to be a traitor. Never. If I could give this ability back to the Mage, I would. In a heartbeat." She raised her eyes to his, her hands reaching to touch him. Afraid to. He looked down at her, torn into pieces by the sight of her battered body. He had it now. Felicia's bitter secret hugged close to her violated heart.

"I want to believe you. I do. And I'm so, so sorry for the pain you have endured, but Felicia, how can I trust you?" The words came out in a strangled whisper. Dominic's chest tightened. Just asking the question felt like a sword thrust into the heart. Her gaze clouded. Hope dying. She stepped back a little, shaking her head.

"I know. I have to prove it to you," she murmured. "And perhaps you still won't believe me. But there's one thing. One special thing that Cerys doesn't know."

"What? What is it?"

Felicia sighed, her mouth screwed into a wry smile. "And there it is. The beating curse of Farsight," she said, almost to herself. "I can't tell you what I see. This is your future. Your decision. Not mine. I cannot influence it, Dominic. I wish I could." She ducked her head as if afraid to see the weight of her betrayal reflected in his eyes. "Some things are fated," she said, her voice trembling with a mixture of regret and sorrow. "But most are not. The path can change, Dominic...and the smallest choices can shift everything. Please don't let my past define your future."

Dominic stared at her. The faintest cry from the white owl brushed his hearing as the bird left its perch. The passage of its wings swept past his head. He swallowed. Caught in the moment, aching with indecision. Her shoulders slumped when he didn't respond. She passed a hand across her mouth. "Mayhap, I said too much."

She reached for his reluctant hands, pressed them close to his fast-beating heart against the delicate, carved figure of a falcon he wore on a leather thong around his neck. A gift from his brother long ago. He could feel the hard shape of it digging into his skin beneath his damp tunic. Under the small pressure, a memory rose of a time in the past when his future lay before him. Rich with promise, and Dominic sure of his humble purpose. How far he'd travelled from the questing, curious lad he'd once been. Now, he was a man, nagged with doubt, aching for peace. Afraid to trust. Her face turned upwards to his.

Beloved. So familiar. So alien. Scarred and still standing. Tears started from his eyes. He couldn't have stopped them if he tried.

A faint, golden glow rose in Felicia's crystal eyes. "The boy with the falcon in his heart." Her words were hushed but powerful. An echo of Master Ash's at Falconridge just a few short weeks ago. The hairs on the back of his neck rose as their magic connected. Unbidden, he turned his palm under her cool grip, his blood tingling at the light contact. A tiny glimmer of hope in a darkened world. He let his head rest on hers. Half reluctant, half yearning.

Her hand twisted within his. "I know you don't believe me yet. But I believe in you. If you are true to yourself, you still have a chance," she said.

Chapter 38
Joran

Hours later, Joran's body trembled despite the heat from the hearth and the sheltering comfort of the blanket Little Bird had draped across his shoulders. He couldn't stop the gnaw of self-disgust beating at the centre of him. The knowledge of how close he'd come to repeating his father's mistakes of forty years before. His dagger lay atop Petronella's Book of Shadows. A grim reminder of just how fine the line had been. His heart lurched. It would only have taken a fraction more for him to lose everything he'd gained. Just a second before he became a man like his father, lost to madness and fear and the seductive lure of power. Outside, the storm still raged, intent on battering the castle into submission.

His hands were clenched so tightly against his knees that his nails bit into the skin, but it wasn't the physical pain he was feeling. It was the horror of nearly losing control. Of nearly giving in to the darkness that had plagued his family for generations. His father's face, a ghost in the shadows, lurked at the edges of his vision. The knowledge of his vast crime had haunted Joran for decades, ever since Theda Eglion had told him of his royal origins on that long journey west. He'd grown to manhood under the care of his kin, the King and Queen of Oceanis. Tortured by doubt and the rising power in his blood, twelve-year-old Joran had grown to maturity, sure he was destined to repeat the cycle. It was inevitable. Surer than fate. Like father, like son. Blood calling to blood.

"Here. Have some of this." Crossing the room, Fortuna poured a cup of valerian for him. Joran wrinkled his nose. "I don't want it," he growled, barely glancing her way. He grabbed the blanket closer, chilled to the bone. What was it that had almost led him to the same fate? A handy weapon, a moment of weakness. He felt the sharpness of it still, even though the blade was now out of his reach. It was better this way. He told himself that. He knew it.

Practical as ever, Fortuna's voice cut through his brooding thoughts.

"You'll take this brew." Her voice was implacable. The same tone she used on his children when they dared to disobey. He opened his mouth to protest, but she pushed the cup into his hand. "Little Bird and I forced some into Petronella," she said on a softer note. "She's sleeping. The door is locked. You must get some rest as well, my lord."

He took a small sip, wincing at the heat on his tongue and handed it back to her. His stiff muscles groaned in protest as he stood, dropping the blanket to the floor. It landed in a heap. A nest by the fireside. So easy to curl up within its warm embrace and go to sleep. Huffing a sigh, he kicked it aside. Petronella needed him. He could hear the echo of her voice, weak and strained, whispering in her restless sleep. And the haunting image of her mind being torn apart by Cerys made him burn with helplessness. He couldn't just do nothing, not while she was fighting. But he didn't trust himself to cross that threshold again.

"I can't sit here like an invalid while Petronella is battling that...thing inside her mind," he muttered, eyes flickering toward the door, where the barrier that kept Cerys at bay was, for now, too fragile. "There must be more we can do to help her."

"If there is, I don't know what it is."

His head dropped to the floor. Fortuna was right; they were battling forces beyond their control. But he couldn't abandon the feeling that if he just did something, tried harder, something had to change.

"She's growing weaker," Joran murmured, his voice heavy. He glanced at the locked door, fear coiling through him. "She said it herself. Cerys is there inside her and growing stronger."

"Through the will of the Shadow Mage, her presence is here," Fortuna corrected him sharply. "Cerys Tinterdorn is not. Nor will be if Sir Fellowes and his men do their duty."

"If they do," Joran repeated, cocking an eyebrow. "We must face facts. There is a lot of empty space beyond our walls. The Queen's Guard cannot watch it all."

"Yet they will try," his friend said. "We can only deal with things one at a time, Joran."

He grimaced, the familiar frustration twisted within him. He glanced at his dagger, harmless on the table. "Send for my sword. If she arrives, I want to be ready."

"You just put your dagger down, and now you want your sword?" A grim smile tugged at the corners of Fortuna's lips. "Inconstance, thy name is man."

"'Tis not inconstancy," Joran shot back, his voice gaining strength. "I have no intention of using a blade against my wife." He paced the room, his body aching from the exertion but still unable to quiet the pounding in his chest. "'Tis preparedness. Good sense. You should recognise it."

Fortuna huffed a dubious laugh, regarding him uncertainly from under her lashes. "You can stop looking at me like that," he said. "My mind is quite clear."

She frowned. "I am glad to hear you say it," she said after a pause. "What happened in there?"

The words hung in the air between them. Weighted and heavy.

Joran paused, his hands clenching. He could feel the words strangling him, a confession he wasn't sure he could make out loud. He turned away.

"It was close," he said, his voice thick. "Too close. I was... I almost..." He stopped himself, the shame bubbling up. "I almost became my father."

The silence stretched between them. Fortuna didn't speak. She didn't need to. She understood.

"I can't lose myself like that," Joran muttered, the weight of it crashing over him again. The self-loathing. The fear of who he could become.

"You won't," she said, her voice steady. "You are not him."

Her words cut through the fog in his mind, and for a brief moment, he found himself holding onto them, even as doubt lingered.

"Not yet," he said softly, more to himself than to Fortuna.

A pause. Then, a spark of hope. Fortuna's gaze softened as she moved closer. "Not ever. You are stronger than you know, Joran," she said. "More than you were when we first met. Your father's shadow is long, but it does not have to define you."

Joran swallowed, his chest tight. Maybe she was right. Maybe he could trust himself if just a little.

Fortuna offered him the cup once more. "Remember this," she said. "When it came to it, you chose not to be your father. You chose. Not Cerys. Not Petronella. You."

Holding the cup, he sank into the fireside seat. His mind flickered to the lingering thoughts of what he almost did. How close he had come to losing control. *It was a choice*, he reminded himself. *I chose not to fall into that darkness.*

He swallowed the valerian brew, feeling the warmth seep down into his chest. The tension in his body lessened, and his thoughts quieted, if only for a moment. He wasn't his father. He wasn't that man.

He set the cup down slowly, the decision to move forward feeling almost as heavy as the choice he had made earlier that night.

His voice broke through the quiet, steady for the first time in hours.

"Thank you," he said simply. For the first time, he could see a way forward, even if it was just a sliver. He was not lost.

She huffed a relieved laugh. "Thank yourself," she said, nodding to the chair by the fire. "Get some rest. It is not over yet."

Joran leaned back, the fire's warmth settling into his bones. The storm outside still raged, but inside, in the quiet of the solar, something had shifted in him. He hadn't chosen to be the man his father was, and perhaps that was enough. For now.

CHAPTER 39
DOMINIC

The villagers of Folly Hall gave the battered group shelter for the night. Dupliss' troops had marched onward to the castle, leaving their fallen behind them.

The fishermen, stoic and resigned, had gathered Dupliss' dead and laid them awaiting burial in an unused shed. The storm still raged overhead, although its wrath was focused further to the South. Branches groaned and lashed against the wind. Rain drummed a tattoo against the wooden shutters. Aldric, shaking with coughs, rested on a pallet near the warmth of the fire. Clem crouched at his side, his eyes dull with exhaustion, watching over him.

Aldric's smile was tired, his face drawn, but he'd roused enough to take some fish stew and lament the loss of his bow.

"I'll buy you another," Dominic said, scraping his spoon around his bowl. "Surely there are none in the kingdom who deserve it more than you."

Aldric flashed him a fleeting grin. "I needed a new one anyway," he said. "I've grown. My arms are longer."

Dominic's head bowed to the table. The remains of his supper blurred in front of his weary eyes. "Aye, you have. Thanks to all the Gods, you still have time to grow more," he muttered.

Aldric struggled upright. "Don't do that, Dominic," he said, his rich copper eyes serious in his pinched face. "Don't blame yourself.

You must let other people bear the consequences of their own decisions."

"I should have listened to Felicia," Dominic mumbled. "We could have avoided this." He shoved his bowl away.

Aldric shrugged. "Mayhap," he said. "But who can say? The attack happened. With or without Felicia's intervention or knowledge. We did our best. All we can do now is live with the results."

Dominic huffed a laugh as he rose to his feet. His mouth stretched in a wide yawn. Never had he stayed awake so long after prolonged use of his magic. He eyed the widow's bed. She was curled up in a corner with a blanket pulled over her shoulders, snoring like a piglet. He wondered whether she'd mind if he collapsed beside her. "So young and such a philosopher," he said.

"You make yourself sound like a doddering old man, dribbling by the fire," Aldric replied. He took a moment to cough. "Old before your time."

"I feel old," Dominic replied. "It comes from having to look after you and Guildford. At least I am not the one dribbling by the fire," he added as Aldric stopped spluttering and wiped his face on his sleeve. Clem dangled a grubby kerchief in front of Aldric's face.

"Find somewhere to sleep," he said. "We need to rest while we can."

"Aye. Call me if you need," Dominic murmured.

Leaving the peaceful cottage, his mind ablaze with all that had happened, he wandered into a stand of oak at the edge of the hamlet. His plodding footsteps disturbed the hollow year-end aroma of half-rotten leaves and fresh loam. The wind whined in the bare branches above his head. Damp and uncomfortable, he shivered in the breeze. His boots sodden with water. Hunger gnawed at his stomach despite the fish stew the goodwife had shared between them. Rubbing his eyes, he squinted in the gloom. The small woodland contained little in the way of shelter. Holly dragged at his cloak as he tramped along a muddy path, watching his feet on the slippery ground. The sudden crack of a breaking branch jerked his head up. He whipped out his dagger, despairing the dull flicker of magical energy left in his palms.

"Who's there?" he demanded. His voice, hoarse with fatigue, bounced off the cold, wet trunks.

There was no answer. He searched the shadows beneath the trees. Scanned the bare branches, waving broad and impatient overhead. But he was alone. Dupliss had marched his remaining forces on. One dark, familiar shape silhouetted against the sky caught his attention. *What's a falcon doing down here at this time of night? So far from the cliffs? Is it injured?* He shoved his hood back and tipped his head. Perched on a slender branch atop a sturdy oak, the bird was too far away to see clearly. To his relief, it spread its wings, soaring into the stormy clouds. Dominic watched it for a moment. His dull mind conjured images of the Grayling in a similar flight pattern, flying high and free above the moorlands in front of the castle. The delight he felt when the magnificent bird responded to his whistle. Trusting him enough to swoop to his wrist. His heart lifted at the thought. "You're the only one the Grayling does not try to murder." The Queen's wry humour bled a slight warmth through him. A memory of the night of his ascension to the ranks of the nobility and his first title, Master of Falcons.

"Aye, we had fun, my friend," he muttered, increasing his stride before the rising gale brought the same creaking branch down on his head. "I hope you are guarding her well."

The stand of oak ended at the Cryfell's undulating banks, where the Folly Hall jetty pierced the water, solid black against the dancing waves. The residents had retrieved their precious boats, swabbed them free of blood and ichor, and moored them to await the morrow. Bumped by the rocking vessels, the worn wooded planks juddered a little under his feet as he made his way to the end. Tired to the bone, not yet able to lie down his worries, he came to a halt. Across the tumbling water, the western bank lay silent and dark. To his right, the water blasted through the gully. A tumult of chaos and danger.

To his left, the river flattened, peaceful and determined. Moving ever onward.

Half hypnotised by the sight of its passage and the undulating patterns caused by the current, he dangled one leg over the edge of the jetty, resting his back on a handy piling. One hand plucked at his necklace, folding the wooden falcon in his fist.

"If you're true to yourself, you have a chance," Felicia's voice echoed in his mind.

Felicia. His mouth thinned at the thought of her. He'd left her donning her clothes, shielding the damage on her slender body from prying eyes. The image of her tears burned into his mind from behind his closed lids as he tipped his head back. Had she betrayed him? Really?

She tried to warn you. You could have listened to her. Ever present, the voice at the back of his mind scolded him. He scowled to hear it. It always reminded him of his mother. Tiny and cheerful. Pecking forever at his younger self. Demanding better behaviour. *She trusted you enough to show you everything. Tell you everything. What about your trust in her? Where's that?*

A groan escaped him. He clasped his falcon talisman in his fist and pressed his forehead against it. "But how?" he demanded out loud. "How can I know she's not still communicating with Cerys?"

"Because she loves you, you dolt." Guildford's voice at close quarters made Dominic jump out of his skin. He leapt to his feet, snatching at the piling to steady his balance. Guildford loomed over him. His face glowed like a pale moon in the darkness. His broad chest was naked in the chill. A rough bandage wound neatly around his arm and waist. Felicia's work.

"For a giant, you are as quiet as a cat," Dominic grumbled, shoving his necklace under his grubby shirt. "Was that you in the shrubbery just now?"

"Pah. You were so locked in thought staring at a pigeon, you'd not have seen the Mage if he sent a thunderbolt in your direction," Guilford said. "Some guard, you."

Dominic raised his brows and shrugged. Guildford was probably right. "It wasn't a pigeon. It was a falcon. What are you doing out here, anyway?"

"Felicia sent me. She said I needed to talk to you."

"Aye? And do you?"

Guildford sighed. For once, his face was serious. He picked splinters of tarred wood from the piling on his side of the jetty. "On the morrow, I'm going after Dupliss," he said.

Dominic's head jerked as a startle of alarm spread through his body. "What?" he blurted, mouth gaping like a stranded fish. "You're leaving us?"

Guildford chewed his lip, his brows lowering over his wolf-grey eyes. "Aye," he growled. "That skinny old bastard wants to proclaim me king. I can't let that happen. He's taken enough from us."

"You can't go after him on your own!" Dominic said. "You'll die."

"My thanks for your confidence in me," Guildford rumbled. "I was planning it the other way around."

"But I need you," Dominic said. "The Queen needs both of us."

Guildford stared at him, chewing a strand of hair that had blown across his face. He shook his head. "You're exhausted, so you're not seeing the entire picture," he said, giving him a mocking pat. "Dupliss wants to put me on the throne. Cerys wants to put herself on the throne. That's two things." He held his massive, blunt-fingered hand in front of Dominic's face. "I can take Dupliss down. I'll get under his guard. Tell him I'm coming over to his side." He paused, his eyes glinting. "And then I'll run him through. And anyone else who gets in the way." He grinned at the doubt in Dominic's face. "While you..." the hand descended to thump Dominic's chest, "you need to save the Queen. Magic is your game, is it not?"

Dominic pulled a dubious face. "I doubt 'twill be as easy as that," he said, rubbing his chest. A warning flashed through his mind before he could stop it. "Did Felicia put you up to this?" he demanded.

Guildford rolled his eyes. "By the Mage's girdle, you can be slow. Nay. She didn't. I've got my own scores to settle with Dupliss over Felicia. He stood by often enough whilst my mother bullied and abused her."

"Hate to say it, but you were a bully, too," Dominic said, stung by Guildford's mockery.

Guildford's gaze hardened. He paused, grimacing.

"Aye. I was," he admitted, his voice low. "In my defence. I was not always the one who started it. That would be you."

Dominic drew himself up to his full height, somewhere around Guildford's statuesque shoulders. "I don't see how that could be," he bit out, remembering the many blows he'd taken from Guildford's massive fists over the years.

"Don't you?" The young giant's eyebrows raised. "Felicia and I were a team before you arrived," he said. "And then, there you were. The Queen's new favourite, sharing our lessons, and Felicia couldn't take her eyes off you in your new hat."

"You jest. She hated the sight of me when we first met. She was only about eleven," Dominic said, scratching his hands through his beard. His mind reeled. "She loves me?" he asked.

Guildford kicked at a coil of rope. "Aye. Always did. She tried to hide it from me. But..." He shrugged, his mouth twisting. "She's my twin. 'Tis hard for her to hide anything from me. I suppose I was jealous."

Dominic raised his brows. "Did she also hide the marks on her skin?" he asked, his tone hushed.

Guildford's eyes were bleak. "I've seen enough," he said, staring out over the water. A muscle ground in his square jaw. "Some of it was my Gods-forsaken mother. She was always cruel to Felicia. I think she always suspected something was different about her. She hated Petronella. Especially after my father died. She always loved my father, of course... Yearned to take Petronella's place at his side. Gods..." He ran a hand through his golden hair. "What a tangle." Turning to Dominic, he raised a phantom tankard in a mock toast. "You couldn't have killed a nastier woman," he said. "My thanks." A wry smile twisted the edge of his mouth. "All you have to do now is kill the other one," he said.

Dominic stared at him with narrowed eyes, a deep disquiet prickling under his skin. "Why are you telling me all this now?" he asked. His fingernails bit into his skin as Guildford looked down.

"You know," he said quietly. "Of course you do." Stripped of his usual bluster, Guildford's face seemed suddenly remarkably young. Dominic's jaw clenched against the sudden dread he felt, blooming like a fresh bruise somewhere under his ribs. "I wish you wouldn't do this," he said softly. "We didn't start off well, but...you're my friend now. My brother in arms."

Guildford's fist clamped his bicep. A warrior's salute. Speechless, Dominic returned the gesture, wincing slightly under the power of Guildford's crushing grip. "I give her into your care and keeping," Guildford said, his tone rough with suppressed emotion. "If I don't come back, there's money there. Talk to the bankers in Blade. The townhouse, my mother's estate... And Aldric. Look after him, too. In my name. Promise me, Dom."

Dominic clenched his lips together, battling to keep his own emotions in check. "You know I will," he said. "If I get through it, I'll look after them both. All of it."

Guildford's head jerked in an unsteady nod. "'Tis well, "he said, standing back. He crossed his arms over his chest. "Good fortune, my friend," he said. "You've taught me what it means to be true. I will not forget."

Dominic's mouth quirked in a half smile. "You taught me what it means to endure," he said. "My bruised body will forever thank you."

Guildford stared at him. The moon pierced the racing storm clouds and glowed from his eyes. In the distance, lightning flickered. The air around them felt charged with tension. Poised on a knife edge. Ready to fall.

"Then whatever the outcome, we are even," Guildford said. "Be true, Dominic Skinner."

He wheeled, his boots trembled the rickety planks underfoot. *Another one*, Dominic thought as his receding figure disappeared, swallowed by shadows. His fingers crept to his necklace, cupping the fragile carving in his hands. His brother had given it to him for luck on Dominic's tenth birthday. He traced the delicate carving with his thumb, running his nail across the familiar curves of its wooden wings. "By the Gods, give me strength," he breathed. "There are so few of us left to fight her."

How long he stayed there, he couldn't tell. Locked in a daze of exhaustion, his emotions ricocheted with the chaos of his thoughts, shredded and hurled by the relentless wind blowing from the north. Always from the North. From the mountains. From Traitor's Reach, where the shadows lengthened and stretched, fingers clawed across the peaceful countryside. Tainting everything they touched with the crushing weight of doubt. Dominic pressed his carved wooden falcon to his mouth. Breathing his dread into it. His fear. His hope. *Let me be enough. Please. If it's the only thing I do...*

At first, he almost didn't realise what had happened. His mind a whirl of wind and feathers, the familiar weight of the Grayling's talons on his shoulder didn't register as unusual. Until the bird pecked him sharply on the ear, and his mind snapped back to reality.

He gasped. The wooden falcon dropped to his chest. He raised a careful, trembling hand, too stunned to move faster. The Grayling sidled onto his wrist, his scaled talons sharp on his chilled flesh. The pain anchored him somehow. The falcon put his fierce head on one side, chattering his familiar greeting. Dominic's heart lurched, caught somewhere between relief and sorrow.

"It is you," he breathed, his voice thick with disbelief. "By all that is holy, what are you doing out here? Are you hurt?" He lifted his arm, squinting in the moonlight, but the falcon seemed hale. No obvious injuries. His feathers neatly folded, his eyes bright. Well fed. Flooded with relief, Dominic raised a cautious finger to smooth the Grayling's fragile head.

The bird pecked at his sleeve. Even through the rough serge, it was hard enough to hurt. Dominic's frozen heart thudded in his chest. "You shouldn't be here," he said, his gaze jerking south to the relentless lightning. Surely, that storm should have passed by now. "You should be there with her." He swallowed. The Grayling's head turned alongside his own. To the castle.

"'Tis the Queen, isn't it?" Dominic muttered, his chest tightening. A shiver scurried across his cold shoulders. The pattering feet of anxiety. The Grayling's talons tightened momentarily, his wings lifting, anxious to move. Dominic clambered to his feet. "Aye, my friend. I understand. We have to go

Chapter 40
Joran

Exhausted and propelled by Fortuna's liberal hand with the valerian, Joran's dreams tangled through his mind. Petronella's rich, ironic laughter tickled his sleeping ears. Theda's fierce blue gaze bored into his as she clutched the hair at his temples. Buffeting wind blew curtains that became sails, filled with a wild, relentless roar, the ground restless and shifting beneath his feet. He dropped his dagger. Watched it slide into the Cryfell, its edge glinting as it disappeared beneath the churning iron-grey waves. Gasping, his lungs full and choking, he followed it. Down, down into its Stygian, unknowable depths. Mistress Eglion leaned over him, her snow-white hair drifting over his face like weeds. "I told you, Joran. I told you what would happen..." Her exasperated whisper, the smell of her pipe smoke. Her ancient, knowing gaze. Eyes still piercing blue. Like the sky. The Court of Skies... "Listen," she hissed over the wail of the storm. "Listen to your heart."

He came to, choking for breath, his head tilted uncomfortably against his broad chest, the blankets smothering his nose. Disentangling himself, he cocked his face to the window. The storm was still howling. An uncertain light showed between the curtains as they rippled. Within the chamber, the candles had burned low. The aroma of beeswax lingered in the air. Clapping a hand to his growling stomach, he stumbled from the chair and stretched his aching neck.

Beneath its peaceful exterior, the chamber ached with tension. He glanced at Petronella's door, ashamed of the relief he felt when he saw it remained locked. Fortuna was nowhere to be seen. Perplexed, he turned in a small circle. What hour was it? He felt as though he'd slept a lifetime. But he'd woken with his mind clear, at last. Crossing to the window, he supposed that was something.

Outside, endless rain drummed from the sullen sky. Water cascaded in gurgling streams from the castle gutters. The gargoyles carved at intervals into its ancient stone dribbled water like salivating beasts, flooding the southern courtyard. It was daytime, he saw, surprised. Beyond the vicious, unnatural storm, a weak winter sun struggled to show its pale yellow face. Servants scurried through the deluge, carrying buckets and sacks as they always had. He blinked. Life in the castle beyond Petronella's chamber walls apparently continued. Despite the growing menace lurking within its walls and the tramping feet of soldiers closing from the countryside. The Queen's Guard patrolled the battlements, hunched against the rain, pikes raised. Watching. Face grim, he shoved the heavy drapes aside as the door breathed open behind him.

"Breakfast," Fortuna said, thumping a tray of meat, bread, and pickles onto the table.

Joran crossed to the table before the platters had stopped rattling. "My thanks," he said, stuffing his mouth.

Fortuna raised her eyebrows. "Valerian worked its magic then," she said, tucking a stray curl under her ornate headdress.

Joran swallowed his meat and reached for more. "Did you sleep?" he asked. Fortuna had freshened her hair and changed her gown. The dark forest green she wore highlighted her copper eyes.

"Aye, Little Bird and I are spelling each other," Fortuna said. "There has been a double guard at your door all night." She turned to the hearth, where a bowl of water waited. "I'll see to our lady," she said, thinning her lips as she glanced at the bedchamber. She set her shoulders. A soldier readying for an unpleasant duty.

"I wish I could help you," Joran mumbled through his next mouthful. "But I dare not trust myself. I am sorry."

Fortuna shrugged. "I know. Even I can feel the weight of the witch's eyes on me in that chamber. And 'tis not me she wants."

"Is there any news? Any movement from Dupliss?"

"I haven't heard. Shall I send Sir Fellowes to you?"

"Please." She nodded, turning to the outer door. Joran tore a hunk from the freshly baked loaf and loaded it with more meat. Fortuna had supplied a flagon of small beer, he noted, tilting the jug. Not wine. He sighed as he filled a tankard. Perhaps it was better to keep a clear head.

Fortuna returned, stooping to the hearth, balancing the bowl on her hip. "Wish me luck," she muttered with grim, gallows humour.

"I do." Biting his lips, Joran swallowed, his mouth dry as Fortuna unlocked the door and shut it behind her. Even that small action allowed a thread of unease to trickle into the solar. A tiny reminder of the darkness that awaited within. His arms crossed over his chest, his face set, Joran returned to his station at the window. "You won't beat me, Cerys Tinterdorn," he muttered under his breath, peering through the sheeting rain to the mist-wrapped moorland beyond the castle walls. "I will find a way. I swear it."

Sir Fellowes arrived at a run minutes later, his moustaches twitching. Raindrops spattered across the rug from his dripping cloak. "News," he gasped, thumping a damp message into Joran's waiting hand.

"At last." Joran smoothed the fragile scroll in his hands, trying to ignore the clumsy tremor of his fingers. Sir Fellowes watched him read, thirsting for Joran's response like a hungry dog waiting for a bone.

"Well?" he demanded. "What does it say?"

"It's from Blade," Joran said through numb lips. "The captain of the garrison there says there have been riots overnight. The Temple of the Mage was ransacked. Petronella's statue smashed." He grimaced, screwing the fragile parchment into a ball and tossing it into the glowing hearth. "Gods damn it," he muttered. "If Blade falls, we are truly done for."

"I'll divert some of our guard," Sir Fellowes said, his face flushed in the heat of the fire. "But this is crawling ever closer. We may have to pull everyone back to defend the castle, Sire."

Joran shrugged. "Our gates are closed. It already feels like a siege," he said. "As long as no-one has the bright idea of poisoning our wells, we can hold out." He grabbed the General's wet sleeve. "Make sure you question everyone on the road," he insisted. "Cerys Tinterdorn doesn't care much about the Citizens in Blade. But she does need to breach our castle walls. She needs that Gods-blasted book. I wish there was a way of finding out where it is."

He eyed the door to Petronella's chamber. It opened with a jerk, and Fortuna darted through it, yanking it behind her. Her lips pursed as she turned the key. "Gods blast it," she muttered, scowling. "'Tis worse in there by the second. That evil bitch has even taken to attacking me for want of anything better to do." She marched across the room and snatched open the window, tossing the dirty water from her bowl into the damp air. "So much for you, witch," she said, slamming the casement shut.

Sir Fellowes' grizzled eyebrows raised. "The witch is in there with our queen?" he demanded. He grabbed his sword. "I'll see to her." Teeth gritted, he plunged across the carpet.

"You won't," Joran said flatly. "The witch is inside our queen. You can't kill her without taking Petronella's life."

The general halted, his shoulders twitching. "Shadow magic," he said, his eyes screwed into slits. "Curse her." He sheathed his sword.

"Exactly," Joran agreed. He sighed. "Petronella knows where her father's Book of Shadows is. She can't tell us. At the moment, she can't even think about it, lest Cerys reads her thoughts." He cursed under his breath, struggling to remember the aftermath of Darius' overdue demise at Petronella's hand six years previously. Wounded and half dead, he had little recall of the immediate events. His jaw clenched. He'd been happy enough to avoid wearing the Ring of Justice. That much he could remember.

"Do you know what became of Darius' remains and his property, Sir Fellowes?" he asked.

The older man shrugged. "No point asking me," he said. "I had no part in Darius Falconridge's army. I wasn't even here back then."

"Little Bird and I searched his chambers before we went to the restricted section," Fortuna said. "No-one has been in there for years. There's nothing there. 'Tis empty. Full of mice and dust."

Joran sighed. "I don't know what else we can do then," he admitted. "Curse it. She has us like rats in a trap. Waiting on her pleasure." He roamed the chamber, familiar frustration burning within him. "Gods, I want to do something," he muttered. "Anything. 'Tis the accursed inactivity that bleeds my soul dry. Petronella is weakening under her control, and I can't stop it." He waved an arm at the window. "And the weather. That's what it used to be, back in the good old days of Arion's reign before Petronella gained her true powers. We are losing our Gods-blessed link with the land. Day by day."

"The Ring of Justice is yours. All you have to do is take it." Cery's voice insinuated itself under his thoughts. Trickling like oily water under Petronella's door into the crevices of his defences.

He ground his teeth. "Shut up, you evil bitch," he croaked, slamming his fist on the stone mantel.

Sir Fellowes regarded him with growing concern. "Are you quite well?" he ventured. "Should I send for Master Mortlake?"

"Try not to worry," Fortuna said, ushering him to the door. "Joran is a member of the Blessed. He is fighting a different battle."

"By the Gods," Sir Fellowes grunted, standing back at the door to admit another messenger. "I hope he has better luck than me." He stopped the approaching soldier with a fist on his chest. "I'll take that, thank you," he said, holding out his other hand.

"But..." the messenger began.

"Not now, man." Sir Fellowes shoved him back out and slammed the door in his protesting face.

"Looked like Jackson, but you can't be too sure these days," he muttered. His jaw clenched with distaste as he registered the sodden parcel the messenger had left in his hand. The carrier pigeon was dead, its battered feathers drenched with cold water, its dainty neck hanging loose in his broad palm. "I think this is for you," he said, passing the poor creature to Joran.

Joran's brow quirked as he accepted the grisly burden. "My thanks," he said, working the message canister gently from the bird's fragile leg.

"Poor brave creature, battling the storm," Fortuna murmured, taking the small body. She smoothed its damp feathers. "I'll dispose of it, my lord."

"Aye." He pulled the message free, a reluctant smile pulling at his lips.

"What this time?" the general barked. "More bad news, I'll warrant."

"Nay." Joran's lips lifted for the first time in weeks. A fragile beam of sunlight strayed through the rain-washed window and spread a thin blade of light into the gloom of the room.

"'Tis from Dominic Skinner," Joran said. "They are loyal. And they are coming."

CHAPTER 41
DOMINIC

Creeping through the misty drizzle like a burglar, a fragile grey dawn lifted on Folly Hall as the group came together in a narrow clearing. Cavorting and bucking, Kismet tossed her head. Rested and fed, she read the tension in the air. The fisherfolk crept from their cottages and went about their daily business, oilskins clamped about their shoulders, shooting suspicious glances at the group preparing for their onward journey. Guildford busied himself with armour and supplies, bartering roughly with the owner of the biggest boat for some dried fish. Felicia stood to one side, her hair speckled with moisture, her face drawn and sombre. She made no move to stop him.

"Aldric, I want you to stay here," Dominic said, pulling on his gloves. "You need more time to recover."

"I don't," the lad replied, squaring his shoulders, his mouth set in a stubborn line. "I will ride with you. I still have a sword."

"We aim to ride with Guildford," Terrill said, settling his hat more firmly on his head as the wind rose. He glanced at the remaining members of his crew. Despite the injury he carried, Fabian stood tall at his side, his grey eyes clear. The lad's eyes danced as they locked onto Felicia. Dominic's eyes narrowed as he read the worshipping expression in the young man's gaze.

The remaining member of the team, whom Dominic had mentally christened 'Fly', tipped his head in acknowledgement of Terrill's words. "We are loyal to Joran and the Queen," he mumbled. His face stretched in a tired grin. "Sometimes, we do things without being paid for them."

"And we are Citizens, after all. Guildford can say he's bringing more recruits. Dupliss was happy to let his men die for him while he watched from the bank. He doesn't know our faces," Terrill added. "Now we've caught up with him, we can take him." He fingered the hilt of his sword almost lovingly. "I owe him for Fabian," he said.

"Watch your own back," Fabian said. "I can still swing my sword. They stabbed the wrong shoulder."

Dominic closed his eyes, some of the tension easing from his stiff back. He'd spent the night trying to process the Grayling's arrival and Guildford's imminent departure, his dreams tangled with dread and writhing shadows. "My thanks," he muttered, cutting a glance at the young princeling as he hefted his saddle onto the General's broad back. "I know he is set on this plan, but I was dreading the thought of him leaving us on his own."

"He'll not be alone," Terrill said stoutly. "We'll march with him. For Joran and the Queen."

"Clem?" Dominic said. "What say you? Are you for the castle or with Guildford?"

Clem lifted a shoulder, his eyes on Aldric. "You are fighting a witch," he said simply. "A member of the Blessed, albeit a dark one, with evil in her heart. 'Tis best I come with thee, where my gifts may aid you."

"And you don't want to leave Aldric. You may as well just say it." Clem shrugged, gave a shy smile. Dominic's lips twitched. "Well then, you may come with us." He swallowed, glancing at the ridge of the widow's cottage roof, where the Grayling watched proceedings with steely interest. "We are agreed, then. We will part ways." His gaze drifted across the clearing, where Felicia was exchanging words with Mistress Haverling, the woman who had saved Aldric's life. As he watched, the stout matron thrust a small bundle into Felicia's hands.

The look of wonder that crossed the girl's face and her immediate gratitude screwed his lips into a forbidding line. He crossed over to them, a thoughtful frown skewered on his forehead. Mistress Haverling shot him a cunning grin from beneath her serge hood.

"Come to your senses, have you?" she muttered, almost to herself. Dominic raised an eyebrow and turned to Felicia.

"Have you decided who to travel with?" he asked Felicia, as she shoved the parcel into the folds of her cloak.

Felicia stared up at him from beneath the wave of her hair. "You, if you'll have me," she whispered. "Perhaps there is still something I can do to make you forgive me."

There was a question in her quiet words. He read it in the softness in her eyes. The shadows under her high cheekbones that bespoke her privation and her exhaustion.

"Give me time," he said.

"Aye, time," the matron said dryly, "Because you have so much of that, don't you?"

Dominic rolled his eyes. He turned his back on her. Soft as the Grayling's feathers, his gaze travelled slowly over Felicia's face. Her eyes on his held the shimmer of starlight. Open and vulnerable, as he had seldom seen before. Transfixed, the chill wind ruffling his hair, he stared back. The Grayling chattered urgently overhead. Calling him back to the task at hand. He blinked, dragging his eyes away from Felicia.

"I think we must leave," he said. He whistled, and the Grayling swooped to his place on Dominic's arm. Without his falconer's glove, Dominic winced slightly as the bird's talons dug into the skin of his wrist. The bird shuffled obligingly further up his sleeve. Felicia's low chuckle turned his attention back to her.

"I could wish my hawk so accommodating," she said.

Dominic stroked the falcon's head with his free hand. "Mayhap, he's learned some manners since we last met," he said. His eyes dropped to her cloak. "Is that heartsease?" he asked, striving for a neutral tone.

"Aye," Felicia patted her pocket. "Mistress Haverling has a stall in Blade market. This is some of her stock." A small smile lifted her lips. She raised a hand to the tendrils of hair escaping from her loose braid, staring at her brother as he fastened his tooled leather saddlebags and leapt astride his pure white charger. "Ah, Guildford. Only the best of everything," she murmured, but her expression was fond as she shook her head.

"How will he fare?" Dominic asked. "Has your Farsight spoken to you? Did you see anything for him?"

"The Mage shows me many things," Felicia said, "but in this, he is silent. The future is not yet written. All depends on the choices of the players." She jerked her chin at her brother. "And we are all players. Whether we agree or understand the game we play or not."

The jingle of tack and the rasp of Guildford's voice as he gathered himself to leave jangled across the clearing. Terrill, Fabian, and Fly shrugged their haversacks over their shoulders and adjusted the straps, preparing to move out. Dominic strode across the distance between them and patted the General's thick, muscled neck.

"Farewell, my friend," he murmured. "Look after your crew."

Guildford glanced around. "Seems hard to imagine they are suddenly my men," he muttered. "I thought they'd go with you."

"I'm taking a leaf out of Aldric's book," Dominic said. "No longer responsible for everyone else's decisions."

"So you won't try to stop me?"

"Nay. I'm leaving it in the Mage's hands. And in yours." Dominic's gaze travelled to the ornate, silver-chased sword hilt resting easily at Guildford's left hip. "Just do what you promised and take Dupliss down. Listen to Terrill. They've been at this game much longer than either of us."

Guildford nodded, his face grave. His glance slid to his sister. Nodding at them, Dominic returned to Aldric and Clem, allowing the siblings a moment alone.

"Is she coming with us?" Aldric tightened Hamil's girth, smoothing his fingers across the horse's flanks.

"Aye." Felicia and Guildford were locked in conversation across the clearing. Guildford waved a hand Dominic's way. Felicia nodded reluctantly. Dominic huffed a silent laugh. He didn't need Farsight to follow the tone of the conversation. He just needed the set of Felicia's mouth. The toss of her hair.

"And there you have it," he said, running a hand through Kismet's freshly groomed mane. "He's just told her to go to me with her needs, and Felicia just told Guildford what he could do with his request."

"You love her, don't you?"

Startled, Dominic's eyes jumped to his young squire. "I don't know," he said, frowning. "She has proven my trust in her misguided. But I've loved her for so long 'tis a habit. Hard to break."

"I don't know what we are riding into. And I know it's not my business," Aldric said, running a hand down Hamil's near hind and checking his shoe, "but seems to me you two need each other like bread needs wine. As one hand does the other." His gaze cut to Clem, busy currying his own mount, a gentle, melancholy whistle rising to tease the chill wind. And then to Guildford. The young man leaned from his saddle and scooped his sister easily into the air with one arm, hugging her close above her protests. "I loved Guildford, but I can let him go," Aldric said quietly. "Because, mayhap, there is something else here for me if the Goddess is kind." He paused, biting his lip as Guildford replaced Felicia on the leaf-brushed ground. "But I don't think there will be any other for you, Dominic. So whatever we face. Don't let Cerys come between you."

"Cerys." Dominic gritted his teeth. His mind clouded with the memory of Cerys' handy work on Felicia's fragile flesh. "She has a lot to answer for."

The Grayling chattered and took off, his wings beating through the mist. "Enough wool-gathering and fond farewells," Dominic said, following the bird's agitated flight, his high, urgent cry echoing the tension spiking in his blood. He vaulted onto Kismet's back. "Come," he said, waving his arm. "The day is wasting. Let's ride."

The group parted company where the way split at the moorland cross-roads, half a day's ride from the Castle of Air. A morass of muddy footprints made it clear Dupliss' force had turned further south.

"Down to Blade," Aldric said, scanning the scrubby moorland and swiping his fringe from his eyes. "They must be going there first to gather more men."

"Then this is where we say farewell," Guildford rumbled. He urged the General closer to Kismet and leaned from his saddle, clasping Dominic's arm in salute. "Good fortune, my friend. Dear sister," he said. "Aldric. Clem."

"Be safe," Dominic said. "Make Joran's day. Bring him a head or two."

"Gods, Dominic, that's a disgusting thought," Aldric said, reaching for his water skin.

Guildford grinned. "Seems a worthy notion to me," he said. "I'll do my best."

He nodded to them once more and wheeled the General. Trudging behind him on foot, Terrill winked at Dominic. "We'll watch out for him," he said. "You watch out for that Tinterdorn spawn. Give her one in the eye for me."

Dominic glanced at Felicia, riding on the pommel of his saddle before him. Her eyes clouded as her brother departed, the General's iron hooves squelching through the sleet-sodden peat, trailed by Terrill, Fly, and Fabian. To the southwest of them, the storm beat at the castle. Circling like a grim fate. Dominic's lips thinned. It reminded him of the dark tornado of energy he'd seen before. Once on the day of the Queen's battle with her father, and then again two years ago, under the temple of the Mage in Blade.

"She's there," he said. "In front of us. Riding into that storm. She's the heart of it."

Clamping his jaw, he turned Kismet's head and urged her on. High overhead, the Grayling followed.

They'd ridden another five miles before the first of the Queen's Guard stopped them, blocking the road with crossed pikes and steely expressions. Water dripped dismally from their feathered helmets. "Name," their captain roared. "State your business."

"Sir Dominic Skinner," Dominic said. "Returning to the castle to aid their majesties." He glanced at Aldric. The lad tipped his helmet back and smudged a hand across his face. Despite his brave words, the journey across the muddy landscape was taking it out of him; his body racked with coughs.

"Any here know this Dominic Skinner?" the captain bawled at his troops.

Silence. Rain drummed down, disheartening and gloomy. Thunder bounced around the cliffs of the castle pass. The Grayling swooped from the sky like an arrow shot from a bow and came to a halt on Dominic's shoulder. Dominic glanced at Felicia. She was glaring at the captain, her eyes flashing with authority.

"You might not know Dominic Skinner," she said, her voice ringing like crystal, "but surely you know me, Captain Dunham. You guarded my rooms often enough when I was a child. I have been travelling with Dominic Skinner and his group for the last few weeks."

Dominic nudged Kismet so that the dubious soldier could see Felicia. She shrugged back her damp hood. The man's eyes widened as he dragged his awed attention from the falcon's golden glare. "By the Gods, lady, what happened to you?" he gulped.

Felicia all but snarled. "A lot. I've been gone two long years. Trapped by the witch, Cerys Tinterdorn."

Dunham's eyes narrowed. "I must prove you are real," he stuttered. "'Tis the only way we can tell the witch has not passed us by."

"Ask Lady Wessendean something then," Dominic ground out. "We have no time to waste bantering words with you whilst our queen and Prince Joran need our help. We have the Grayling here. Is this proof enough for you? That we travel with the Queen's treasured bird?"

The man's eyes crossed. His eyes traversed Felicia's gaunt face like a man seeking a route across a hastily drawn map. Shivering under his cloak, Dominic forced patience into his weary mind, clutching his fists against the urge to blast the group aside with a well-aimed kick of his power. His shoulder stung under the clutch of the Grayling's talons.

"Hurry, man," he snapped. "If you know my Lady of Wessendean, there must be something you share the witch would not know."

The captain's gaze snared on the Grayling. He cleared his throat. "Your own bird, my lady. I know you have one. What is her name and species?" he asked. His troops stood taller, their hands firm on their pikes. White-faced, waiting for Felicia's reply, the captain dropped his arm. The pikes lowered. Their owners took an attacking stance, their weapons poised to pierce Kismet's chest. A muscled ground in Dominic's jaw. He readied his power in his fist. He'd be damned if he let a simple soldier touch a hair of Kismet's coat.

Felicia swallowed. He was surprised to see her cheeks pinking under his gaze. "She's a merlin," she said, her voice soft. "I miss her." She paused. Adjusted her hood, rearranging it to avoid the worst of the weather.

"Her name?" Dunham insisted. "Come now, I heard you often enough singing to the blasted thing when you thought no-one could hear."

Felicia waited an irritating amount of time. Kismet hung her head, snatching at the west grass. Aldric sighed, drooping in his saddle, almost falling as Hamil copied Kismet and pulled the reins from his grasp. Clem wrapped a hand around his wrist, jerking him back to his seat.

"Her name?" the captain insisted. He drew his sword. Eyes narrowed, his blood pounding, Dominic drew his.

"Dominica," Felicia murmured. She ducked her head. Dominic peered at the top of her hood, his heart all but bursting in his chest.

"Dominica?" he hissed.

Ahead, the captain nodded to his colleagues. The pikes lifted. The troop split neatly to line the rutted track.

"Dominica?"

"Oh, shut up."

"Pass," Dunham said. "And Godspeed."

Still teasing Felicia, they jogged on, the horses splashing and sliding through the tussocks as the moors sloped sharply downwards. A rising mist spread tendrils of smoke-white vapour towards them as they continued. The storm over the castle grew ever louder, the day darker. Their spirits lower. Burdened by fatigue and hunger.

"Tinner's Ridge," Dominic murmured, his voice blurred by weariness. "Just Featherwood to get through, and then we are nearly home." Heartened by the thought of food and dry clothes, he spurred Kismet on towards the trees. The smell of loam and wet mud bloomed under the steady clop of Kismet's hooves.

"Can't come soon enough," Aldric grunted, grabbing the pommel as Hamil slipped on a loose stone. "Remind me never to go on any type of journey with you ever again."

The day closed upon them almost completely as they crossed the boundary into Featherwood. Trees crowded close. The paths were narrow and clogged with half-frozen mud. Dominic squinted through the gloom. Chased from the moor side by another storm, they'd raced down this path weeks ago, attended by the Court of Skies. It was here that the Queen had suffered her near-fatal riding accident after her last hawking party. His hand crept to his sword, sweeping the undergrowth for strangers or assailants. It was hard to make anything out in the soft-focus gloom. He frowned, his shoulders rising with tension.

Less comfortable in the cloistered arms of the forest, the falcon soared above the treetops. The Grayling's sharp warning cry echoed to them, eerie in the blackened sky. Dominic's gaze flicked aloft to his grey shadow, circling through the mist, thunder growling above his wings.

Twisting suddenly in Kismet's saddle, Felicia startled upright. "This place," she said, grabbing his sleeve. "I've seen it before. There's something here. I know it. Be ready, Dominic. Don't let them catch you unprepared." Her eyes were dark, darting puddles in her thin face. Dominic clenched his fists. Summoning his Blessed gifts sapped his already depleted energy. "On guard," he muttered. Tightening his knees against Kismet's sweating flanks, he drew his sword. The whip of steel sliced through the hazy air, echoed hastily by Aldric and Clem. Eyes wide, they pressed on in single file, alert for danger.

The attack, when it came, was sudden and vicious. A small force of foot soldiers converged from both sides of the narrow path, emerging like ragged phantoms from the shelter of trees and the tangle of shrubbery. Kismet reared automatically. Felicia gasped, clutching the saddle. Forcing the mare's legs to solid ground, Dominic gathered defensive power in his fists, blocking the strike of a fiercely swung staff. The quiet forest rang with the silvered song of steel and the pants and gasps of fighting men. Aldric and Clem thrust and parried. Hamil kicked out. A peasant sank into the mud at his plunging feet, clutching his thigh. Lips tight, Clem turned his own mount in a small circle, his sword flashing.

"Take heed, they are Citizens, not soldiers," Dominic yelled. He blocked another blow and flicked his sword arm backwards. His attacker screamed, his mouth gaping at the spurt of blood from the deep gash in his wrist. The Citizens wielded little in the way of weapons. But they made up for the lack with ferocity and dogged determination. Thin and ragged, they hurled blow after blow at the beleaguered, angry horses, determined to unseat their riders and force the small force to engage. Hampered by Felicia's slim form, Dominic shielded her as best he could from the long reach of the heavy clubs. She screamed as a burly fellow broke through Dominic's defence and aimed a blow at her left shin. Biting his lip, Dominic's brow lowered. He didn't want to kill anyone, but this attack could not go unanswered. Eyes narrowed, his battle cry shivered the remaining leaves on the thrashing branches as he reversed his blade, thrusting it deep into the man's chest.

Felicia's gasp alerted him to another attack on his left side. He twisted in his saddle in time to see the Grayling throwing himself from the sky, screeching like a banshee. The magnificent falcon emerged from the mist like a thunderbolt, talons outstretched, aimed at his assailant's face. The man jerked to one side to avoid him and came back swinging. Undaunted, wings thrashing, the Grayling wheeled and returned to the attack. His angry screech twisted with the skeletal trees, beating their naked arms against the sky. Leaving Felicia to hold on as best she could, Dominic threw a frantic block between them as the man's wheeling staff whistled through the damp air, aimed at the Grayling's chest. The man stumbled against the solid wall of Dominic's will and rebounded. Dark eyes fierce in his face, Aldric commanded Hamil forward. He leaned far over his mount's neck to knock the rough-hewed staff from the man's fist. Panting, Dominic threw an urgent whistle skywards, beckoning the enraged falcon back to the safety of his wrist. Behind them, Clem finished the last of the Citizen soldiers with a hard strike to the temple from the butt of his dagger. Heart thudding in his breast, Dominic turned to Kismet, surveying the group of battered Citizens with a thunderous scowl etched into his forehead. Safe in the curve of his arm, he felt Felicia's breath tremble against his left cheek. The Grayling chattered his disgust, his talons biting through Dominic's sleeve as he sidled up and down his forearm.

"Be calm," Dominic murmured, "we are all safe." Biting his lip, he wished he had the Grayling's jesses and hood. He jerked his head at Aldric. "Do you have a spare strip of leather I can use for the Grayling?" he asked. "I daren't let him go. The Queen would never forgive me if something happened to him."

Aldric shrugged and reached into his pouch. Dominic ran sad eyes over the small band of warriors who had fought in vain for their beliefs. Of the attacking party, three lay dead, rain already pooling in the hollows of their cheeks. The remaining four nursed various bloody injuries between them.

"You'll get what's coming," one of them threatened, clutching the tattered remains of his sleeve over the savage gash in his upper arm. "They're closing on the castle. All of Dupliss' men."

"We have no wish to fight Epera's Citizens," Dominic hissed, righteous fury sizzling through his blood hot enough to set the dripping forest ablaze. "By the Mage, what are you people doing? Don't you understand the hand of the Shadow Mage in all this?"

"Guildford. We want a Citizen on the throne." Their leader's thin lips set into a stubborn line, harsh as a blade's edge. His eyes were empty of everything except blind belief. Dominic surveyed him with a twist to his brows, exchanging a glance with Felicia. She shrugged one shoulder. "They are bewitched," she murmured. "Like so many. Transfixed by dark magic and empty promises. Don't waste your breath." But her face was sad, her narrow shoulders slumped.

Mouth dry, Dominic gestured to the fallen Citizens. "Guildford of Wessendean is loyal to our queen. They have lost their lives to a cause that never existed," he said.

"Prince Guildford is the rightful king." A second tattered Citizen stepped forward, ranging himself with his companion, head flung back. The same absent, stone-cold belief clear in his dark eyes.

Giving up, Dominic took the strip of frayed leather Aldric handed to him and wheeled Kismet, eager to put the cold, dark trees at his back. Felicia was right, he thought, winding a loop around the Grayling's sturdy leg and another one around his own wrist. The Grayling glowered at him and pecked at the restraint. The people were entranced. There was no arguing with them.

"See to your dead," Dominic said, the words harsh in the back of his throat. Squeezing his heels against Kismet's flanks, he led his force onward, still alert for more attacks. But the only thing travelling with them now was the rain and the storm. Beating at their senses, churning like a slow, unmoving tornado with its centre revolving directly over the Castle of Air. The hair on the back of his neck rose as they approached. The massive fist of the Shadow Mage seemed to hold all beneath it within his fearsome grip. Dominic could sense his remorseless eyes on them. The pressure building into a headache of fearsome proportions. They rode on into the eye of the storm. Tiny pieces, mere dots against the sweep of the valley that separated them from the ramparts. Insignificant as ants.

CHAPTER 42
JORAN

In Petronella's solar, his mind racing with plans, Joran stared at Dominic's rough scrawl.

"What does it say?"

Little Bird's voice at his shoulder made him jump. The edges of his lips twisted into a half-smile as he looked down at the girl. She stood beside him, neat and prim in a fresh gown and apron, her eyes bright.

"Little Bird, I didn't hear you come in." He nodded at the curling page. "'Tis from Sir Skinner. They are coming home," he said. "That should please you."

"He is?" Her tone brightened. "That's good news," she said, a smile curving her lips. "It's been such a long time since I saw him. When will he arrive?"

Joran grimaced. "I have no way of knowing," he said. "I hope not long. We have little time left to us." He screwed the message in his fist and lobbed it into the grate. The flames flared around the parchment.

"Aye." Little Bird's periwinkle gaze flicked to Petronella's locked door. "How does the Queen?" she asked.

"Fading under the witch's torment," Joran replied. His chest tightened. The words tasted like ash in his mouth. Bitter with defeat. "Don't go near that door, Little Bird. 'Tis safer if you stay away."

"But what about your ring? Don't you want it? You could fight her with it."

Joran glanced at her as he took a seat at Petronella's desk and pulled a blank piece of parchment towards him. Little Bird regarded him with her head on one side, alert as a sparrow pecking for crumbs.

"'Tis not safe for me in there, either," he said, plucking a quill from a pot on Petronella's desk and dipping it in thick black ink. "Mayhap not for any of us. You saw how I was when I came out."

"Aye. But I don't know how you will fight her without it. The Queen might die." Little Bird's voice was small. She busied herself around the room, rearranging the blankets Fortuna had left already piled on Petronella's trunk, sweeping the hearth, her fingers nimble.

Joran scowled. Little Bird's comment only reminded him how lost he was amidst the turmoil. How fragile his grasp on sanity. He bit his tongue on the desire to snap at her. "How are the children? Did you and Fortuna decide on a replacement?" he asked, trying to turn the conversation.

"A girl called Primrose Winterbane," she said. "Fortuna thought she might be good. She has lots of brothers and sisters." Her face twitched into a grin. "She's also very plain," she added, in a whisper, "so the guards' heads are not like to be turned. That's what Fortuna said, anyway. She seems nice enough."

"'Tis well," Joran replied absently. Bending over his parchment, he scribbled a quick message to his uncle, King Merlon of Oceanis. Sanding it carefully, he blew across the page and rolled it into a scroll, sealing it with wax warmed at the single candlestick. He pressed his seal into it. Little Bird watched with interest.

"So much power in your ring, though," she said. "Is it like the Queen's? What would happen if you put it on?"

Joran's eyebrows raised. "I don't know," he said, scratching his chin with the tip of his quill as he pondered her words. He turned his palm where the signs of both the Mage and the High Priestess tangled deep in his blood. "That's a good question."

"What happened when the Queen banished the Shadow Mage?"

Joran frowned. "So full of questions today, my maid," he teased. "Lots of things happened. She called on the power of the Mage. The power of light. There was a massive surge of energy, and when it ended, Lord Falconridge lay dead, the Shadow Mage had vanished, and we had to replace a great deal of very expensive stained glass."

"And Petronella became the Queen?"

His smile softened. "Petronella was always a queen. She just didn't realise it at first," he said.

Little Bird's face furrowed into confusion. "Why not?" she demanded. She bundled herself into the chair by the fire, looking so like a child requesting a bedtime story that Joran gave up trying to compose his next message.

"The Queen's ring didn't work for her at first. Not until the heartsease she took every day wore off. She didn't know she was Blessed by the Mage," he explained. "That came later. When we touched for the first time. It was like a thousand stars all shining at once. It scared us all."

"It knew you?" Little Bird's eyes were wide and curious. "Right from the beginning?"

Joran frowned. "I suppose it did," he said reflectively. "It made us both realise that we were meant to be together. But neither of us was ready to believe it." He shrugged. "Love is a funny thing," he said. "Sometimes it creeps up on you, and sometimes you just know. Immediately."

"Does it?" She turned away, staring into the fire, her vivid young face hardening in thought.

"You loved Will Dunn, didn't you?" Joran said gently.

"Will?" Her gaze snapped to his.

"Aye, Will Dunn. Your young man."

She bit her lip. "Aye, I reckon I did. Do"

"So you know what love is," Joran said. "How it can be."

"Aye..." Her voice trailed off as she wiped her eyes.

"I'm sorry," Joran muttered. "I did not speak to upset you. I know you must miss him."

Little Bird scrubbed her cheeks with her apron. "I must see to the children," she mumbled. "I will send Fortuna to you when she wakes." She scrambled from the chair. Forgetting to curtsey, she all but bolted from the room.

"Well done," Joran muttered to himself. "Best leave the sympathy to Petronella. I'm surely not good at it." He gritted his teeth at the thought, his eyes wandering to the locked door. Shoving the parchment aside, he crossed to it and pressed his ear to the thick oak panel that separated him from his wife. The door was icy to the touch. A charged silence brewed behind it. A watchful, waiting tension. Heavy with anticipation. He leaned his head against it, his blood chilling with the darkness of his thoughts. *Fine King I am, Petronella,* he thought. *Little Bird is right. Your powers vanquished the Shadow Mage. Why should mine not do the same? All I have to do is take what is rightfully mine.*

His lips pressed together. He glanced over his shoulder at the outer door through which Little Bird had darted, as if all the Shadow Mage's minions were after her. His fingers twitched as they closed on the cold iron key waiting in the lock. Light, mocking laughter filtered to him through the wood. Throat dry, his heart racing, he snatched his hands away and retreated, trembling, to the desk and the dubious protection of Petronella's enigmatic Book of Shadows.

"Mage, take it," he muttered, picking up his quill and wiping a prickle of perspiration from his brow. "I hope you have answers, young Skinner. Because I don't. Not a one."

CHAPTER 43
DOMINIC

Viewed from a distance, the Castle of Air claimed attention, dominating the pass to the northern ranges as it always had. Petronella's familiar standard drooped under the weight of the unmoving storm, the flags too sodden to manage more than a faint flap in the gale. Up close, the ancient grey stone dribbled water, alive with the thunder rebounding against its ancient walls. Even in this sorry state, clattering up to the north gate still felt like coming home. Saddle-sore and weary, Dominic argued his credentials with the Chief Gate Guard, Tim. The man tipped a salute as Dominic led his soaking party under the battlements to the northern courtyard he'd left so many weeks before.

Faces grim, the stable staff raced across the straw-strewn puddles to tend their mounts. Aldric dismounted with a tired sigh, his head twisting on his shoulders as he looked around. Felicia slid from Dominic's arms into the support of a stable lad, pulling her hood from her shoulders. Dominic threw his reins over Kismet's head and all but fell to the familiar cobbles. The Grayling shrieked, batting his wings as Dominic lurched, his legs numb from the long ride and the surprise attack.

"Look to our mounts," Dominic said. "They have travelled a long way."

"Aye, lord." The youngest member of the groom's team stared up at him with eyes like full moons. Dominic glanced down and blinked.

The lad could have been him eight years ago. Dazzled and trembling in the presence of the powerful courtiers. The only difference was that this young lad looked well-fed. Still grubby but less ragged than Dominic's former self.

"My thanks," he said, flipping the youngster a sixpence. Grasping Kismet's reins in one hand, the lad snatched the coin as it twisted in front of his eyes. Dominic gathered the folds of his cloak, eager to enter the castle and into somewhere dry. Huffing a sigh, he ran his free hand through his dripping hair and forced his stiff legs up the broad stairs into the body of the castle. The Grayling rocked with his stride, garnering curious glances from the startled castle servants hurrying along the dimly lit passage leading to the court chambers.

Long accustomed to the wide-open vistas of Epera's mountains, the corridors seemed to close around Dominic the further into the castle he walked. Glancing at his companions, he wondered whether any of them felt the same way. Rushlight and oil lamps flickering at intervals shone moody circles of light between the suits of armour and priceless tapestries on the walls. The whisper of their return swept with them. Scowling, he nodded at the familiar faces of servants and nobles. Fellow members of the Court of Skies. Evaded their clutching hands. His shoulders shrunk from the iron weight of their stares. Despite the familiarity, he felt somehow detached from them. Someone changed and larger. No longer fitting his skin. "That's Skinner, isn't it? But where's Guildford?" the whisper echoed behind him. "There's fighting down Blade way," someone else said. "Mayhap, he's there. The Citizens want to put him on the throne." Dominic's fists clenched at his sides. He had no way of knowing how Guildford fared in his personal battle with Dupliss.

Felicia's face was a mask of blankness. He glanced at her, thin and proud, as she strode by his side. Ignoring the thread of gossip that followed her. "That's Felicia of Wessendean. Wasn't she dead?" She cut a glance at Dominic. He rolled his eyes in response.

"Aye," he muttered. "It has started already. Welcome home."

Stoic and determined, they paused outside the Great Hall. The servants had already prepared the room for supper. Thick earthenware jugs and pewter tankards punctuated the tables at regular intervals. The familiar smell of roasted meat and spices wafted to them from the far door leading to the castle kitchens. Clem's face lightened slightly as he spied his kinsman, tuning his lute by the fire.

"No sign of the Prince down here," Dominic muttered, poking his head into one of the Council Chambers. He scratched at the scars on his wrist caused by the Grayling's talons. The Grayling pecked the back of his hand. "It doesn't feel right, does it?"

"Nay." Felicia peered into a room on their right. "That's my lord Chamberlain's office, isn't it?" she asked. "He's not there."

Feet dragging with weariness, their search took them through the crowded gallery where more courtiers gossiped and diced. Danced and drank. Stares and whispers trailed their passage. They paced up two more flights of stairs.

"The Queen's wing," Dominic said, his concern mounting. "Of course."

"Do we not need to change into something more fitting?" Clem said.

"I really don't think she'll mind," Dominic muttered. His magical senses were tingling an alarm the closer to the Queen's wing they travelled. It was colder here, away from the enormous fireplaces and crowded public spaces. More claustrophobic. The stone walls gave way to ornate panelling. Dark oak, worn with time. Beeswax candles in place of rushlights. But his shoulders pricked with tension. His power built in his hands. "Stay close," he said as they reached the last corner, passing the narrow corridor that gave way to Fortuna's chambers.

The double guard stopped them as soon as they set foot in the Queen's wing.

"Hold," their captain said, his sword aimed squarely at Dominic's chest. The Grayling chattered furiously. Dominic ducked his head to avoid his beating wings. The soldier glanced at it. "The Queen's bird? We thought he'd flown," he said before he could stop himself.

"Aye. The Grayling," Dominic snapped. His power lunged from his fist and pushed the man's sword to an upright position. He was tired and heartily sick of having to prove his identity to every guard who asked. On their journey across the moorland from Fortune's Hall, they'd hit the same obstacle at least five times, as well as the Citizen's attack in Featherwood. The soldier's dark eyes blinked in astonishment. He tried to force his arm back down. Dominic ground his teeth and increased the pressure.

"I swear upon my soul I mean the Queen no harm," he said, taking a step closer. "I have sent a message to Prince Joran. He is expecting us."

Unable to counter Dominic's Blessed power, the captain waved at his subordinates. "Get the Prince," he snapped.

Tapping his foot, Dominic waited, his unease growing by the second. The Grayling chattered at him again, turning his head down the broad corridor.

Joran's swift footsteps echoed on the ancient stone as he strode towards them. Dominic's eyes widened. The Prince had lost weight. Heavy shadows ringed his famous aquamarine eyes. An equally heavy beard outlined his jaw. He looked as though he'd not slept in weeks. His clothes were rumpled and wine-stained.

"Dominic Skinner. What did we discuss the last time we met in my study?" the Prince's voice grated with fatigue. Dominic's jaw hardened. He could have done without the reminder of their last tense meeting.

"You told me to kill my uncle, Terrence Skinner," he said.

Joran relaxed visibly at his words. He reached a hand to the panelled walls as if glad for their support. "And the others..." His lips thinned as his fierce gaze landed on Clem. "Declare yourselves."

Dominic sighed. "They don't have to. You know Felicia of Wessendean. Aldric Haligon," he stepped aside so Joran could see them better in the dim light. "The fourth is Clem. A Blessed musician and soldier. All have travelled with me day and night for the last few weeks."

Joran's gaze roamed over them, his eyes widening as they registered the change in Felicia. "My Lady of Wessendean," he murmured formally. "You are under arrest." The Queen's Guard snapped to attention, closing around Felicia, alert as bloodhounds. She froze on the spot, her chin raised, daring them to lay their hands upon her.

"What?" Dominic's voice snapped like a whip in the quiet corridor. "We travel the length of the Gods-blasted country to come to your aid, and this is your thanks?"

Joran raised a brow. "I am placing her under house arrest until she can prove her loyalty to me and the Queen," he said, gesturing to the guards. "Dupliss wants to place Guildford on the throne. There are rumours the lad has joined forces with him. And what are you doing with the Queen's falcon?"

Dominic rolled his eyes. "I would trust Guildford of Wessendean with my life," he said. "In fact, I often have. If there is a more loyal subject, I have yet to meet him." He stretched his tired body to his full height. Joran still topped him by an inch or two. Almost nose to nose, he glared at the Prince. "You will take Felicia of Wessendean over my dead body," he said. He heard Felicia's light, surprised gasp hidden behind her hand. "Guildford is ready to engage Dupliss, hand to hand. That is his plan. He will give his life, if necessary, to bring the man down."

Joran pinched his nose. Dominic wondered whether he had the same crushing headache that had afflicted him from the moment he set foot on the castle grounds.

"And can you vouch for Lady Wessendean?" Joran demanded. "We are in dire straits. The witch, Cerys Tinterdorn, is attacking the Queen on every level. Through Dupliss and the Citizens. And through a fierce psychic bond we cannot fathom. The Queen is dying under the onslaught. Her link to Epera is fading. There is nought I can do to prevent it." A wealth of sadness underlay his words. Dominic looked at him more closely, noting the faint tremor in his hands. The new lines on his face. His eyes widened. The Grayling dipped his head, almost in acknowledgement of Joran's sad words.

"But you can prevent it, my lord," Felicia said, taking a step forward. "She has not yet found the black Book of Shadows. If she had, she would have won by now." She turned to Dominic, grabbing both his hands in her thin, grubby palms. "When I was in the mountains," she said, "we talked. Your uncle and me. Whenever we could, when we were both free of the Shadow Mage, and Cerys was elsewhere. He never told me where the Book of Shadows was, and we know it is not at Falconridge. We looked. Cerys looked."

"Aye?" Dominic said. "She has the Blade of Aequitas but not the book. Get to the point."

"Your uncle was always adamant that you knew where that book was. Isn't that what he told you as he passed?" Felicia's gaze pierced him through. Familiar dread clenched Dominic's chest. "But I don't know where it is," he said. "Why should I?"

"It has to be here," Felicia said, her lips thinning in the stubborn line he knew so well. "Where else would it be if it's not at Falconridge?"

"It's not in his old chambers nor in the restricted section," Joran said, ruffling his hand through his hair. "Fortuna and Little Bird already looked."

Dominic shook his head, pure fatigue battling with the expectant look the beleaguered Prince threw at him. "But I don't know," he said. "I wish you wouldn't look at me like that." He wobbled, the corridor a sudden, dizzying swirl of candlelight and shadows.

"My lord," Fortuna's voice, sure and capable but tinged with a thread of panic, echoed down the corridor as she leaned out. "Come quick. The Queen needs you."

Joran's gaze flared at her words. He waved them onward, herding them like sheep to the Queen's rooms. Dominic flinched at Felicia's fierce grip on his left hand, matched by the talons of the Grayling riding his right arm.

"Stay true," Felicia muttered as they passed under the heavy guard into the cluttered warmth of the Queen's suite. Glancing at her face, he wasn't at all surprised to see the golden glare of Farsight illuminating her pupils.

Dominic bit his lip at the changes that had taken place in the Queen's apartments since his departure. The once welcoming chamber ached with the sense of creeping evil. Deep shadows lurked in every corner. His skin crawled. Feathers ruffling, the Grayling scurried the length of his makeshift jess to his shoulder and tucked his beak as close to Dominic's hood as he could get. Dragging his hand free of Felicia's crushing grip, Dominic stroked the bird's head. The Queen's bedchamber door was shut. His gaze snared on the heavy iron key standing in the lock. The room smelled strongly of rain and valerian. Books and scrolls cluttered her desk. A pile of soiled laundry lay in a bundle by the hearth. Frowning, he glanced at Fortuna. She'd lost weight, he noticed, her figure still shapely but slender. Worry had carved indentations in her broad copper forehead. Sullen firelight glinted dully from her golden rings.

"Where's Little Bird?" he asked. "Is she well?"

Fortuna threw him a harried glance. "Aye, she's with the children," she muttered. "Nay, 'tis the Queen. She is too quiet. I fear..." She swallowed. The look she exchanged with Joran and the Prince's blanched cheeks filled him with dread.

"What has happened to the Queen?" Dominic demanded. "We came across the Grayling at Fortune Hall. 'Twas like he was looking for us."

"The Grayling," Fortuna's expression softened momentarily as it flicked to the bird. "Well, 'tis good you have him," she said, "but I fear we are too late. I went to the Queen with her dose of valerian, but..."

As one, they turned to the Queen's door. Dominic risked a glance at Joran. The Prince stared at the thick oak panel like a man in the grip of a waking nightmare, his fists clenching and unclenching at his sides. Thunder rattled the windows.

"My lord, don't you wish to go to her?" Dominic asked into the waiting silence. Joran stared at him, his expression anguished.

"I wish it more than anything," he muttered. "But Cerys Tinterdorn lurks within. And she will not allow us peace."

"Does the Queen still guard your ring?"

Joran nodded jerkily, his hand running over his mouth like a man in desperate need of a drink. "She does. The thought of it is tearing me in two," he said. "I know 'tis mine to wear and wield. But I am so afraid I will turn into the tyrant my father became. I nearly took it to kill Petronella just a few nights ago. 'Tis what Cerys wants. To show her power over me. For me to kill my wife with that ring, just as my father did my mother."

Their gazes clashed. Dominic felt the weight of Joran's dread mingle with his own. "And thus lose your Blessed gifts. Like old King Francis," he murmured. "Cunning witch. Using your own fears against you."

"Don't let her win." Aldric's voice was quiet in the crushing silence. "'Tis what she wants. Remember, the Shadow Mage is in this room. Just as it was in the mines. Your thoughts are not your own." Sturdy and determined, Aldric cleared his throat on a racking cough.

"Fortuna knows it," he added. "That's how she can stay strong. Cerys Tinterdorn cannot bring her force to bear on someone from Argentia." He exchanged glances with Fortuna, who raised her eyebrows and nodded.

"To date, the witch taunts me with her possession of Petronella, but you are right, Aldric. My worry is for Joran and our queen, not myself," she said.

Then I will attend the Queen with you. We can check on her together," Aldric said. "Cerys has had little effect on me, to date, apart from making me hate her. She can taunt me if she wishes. But I say we take the Ring of Justice. 'Tis Joran's now, to have and to hold. That much, at least, we can do."

Dominic turned to him. Tall and serious, the lad looked more like a physician than a soldier with every passing day. His counsel well considered.

"That sounds like good sense," he said. "Cerys knows how powerful your ring is. 'Twould seem likely she does not really want Joran to have it. Using his own fears to prevent him from taking it would suit her twisted logic. But you could hold the ring for Joran until he is ready. By your leave, Sire?"

Indecision twisted across Joran's face. "Mayhap taking the ring will remove a piece of Cerys' bargaining power. If I can call it that," he murmured. "But I bid you keep it from me." Clenching his jaw, he nodded to Fortuna. "By all the Gods, I pray my queen lives. Go to her. Take it now," he said.

Fortuna and Aldric crossed the floor to the bedchamber door. Fortuna turned the key and cracked the door open. An icy chill emerged to greet them, twining around their ankles like a cat come in from the cold. Dominic shivered as the door snicked shut behind them.

"She wants the Book of Shadows. She cannot complete her plans without it," Dominic said, straining to hear what was taking place behind the closed door. "We still have a chance if we find it before she does. And she is not here yet."

"In shadows deep, the truth lies hidden,
Silent, 'til his heart is bidden.
Blood of blood, and son of kings,
Together, they must bind the rings.
One must break, so one may rise,
A falcon's flight to pierce the skies.
And when the shrouded crown is riven,
The light, once lost, shall be forgiven."

The Falconridge prophecy issued from Felicia's dry lips like a whisper from the Gods. Dominic blinked, his mind jumping back to the Falconridge family chapel and Master Ash's lifeless corpse. Felicia had wandered across to Petronella's desk. She leaned against it, one fragile hand on Petronella's Book of Shadows. Candlelight blurred and flared with her breath. Felicia's eyes stared at nothing and everything. Gold to their heart.

"What is she saying?" Joran blurted. "Is this Farsight? What does she mean?"

Biting his lip, Dominic fumbled in his pouch, fetching out the fragile paper upon which Mistress Eglion had recorded her vision. He passed it to Joran, who read the prophecy with his lips moving, eyes darting across the close lines, seeking clarity. "Mistress Eglion?" he asked, fixing on the neat signature etched with careful brushstrokes at the bottom of the page. "Where did you come by this?"

"Hidden under the altar at the Falconridge family chapel. There's more," Dominic mumbled as Felicia took a breath and started the prophecy again. He handed the Skinner family tree to Joran with a wordless shrug, still unwilling to believe the contents. Tugging at his beard, Joran stared at it. Turning to the candlelight for a better look. He raised an eyebrow.

"You are related to Petronella?"

Dominic swallowed. He avoided the Prince's piercing gaze and looked at his muddy feet. "Apparently, yes," he muttered. "Distantly. I think that's what one bit of the prophecy means. 'Blood of blood'. You must be 'son of kings'."

"By the Mage, that explains a lot. But how do we 'bind the rings'? What does that mean?" Joran's brow creased. He crossed to Petronella's desk and shoved Felicia out of the way. "If you are of Petronella's blood, you can read this," he said triumphantly, slamming his hand down on Petronella's book. "Try it."

"What? No!" Dominic said, terrified. He clasped both hands across his chest, over his fast-beating heart. "That's the Queen's," he said. "I can't possibly touch it."

"Read it, Dominic. Please try. It will not let me in." Dominic's eyes widened. Joran's voice was softer than he'd ever heard it. Stripped of impatience and privilege. Just a man, flayed and raw. Desperate for aid. Swallowing, Dominic joined the Prince and pulled the heavy volume towards him. The Grayling leaned over the book with him, his beak nearly touching the leather cover, his wings beating for balance. Heart in his mouth, Dominic was conscious of the listening evil lurking just a few feet away through the closed door. Thunder growling in his ears like a rabid wolf, he lifted the cover.

His gaze swam. Under his touch, the book relaxed like a willing woman in the arms of a lover. He stroked the ancient leather, admiring its burnished sheen. The pages crinkled a greeting. He blinked as the ink ran and changed. The ancient script, a world of flourishes and swirls, twisted under his tired eyes like waves on the Cryfell.

"What am I looking for?" he asked.

Joran shrugged, fascinated. "What can you see?" he asked. "It looks as it always has to me. Reads more like an ancient history book. And a boring one, at that."

"Nay, 'tis...spells. Teachings, prophecies," Dominic said in wonder, leafing through the stiff pages. "All worked by different Seers over centuries...but 'tis hard to see them clearly..." He turned a page and then another. "Some of them must not be fixed," he said, raising his eyes to Felicia, still staring into the distance. Her lips were moving, but no sound issued forth. "Felicia said the future is hard to see. She says sometimes we can change it... Here's something..."

He paused, squinting at the archaic script. "The Mage's law is inviolate..." he quoted. "The Blessed will wield their gifts with discernment. Only the Mage judges who are worthy to act in his name..." He huffed a quiet laugh. "I learned that well," he added. "Two years ago."

Joran frowned. "How so?" he demanded. "I never heard the entire tale."

Dominic sighed. "I used telekinesis against Aldric's former master," he mumbled. "Broke his neck when he threatened to kill him. The Mage stripped my powers from me."

"By the Mage's girdle," Joran swallowed. "But you have your gifts now?" he asked. "The Mage changed his mind?"

Dominic shrugged, still uncomfortable at the memory of Arabella of Wessendean's ruined, screaming face disappearing forever into the inky void and his frantic prayer to the Mage to help Guildford, his greatest enemy.

"Apparently. Maybe that's what Felicia means when she says we can change the future," he said, swallowing against his dry throat. He reached for the pewter jug on the table automatically before remembering where he was. He snatched his hand away. "Apologies," he said.

Joran grunted and waved a hand. "Take what you want. The others, too. A fine welcome I've offered you." He turned on his heel. "Keep looking, if you will," he said, bending to the hearth and adding more wood. "But hurry, I pray you. We must find that book. Before Cerys does." He stood up, his head on one side, as a mighty slice of lightning sizzled into the room. They jumped, clapping their hands over their ears at the raging peal of thunder that followed on its heels.

Aldric and Fortuna emerged from Petronella's bedchamber at a run, their faces pale. Aldric slammed the door, turning the key with both hands. The door rattled behind him, the handle jigging furiously as the occupant attempted to batter it down. Fortuna held the Ring of Justice in her fist. The heavy jewel glowed in the candlelight, dangling from its chain like a pendulum, twisting slowly. Transfixed, Joran stared at it as another blast of thunder rocked the castle.

Aldric pressed his cheek against the door. "Well, the Queen, or whatever is inside her, is alive," he said. "Powerful. And she didn't like us taking it." He wiped perspiration from his face with a trembling hand. "She didn't like it at all."

CHAPTER 44
JORAN

Magnificent, enigmatic, the ring twisted in front of Joran's eyes. His palm tingled in its presence, as it always had. Seeking a union.

Fortuna's wide eyes locked on his from across the carpet. "What shall I do with it?" she whispered. "Are you ready to take it?"

Joran bit his lip. The lure of power tugged at his mind. Felicia of Wessendean was still muttering her prophecy and didn't appear likely to stop. He could recite it by heart now. Poised at the desk, still leafing through the Book of Shadows, Dominic Skinner's vivid blue gaze locked with his. Shadowed by candlelight, muscular but more slender, his cheeks hollow, he looked every inch the Blessed knight he was. Valiant and determined. Honed by experience. Very unlike the pampered nobleman who had left the castle but a few short weeks ago, tasked with killing his own uncle. Perched on Petronella's desk at Dominic's side, the Grayling helped himself to the remains of Joran's evening meal. His speckled head raised as he felt the weight of Joran's stare, his head twisting, studying him. Joran frowned. He could almost feel the bird's judgement upon him. He blinked as the bird swooped from the table, circled the room, and came to rest on his shoulder. Dominic's lips lifted in a half smile. "He knows you," he said, turning another page. "Guard your ears. The Grayling's version of love language is like to take them from your head."

"Thank you." the words left Joran's lips involuntarily. "You did everything I asked."

Dominic gave his familiar half-shrug. "Almost," he said. "Dupliss eluded us. I pray Guildford has completed his task. He is a brave warrior, my lord. I hope you believe it."

Joran raised his eyebrows. "'Tis hard to trust a Wessendean," he said.

Dominic's gaze drifted to Felicia. "Aye," he said quietly. "Their mother was both vicious and deranged. And yet, her children are stronger than you can imagine. Truly of the Eagles." He hesitated, one hand rising to toy with a carved wooden falcon hanging at his breast. "I need to tell you that Felicia was the traitor you sought," he said slowly. "'Tis her Blessed Farsight that Cerys used against you."

"What?" Joran's head raised, instant rage sparking in his blood. "You brought a traitor here? To the Queen?" He took a pace, intent on seizing the fragile girl as she stood, wrapped in her Blessed gift. He grunted in surprise as Dominic raised a casual hand. Power crackled and Joran rebounded from the invisible barrier the young knight conjured between them. "What are you doing?" he snarled. "There is only one outcome for a traitor such as she. You know it. Put down your guard at once."

"Nay." The young man didn't need to raise his voice. But his willpower was formidable. Joran flattened his lips as he tried to force his way through and then stopped, realising how foolish he looked. "You had better explain," he said. "I will listen."

Eyes flashing blue fire, Dominic lowered his hand and raised his chin. "Felicia's story is hers to tell, or not, as she wills," he said. "I was furious as well, at first. But I have seen the evidence carved on her skin. Cerys tortured the information out of her. Felicia tried everything she could to prevent Cerys from using her Farsight against us. Battled to remain free of the Shadow Mage. And attempted to prevent the worst of her visions from coming true. And by the Gods, she succeeded." He paused, his face flushed. "So, I swear, my lord, that if you touch one hair of her head, I will hold you to account for it. Their mother was a traitorous bitch, but both her children are loyal. I swear it on my life."

Still perched on his shoulder, the Grayling pecked Joran's ear and swooped to the mantel before he could bat him away. Scowling, Joran swiped at the wound and glared at the bead of blood on his hand. It smeared eerily over the sign of the Mage pulsing dimly in his itching palm.

"You'd better hold on to that ring, Fortuna," he said, casting a mock glare in Dominic's direction. "Lest I am tempted to use it on all my most loyal allies."

Aldric's gurgle of laughter broke the tense silence. Felicia stopped gabbling and swayed on her feet. Slipping an arm around her, Aldric helped her to a chair.

"'Tis alright," he said in answer to Dominic's unspoken question. "She's well." He fetched a drink for her. Felicia sipped, her grey eyes glassy with weariness. Joran's eyes narrowed as her sleeve slipped from her wrist, revealing the white lines of healed scars disappearing up her arms. He flinched. Felicia's gaze, when she turned it upon him, held a vast question. But at least this one he could now answer.

"You are welcome at court, Lady Wessendean," Joran muttered. She swallowed and buried her head in her cup.

Watching the interaction, Dominic's shoulders relaxed. He returned to the vast Book of Shadows, a fine line of concentration appearing between his brows, flattening the pages a little more to read something more clearly. His light gasp drew Joran's attention.

"What's this?" Dominic said.

Joran took two quick strides to the desk. Dominic tugged at something small and shiny, lodged securely between the tight binding of the ancient pages. "'Tis a key."

Dominic held it out to him. Fortuna dropped the Ring of Justice unceremoniously into her apron pocket and leaned over their shoulders. "What does the page say?" she asked.

Joran held his breath as the lad slanted the book towards the candlelight and traced the text with his fingers.

"Did you say you looked in the restricted section?" Dominic whispered.

"Aye, we did," Fortuna said. "We brought back everything we thought would help us with Petronella and the Shadow Mage." She waved a hand at the pile of books taking up valuable space on the carpet. "There's nothing there."

"Do you know something?" Joran's voice felt rough in his throat. He glanced at the bedchamber door. A tomb-like, listening silence emanated from the chamber, underscored by the continual growl of thunder. Of a sudden, the shadows in the room felt darker. More solid. "What does it say, Dominic? By the Gods, speak up."

"I remember something..." Dominic's eyes drifted far away. "Something my uncle said when he was explaining to me about misusing the Mage's gifts. He was overcome that day. Battling with the Shadow Mage in his mind. I saw it. 'Twas terrifying."

"What about it? What does the book say?" Joran clenched his hands behind the back against the urge to shake information from the lad.

"'Tis not what he said, it was where we were at the time..." Dominic murmured. He glanced at the locked door and dropped his voice to the merest whisper. "I couldn't concentrate. My uncle told me about Darius' Dark Army and his place as a founding member. I remember how much he had to fight to stay with me, in the light. There was something there. In the restricted section. I could feel it watching me... And the writing..." He stared at the page, his eyes rising to meet Joran's urgent stare. "It's a library reference number. It is still in the restricted section," he said. He turned the key in his palm. "It's just not on a shelf."

CHAPTER 45
DOMINIC

The key twinkling in Dominic's palm was surprisingly heavy, despite its small size. Dominic clenched his fist around it. He straightened from the desk. "This is it," he said. "What Master Ash sent us to find."

Joran's eyes darted to his wife's chamber. "Go, go," he breathed, flapping his hands at them. "Hurry, please!"

They left the Queen's apartments at a run. Felicia's feet flew at Dominic's side, her braid bouncing down her back. The Grayling clung like a barnacle to his wrist; his chatter echoed along the endless corridors. Aldric and Clem brought up the rear, hands on their swords, daring any to stand in their way. No-one did. Courtiers and servants alike flattened themselves against the dusty tapestries lining the walls, their mouths open like nestling chicks, waiting to be filled with more gossip. Dominic's thoughts raced in time with his thumping feet. His heart pounded with relief. The answer was here. So close. All he had to do was find it.

They skidded to a halt outside the Great Library, the familiar environment of their childhood schooling. Muttering apologies, they dodged around scholars and students browsing the stacks. Storm light flickered against the vast windows. Outside, the thunder had stopped. The sudden silence after hours of noise was startling. The familiar smell of parchment and the acrid aroma of the many oil lamps clogged their nostrils the further into the depths they travelled. A half-smile twisted Dominic's lips as he passed the scene of the most dramatic incident of his school days. He exchanged a glance with Felicia, one eyebrow raised.

"Aye," she panted back. "You owe me a gown. I never could remove the ink you spilt all over it. It was my favourite, as well." His hand brushed hers. A fleeting touch that tingled in his senses. Felicia let her hand linger. He took it, pulling her close to his side.

"I'm sorry," he muttered. "If we get through this, I promise I'll buy you another."

Hand in hand, they wound through the economics section and fetched up in the oldest part of the library, where Epera's huge history collection stretched around them. Clem's murmur of fascination went unnoticed by Dominic. He paused in front of the unassuming dark oak door carved with the repeating sign of the Mage.

Heart in his mouth, he tried the handle. "Of course, it's locked. By the Gods, I'm an idiot. Who has the key? Is it with the Chief Librarian?" His hand shot to his mouth, panic flaring. "'Tis not with the Queen, is it?"

"Since when does a telemantist need a key?" Felicia said. She rolled her eyes at him and gave the handle an experimental rattle. "If the room wants you in it, I'm sure it will open," she said.

"Go on, Dominic," Aldric muttered. "Else, I'll have to go find the librarian, and that could take too long."

"Alright." Grimacing, Dominic settled into his power, stretching his fingers to the empty keyhole. He dug deep, locked into a mental battle with the ancient forces that had crafted the door. His mind whirled with the many author's voices packed behind its ancient planks, each apparently demanding proof of his purpose. Felicia shifted impatiently at his side. Clem's hum softened the spirits of the books behind the door. They calmed slightly. He could almost feel them stepping back. Releasing their hold on the workings of the lock. He drew a breath and swiped perspiration from his forehead as the lock clicked. The door swung open into blackness. Inviting them in.

Ever practical, Aldric plucked a lamp from a hook on the wall.

"Wait here," Dominic said, taking it from him. He urged the Grayling onto Aldric's fist. The Grayling gave him a filthy look and sidestepped reluctantly away. Aldric gathered his jesses. "Thanks. There may not be room for all of us."

Nodding, Aldric stepped back, taking up a guard on one side of the door. Clem took the other side without asking, eyes steady, his sword ready in his fist.

Together, Dominic and Felicia took a nervous step into Epera's most fiercely protected collection of magical works. Dominic raised the lamp. Gaps in the crowded shelves loomed like pulled teeth. A haphazard collection of single pages and unrolled scrolls, evidence of Fortuna's hasty search, littered the floor. The magic in the room reached into his blood. Seized the power there. The hair on his head lifted in response. Wide-eyed, Felicia gasped, staring at the beat of the Mage in her own palm.

"I've never seen it so clear before," she said, turning her hand over so Dominic could see it. The sign of the Mage. A rich, deep blue pulsing in time with her heartbeat.

"Do you accept it now?" Dominic asked, his voice hushed. Surrounded by the living heart of Epera's magic, he needed to hear her voice. "Your Farsight is neither a blessing nor a curse," he whispered. "Surely, you of all people understand 'tis what you do with your visions that count the most."

Felicia closed her fist. "Aye," she whispered, stroking her fingers over the nearest volumes. "I am Blessed." She trailed the same hand from the books to his arm and then up to his bearded cheek. "And not just by the Mage." His skin prickled where her fingers touched, her gaze wide and searching. "Am I ruined in your eyes, Dominic?" she asked. There was a tiny hitch in her voice. The smallest tremble to show

how much his answer meant to her. He turned his face into her palm, pressed his warm lips against her skin.

"You have never been more beautiful in my eyes, Felicia," he said. "That witch may have wounded you outside. But that is not what I see when I look at you." Gathering her small, oval face in both palms, he pressed a gentle kiss to each of her fluttering lids, one on her forehead. The next on her soft rosebud mouth. "I see someone strong, and brave, and true. You are my life, heart and soul, my beautiful Felicia," he whispered. "Believe it."

She smiled. Dominic blinked. He'd seen sight of it so seldom and never like this. Meant just for him. Warm and molten. Aldric's clearing throat was the only thing that stopped him from pulling her into his arms right there and proving his need for her on the dusty floor.

"Focus," Aldric hissed. "Aren't you looking for something?"

Dominic shook his head, a wry grin on his face. "A funny thing. I had a dream about you once," he said, raising the lantern again. Felicia's precious face glowed in its golden light. "Right after you disappeared, and I missed you so badly. In my dream, I thought I could hear you calling me."

"I probably was calling you. I spent most nights in the dark trying to remember your face. What's funny about that?" Felicia said. She glanced down, searching the shadows for some sign of the elusive black Book of Shadows.

"What's funny was that in my dream, you were calling me from in here," Dominic said. "I thought this was where you were."

Her eyebrows raised. "A man of Farsight," she teased. "What are we looking for?"

"Something with a lock," Dominic said, turning. The oil lamp passed across the shelves, travelled into the darkest corners. A glass case rocked in its light. Felicia gasped. A fragile creature, metallic and beetle-like, glared at them from behind its thick casing.

"By the Gods, what's that?" she muttered, taking a careful step back.

"Something that can't get out with any luck," Dominic replied. He dropped to his knees, scouring the lower shelves. "Here," he said. "These are boxes, not books. Hold this." He handed her the lantern. The row of boxes was old. Coated with dust, peppered with wood-worm. He hauled them out, but none bore a lock the size of his key. One crumbled under his touch, spilling its former contents into a dusty pile at his feet. He pushed the battered scrolls gently aside. "There's a job for the Chief Librarian," he said, reaching behind it for something else. Something small and black. The heavy wood prickled his fingers with a touch of acid. He scrubbed his hands against his damp cloak and stood back, ushering the box out with a quick boost of his energy, unwilling to touch it.

"Is that it?" Felicia stared at it. Almost innocuous. Plain blackwood. It gleamed dully under the lamplight, so shiny it seemed even dust was loath to touch it. He fumbled with the key. This lock turned easily. A strong smell of concentrated ink and something worse. Something tar-like and sticky oozed out. He clenched his teeth.

"This is it," he said. "I remember it in Falconridge's possession. He had it on the march to Sunira. I saw it once when he thought he was unnoticed. That's what he used to call his Dark Army."

Swallowing against a sudden surge of nausea in his belly, he doffed his cloak and folded the book within it. The Grayling chattered at him as he ducked through the low door.

"We'll have to send the librarian to lock it," Aldric said. "Do you want the Grayling back?"

"Aye. I'll lift this." Dominic unwrapped the bundle and used his gift to hold the book in front of him without touching it. His skin crawled even at that distance.

"Nay. Wrap it up again. I'll carry it," Aldric said, glancing at his expression. "You'll only draw attention to it, else. And the quicker we move, the quicker it will be over." He handed the Grayling back to Dominic. The bird lunged away from the book to the length of his jesses, his wings beating with fear.

"Hush now." Dominic reached a wary hand to the snapping beak and put another few steps between them and the book. "Be calm, my friend," he murmured. "I won't let anything harm you." The bird shuffled closer to him. He petted it gently, smoothing the tremors that shook his fragile body.

"If we only knew what we were waiting for," Clem muttered, falling in next to Aldric.

"Oh, Cerys is coming," Felicia said as they marched back through the stacks, stalked by the irritated glances of ordinary students. Her eyes narrowed. "I reckon she's already here. It's what she wants. For us to do all her dirty work for her."

She glanced up at Dominic's frown and shrugged. "'Tis how she works. A sucking parasite. I thought you'd guessed that by now."

Clem drew his sword, taking a pace closer to Aldric. The younger man marched, his jaw locked with distaste.

"I'm only half Eperan," he said as they left the library and tramped back to the Queen's quarters. "But I can still feel this thing sapping my strength."

Propelled as much by disgust as fear, the group increased their stride. Dominic's heart pounded in his chest. He glanced at Aldric. The lad's jaw jutted. His breath came in pants. "It's like that night under the temple," Dominic murmured. "Like a dream. Do you feel the same? As if we are walking but going nowhere?"

"That's it," Aldric snapped, leaning into the force that wanted to hold them all back. "Just the same. It's getting harder. Probably worse for you."

"Stay true," Felicia muttered, gripping his elbow. They were pushing through the mass of courtiers in the long gallery. The crowd appeared to have grown to twice the size. Hands reached out to claw at their shoulders. The dark, open mouths leered like gargoyles. Their breath pressed close and hot. Like monsters from a nightmare.

Unable to clear it, Dominic shook his head. "'Tis an illusion," he muttered. "Just an illusion."

Sword still in hand, Clem's eyes narrowed. He took a breath and flung back his head. Dominic threw him a glance as he raised his voice. The rousing melody of "Where the Robin Roves" bounced around the gallery. The Grayling relaxed his punishing grip on Dominic's wrist. He took a breath. The simple normality of the soldier's drinking song threw its raucous melody into the swirling ribbons of dark energy emanating from the black Book of Shadows. Clem's gift couldn't counter it fully, but some of the clutching hands withdrew, the gaping mouths stretched into laughter. Snatches of song came back to them as the courtiers took up the round. Clem stopped singing as they pushed their way up the staircase. Dominic risked a glance back. The courtiers had grown strangely silent. They stood, watching from the base of the staircase, a richly dressed company, warm in their silks and velvets. All quiet. Staring.

Waiting.

The Queen's Guard on Petronella's corridor let them pass without a murmur. Dominic raced through the door to her apartments and skidded to a stop. Joran stepped towards them and then came to a halt as Aldric dumped his burden on the desk and stood back, scrubbing his hands down his breeches as though they were burning. He lurched away, clutching his stomach, one hand to his mouth. Fortuna pressed a glass into his hand. Aldric took it, his eyes widening at the girl lingering near the window seat.

"Little Bird!" he said.

Joran ignored them. His gaze hardened. "You found it then," he said. He seemed in no hurry to examine the contents of Dominic's damp cloak. Perhaps Joran could feel it, too. The drifting evil in its pages. Dread curled through the room despite the warmth from the merry fire twinkling in the grate. The chamber seemed made of shadows.

Little Bird stared at him from within Aldric's loose embrace. Dominic drank her in. Her neat nursery garb, her bobbing curls under her cap.

"Dominic..." she said. He waited, the memory of her last crushing words swirling through his mind. Her loss, her bitter grief at the death of Will Dunn. She'd sworn never to forgive him. She looked well now, he realised with relief. No sign of sadness in her eyes. She was grinning, her blue eyes alight. Glad to see him. The leaden weight of guilt for hurting her so badly lifted a little from his battered heart. He strode towards her, a smile lifting his lips.

"Dominic..." He ignored Aldric's hushed warning in his delight at seeing her again. The Grayling screeched in his ear. He paused, raising a hand to shield his face from the bird's batting wings.

"Bird," he said. The girl ignored him. Her eyes flicked to the small black book, squatting like a malevolent toad on the desk.

"That shouldn't be there," she said, crossing to it. Her skirts hissed across the carpet. "Not so close to the Queen's book."

"Dominic..." Aldric's voice was urgent now. He darted forward, lunging for Bird's skirts.

"Nay, Bird, don't touch it. 'Tis evil..." Dominic moved to stop her, but she was quicker. Her nimble fingers closed on it. She whirled, clutching it close to her heart.

"My thanks, Sir Skinner," she said. She crossed the room in a heartbeat, snatched the key from the lock of Petronella's quiet bedchamber and let herself in.

"Bird..." He lunged after her, still not understanding. "Come back, don't go in there..." The Grayling raised his voice again, his wings thrashing. He swooped to the limit of his jesses, lunging after the girl. Stumbling after him, Dominic drew him back before he hurt himself, cradling his wings, hardly noticing the striking of his beak against his chest in his fear for Little Bird. "By the Gods, what's she doing?" Reaching the door, he struggled to open it.

The quiet snick of the key brought him up short. A woman's satisfied laughter followed. Mocking. Delighted. That laugh had haunted his dreams for years. Dominic glanced at Joran. He stood like a man on the edge of a cliff, completely bereft, his mouth working. He buried his face in his hands and then raised it, eyes scorching with rage. Fortuna's mouth hung open in shock. Fast on the heels of it, her anger blazed across her face.

"The conniving bitch," she hissed, slamming a heavy fist on the mantelpiece so hard the candles jumped in their sticks. Panic beating through him, Dominic's gaze jerked to Felicia. She sighed, reading the question in his eyes. Shook her head. "My Farsight never showed me this," she said.

For a second that seemed to last a lifetime, no-one moved. Then Joran shot across the room and hurled himself at the locked door, shouting obscenities at the top of his lungs. "No! Petronella! Petronella!" Alerted by the noise, the Queen's Guard entered, stomping across the room to the door. "Open it!" Joran commanded. "Get it open."

"Sire." The guards tried their best. The door jerked and rattled on its hinges. But the ancient planks held firm. Ice gripped the room, trickling from underneath the locked door. One by one, the flames in the hearth flickered and died. The candles followed. Outside, the storm gathered power, wailing and shrieking against the battlements.

"Wait," Dominic said. "Stand back."

Gathering his power this time took everything he had. He forced himself to concentrate. Blotting out Joran's shouts of rage, his beating fists at his wife's door, the howling wind, the Grayling's screech. His breathing slowed. He closed his eyes. Raised his hands. He didn't bother with the lock. Instead, he rode the force of his telekinetic gift beyond it, searching for the key. Cerys had dropped it to the floor. He could sense it. The hard iron. Cold on the heavy carpet, Bound in ice. His fingers moved, tracing the shape of Cerys, standing at the foot of Petronella's bed. Deep at the heart of him, he felt her triumph as she drew the Blade of Aequitas from her apron pocket. She cracked open the book. There was so little time. Forcing himself to remain calm, he withdrew, little by little, hoping the witch wouldn't notice. Dropped his power back to the floor. Enveloped the key. Drew it to him. Slowly, slowly, over the edge of the rug. Across the short span of oak floorboards, cringing at the scrape of metal on wood. Back, back. Under the door.

"Ah!" Joran pounced on it, his fingers trembling as he shoved it into the lock. They advanced as a group. Joran and Dominic, his head whirling with dizziness, in the lead. The Blessed of Epera.

And the witch.

Petronella's bedchamber was cold as a tomb. Entranced by her own power, Cerys didn't turn. Stripped of her disguise, she faced the bed, her long dark hair a scribble of ink against the white of her dress. Petronella lay on her back, her dark hair blending with the shadows that crawled across the floor, inching from the walls. Dominic's heart sank as he spied the Ring of Mercy, almost completely black. The book floated in space in front of Cerys. She did not need to hold it. Dominic's skin itched with disgust at the words issuing from her lips. He couldn't understand them. They were a language he didn't want to know. Ugly and guttural. Crawling with malice. His mind wanted to retreat from the sight. *Mage help us. She'll take her soul. She'll take everything.* Silent for once, the Grayling pecked 099999op- at his arm, struggling to free himself from his restraint. Cerys' voice rose. Dominic's skin prickled. His hands stung. Battered and bloodied by the Grayling's beak as he battled for freedom. Joran's face was grim. He fingered his dagger, looming behind Cerys, prepared to use it and be damned to the consequences. Cerys raised her knife. Joran raised his own. Felicia's hand shot out, clamping on Joran's sleeve, pleading with her eyes. Still struggling, the Grayling snapped his head around, his eyes locked on Dominic. Intent. Pleading. Urgent. His golden glare turned back to Petronella, defenceless, exhausted from her constant battle. A memory flashed to him, even as Felicia whispered the sentence deep in his mind. "*He who holds the Grayling, holds the crown. Let him go, Dominic. Let him go.*"

"*It's the Grayling. I can't. I can't.*" His reply came from the depths of his heart. The Grayling. His beloved companion. The beacon of freedom and hope that shone forever in Dominic's heart. He couldn't lose him. He couldn't. Tears spiked his lashes. His fists convulsed on the Grayling's jesses. The familiar weight on his wrist, the freckle of his silken wings. His golden eyes proud and wild. A symbol of everything he cherished. Love and loyalty. The bird had been his guide and protector. Had brought him back to this moment. To Petronella. The Grayling chirped. Just once. Soft. A question. He cocked his head.

Felicia's eyes held a desperate certainty as they locked on him. Reading his sorrow. His denial. She shook her head. "*Dominic, you can't carry it all. He's giving his life for both of you. Trust me. You must. Dominic, please. If you love them both, let him go.*" His heart thundered in his chest. But Felicia was right. As Aldric had been right. Not everything was his to control.

Cerys' voice rose to a triumphant crescendo. She hurled the blade of Aequitas. Time seemed to slow. The lethal blade twisted in space, trembling, its runes singing an ancient song. A blend of love and hate combined. His heart flooding with grief, Dominic opened his trembling, clutching fingers. He let go.

And the Grayling soared. His wings stretched. He had chosen. A defiant beat of purpose against the battle of the storm. A blur of feathers racing the blade. Faster than thought. He came to rest on Petronella's chest. The Blade of Aequitas tore through him and pinned him to his mistress's breast. His head fell back, and a screech of defiance echoed around the room. His beautiful wings batted once. Twice. And then were still.

The room stood silent. Even the storm held its breath. The creeping shadows halted their advance. But they didn't leave.

The Queen didn't move. Pinned to her pillows, cradled by the wings of her precious falcon. "You are worthy of the Falcons, Dominic. Your heart is true." Joran's hoarse whisper drifted to him dimly. Dominic stared at the bird, tears flooding his cheeks. His wrist felt too light without the bird's fierce presence. The world too quiet without his demanding chatter. *Why? Why did you have to go?* His hand drifted to his chest, where the carved wooden falcon dangled from its leather thong. He crushed it in his fist, welcoming the pain of the worn wood against his palm. But the shape felt subtly different. The edges sharper. Blinking, still wrapped in grief, he stared at it. A delicate silver falcon, his wings outstretched, forever caught in mid-flight, hung from a silver chain.

"The boy with the falcon at his heart." Felicia's whisper, deep in his mind, drew him stumbling to his feet. He stared at her. Locked in his loss. Uncomprehending. *"The Mage honours your sacrifice. And your service. Blessed Knight of Epera,"* she murmured. He stared at her, choking back tears. Her familiar smile was gentle under the blaze of gold in her eyes.

Cerys screamed. A howl of rage that came from the very depths of her soul. It froze the marrow of his bones. Joran grabbed her as she hurled herself at the bed, clutching for her blade, intent on trying again. Gritting his teeth, he held on, hauled her back, his grip tightening as she struggled. Clutching his silver falcon, Dominic watched as her disguises shifted across her face. First a soldier, then Celia. Another soldier, unknown to him. And then Little Bird. Then Cerys again. Tall and slender. And so like the Queen. They could be twins. His devastated heart stopped at the wildness in her face. She clawed at Joran's fingers.

"You bastard," she choked. "That ring should be mine. It should be mine. I was the next daughter. Not her. Not her. And she killed him. She killed my father! She should be dead. I hate her. Hate her."

Her words tumbled into the waiting shadows. Felicia took a step back, beckoning to Dominic. He stepped to join her. Took her hand. It tightened on him. Her presence was solid and warm at his side.

"What now?"

Her smile again. Soft and expectant. She put her fingers to her lips. *"Wait,"* she said.

CHAPTER 46
JORAN

J oran's fist clenched as he watched the Grayling's last flight, his last act of love for his mistress. His heart ached not just for the sacrifice of the bird but for Dominic. For all the weight that this act carried. His voice, when it finally came, was hoarse. "You are worthy of the falcons, Dominic. And your heart is true." The words came not just as praise but as a recognition. A bond formed in shared loss, in the commitment to protect those they loved. In his arms, Cerys Tinterdorn writhed like a feral cat. He grabbed her, too terrified to let go. Petronella lay in her bed with the Grayling pinned to her chest like a badge, a bloom of blood spreading from the wound in his chest. The Blade of Aequitas quivered as the falcon's faltering wings sagged and stilled. *No.* His heart clenched in his chest. The chilled blood in his veins froze. He watched his beloved wife over Cerys' head. The woman's crazed ravings ravaged the atmosphere, a constant stream of curses gobbled by the waiting shadows. He ignored her. Willed Petronella to move.

She didn't.

An ice-cold rage rose within him, burning in his chest. His grip on Cerys Tinterdorn increased. Felicia of Wessendean's grey eyes glinted in the gloom. She shook her head. Somehow, the action calmed him. He heard her voice, cutting easily through the fraying blocks he'd placed on his telepathy, too exhausted to bolster them. *"Wait,"* she said.

Dominic Skinner stared at the Queen with tears standing in his eyes, his lips clamped together, his whole body trembling. Leaving Felicia's side, he crossed to her, cradling her dangling fingers in his own. Pressing a kiss to her hand. He lifted a gentle finger to stroke the Grayling's motionless feathers.

Dead. Is she dead? Joran's mind couldn't comprehend it. The young lad, Aldric, choked back a sob. Cerys shuddered in his iron-hard grip, still keening. He hardly dared let her go. Clem stepped up, clamped a hand around her arm, and held her close against his broad chest. He nodded at the bed.

Grief opened up in Joran's heart, wide open and fathomless. He had the sense of his older self clutching that cliff face, like so long ago, and Petronella, no longer there to save him. He could let go. Fall. He would never stop falling. He knelt at his wife's side like a man in a dream. Picked up her slender hand. Fragile in his. Long fingers. A scholar's hand, he'd teased her, so long ago. Made for scribbling. He touched his lips to her ring, honouring her as his queen. But the fragile circlet of gold decorated with its priceless diamond resisted his fingers when he tried to draw it from her.

Sitting back on his heels, he frowned at it. According to what he knew, when a queen died, the ring would leave her hand. Her bond to the land broken.

His head jerked to Felicia. She smiled at him.

"I can't take her ring," he muttered.

"No."

"So she's not...?"

"That's right."

"By all that's holy."

Felicia's eyes flickered gold. "The future lies in your hands, lord," she whispered. "Complete the prophecy."

"Together, they will bind the rings..." Dominic Skinner's voice was hushed in the taut atmosphere. Ever practical, Fortuna roamed the chamber, using her flint to relight the candles. A welcome glow went some way to ease the tension. She came back to the bed and dug in her apron pocket. "I think you need this," she said, but her fingers trembled as she handed it to Dominic.

His calloused palm shaking, Dominic took the jewel from Fortuna. He held it out to Joran, his vivid eyes alight with hope. The diamond faces twinkled at him in the candle glow. Joran stared at it. In his memory, he watched it drop from the Grayling's beak. The valiant bird carrying a part of Petronella's soul. And her voice echoing down the years. *'Tis yours. Please take it.*

To his astonishment, Dominic knelt at his feet. "I pledge my allegiance to Joran of the Eagles. King of Epera," he said, his voice full and firm. "I am his liege man of life and limb. Now and always." Clothing rustled as the rest of the group followed suit. Joran swallowed, his heart racing. All those years of frantic denial. Of doubt. Running from the past, too afraid to claim a future. The Shadow Mage was still here, in this chamber with them. Perhaps it always would be. But those shadows were not as monstrous as they had been. It was time. Long past time for him to make his bond with his country and his God.

Joran's fingers shook as he held them out. Dominic's half-smile tugged at his lips as he placed the heavy jewel reverently on the forefinger of Joran's right hand. Cerys' moan of defeat underlaid the subtle pressure of the ring as it sought the bond with Joran's soul. To his surprise, there were no crashing thunderbolts, such as had accompanied Petronella's dramatic banishment of the Shadow Mage all those years ago. Instead, the Ring of Justice settled on his flesh like a weary hound after a long day's hunt. Comfortable. At peace. His shoulders relaxed for the first time in years. The dreadful doubt lifted from his mind. *"You are not your father. You passed the test. Now, rule with honour and justice. In my name."*

He blinked; the Mage's voice in his head was surpassingly gentle. Forgiving. His brow quirked. He had never thought the Mage could be anything less than stern. The demanding hand of a domineering father. He smiled.

"Petronella…" Brushing his hand across Dominic's rough head, honouring his grief, he leaned down and took Petronella's hand in his.

Their rings kissed. And ignited.

The shadows cringed in the blinding light that flooded the chamber, scurrying like fleeing rats in the face of a storm. Cerys gasped, shielding her face, turning against Clem's chest. He held her gingerly, deep distaste in his face. Joran's gaze locked on Petronella. Her hand shook within his grasp. He could feel their twin powers building. Twisting. Combining. A surge of energy started somewhere at the base of his spine, rippling upwards. Through his pounding heart, driving the ache from his head. Onwards. Upwards, seeking a union with a god. The Grayling's fragile body glowed with light, so bright it hurt his eyes to see. He blinked. Just once. When he opened his eyes again, the bird was gone. Heart in his mouth, he brushed the deep neckline of Petronella's bedgown aside. The white shape of the Grayling's wings stretched protectively across her breast, undulating faintly under her pale skin. A blessing from the Mage. The return of the untainted fragment of her soul guarded tenderly in the heart of her falcon. The Blade of Aequitas lay lengthwise on her body, alongside her staff, stained with the Grayling's lifeblood.

"Joran…"

Petronella's eyelids fluttered open, and the sapphire depths of her eyes caught the light like newly emerged stars. He could fall into those eyes, he thought wildly. Fly in them. He lowered his lips to hers.

"You're here. With us. Thank all the Gods." For a moment, she seemed distant, still tethered to the spirit world, but then she blinked and smiled faintly. Her touch, weak but sure, found his hand.

"The Grayling is here," she whispered, as though speaking not only to him but to herself. "He's part of me now." Her eyes drifted around the chamber, smiled when they met Dominic's, still wet with tears, kneeling at her side. "You let him go," she said, her voice faint but growing stronger. "We thank you."

Cerys' snarl snapped his head around. He looked up. Cerys hung in Clem's arms. Her hair covered most of her face, but her eyes were still wild. Black as night. The storm outside was quiet. But it was the silence of something hidden and waiting.

"Open the curtains, Fortuna," he murmured, still clasping Petronella's hand. It was cold in his grip. Their breath weaved in the chilled air. At the corners of the room, the shadows still lurked.

Beyond the windows, the world presented an eerie sight. Heavy clouds, circling like pacing wolves, revolved slowly around the Castle of Air. Blotting the familiar skyline and the wheeling stars. They held a vaguely crimson cast in their ebony depths. The wind had died almost entirely. His ring pulsing on his finger, Joran's eyes narrowed.

"The Shadow Mage is still here," he said. He turned to Cerys. Clem had not loosened his grip, even though the woman had stopped struggling. The soldier's face clenched with the effort of holding his stance.

"Dominic, take the Blade of Aequitas," Joran commanded. "Guard it well. We will need it on the morrow."

The young knight retrieved the dagger, turning it thoughtfully in his fist. "What do you mean to do with it, my lord?" he asked.

Joran's lips twisted. "Tomorrow, my queen and I will judge her," he said. "In full view of our court and our people. The blade will play a part in that. For now, she can stay tied in here. Take the book from the room. Back to the restricted section if you can bear to carry it so far. We will destroy it. I want a full guard placed on the door and another in the courtyard outside, watching the window."

"Aye, my lord. Your Maj." The grin Dominic turned on Petronella transformed him into the charming young courtier that lurked beneath the grime and muck of his long journey. Petronella's lips twitched as he took her free hand and planted a robust kiss on the back of it. "You can go and get cleaned up," she said, smoothing his rough beard. "I've forgotten what you look like. And Dominic," she paused, reaching for his sleeve as he stood, "the Grayling is not gone." She brushed the fragile silver chain that hung around his neck. Pressed the falcon to his breast. "He's here. Remember him well."

The lad nodded, his eyes blurred. He stepped back and bowed. To them both.

Joran stooped, lifting Petronella easily in his arms, staff and all. She weighed hardly anything. Her long illness had carved pounds from her already slender frame. Her pregnant belly rounded against her stained nightgown. "You'll stay with me tonight," he said, holding her close against his beating heart. She rested her dark head on his shoulder. Pressed a kiss there.

"I should hope so," she said.

He nuzzled her hair. "And tomorrow, we will rid ourselves of a witch."

Chapter 47
Joran

Commanded by Sir Colman, the magnificent throne room of the Castle of Air thronged with people as the temple bells rang for midday. Courtiers, nobles, merchants, and servants, some Blessed, many plain Citizens, vied for space, craning their necks, alive with speculation. Outside, the sullen storm shed a dull, crimson light over the surrounding countryside. Suffocating and heavy. Ready to roar.

Joran stood on the dais, with Petronella at his side, facing the avid crowd. Behind him, dragged from storage just that morning, was the throne Petronella had first commissioned for him years ago. A twin to hers. The silver glowed under the light of the many candles, but the oppressive atmosphere cast gloomy shadows through the new stained-glass windows. Petronella stood tall and proud, slender as a reed. Only Joran knew her staff was not just there as a symbol of her status as the nation's seer. He could feel her tremble as she placed more weight on it.

"We'll make this quick," he whispered.

"'Twill take as long as it takes," Petronella said, deep in his mind. He edged a glance at her. Stoic and determined, she'd refused all suggestions that she rest.

"As you will, my lady," he replied. He straightened his back and nodded to the guards. The Lord Chamberlain, his staff of office proud upon his portly chest, pounded his staff of office three times on the tiled floor. A hush descended through the packed court. Prickling

with tension and expectancy. The tall, carved doors of the throne room opened.

Joran's eyes narrowed. He'd ordered the witch surrounded by Clem and the most stalwart members of the Queen's Guard. At his request, Dominic Skinner brought up the rear, ready to use his Blessed gifts should she make a bid for freedom. Cerys Tinterdorn shoved her hair back and glowered at him. Tall though she was, her guard topped her by several inches. Their footsteps were loud as they escorted her down the long aisle from door to throne. She walked stiffly, her face stamped with fury, her hands straight by her sides. As Joran had ordered, the guards aimed their naked blades at her back. He could take no chances. The black Book of Shadows waited on a stand at the bottom of the shallow stairs. Joran's gaze fastened on it, in no doubt of its imminent fate. He would have destroyed it last night but for the need to make this judgement of Cerys a public display. He knew the outcome would circle Epera before dusk. Whatever that outcome was. His thumb caressed the heavy diamond of the Ring of Justice, reassured by the steady beat of Mage power in his blood. His jaw clamped. Justice at last. The thought of it warmed his senses.

Ranged a step below him and Petronella, Aldric, Fortuna, Little Bird, and Felicia stood in a solid line. Allies. Friends. There was a gap where Guildford should stand. Joran's fists tightened against his thighs. They had received no word of Guildford's fierce pursuit of Dupliss. No word of fighting at all. It was as if the crushing fist of the storm held the entire nation in abeyance. A more deadening version of Dominic Skinner's blocking ability. Its power seemed to hold the gift of time, releasing it slowly, one parsimonious grain at a time. Seconds as minutes.

The guard drew to a halt, stamping their feet smartly to attention. His lips thin, eyes narrowed in concentration, Dominic Skinner halted with them, holding the woman in a Blessed prison of his own devising. Joran could see her fighting it. The furious glower she tossed behind her. Dominic merely glared back and increased his energy. Joran lifted an eyebrow. How that lad had grown in the passing weeks. Quieter. More determined. His blue eyes were vivid with energy and steely purpose. His Mage-forged silver falcon blazed on his breast. A Blessed Knight of Epera. Joran smiled. The stultifying envy that hounded him when he viewed the former stable boy and tanner's son was gone. Replaced by respect and gratitude.

Joran raised his voice. "Cerys Tinterdorn, you stand before us to hear our judgement on you and your crimes."

"Piss on your judgement," Cerys spat. She raised her chin, her eyes black as the mines in which she was born. The crowd hissed and jostled. "I am the rightful Queen of Epera. Darius of Falconbridge's second-born daughter. You don't have the right to judge me."

Her claim rang in the air. Joran could sense Petronella's interest now that the woman stood in front of her.

"She's so like our father," she murmured in his mind. *"When he was younger. Perfect and cold. So sure he was right."*

"Right..." He huffed a sigh. *"Cerys' right is everyone else's wrong, and yet look what damage she has created, just like your father,"* he replied. He tipped his head to one side, considering his options.

"'Tis not her fault. Mayhap, she never had a chance." His wife's mental voice, ever gentle, stroked his senses. *"I would have spared my father, but madness had claimed him years before. He would never have stopped. This judgement belongs to you."*

"Aye." Fingers tapping at his thighs in time with his thoughts, Joran stared at Cerys. She raised her chin. Challenging him to do his worst to her. *I could end her here,* he thought. *In the past, I wouldn't give her a second's grace.* His brow creased under his frown. *But I am not the same man today.* He blinked with the realisation. *I do not wish to kill her.* Turning his palm, he stared at the undulating pattern of the Mage's symbol, forever chasing itself. *Circles,* he thought, his logical mind grasping at the concept, trying to will it into focus. *My thoughts*

are my prison, as much as Cerys'. But I can choose. I am free to choose a different path. A different ending. Not in revenge. Not with anger. But freely. Impartially. With justice.

He raised his voice. "Cerys Tinterdorn, daughter of Darius of Falconridge and Juliana Tinterdorn, you stand accused of high treason. Threatening the life of our sovereign queen and the brewing of insurrection and civil war within the environs of Epera. How do you plead?"

Stubborn and wilful to the end, Cerys clamped her lips together. She tossed her head.

"Do as you will," she sneered. "Only I have the right of judgment on my soul."

"Only you?" Joran glanced at Petronella. She nodded, her steady gaze fixed on the woman before her.

"You called on the strength of the Shadow Mage to aid you," Petronella said, her voice colder than ice. "The same dread force our father unleashed upon our land. I banished it then. Together, we will banish it again. This time, for good. Starting with this Book of Shadows."

"You will never get rid of the Shadow Mage," Cerys said, her lip curling with derision. "It lives within the hearts of men. Surely you know that. Even now, your Citizens rise against you. Led by Count Dupliss. And where is your brother, Felicia of Wessendean? Is he as traitorous as you? Has he not left to fight with Dupliss for his crown?" She stood with her hands on her hips, head held high, sure of her challenge.

Felicia straightened, poised and slender as an arrow. Joran raised a hand for silence as the courtiers surged forward, their shouts of surprise and derision blistering the air.

"Hold!" Joran shouted. "Felicia of Wessendean is loyal to the crown. I will not hear a word against her."

"Nor against me, I hope." Guildford's powerful voice carried effortlessly across the vast chamber as he entered, batting the guards aside. He strode to the dais, muddy to his eyes. A roughly tied bandage decorated his forehead. Equally filthy, tall and well-made, his spurs ringing with his stride, Fabian walked with him, a tired grin tugging at his lips. The courtiers gasped again. Joran groaned inwardly. Leave it to Guildford to make an entrance. He waited, one eyebrow raised, as the young princeling reached them. He threw Cerys a casual, dismissing glance. She tossed her hair, her jaw set with hatred. Without ceremony, Guildford swung a coarse woollen sack in front of them. Something heavy and round rolled inside. The copper tang of blood hit Joran's nostrils as the sack hit the floor with a thud. Guildford flung his head back, his pale grey eyes alight with triumph.

"As you commanded, my lord," he said, dropping to one knee. "Dupliss is dead. By my hand and with the aid of my friend, Fabian of Warnham. But I am deeply sorry to report the deaths of your friends, Terrill and Fly." His face sombre, the young man at his side also knelt. Head lowered. "We pledge our allegiance to you, Joran of the Eagles, and Petronella of the Falcons. As your liege men of life and limb. Freely and fully. I have declared such on the steps of the temple in Blade, my lord. The rebellion is over."

Joran let out a heavy breath, the weight of his relief palpable. "And I'm sure every soul in Blade heard you," he muttered with a half-smile. He raised his voice, addressing the room. "You are right welcome, Guildford of Wessendean, Fabian of Warnham," he said warmly, motioning to the dais. "We honour the sacrifices made by our friends on Epera's behalf.. Take your places as our allies. Join us as we make our judgment upon Cerys Tinterdorn."

The grin stretching Guildford's lips beneath his beard vanished as he ascended the stairs with Fabian, their cloaks trailing mud over the tiles. Joran waited as the crowd settled once more. He allowed a long breath to escape his lips and sent a prayer of thanks to the

Mage. Guildford and Felicia of Wessendean. The son and daughter of a former king. United under the Eagles at last. Petronella stepped forward to join him, sliding her long fingers to his.

"Your plans are in disarray, it seems, Cerys Tinterdorn," she remarked. "Apparently, some men remain immune to your shadows. Have you anything to say before we rid ourselves of this evil artefact?"

Cerys narrowed her eyes. "'Tis our father's life work. You can try," she sneered.

Taking a breath, Joran clasped Petronella's hand more firmly in his. Their joined rings flared. Darius' Book of Shadows caught fire where it lay, a sulk of flame and smoke. It didn't alight. Instead, it glowed, first red, then white as metal in a forge, sparking with black energy. A cry emerged from its wounded heart. Soft at first but growing louder. More anguished. The shrieks of the tortured souls whose suffering had contributed to its writing. Aware of the pain in Petronella's face, the tremble in her hands, Joran gritted his teeth and increased his energy. One by one, dark shadows emerged from the molten pages. The crowd gasped, pointing at familiar faces as they blurred and burned, dissolving in front of their eyes. The Winterbane clan moaned at the sight of Juliana Tinterborn's image drifting from its pages. There were many others. Former members of the Blessed, lost to the mines at Traitor's Reach, their energy harvested and forced into a book that enslaved their Blessed gifts and twisted them to evil. Their shades rose with the smoke. The pages that had held them writhed and melted in the crucible of Mage power. Petronella gasped as her sister Janna's beloved face emerged at the last, her face white and sad beneath her russet curls. Cerys wailed as the book burned. A single piercing note that forced many spectators to clap their hands to their ears. Jaw locked, brow clammy with perspiration, Joran poured more energy into their joint bond, willing Darius' black book into oblivion, his obsessive years of study into nonexistence. Peace for the Blessed souls cursed and bound within its pages for so long.

The book died as Janna's soul left it, crumbling to a harmless pile of smoking ash. The guards jumped as Cerys dropped to the floor, writhing in pain, clawing bloody strips from her own skin.

Joran let go of his wife's hand. She stumbled a little and caught herself with her staff, passing a hand across her brow. The chamber stank of charred flesh and hot metal. Dominic's face was whiter than chalk, but he kept his hands steady. Joran's face creased into reluctant admiration as the lad stretched his gift. Caught Cerys' clawing fingers, pinning them gently to her sides, where she could not harm herself further. He shook his head to see it. That kindness in Dominic that powered the heart of him. The urge to help. Even for such a stricken soul as Cerys, intent on destruction.

"Cerys Tinterdorn. Stand." Joran's command echoed around the walls of the immense chamber, bouncing from the ancient weapons that decorated its walls. The woman took no notice of him. Perhaps didn't even hear him. The atmosphere had lightened slightly as the black Book of Shadows released its hold. But the storm outside still circled. A silent predator. Joran's jaw hardened. It was clear where the remaining evil lay, locked in the woman before him. There had to be a reckoning. It was time. He loosened the Blade of Aequitas from the temporary sheath strapped to his thigh. The weapon was a marvel of balance. Intricately carved runes gleamed across every inch of its surface. It trembled in his gasp. But his fingers were steady on its hilt.

"Stand," he said again. Reading his determined gaze, Dominic urged Cerys Tinterdorn to her feet. Joran strongly suspected he was propping her up. Petronella had recovered herself. She leaned on her staff, every inch the Queen and seer of Epera, her face a mixture of resignation and determination.

"Your choice, my love," her voice whispered in his mind. *"Choose wisely."*

Completely silent, the crowd waited.

Joran stared at Cerys. The woman whose manipulative mind and ruthless vision had conspired to steal the kingdom from its rightful king and queen. Pinned in place, Cerys raised her chin. Blood oozed from the scrapes and cuts on her arms.

"Why?"

His quiet question seemed to disarm her. Her eyes darted around the chamber, seeking a way out. She struggled but, by now, appeared to realise there was no way to break free of Dominic's iron control. "Before I cast judgement, I would understand," Joran said. He turned the blade in his hand. The runes twisted in a dizzying swirl. Cerys watched him, a glow of repressed triumph buried deep within her black eyes. "You have tried in every way possible to breed division and sow hatred amongst us. Citizen against Blessed. But there is no reason for it. None. King Francis has died, and his prejudices died with him. They are not mine. Not Petronella's. You are waging a war against a non-existent enemy."

"She killed him." The woman's face twisted. She pointed at Petronella, her cold, beautiful face ablaze with hatred. "You killed him. Your own father. A Citizen. Tell me that is not your prejudice."

Petronella raised an eyebrow. "I killed a madman intent on enslaving every nation of Arcanis," she replied. "I killed the man who murdered our sister in front of my eyes when I was but eight years old. You have just seen the remains of the poor souls who lost their lives at his command. Including your own mother. Our own sister. The first of so many. I gave him a chance at redemption. He could have saved himself. But in the end, 'twas not I who ended him, but the will of the Mage. 'Tis no great honour to know him as my father."

Cerys' lips drew back in a snarl. "You don't know about my mother. You can't."

"Oh, Cerys, do you truly think I would not walk within your mind whilst you were so conveniently attacking mine?" Petronella said. "I know you. I have suffered with you. Your hurts and your sorrows. Your hopes and your fears. I see the lost child. I see your fear of our father. 'Tis the same fear I had of him. His power. His rages." Her voice was clear, commanding the attention of everyone in the room. She took a step towards the edge of the dais. Her seer's staff glowed in her hand, along with the compassion shining in her eyes. "That was the only way of saving yourself, wasn't it? Binding yourself to him. Turning a blind eye to his every cruelty."

She had her sister's attention now. Cerys bristled under her words, struggling with the truth reflected at her. Gentle but remorseless, Petronella continued. Pinning her sister with her gaze. "You could have run, Cerys. He wouldn't have cared. He had no more use for you than your poor mother once he'd forced her to his will. And yet you stayed at Traitor's Reach. Hoping for a morsel of attention. A second of his time." She paused, nodded as if in confirmation of her conclusion. "Aye, that was your choice, Cerys. Only yours. To become like him." She bit her lip, her voice lowered. "I would laugh were it not so sad." Drawing a steadying breath, she stood a little taller, Epera's Queen. "You need not explain yourself to me, my sister. I understand." She nodded at Joran, squeezed his fingers in reassurance. "But the King of Epera bears the Ring of Justice. The judgment lies with him." Her voice rang around the room as she stood back.

Cold and triumphant, Cerys smirked. "You can't kill me with that," she said, waving a hand at the Blade of Aequitas. "Those are my runes on that blade. Etched with my blood."

"But this is the knife that cuts both ways, Cerys. Your mother bound it with love. You cursed it with hate," Petronella said. "And perhaps, 'tis her judgement on your actions you most fear."

She said no more. Stood back so that Joran had room. He could feel her presence in his mind. Steady and comforting as ever. He turned the Blade of Aequitas in his hand, aware of the court's eyes upon him. Cerys' black eyes bored into him. Taunting and savage.

"Go on, throw it," she said through bared teeth. "It won't kill me. You'll see what happens when I throw it back."

"No. Mayhap it won't," Joran said, testing the weight of the blade balanced across his palm. He met her gaze, no longer bound by her threats. The more Cerys fought to deny Petronella's words, the more he saw the truth of her. A broken child, clinging to her shreds of power. "You are a lost soul, Cerys Tinterdorn," he said, his tone crisp and true. "And this is your dark magic. Bound by your mother's blood and your own." His ring pulsed in his palm, flashing like icy fire down the length of the blade, igniting the runes. "But it was never your blade. It leaves my hand as a neutral force. For justice and for the good of all. In the Mage's light."

For a second, he hesitated, collecting himself for the act. A vision flickered in the back of his mind. A dim memory of an old man standing over a bed and the start of terror in Joran's infant heart as the man's ring flashed white fire, and the room filled with his father's rage. His remorse. His shadows. The start of a dark journey for his beloved nation. *No. I am not my father. I choose justice. In the Mage's light.* The diamond pulsed in his palm as if in acknowledgement of his thoughts.

"You have earned the right, my love," Petronella whispered deep in his head. *"Do not hesitate. I am with you."* Lighter in heart, he raised his hand in his first act of judgment as Epera's King. But the shadows that had haunted him for so long were absent. His thoughts were as sharp and true as the blade he held. Untainted by revenge or the need for control. The heavy responsibility he had once so feared had given way to a burden as light as the touch of a falcon's feather. Right and natural.

Petronella's hand slid into his as he threw the knife. The crowd drew a breath. Thunder growled. Low and threatening. The many decorative weapons nailed to the throne room walls shuddered as the energy grew, drawn from the land. Connected with the sky. Light from their rings combined, anchoring their joint power. Balancing justice with mercy. The blade flashed silver and gold along its gilded edges, slicing through the charged air. Dominic dropped his block in the instant before the gilded point pierced Cerys' chest. There was nothing she could do to stop it.

The crowd drew a breath. Waited. Cerys gasped. Dominic took a couple of steps away as she swayed. The flashing runes discharged in a blinding dance of red, white and deepest black. Cerys stumbled. "NO!" her shout blistered the air. "No!" She grabbed the blade with both hands, tried to tug it free. The knife remained where it was, dimming as the runes dissolved, their power spent. Cerys sagged to the floor, her hair falling over her face. Sobbing. It was the voice of someone much younger. "Why?" she whispered into the fall of her hair. "Why was I always so alone?" Abandoned. Lost in the dark. Stumbling through ancient tunnels, chased by her demons. The quick mental impression ran through Joran's mind as he looked at her. He swallowed and glanced at his wife.

"Is that what you see, as well?" he asked.

Petronella nodded. *"Lost and alone. And no-one to care. That's what she understood. 'Tis what hurt her the most. Her most terrifying memory."*

All around them, the shadows lifted. A wind arose. Rushing from the south. Welcoming as spring after winter. The storm released its crushing fist reluctantly. The courtiers blinked as if people were waking from a dream, turning to each other. Clasping hands. Their chatter rose. Swift as the starlings darting from their roosts to chase each other across the clearing sky.

Joran's breath left him in a rush. Cerys didn't move. Dominic stooped to her. Her face turned whiter than the tiles she laid upon. The Blade of Aequitas dropped from her chest into her hand. A dull knife. Of common design. No longer the gilded, decorated weapon it had been seconds before. Dominic collected it with a wave of his power before Cerys could hurl it again.

Joran peered at her more closely. She still had the look of his beloved Petronella. But this woman lacked in some indefinable way. Her cold glamour spent.

"My powers," she whimpered, stretching her hands as if she couldn't believe what had happened. "What have you done with my powers?"

"They are gone, Cerys," Petronella said, her voice soft. "The Mage has judged you for your actions."

"No. It's not fair. No, he can't. He must give them back." Cerys twisted wildly on the spot, searching the room as if she could see her powers lying like discarded toys on the floor, ready to be gathered. "I have nothing. You did this!" she moaned at Petronella. "You!"

"No, my sister, you did this to yourself." Petronella used her staff for support as she navigated the stairs. "But you have time now. Time to heal. We will help you if you wish."

Cerys struggled with the idea. She shook her head, scowled under her brows, checked the watchful room of strangers like a wounded animal, broken and afraid. Shaking his head, Joran ran down the steps.

"Calm yourself," he said. "'Tis over, Cerys. The Mage has stripped your powers. But the Blade of Aequitas has severed your connection to the Shadow Mage. You are free of his darkness. Freer than you have ever been to make your own choices."

Shaking, the woman stared at the hand he held out to her, lingering on his ring, and then raised her eyes to the circle of faces that surrounded her. Not just Joran's. But Petronella's. Dominic's. Felicia's. Every member of the Court of Skies. Citizen and Blessed alike. The defiance left her all at once. One last shadow drifted from her and twisted aimlessly into the air. Cerys blinked as she watched it vanish, her hands wrapped around her chest, choking with sobs.

Petronella knelt at her side. "You are my sister," she whispered. "As I am yours. If you will let me."

They waited. Outside, the storm dissipated as if it had never been. Pale winter sunlight sent its golden fingers into the depths of the room.

Cerys turned to him, her eyes wide, blinking rapidly as someone emerging from a savage nightmare, her face streaked with tears. Joran smiled. The darkness had faded from her eyes and left a rich, dark emerald. Mysterious as the deepest forests in Epera's most unexplored valleys. Verdant and full of potential.

"He no longer owns you, Cerys. You have a choice. What say you?" Joran urged. "Will you let us help you?"

She struggled to her feet, fragile as a wand of mountain ash, but her gaze was steady.

"I will try," she said.

EPILOGUE
THREE MONTHS LATER

A fresh spring breeze fluttered the standards crowning the battlements of the Castle of Air. The bustling courtyards swarmed with Eperans of every ilk gathered from far across the nation in celebration of Dominic and Felicia's wedding. Petronella and Joran had commissioned a new standard for the occasion. The King and Queen watched proudly, his hand on her growing belly, as their soldiers hoisted them aloft. The grey and pale blue of the Falcons entwined with the royal blue and black of the Eagles. Two birds facing each other. Linked by two rings, twisting together. The sign of the Mage. The castle's starlings circled them, swooping to roost as the pale spring sunshine gave way to the star-washed evening.

The same motif decorated the famous hammer beams of the castle's . Undulating lazily in the warmth from the huge hearth. Petronella had spared no expense to trim the castle's gathering place in a manner fit for the wedding feast of a Blessed knight and his bride. The royal banners interspersed with the one she'd gifted the newly wedded couple.

"It looks well, Dominic. Do you like your new standard?" she murmured, leaning on Dominic's arm, one arm around her swollen belly.

Dominic grinned. "Very much," he said, raising his voice a little as Clem started a risque version of 'Where the Robin Roves," with much nudging and knowing looks from the raucous gathering. "I never thought to see falcons and owls combine with eagles and serpents on one flag."

Petronella laughed. "Aye. It was difficult to get the balance of the quarters right. The Master of Heralds and I enjoyed our arguments immensely," she said. "Did you enjoy the ceremony?

"Aye. I am now wedded but not yet bedded," Dominic said, shifting impatiently from foot to foot as the servants started the long task of clearing the tables to make room for the entertainment. He glanced over the room, where Felicia and Joran were chatting to Tom Buttledon and Mistress Trevis. Tom had lost his arm in the end, despite his loving wife's nursing ability. But his familiar, teasing smile wreathed his face. Sensing Dominic's gaze, he raised his glass in salute.

"Hah," Aldric said, punching his arm. "Has she still not given in to your undeniable charm?" Fabian chuckled, his eyes alight with merriment. He'd become a well-respected member of the group over the last few months.

"She said she'd make him wait," Guildford said, his grey eyes dancing with mischief. "Better give them a very long time in bed tomorrow, my friend."

The three exchanged grins. Fortuna's shoulders shook with mirth. Dominic scowled at them. "Some things are worth the wait," he said, primly.

"Aye. You should know." Chortling, Aldric and Guildford clashed tankards over his head.

"What say you, Little Bird?" Aldric asked, cutting his gaze to where Little Bird perched like her namesake on the edge of a wooden bench, her face tilted to the waving banners.

"I say you should stop teasing him," she said.

Dominic swept her a bow. "Thank you," he said. "Someone on my side, at last."

"Aye, well," Bird said. She glanced up at him, then away. He left the others and stepped across to her. Their relationship had altered over the long separation and Bird's grief for her beloved Will Dunn. Little Bird blamed herself for Cerys' last cunning disguise, disgusted at the lengths to which the older woman had gone to gain access to Petronella's chambers. Felicia and he had been battling her over it for months. Little Bird still somehow thought it was her fault. To date, she'd yet to spare Cerys Tinterdorn a glance.

"Will you wish us good fortune, Little Bird?" he asked, handing her a gift of marchpane wrapped in a blue ribbon he'd chosen to match her eyes. "There is no-one's blessing I wish more than yours."

She swallowed, toying with the lumpy package. "I wish you every fortune," she said. "I wish Will was here to say it himself."

"Aye." He fumbled in his pocket. "I found this the other day, buried in my old pack," he said. "I could kick myself for not remembering it sooner." He dug in the pocket of his tunic and handed her a package. Grimy leather, tied off with a frayed binding.

Bird stared at it. "What's this?" she asked.

"Will wanted me to give it to you." He bit his lip at the instant outrage on her face.

"Typical. You remember it now? Months afterwards?" she demanded.

Dominic shrugged, awkward under her glower. "Mayhap 'tis better now," he offered, turning so he shielded her from the curious glimpses of their friends. "When your grief is not so raw."

She bit her lip, taking the package onto her narrow lap. "He really left this for me?"

"Aye. I won't watch you open it if you don't want me to." He drew away a little, watching the graceful dip of her neck as she bent over it.

"Nay. Stay. Won't you?" She drew him back to her side, took a breath, and pulled at the rough bindings. Several large coins tumbled onto her new brocade skirts. She gasped, fingering the money. "This is too much," she whispered. "Look, there's an eagle. Another eagle. Where did he get this?"

Dominic chuckled. "I guess he probably won it," he said. "Aldric taught him how to gamble on the march north, and he was a most willing pupil. And he would have saved his pay. Ever practical, that was our Will."

"What's this?" Her nimble fingers pounced on a circlet of gold. A tiny, fragile thing. Big enough for a girl's ring finger. Little Bird gasped. She turned it in her hand but made no move to put it on. A tear rolled down her cheek.

"There's something else in there," Dominic murmured, touching a gentle finger to a ragged piece of parchment sticking out of the bag.

Little Bird swooped on it. Unfolding it in a frenzy of urgency. "Careful, love, you'll tear it," Dominic said.

"I won't." Her lips trembled as she read the blocky capitals scrawled in Will's stilted, untutored hand. She clapped her hand to her mouth. "He's left me his cottage on the edge of Blade that came to him from his parents," she whispered. "Says we would have lived there together. Oh, Dominic."

Dominic slid a gentle arm around her shoulders. "He loved you, Little Bird. He left Aldric and me a message, too," he said. "And we promised we would look after you. And we always will. If you wish it."

She turned in his arm, snuffling like a piglet. A wry grin on his face, Dominic handed her a clean kerchief. "One day, I'll give you away at your own wedding," he said carefully. "And you can be sure your Will Dunn will be standing right beside you, wishing you love. All he wished for was your happiness, Bird."

She heaved a giant sigh and blotted her eyes one more time. "Aye," she said. "But no more tears. Not on your special day. Look. Your bride has finally decided you are worth her company. Mind you, don't tread on her new slippers." She handed the damp cloth back to Dominic, collected her precious coins, and scampered across the stone flags, strewn with last year's lavender. She grabbed Aldric's unresisting hand as the court musicians gathered around Clem and started a sprightly galliard. Aldric grinned as she tugged him into place, pinking slightly under Clem's wink.

Dominic rose to his feet, his face wreathed in a broad grin as Felicia swept to him, resplendent in pale blue, her face rosy. A fragile lace ruff circled her slender neck. The train of her gown dusted the floor. Her long, dark blonde hair lay loose on her back, bound by blue ribbons and lace. He bounded to her side with as much grace as he could muster. Re

"So eager a groom," she murmured, handing him a thick pouch of coin. "Guildford gave me this for you earlier on."

"That dowry again?" Dominic raised his eyebrows.

"Are you glad to take it this time?"

She glanced up at him from under arched brows, a wicked gleam in her eye. "You can hold it for a while," she said. "Until I demand it back. How else are you going to keep me in clothes?" She turned a neat circle before him.

"A vision, you are to be sure," Dominic said. "Come, my beautiful wife. Let's dance."

She arched a brow. "Dominic Skinner, dancer?" she said.

He grinned. "Aldric is more graceful. Guildford will throw you in the air three times before he catches you," he said, sweeping her a courtly bow. He took her hand and pulled her close. "I promise to stand on your feet and crown you the queen of my heart despite my clumsiness. Will you have me? As long as Fabian doesn't mind, of course."

"You shouldn't worry about Fabian," she murmured, dipping in a curtsey, making room for Joran and Petronella in the circle of dancers. Laughing, Guildford and Fortuna joined the line. Aldric and Little Bird completed their set. "I had to save him on the boat that day."

He threw her a perplexed glance. "Why?"

She grinned, glancing at Guildford. "If I hadn't, Guildford would not have been successful in his pursuit of Dupliss. He needed Fabian to watch his back." She pressed a finger to her lips. "Don't ever tell the big oaf it wasn't all his own work."

The court musicians played their opening chord. A triumphant flourish in a major key. Dominic's magical senses prickled, his heart alight with a new sense of the future. There were estates to run. A tanner's business to find a buyer for. A young peregrine falcon to train and gift to his queen. His face flushed with pleasure as he looked at Felicia. His heart's love, her face alight with laughter, her eyes aglow with light.

And there were no shadows. Nothing he could not face.

He was not alone.

"In shadows deep where whispers weep,
A blade of fate lies cast,
Aequitas, the soul's eclipse,
A curse from love's lost past.
A token turned to fate's cruel hand,
To sever bonds unseen,
Beware the heart that wields this blade,
For night and day convene.
Aequitas, the knife that cuts both ways,
In balance, true, its power sways,
A whisper dark, a beacon bright,
It holds the realm's own fragile light.
Prophecy in ancient lore,
Foretells of times to come,
When kingdoms rise, or kingdoms fall, beneath the blade's cruel
hum.
The bearer walks a path unknown,
Through shadows, thick and thin,
For light and dark both mark the path,
Where destinies begin.
Aequitas, the knife that cuts both ways,
In balance, true, its power sways,
A whisper dark, a beacon bright,

It holds the realm's own fragile light.
To wield this blade of fateful edge,
A heart must find its peace,
For good or ill, its secrets spill
And bring the world release.
The runes that bind both kind and cruel,
Hold truth within their lines,
In hands of those who understand,
Its power intertwines.
Aequitas, the knife that cuts both ways,
In balance, true, its power sways,
A whisper dark, a beacon bright,
It holds the realm's own fragile light."

AFTERWORD

Thank you so much for reading *King of Swords*.

I hope you've enjoyed your journey through Epera, the land of the Swords.

For those of you who love tarot, you may have noticed plenty of 'easter eggs' woven throughout this story—subtle references to various cards and scenes inspired by the imagery of the swords minor arcana. The world of Epera itself is steeped in the motifs of the swords suit: daggers, blades, mountains, wind, feathers, birds, and ice all come together to evoke the stark, cutting energy of this tarot suite. Each of my major characters faces a personal struggle, grappling with self-doubt and battling their inner demons in pursuit of peace.

I've also incorporated elements from the major arcana, particularly the card most aligned with the swords suit—*Justice*. The theme of the *Saga of the Swords* is built on the delicate balance between justice and mercy, both for others and ourselves.

If tarot is new to you, I truly hope you've still enjoyed this series as an epic adventure, with characters you can relate to and a world you can immerse yourself in!

And if you'd like to discuss anything from the book, please feel free to reach out—I'd love to chat!

In the meantime, dear reader, my blessings to you.

Until next time.

CC x

Acknowledgements

I'm so excited to have finally reached the conclusion of Saga of the Swords. Nearly three years ago, during lockdown in the UK, the idea of Tales from the Tarot came to me like a bolt from the blue. An opportunity to explore the world of the tarot from *inside* the deck. To go for a ride through a mystical medieval landscape and see what I could discover.

Saga of the Swords is the product of many hours of thinking, writing and communing with both the tarot and with nature. But I also couldn't do this alone. Many thanks to my wonderful editor, Natasha Rajendram, whose enthusiasm, expertise and attention to detail have enabled me to bring this saga to life.

Many thanks also to my wonderful ARC readers, Aly, Joy and Gayle. Thanks to all of you for your support and encouragement.

Last, but never least, my heartfelt thanks to my wonderful husband, Jim – and our menagerie. Thanks to Bingo, Blue, Rosie and Daisy for keeping me company at my keyboard. And Jim, without whose solid support and unwavering faith I would probably never have started.

CC x

ALSO BY CHRISTINE CAZALY

SAGA OF THE SWORDS
Seer of Epera (prologue)
Queen of Swords
Page of Swords
Knight of Swords

COMMENCING 2025

VOLUME 2 OF TALES FROM THE TAROT
WAY OF THE WANDS

Set in the harsh desert world of Battonia, *Way of the Wands* is a series of epic tales full of passion, adventure and romance. It all kicks off with a prologue novella, *The Shattered Wand*. The full series will begin with Nino Lombard. A young man with a passionate heart, and a lot to learn in *Page of Wands*.

Watch out for it in 2025!

amazon.com/Christine-Cazaly/e/B0BBJW5VWS?ref=sr_ntt_s rch_lnk_2&qid=1661516964&sr=8-2

facebook.com/christinecazalyauthor

bookbub.com/profile/christine-cazaly

goodreads.com/https://www.goodreads.com/author/show/22 759981.Christine_Cazaly

Facebookhttps://facebook.com/christinecazalyauthor

GoodreadsChristine Cazaly (Author of Queen of Swords) | Goodreads

BookbubQueen of Swords (Tales from the Tarot) by Christine Cazaly - BookBub

Instagram https://www.instagram.com/christine_cazaly/

AmazonAmazon.com: Christine Cazaly: books, biography, latest update

For updates, recommendations and giveaways, join my newsletter and get Carlos and the Mermaid, a FREE short story, set in Oceanis, the Kingdom of Cups. It's inspired by the tarot card Five of Cups. You can join my newsletter at https:/christinecazaly.com

Join my newsletter for progress updates and to be notified when my next books are due for release!

Printed in Great Britain
by Amazon

56627393R00229